THE SUN ROAD

THE SUN ROAD

Hannah MacDonald

LITTLE, BROWN

A *Little, Brown* Book

First published in Great Britain in 2003
by Little, Brown

A CIP catalogue record for this book
is available from the British Library.

ISBN 0 316 86189 8

Typeset by Palimpsest Book Production Limited, Polmont, Stirlingshire
Printed and bound in Great Britain by Clays Ltd, St Ives plc

Little, Brown
An imprint of
Time Warner Books UK
Brettenham House
Lancaster Place
London WC2E 7EN

www.TimeWarnerBooks.co.uk

For Vivi – my mother
and my first piece of luck

Acknowledgements

Thank you to Sam Boyce, Tara Lawrence, Eve Claxton and Hannah Weaver for all their incredible help. Thank you too to Deborah Amlot, David Nicholls and Phyl MacDonald for their support. A particular thank you to my father, Robert, who bought me my first dictionary. Finally, thank you and more to my much-loved husband, Paul.

The Goddess Fortune be praised (on her toothed wheel
I have been mincemeat for several years)
Last night, for a whole night, the unpredictable lay in my
   arms, in a tender and unquiet rest –
(I perceived the irrelevance of my former tears) –
Lay, and at dawn departed. I rose and walked the street where
   a Whitsuntide blew fresh, and blackbirds
Incontestably sang, and the people were beautiful.

John Heath Stubbs

Contents

PART ONE

1. Martin and Paul

Leicester, 1969

They are two small boys walking down the street. One would come up to your waist and the other up to your thighs. In slow, tired moments the littler of the two might reach and place a hand on your leg for support, as if you were a tree. The heat and light pressure of his small palm would work through your trousers and you would probably reach down to ruffle his head, your hand covering from the front to the back of the scalp, like some everyday priest. The two of them feel warm and wriggly – their faces are still pudgy – and on your lap, in your arms, they squirm like animals flattening grass or treading down earth, making a cave out of your embrace.

When undressed they are smooth and grabbable, their flesh moulded around soft, developing bones. Sometimes their mother thinks their limbs could be snapped, that Paul's thin wrist could easily be bent to a wrong angle and splintered inside, like a bird's wing.

Martin is older and slightly taller. He walks with purpose while Paul still seems to be dawdling in childhood, paddling his hands through the air of a stirring, chaotic world.

They are only little, and dressed in brightly coloured clothes. Martin chattering, on their way to the swimming pool, Paul stumble-walking with one hand stretched out ahead, as ever, high and far to an adult. It's a wonder one arm isn't longer than the

3

other. Paul has dark hair in a pudding-bowl cut, browner skin than his brother, a stubby nose and glistening eyes, and as he is pulled along almost sideways on he registers passers-by with an oblique stare. He doesn't much like swimming so he is in no hurry.

Martin is in a hurry though. He is fairer and prone to allergies – eczema and agitation. He doesn't sleep very well and sometimes wets the bed. He doesn't know why, only that it's inappropriate. He is a big boy now and yet he is constantly assailed by some urgent desire – to pee, to cough, to itch, to cry. He tries to dodge them, to preempt the urges; leaving the table before he's finished his tea, checking out the shallow end of the pool for bombers, climbing in carefully before anyone teases him to dive. Bombing is not allowed, but like so many things (swearing, spitting, shouting, stealing) people do it anyway. Is it not allowed because so many people are doing it already? So many that the ones like him, who are bound to do as they are told, must be bound to good behaviour. Someone must behave, he supposes.

They reach the local baths, which have only been open since the start of the year. Their dad, Gavin, holds the door open for the two of them, ushering them with grand movements through the arch beneath his right arm. As if he had just marched a whole orphanage of the things over from China, thinks the woman behind the counter. Gavin likes being a dad. He likes the noise and value of it, and he loves their trust and their big clear eyes. In them he can go back to the beginning again and create friendly worlds of talking animals and happy planets.

'One adult and two children,' he says, pulling a small leather purse for change out of his summer jacket pocket.

'Five bob altogether,' she says and he counts out the coins in front of her. She slides them noisily off the counter, long red nails scraping the surface, and, when she's done, looks under

4

her fringe at the half-moon face staring up at her and the curled hands sitting on top of her counter. She winks at Paul and his eyelids lift in surprise, as if he's just seen a shooting star.

Gavin herds them through the reception into the men's changing rooms. Unlike the swimming pools of his youth, you don't change in curtained cubicles round the edges of the pool – unpeeling your pants below the strip of material like some bawdy seaside postcard. Here you have silver lockers with keys and wooden cubicles with doors, as well as a central changing area for schools and groups – and families.

But Martin has other ideas. He likes the privacy of the stained teak cubicles; it's warm and cosy, possibly even a little smelly, and it feels a very safe place to get undressed in. It even has a lock.

'You don't want to go in there, Martin,' says his father. 'We'll be ready in two ticks. Come on, son.' He reaches out for Martin's shoulder but the boy flinches away and locks himself in the teak cabinet. Gavin sighs and sees himself as a big fat man in a changing room with a scared son who'd rather not be near him. He looks at Paul slowly undoing his laces. He is concentrating very hard. 'Sometimes,' Paul says in a considered way as his father takes over, 'I think things are harder to un-do than do-up.' His sensible brown lace-ups are very scuffed and have gone beige and bulbous at the toe. They used to seem ever so long, great flappy things at the end of his feet, but now they are tight and grubby like Chinese bandages. His mother would have put him in his new summer sandals, which are two bands of sharp-edged pale blue leather, but Gavin thinks they make the boy look like a girl.

After five minutes of goosebumps and awkward manoeuvring, of stepping in and out, of trying to hide one's private parts, they are ready. Now they must visit the wet toilet – which scares Martin because there's no way of telling one kind of wet from the other – and walk through the chilly Verruca Pool. Verrucas came in the same hushed, threatening category as head lice, bottom worms and tramps. Sometimes Martin sees people in a single white sock, hiding their verruca. Only not hiding it because they are as good as branded in their plastic socklet.

There is a small paddling pool on the way out of the showers, for rinsing your feet before entering the main hall. The cold water slaps ankle-high and sometimes there's tissue floating on the top. The water dribbles through a pipe in the wall and drains slowly out of a mouth-sized gap in the ceramic tiles. It reminds Martin of the lips at the top of their bathroom basin. A nice, white, clean basin, with a small black hole leading to pipes and sewers and rats.

The machinery and innards and, yes, the rats of the Leicester Recreation Centre are equally hidden, only to be sensed when a staff member in shiny tracksuit bottoms opens a Restricted Entry door and heat and noise slips out. Or when Martin, clinging to the edge of the shallow end, presses himself to the corner and hears the blue chlorinated water sloshing and draining with a heavy slurp, in rhythm with the crowd-made waves that pull him away and then push him hard into the white tiles.

The animal sound of the glug and the echoing shouts of the gang on the other side of the pool make Martin want to cry with panic. He's all alone because he got in before his dad and Paul had made it down to this end. He already has water in one ear and chlorine in his eye. He's nose to iron with a grate. The water, and a brick-coloured corn pad, is flowing away fast, and he's spluttering.

'What you doing down there?' says his dad. 'You'll get sucked down the drain, hiding in the corner like that.' His father is right beside him, unclasping his hands from the rim, turning him round and giving him a big hug, like the little boy he is, and whirling him round and round in the water. They both splutter and laugh and Martin screams 'Dizzy, dizzy' as they stagger, buoyantly together.

Paul is floating inside an inflatable ring with seashells and seahorses on it and he also has water wings, orange ones, but the left one isn't plugged in properly so it's deflating. If he doesn't pay attention he'll just go round and round in circles, like a maimed bee. But he's okay for the moment, bobbing and flapping around the shallows, looking down at his enormous white legs and the dolphin-like body shapes deep below. Martin looks at the water inside his own ring. It looks blue from far away, at the other end of the pool, but then when he tries to capture it, inside his plastic swimming ring, it is clearly colour-less like any old water. This is the ring he used on the beach last year. His dad pretends that going swimming is like going to the seaside, but it doesn't seem right to have seashells on your ring at the swimming pool. He will make them buy him another one. The only similarity between seaside and swim-ming pool is that there's water in both places. You don't have to pay to get in the sea. And the sea goes on for ever, out and out and down and down. The pool has a floor that you can see. 'What happens next, after the bottom of the pool?' Martin asks his father.

It's no different from any other building, on any of the streets in Leicester, his dad tries to explain. Gavin likes making the world clear. But what happens below the streets *is* mysterious – there is matter and interruption, cased pipes criss-crossing deep below the streets, cables higher above, sewers cutting a swathe like the new M1 through great areas of earth. Paul asks about the worms and the rabbits and the moles and he imagines the world as a circular cross-section, small mammals and organisms digging around the pipes and tunnels as if in a muddy adventure playground.

There are only certain members of staff permitted to go down to the generator and pump room. Keith is one. He's not an engineer, he's a Life-Saver, but George, who is one of Leicester's forty municipal engineers, has, like a vicar, many parishes to attend to and only comes in once a week. Keith has been trained in pool maintenance and it is his responsibility to check the system four times a day. It is a useful responsibility as it gives him more status and more money than the rest of the pool-side staff. He has high hopes of being made assistant manager by the end of the year. The leisure industry is a growing business, he reckons. These days he has five different pairs of nylon track-suit bottoms, in all colours of the rainbow as his mum says, who washes them by hand for him every Saturday night.

It is four-thirty in the afternoon. The pool is now closed to new swimmers. Keith is a bit late with his fourth check but he has been struggling with the last clue of the *Mirror* crossword and as he leaves the staff room, crosses the entrance and goes through the Restricted Entry door he is still trying to puzzle out what is eight letters long, begins with an A and means 'Need – for all sorts of things'. He stops for a second as he shuts the door. Something is different. A bit odd. What? He walks slowly down the steps to the generator room and as he reaches for the light switch the answer to both questions comes to him.

They'd been in the pool for forty minutes now and they were the last people left. Martin's fingers were beginning to prune so Gavin told them they had another five minutes and that, yes, they could both have a packet of crisps from the cafeteria. Once he'd said that, though, it seemed to Martin and Paul that they'd like to get out right now. They'd come swimming, they'd got wet and splashed a lot. They hadn't been that keen about it but now it was done, the bombers had been avoided and there was something else, salty rather than watery, in the offing. Martin thought about this as he climbed carefully up the steps out of the shallow end, his trunks bagging and slipping with the weight of collected water. He reached behind and held up his trunks with one hand, gripping the rail tightly with the other. It was interesting how things passed, like hours in the pool. And long, dark nights. It could have been worse, he thought.

The two words came to Keith in a hurry: Appetite and Gas. And only when that millisecond word placement was done did he realise what that meant and move his hand away from the light switch. A strong smell of gas meant a leak in the building's heating system, and a strong smell meant a large leak – a dangerous leak. He stopped, his head empty with panic, at the bottom of the stairs, not knowing what to do. 'Fuck,' he said to himself, 'fuck, fuck, fuck . . .' And he turned and ran back up the stairs, slamming open the door into the reception, charging through a perfectly normal Saturday afternoon towards the manager's office.

Howard Shorter had a poolside office. It was rather impressive. And it had its bonuses on Ladies' Afternoon. When Keith burst in, Howard had been watching a fat man slither and slop his way around the pool edge, his kiddie in his arms. Shouldn't carry 'em, Howard thought, he'd seen too many accidents that way. No point in tapping on the windows though, they never heard – the glass was too good and thick. Keith came in without knocking – out of breath, stumbling over his words. He was sweating under his red tracksuit and Howard shrank from his unattractive urgency. Keith did not look in control.

'Good God, what's the matter? Slow down—'

'I didn't know what to do. We have to clear everyone out,

shut everything – there's a gas leak downstairs – the heating system. It's really strong.'

'A gas leak?' Mr Shorter looked relieved. 'Well, that's not too bad, is it? We can deal with this – that's what we're trained for. Go and shut the system down. Go on.' He looked hopefully at Keith, who seemed to be about to cry. His shiny face screwed up like he'd just stubbed his toe and he said, 'Please, Mr Shorter, get everyone out. Please.'

And he went over to the panoramic vista of his boss's office and began to hammer on the glass, shouting at the last straggling family, 'We've closed, you've got to get out.'

'Keith.' Howard was on his feet. He lunged round the side of his desk, a large man moving unusually fast, his heart pounding with anger. 'Get a bloody grip. Go and turn the system off. Shut down the supply. Go on, get on with it.'

But Keith shook his head, panicking. 'I can't, I can't, it's gone, I can't remember.'

Howard stood still, frowning at the lumpen boy in amazement, and then picked up the phone. 'Melanie. Set the evacuation procedure in motion. As practised. Everyone must be out within three minutes.' He put his hand on the cradle and then, with a jabbing finger, dialled the emergency number that was Sellotaped to the wall behind his desk. It was all going to be fine. They had procedures.

Paul watched the man in the red tracksuit in the glass room up above. He was hitting the glass. Paul would have thought that was rather dangerous. It might smash and the red man might fall out. He might land in the water, but then there was no telling, he might land on the hard plastic spectator seats around the edge. Which would hurt.

Downstairs in reception, the Restricted Entry door swung

slightly. Keith hadn't shut it properly in his scramble. Sarah, behind the counter, with the wink and the red fingernails, stopped mid-nail-filing and looked up. She'd just caught the strong, nauseous smell. Down the corridor, beside the door to the basement, came two young lads. They were making a racket and Sarah, distracted by disapproval, scowled at them. They stopped, one of them fumbling in his pockets, and Sarah watched them until she caught another toxic gust and stood up in dismay. Picking up the phone, she felt a slight panic rise in her heart, her fingers fluttering urgently through the new phone list. As she stood the boy on the left, still standing at the entrance to the corridor, put a cigarette in his mouth, took out his Swan Vestas and flicked the match. Sarah's ear was to the phone and she turned back to look at the boys. She saw the match travel to his mouth and as she said 'Stop' he lit his cigarette with a single touch and threw the match aside. It arced through the air, its small, blue-hearted flame still burning, tracing a semi-circular line like a yellow sparkler at night, falling swiftly and softly through the warm, humid atmosphere. It began to descend, Sarah watching it travel, mouth in mid-cry.

From now on there are only the minutest measures of time.

The air erupts. The entire reception area, Sarah and the two teenagers with it, is flung into a red-black explosion of fire that consumes the building's interior within five minutes. The sounds of metal rending and stone collapsing are like a memory of war. The noise rips through the burble of the town and can be heard two miles away. People stop in shops, on streets, at their sink, as if the sound has snatched a heartbeat.

Martin and Paul and Gavin had nearly reached the exit to the changing room as the match flew. The space between a footfall gave the beginning and end. They were so close to the source that there was no gap between sound and explosion. No gap for

11

Paul to turn his head as he sat on his father's hip. Or for Martin to get scared. Or for Gavin to throw himself and his children to the ground. They were simply walking slowly when in the space of that footstep, in the midst of a breath, they were lifted off their feet and thrown into the air like a plastic model of a family of three. One moment they are walking and talking, the next they are blasted by such a great roar of heat that Gavin thinks the end of the world has come. For all his bulk and brave love they are nothing in the face of this liquid rush of fire. Faces wrenched by the power of the explosion, they are thrown, separately, into the water, travelling on the wave of fire, landing in the pool with chunks of brick and metal from the building's innards. The fire travels so quickly that it seems as if it were sent from the sky with one pointing finger, but actually it travels like a tidal wave through walls and doors. Up in his office, for one unrecordable, infinitesimal second, Howard watches a family fly and a building erupt in on itself. The plate glass shatters and Howard is thrown out of his office and into the burning seats below. Shards of glass rain down. The fire has reached him and is licking him raw when a jagged pane of glass plunges into his stomach, the sharp coldness in his belly killing him first.

They are alive as they hit the water, Martin thinking with clarity that something has gone wrong, Paul screaming not thinking, Gavin beginning to shout his children's names. They feel the liquid around them and the fall of wreckage, but the water is no longer cold. As the fire storms the centre and consumes every burnable trinket in the pool hall – the towels, the 'No Bombing' signs, the abandoned plastic rings, the anoraks, the seats, the steps – as it cracks the tiles and pounds at the asbestos roof tiles, as detritus lands in the pool in flames, made from such creative chemical compounds that they simply burn while floating, the temperature of the water in the pool begins to rise.

12

Gavin is surrounded by flames, burning boats of debris around him, and the heat of the air makes breathing almost impossible. It's hard to open his eyes properly but he flounders in the water, feeling out for the small soft bodies of his boys. He shouts, or at least he opens his mouth and cracked whispers of the boys' names emerge. He can feel the water getting hotter, tightening on his flesh. He ducks down into the pool and tries to open his eyes. Things fall languidly in front of him; there is a forest of bricks, pipes and poles down there, floating slowly through the murky hot soup. He comes back up, spluttering. There is hardly any air to breathe and what he can inhale cuts into his throat with its heat and bitter taste. He coughs and would like to close his eyes and his lungs for a minute to rest but his children are somewhere down there so he forces himself to breathe out and kick back below the surface. He tries to swim forward but the water is so hot that the breathtaking white pain could come from swimming in ice. His body is growing redder and redder and the tender parts of his flesh are burning through one layer of skin after the other. His groin stabs with pain. Again he opens his eyes under the water and can feel them begin to burn, his lungs tight. Suddenly in front of him he sees an arm, then a leg sinking through the water. He lurches with painful slowness through the thick liquid and reaches for the child's arm. He tries to grasp it but bits come off in his hand. The flesh is soft and disintegrates under his touch. Gavin knows he must breathe now, his whole chest is ready to burst, but strangely his mind takes the time to think how bizarre it is that they may die in a swimming pool. He has time to wonder how it came to this. He moves his hand up, trying to get a grip on the child's limb, and then pushes himself to the surface, pulling the boy behind him. But the water has begun to boil and though Gavin is only five feet from the pool's edge he might as well be lost in the Red Sea. He gasps one final burning breath as his heart seizes and stops.

His grip on Paul's arm loosens and their bodies are moved apart. Their three corpses move and sink below the floating flames, far apart at the deep end.

2. An Ordinary Mother

The next day is Sunday and it rains. Leicester watches the skies empty, awed by the force of the fall, and everyone, with the unity that arrives with tragedy, feels the weeping of the air. Most sit in, solid on sofas before the TV or scraping chairs in the kitchen, heads bowed over papers and tea. They ring their parents and children and walk through the streets to churches or corner shops with the heavy grace of pallbearers. In the park steady dogwalkers frown at the shouting footballers, their own unfinished sentences circling above their heads.

Twelve people have died in the Leisure Centre tragedy: Howard Shorter (Duty Manager and father of two), Keith Adams (Pool Attendant/Life-Saver and son), Sarah Lord (Receptionist and divorcée), Gemma George (Pool Attendant and fiancée), Meg Dee (Café Supervisor, mother of four), Bob Akiwa (Cleaner, father of six – two deceased), Keith Brown (Apprentice Blacksmith), Ted Smart (School-leaver), Gavin Jordan (Father and Decorator), Martin Jordan (Seven, blue eyes), and Paul Jordan (Five, brown eyes). Nine families taken apart.

It's noon the next day at Leicester mainline train station and Lizzie is on the way home to her own particular family. She's standing at the bus stop, drops of early morning rain trickling down the plastic-cased timetables. If you were to see her now you'd think she was a very ordinary raincoat with a woman

15

inside. She is of an indefinable age, somewhere between twenty and forty, and has neat brown features and a short wavy hairdo that is so transparently man-made that you just presume she needs the artificiality, the help. But in fact Lizzie is only twenty-six, and is one of those women who takes you by surprise. She will suddenly turn up at a parents' evening in a plum-coloured jumper that will make men give up their seats while the other women feel cross. It would be all right if Lizzie made an effort all the time, but to surprise one like that is somehow unfair; appearances are a serious game and there are rules.

Now she stands at the bus stop looking composed – her hands clasped in front of her, her handbag swinging slightly from the net of her fingers. Occasionally she rocks backwards and forwards on her low, navy court shoe heels, betraying a slight impatience. At her side is a small green overnight suitcase, inside which is a new, unworn nightdress – silky lemon with lace – a change of knickers, a slip, a cream skirt, the plum jumper and her washbag. A car pulls up at the bus stop but she looks straight through it. She knows it won't be for her. Gavin needed the car this weekend to take Martin to a football match on Sunday morning. There's a man standing next to her, who's been twitching in a worrying way and now he's starting to talk to himself. She feels a familiar rise of tension, her poise becomes more rigid, her breathing a little faster. She sometimes thinks she is cursed to attract – that she's magnetically programmed to attract – every oddball in Leicester. It seems like everywhere she goes there's a woman with mad hair and overflowing bags, a young man talking to himself, an old man revealing himself. She can't believe there are really that many strange, sad people out there – she really believes they come and find her. Even when Paul was christened there was some tramp muttering rude things from the back of the church. She'd asked the vicar to eject him but the vicar had just said that it was God's House.

Gavin had placed his hand on Lizzie's arm to try and calm her and she'd thrown it off with a gesture that was too large and forceful for God's House. The vicar had looked at them both as if it were they, not the bloody tramp, who were unclean.

The Twitching Boy gets in the Rover that's just pulled up and Lizzie relaxes now that there's nothing funny or potentially disturbing around her. What would people do, Lizzie sometimes wonders, if she took it into her head to suddenly start talking in funny voices or shouting in the street? What would happen if we all started to do it? It'd be Bloody Mayhem. Bloody Babel. For all sorts of reasons Lizzie thinks you have to stick at things and put a respectable face on them.

Lizzie is scared of compassion; it's a purifying draught and she's none too sure of her mind's balance these days. If she stares hard enough at one spot for a few minutes she can reach a state of complete uncertainty as to her next movement. She can scare herself silly with possible unpredictabilities. For all she or anyone else knew she could take the number twelve bus instead, away from the street she lives in, away from her home at number twenty-seven Haverhill Crescent, away from her husband and two little boys, away from the neighbours and the beige wallpaper she'd mistakenly chosen for the bathroom. Physically speaking there was no reason why she might not do that. Free will, she'd always thought, was a decidedly mixed blessing. But she allows herself only a minute to dwell on these obscene possibilities, like an adolescent with the door locked, before the number eighty bus arrives.

Lizzie, head of the queue, climbs on the bus with its suburban camouflage of magnolia and green. She asks a man to make room for her and sits beside the window, her hands clasped in her lap. The motion of the bus and the passing of street-walkers' faces relaxes her mind-lock, and although she tries to block them suppressed images begin to seep out. She sees two bodies in

17

bed, her own white torso laid out to brazenly face the ceiling, legs folded, knees high, fingers and nails curled, gripping at his skin. When they are apart Roger is more real. When they are together she can hardly believe he is there, that he is a proper man, the professional business manager of the old people's home where her own mother now lives, and that he is choosing her as his romantic heroine, picking her out as his quest. She is an ordinary, respectable, twenty-six-year-old mother-of-two, with a lover in Harrogate.

Gavin and the boys will not be home yet which is a good thing. Last time she returned from Harrogate she collided head-on with guilt at the front door. It is better if she has time to gradually reacquaint herself with her home and family, and with herself. She will need that half an hour's practice before she fits in properly with her constructed world. She has her place and with the strange dual certainty of infidelity, passion solidifying what it betrays, she believes she must keep it.

It's a fifteen-minute journey on the bus, past the shopping arcade, the Co-op, the new grammar school, the church, then down the steps of the bus into the breeze at the junction between West Avenue and Poplar Street. She is conscious of every step, sensitive to the sounds of the infrequent cars, the birdsong, a radio filtering through the gardens. She blinks in the sunshine that flickers fast in and out of clouds, chasing her through the shade of houses and trees. She feels as if she might have a spotlight on her, that the odd person she passes can see a strangeness in her, as if she were one of those so allergic to the world that every element feasts on her. She turns right into her street, swapping her overnight bag into her other hand, rooting blindly for her keys in her handbag, feeling round the bags of boiled sweets she has bought for the boys.

She opens her front gate, noticing that its latch isn't down –

a reflex thought. When Martin was a toddler and they'd first moved here, he'd had a habit of wandering down the side-alley, out of the back garden, into the street. There wasn't much traffic on this new housing estate but the few cars went quite fast. She closes the gate carefully behind her, even though Paul is now old enough to know how to escape, and walks up the short path to the front door. She puts a key in the bottom lock and turns, but it isn't locked, which makes her tut. So she juggles the keys with one hand for the silver Yale, but before she can use it the door gives and is opened slowly.

It is her mother-in-law, Rose. Lizzie is jolted with surprise and her head moves back slightly as if there is a wasp in her face. Rose has a key because she babysits sometimes, but she's not meant to be here now.

'Gran,' she says, because that's what everyone calls her. 'This is a surprise.' Lizzie puts a foot on her doorstep, to enter her own house, but Rose doesn't move. 'You all right?' Lizzie asks in the rather brittle tone she reserves for her mother-in-law. She looks at her with a half-smile and notices that Rose looks awful. Grey in the face, with a peculiar cardigan on. It's several seconds before Rose speaks, just long enough for Lizzie to experience the strangest sensation. She's holding her breath and her skin is pricking. Without reasoning she knows there's something wrong.

'Rose,' she says, 'what's happened?', desperately flicking through the options in her head, thinking that, yes, it's probably George, Gavin's father. George has probably had another turn and might even be in hospital.

And then Rose says, 'Come inside,' and she moves aside to let her in. Lizzie steps into the hallway, Rose closes the door and before Lizzie can put the bag down she sees a policeman at the door to the kitchen. There's something wrong. The panic builds like air not breathed out and she turns to Rose and says, 'Where are the boys?'

Rose looks her straight in the eye and says, 'Oh Lizzie,' and streams of tears begin to funnel down her face. Lizzie wheels round to the policeman, still in her raincoat with her bag in her hand, and says, quite quiet and taut, 'What's happened? What's going on?'

The policeman steps forward, meeting her at the bottom of the stairs, and puts his hand on her arm. 'I'm sorry, Mrs Jordan. I wish I didn't have to . . . There's been an accident. Your husband took your sons to the swimming pool yesterday at around four. There was an explosion and they all . . .' He pauses. 'Passed away. Immediately. In the accident. In the pool. Together. All together.' He swallows. He has wet eyes. He holds her arm, thinking she should sit down, he should take her into the lounge. She should sit down. She still has her coat on, for God's sake.

Lizzie's eyes flicker, frightened. 'No,' she says to the policeman, because obviously this is a mistake. They're at the football. 'No,' she says, shaking her head too fast and hard. 'No, they're at the football. They didn't go swimming. Paul doesn't like swimming. You've got the wrong family. I spoke to them in the afternoon. They never said they were going swimming.'

The policeman is trying to apply pressure to her arm to get her into the lounge. He's never done this before. He's sure she's meant to be sitting down. Does he answer her, or is she in shock? He doesn't know.

'I'm sorry, Mrs Jordan, but we've identified them. I'm ever so sorry, but it's definitely them.' He's never seen someone's face drain before; he's never seen someone swallow such news. Three deaths. It's as if all her strength is sliding out of her. Her jaw goes slack, and then her mouth opens into an ugly hole and as she begins to scream and falls hard on to her knees, saying 'No' over and over again, so high and so raw, he knows he should have got her onto the sofa first.

* * *

20

The next day is Monday. It rains then too. And the day after. And after, and on. The city lumbers slowly, forgetfully into the future while the repercussions of the explosion are hidden in unwelcoming buildings – crematoriums, courts and the offices of Allied Insurance. No matter, Lizzie will never remember these days anyway. They have been lost. They have dropped off the abacus. And it is only when Roger arrives from Harrogate and finds her sitting alone, a stuffed donkey in her lap, her fridge full of well-meant rotting stews, that her days are reclaimed and become more carefully numbered. She is three months' pregnant with Roger's child.

It's difficult to believe in the sanctity of life when your children come and go so quickly. Martin and Paul now sit mute in a photo frame at the back of the mantelpiece. It is important to Lizzie that they don't feel excluded. Beth is born in February 1970, rudely alive, and Roger hides his delight so as not to upset Lizzie, once his secret and now his wife and no clearer to him for all that.

3. Kamikaze

Eight years later, South London, 1977

Jacob Frederick came slowly down the stairs in his wife's dressing gown. He yawned, screwing his eyes up tight, showing as much exhaustion as he felt, then trod on something slippery and cold. He swore and picked a red Wellington boot from off the floor. A collection of coloured boots lay flat on their sides like dying fish by the front door. Hands on pink velour hips, Jacob counted them out loud. Eleven. They had found every boot in the house and dumped them in the hall. It wasn't even ten o'clock.

He walked through the lounge, still carrying the boot. He and Rachel had recently opened up the two main rooms so that from the front door you could see straight through the house. It gave more light and made the house feel modern, more designed, less poky and Victorian. But it meant that Jacob was reminded of his limits every time he came down the stairs in the morning. If he'd been more of a thinker he'd have realised that he was irritated by not being able to pretend there were six more rooms hidden somewhere.

He scratched his belly as he walked; what with the yawning and the bending Rachel's dressing gown had bunched up uncomfortably in the middle. He needed a deep tan cup of tea to put some strength in his blood and settle his mood.

Four children and his wife were sitting eating sausages at their kitchen table as Jacob came in. At the sight of his father Dave, his nine-year-old son, shouted 'Daaad' with dismay. Jacob was stood in the doorway, dressing gown separated, his penis right in his family's eye line.

'Dave!' he shouted back, gesturing fiercely with the Welly.

'Jacob,' his wife winced, nodding downwards at his cock.

He looked down, raised his eyebrows in recognition, tugged at the pink velour, then looked up and smiled at each of the children.

'Dan, Greg, Dave, ohhhh yes, and Beth Standing.'

They'd started to giggle, Dan and Beth. They usually did. Giggles swallowed like bubbles, pink faces squirrelled away into polo necks and scarves.

Jacob drew up a stool, took two sausages and a cold piece of toast. 'So, what's with the Wellington explosion? Have you actually all decided you'd like to go for a walk? Because I know what happens when you decide you want—'

'Daaaad.'

'Look outside.'

'Stupid.'

'Dave . . . don't call your dad that.'

Heaving giggles from the end of the table.

'LOOK AT THE SNOW!' Dan suddenly shouted far too loudly. He was an unnerving child. There was silence in the kitchen.

Jacob looked out of the window. 'My God, you're right. Who left all that white stuff there, then? We should go sledging.'

'My mother's coming for lunch,' said Rachel.

'Must she?' said Jacob. Rachel laughed and then stopped abruptly, remembering her mother's grandchildren.

'Yes.'

'Granny doesn't like you either,' said Greg.

'No?' asked Jacob mildly.

'No. I asked her. She told me. She said you were a . . . a something that means a show-off.'

Rachel enjoyed this for a moment before saying, 'That's enough, Greg.'

Jacob looked at Beth, which made her nervous. Dan's dad was unpredictable. Not like hers. He made jokes that she didn't know how to answer. 'Have you got a grandma?' he asked her.

She shook her head. She was embarrassed and looked to Rachel for help. Rachel could handle anything. She was calm and glamorous and fascinated Beth. But Rachel was reading a paperback book. At the *breakfast table*.

'Well, I wouldn't worry about it,' Jacob said. 'You're not missing much.'

'Why haven't you got a mum?' said Greg to his father, relentless as ever. 'Where's your mum?'

'Dead,' said Jacob. The children looked surprised. Dead is a four-letter word. They were used to the euphemisms. Then Jacob pointed his fork to his chest. 'And in here.' Rachel snorted with laughter once more but did not lift her eyes from the page. Her long plait wrapped round her hand like a brunette pet.

Overnight, the long street where the Fredericks and the Standings lived had been transformed into a glacier-white runway. Their houses were directly opposite each other and their children had slept through the soft, grey daybreak and awoken to find London had grown a new skin. At nine, Lizzie and Roger Standing's seven-year-old daughter Beth had dressed quickly and gone to knock for her friend Dan. She knew she had to be quick; it wouldn't last for ever.

By ten-thirty Dan, his brothers and Beth had eaten sausages and then churned the snow in his back garden into a grey gruel. So the two of them crossed the road to Beth's house, stopping to sweep great lengths of snow from the front garden walls. They

24

went through the side gate into her back garden and began making a snowman with fierce, breathy concentration.

They were in the same year at school and had known each other for as long as they could remember. Like twins, they mirrored each other's movements and moods but, unlike twins, had a choice of houses. Rachel and Lizzie had both arrived in Delia Street in 1970. They had never made friends in the same way as their children but they had quickly recognised how happy their children were in each other's company. Rachel had always thought that since Beth was Lizzie's only child it was generous of her to allow Beth to spend so much time at their house. A woman other than Rachel might have felt she had enough kids as it was, without Beth's constant presence, but Rachel liked children.

For Lizzie, the sight of Beth playing with other boys provoked much more complex emotions. Allowing Beth so much freedom, so much access to someone else's brothers, was the most selfless gift she felt she could give her daughter.

After all, Beth was the result of an adulterous affair, the result of an afternoon spent lustfully while her two sons and first husband died in a fire. The less Beth knew of her, Lizzie thought, the better.

So when Lizzie came into her bathroom at about eleven that morning and saw her daughter through the window she was caught off guard. Her emotions flared before she could deaden them. They looked so sweet playing together that Lizzie had to breathe in sharply to break a sudden spasm of emotion. She clutched her coffee cup tight, watching their bright Woolworth's colours flashing against the sheer white. They screamed happily, shoving great handfuls of snow down each other's backs, bending, bouncing fast like toys.

Beth's hair was loose, flapping in her wet, white face and getting stuck to her lips. It was almost unfeasibly thick above

25

her small, bundled body. Roger had said it was about time that she got it cut but Lizzie hadn't replied, as if the descent from childhood would begin with the loss of hair.

The children didn't know they were being watched but Lizzie knew that if they did catch sight of her at the double-glazed window, in her green dressing gown, brown hair in a pony-tail, the tempo of their game would change. Her daughter would become self-conscious, suddenly dislike her woollen hat or trip on a paving stone. My child is wary of me, Lizzie thought, she's uncertain of my feelings. But, oh, they looked so happy in the snow, like small animals whipping through scraggy bushes.

Lizzie could feel how cold their small hands would be when they came through the back door, fingers in icy curls, tight like new bracken fronds, struggling with zips and bows. Their noses would be flushed and sniffing and their bellies warm under jumpers.

She loved the physical perfection of her child and didn't want her to grow, didn't want to lose easy access to her child's soft flesh. Lizzie often went softly into Beth's room late at night, when the television had been turned off and the windows shut, to stroke her new skin and wonder at her dormant future.

She tried to remember what she had known when she was childless, before rationality was an unachievable luxury. Strongest of all was the memory of clarity, a sense that she might have once walked down roads with a single purpose. Strange that before she had any children she knew exactly how to bring them up. Now things blurred until an urgent instinct either to protect or chastise gave her impetus, but she wondered what kind of mother this made her. She was damaged goods and could only do her best. The best thing, she had long ago decided, was to not inflict too much of herself on the child. It was Roger who provided the comfort, the softness; Roger who pretended that all was right with the world, that it was waiting for Beth in a smiling way. It was an unnatural dynamic but in calmness she admitted there was no other way of doing it right. After all, she thought, remember how little she had been led to expect of life. Better that Beth was an entirely different creature. She told herself that all children, and so all adults, must have, would always have, something to blame their parents for. But she also knew that those truths of childhood turned into keystones of personality. And she knew that decoding those keys could be punishing for anyone who tried to love them.

It was confusing – the nature of a heart that loves painfully and is selfish for love. The adoration in a child's eyes could swell a mother, lull one dangerously into the hope that intimacy brings. But the heart is a romantic muscle, she thought, one that waxes and wanes within the hour, and she had established something much more valuable within her household – safety. She would always be there.

Down in the garden, under Lizzie's gaze, Beth told Dan that he was useless at making snowmen. He shrugged and wandered out of the side gate into the street, leaving her standing in the garden, eyes roaming everywhere but up for distraction. Lizzie drew back from the bathroom window, pre-empting rejection, and crossed over the landing to Beth's bedroom. She would collect clean, dry clothes to confront her with.

It took a year before Lizzie could reconcile herself with Beth's presence, and after seven she had yet to reconcile herself to her reaction to it. Sometimes it was hard to concentrate on sorting the washing for the swirling mantras of guilt in her head. She had hated Beth for whole hours, for her screaming life force, for her greed and primitive pleasures. She was so rudely alive. Sometimes Lizzie had wanted to slap her into silence. She'd usually walk away and leave her screaming, to stand in the bathroom with her head pushed hard against the wall. How could she have wanted to punish a baby for just being a baby?

Beth looked nothing like her brothers. She had Roger's darkness, his dark brown eyes and heavy lashes and pale skin. She hadn't seemed like an English baby; there were no milk spots or flare-ups. Her baby skin hadn't burned red after a cold wind or a strong soap as Martin and Paul's had.

Lizzie had acted on automaton for years, it seemed. How else was she supposed to get through, except by drawing on her memory bank of the way people were meant to behave? Unless she took Valium her brain raced through whole cities of other lives they could have lived, other decisions she could have made, other directions taken. At its worst there was no difference between sleep and consciousness. She paced the sitting room creating Faustian pacts, willing an amoral God to turn back time, to turn her into something else, to take her away, to breathe life back into them. She tempted, willed madness because it was her only possible chance to find them again. But then, in the calm of exhaustion, she was scared by her descents into pure anger, was scared of when it would next come.

She had a glassy look to her eyes for those first two years. It must be hard for Roger, she would think, finding a wife finally through disaster, ending up with a shell of a person who couldn't think how to feel, when he'd seen her in his bed so lost and so someone else.

Three months after Beth's birth she'd forced Roger to touch her again. It had been only fair. He'd been very patient and if he were to wait until she felt stronger (as he'd said, promising that it really didn't matter) he'd have been waiting for ever. She couldn't think when she'd be able to make a pronouncement about herself. If it weren't for Beth and the fact that she was her mother, she'd never have got out of bed again. What could

28

possibly be the point? Life lay ahead, unaccountably long.

She wasn't learning to live with it. She kept breathing because the only alternative was killing herself. Although she wasn't religious, she was an Anglican product and scared of the eternal confrontation of death. She despised her weakness in not simply following her sons. Yet someone needed to be alive to remember them. Each night she got up to check on Beth because not to would take a decision. She took her pills because they robbed her of the raw energy to scream.

Sometimes she wondered whether Roger would tire of her. And on the whole, not least for practical reasons, she knew this would be a bad thing. She might one day remember how to appreciate him. In the meantime he didn't fuss her, and that was the best she could say of anyone.

He was overawed by his child, but she knew he was muted by her loss. He held Beth like a gift, not wanting to presume or consume too conspicuously. Beth made him smile, and Lizzie remembered thinking what precious things his curling, wide-mouthed smiles were.

Some nights Roger saw Lizzie flail halfway across the bedroom, woken from the same nightmares straight into rage. And he leaped up and grabbed her tight, let her drum her fists into his chest rather than the wall, or worse. He stopped her from drawing blood. But she knew she had sometimes put Beth down on the settee with more force than she needed to and left her crying longer than other babies. But what could she do for a child beyond feed it? She knew how it could end.

But Beth grew and years passed, and there seemed to be no end to life. One afternoon when Beth was a toddler, and had been laid down for a nap, breathing with a gentle wheeze, her little finger flexing, Lizzie went in to watch her. Lizzie stroked Beth's cheek with half of her own finger and thought how small and powerless Beth was, and then how extraordinary it was that

29

she grew so relentlessly. Lizzie had to admire it. She thought that her daughter might grow to be a fighting thing, surviving as she was with only half a mother. Now that Lizzie had decided Beth was never to know about Martin and Paul, she hoped that her ignorance of her mother's loss, combined with the fact that Lizzie would never spend a night apart from her, would balance her world rightly in the end.

From the top of the stairs she watched her daughter wrestling with her yellow boots, a hard-pressing feeling of something very like love in her chest. Lizzie sat down next to Beth and helped her to untie her Wellies. Out of the gentle moment came Beth's voice, loud with daring: 'Why don't I have a grandma? Dan has one. Why don't I?' Lizzie was shocked. Beth wasn't a questioning child. She was a solemn, silent little girl who rarely asked questions and left her mother unprepared for this kind of challenge. Lizzie felt a welling helplessness. And a flickering desire to give her seven-year-old daughter a sharp kick down the stairs, punishment for the unerring accuracy of her question.

Because I abandoned my senile mother in a home, she thought. Because your father had to choose between his family and me. Because my sons died in a fire while I was with your father. Because I can't tell you. Because you're a child and I don't want you to suffer too.

She got up and left Beth on the stairs, legs skewed, and said, 'Your dinner's ready,' sharply through the banisters.

Unusually, the snow lasted through lunch and into the afternoon. So the tobogganing trip was on and at 3 p.m. Jacob told his mother-in-law to make herself at home, shut the front door and saw the last child scramble into the back of his red Cortina. Someone slammed the door shut. It made a muffled noise and

30

he noticed a swathe of red anorak sticking out. He looked at it and decided against bringing it up; there would only be an indelible black stripe across it and someone was bound to mind. Rachel was sitting in the passenger seat while Jenny Garland, from number 24 Delia Street, fourteen years old and aware of it, was in the back on the left, with Beth perched awkwardly on her knee. Then came Greg, his youngest son, who was small for four, followed by Dave and Dan.

Beth sat very still on Jenny's knee, trying to avoid too much bodily contact. She thought that maybe Dan was still cross with her comment about his snowmen, because he hadn't made sure they were sitting next to each other. But her mother hadn't let her stay at home.

'Don't be silly, it'll be fun. You've never been tobogganing before.'

Beth looked out of the window and wondered why her mother called it tobogganing and Dan's family all called it sledging. It wasn't the only thing her mother did differently. She made her say please and thank you for everything. Even a banana. She didn't go to the cinema like Dan's mother, she just went to the shops. She didn't keep a crisp drawer, or a biscuit drawer like her friend Katie's mother. She didn't wear jeans. *She* wasn't allowed jeans either, thought Beth. The connection was a grim revelation; she didn't have any jeans because her mother didn't, which was a much harder battle to win. Her mother had told her she couldn't have them because they didn't look nice, which was, Beth thought, just silly – so silly in fact that she should have known it was a lie.

She'd have to be nice now, in the car, on fat old Jenny's lap. She could tell from everyone's silent behaviour that this was a special treat the adults could have done without. She and Jenny, as the outsiders, would both have to be particularly nice, although Jenny didn't seem to be trying very hard.

31

'Thank you for taking me sledging,' said Beth suddenly at the traffic lights. Jenny gave her a nasty look. Dan turned to her and stuck out his tongue, just as his mother turned round to smile and say 'It's a pleasure' to Beth. Catching him in the act Rachel reached her hand out behind her and gave a slap to a leg dangling from the back seat. The wrong leg, as it happened. Greg yowled suddenly with hurt surprise and broke into crying noises, at which point Dave shoved Dan in the ribs with an elbow. Dan elbowed him back and the two of them merged into a wriggling mess. Beth wished she'd never opened her mouth and watched the mayhem with the disdain of an only child.

'STOP,' Jacob shouted, swerving to the side of the road and turning round to remonstrate, leaving a weekend driver beeping angrily in his wake. Beside him, Rachel set her jaw against possible collisions. There was a second's silence. Jacob's children looked bored, and Beth scared, by this display of temper.

'Jacob,' Rachel said quietly, 'you always just stop in the road. You can't just stop in the road.' If only she had learned to drive, she thought, each journey wouldn't have to be an exercise in restraint.

'Do you have another fucking suggestion?' Jacob said irritably, putting the car into gear. Rachel turned her head away slowly and looked out of the window.

In the back, Greg brightened suddenly.

'Dad said the F-word.'

They reached the Downs thirty minutes later and parked in the middle of a long row of family cars. The children had pressed their noses to the windows like dogs, smelling the edgy freedom of the cold air and snow before they arrived. Almost before the engine was turned off they scrambled out of the car and on to the road. Then they wound back behind the Cortina and charged up the banks of mushed snow and old grass, Rachel's shouts of 'I said the *other* door' carried away by the noise of a passing van.

Rachel and Jacob collected the two sledges and a couple of old trays from the boot. Jacob suddenly reached out and put his arm around her.

'Sorry. Are you all right?' he asked. She nodded. She did love his transparency. His childish sweetness. 'Do your coat up and tie this up too. It's cold.' He took the ends of her blue scarf and knotted them tightly at her neck, then kissed her on the tip of her red nose. Rachel had always had a feline appeal, lithe and shiny, but in the midst of a winter so fierce that their water pipes had frozen and she hadn't washed her hair with anything other than Schwarzkopf's dry shampoo she looked dull. She hung back as they laboured up the bank, metal and wood clashing against their legs, and loosened the scarf.

Beth, Dan, Greg, David and Jenny (now flushed and looking more like a well-fed twelve-year-old) were halfway up the first slope by the time Rachel and Jacob caught up with them. Dan was holding Greg's hand as he scrambled and spluttered and slid to keep up with them.

'When I get to the top,' he was saying breathlessly to no one in particular, 'I'll see the whole world. Granny's house, our house, Spain . . .'

'Stupid, you won't see Spain, we're in Epsom,' said Dave. He spoke with some authority because they'd been on holiday to Spain that summer.

'Shall,' said Greg doggedly.

Jacob, as he reached the top of the hill, was suddenly enchanted by the Brueghel-esque scene around them. Like a fairytale giant he watched small figures scurry below – children bombing down the slope, minions pulling lucky ones back up the hill. He scooped his youngest son, who thought he could see Spain from the North Downs, under his right arm like a load of washing.

Greg screamed with delight, his windburned features muddled with joy.

'Got you, got you, got you,' yelled Jacob, twirling him round and round, bumping into the others until Jacob, losing his footing, collapsed into a heap of sledges and sons. Everyone laughed except Greg, who cried, again, until he was picked up, de-snowed and kissed by his mother.

At the top of the hill people shuffled their bums into place, kicked off with their feet, fathers with legs bent like water-boatmen, limbs too long and stiff, and moved slowly down the hill. But as the sledgers came level with a line of fir trees their trays and toboggans and bin-bags picked up speed. Whooping shouts rose into the air and, just for a moment, the month of February had a purpose.

Dan and Beth fidgeted on the sledge as Jacob explained to them how to steer and slow down, but they weren't listening. Beth wrapped her arms tightly around Dan, who was almost the same size as the giant bear Jacob had won for her at the Midsummer Fayre on the common last year.

'You're squashing me,' Dan said indignantly, his face frowning as he tried to shoulder her off.

'I might fall off,' said Beth, squeezing her arms around him tighter.

'Hold on,' said Jacob, shoving the sledge away with his foot, 'and remember to steer.'

They moved embarrassingly slowly down the slope, curved slightly to the right and, gathering their own inertia, ground to a halt.

'Stupid thing,' said Dan, cross. Beth wriggled furiously behind him, trying to push them on, but Dan was already climbing off. Jacob, laughing, scuffed through snow towards them. 'You didn't get far.'

'Shut up,' said Dan. He could be very rude to his father

sometimes, particularly in front of Beth. But Jacob didn't care about things like that much.

'Be like that then,' Jacob said, shrugging. 'Come on, Beth.' He picked her up, sat on the sledge, put her on his lap and kicked them away.

Beth felt funny sitting on someone's lap who wasn't her dad, even though Jacob had won her a giant bear and had picked her up thousands of times and had even told her off in the same way that he told off his own children, which had made her cry rather than sulk. But then they began to pick up speed and her mouth opened wide, swallowing the fast-rushing air, tasting the sharp coldness of the snow as it flew like fireworks from the runners. In her ear Dan's dad whooped loudly and, as they swerved to the left to avoid a group of heavy-puffing boys, she too screamed with pleasure. They came to a halt and, giddy with rare, burbling excitement, she began to pull Jacob back up the hill.

Rachel, ostensibly helping Greg to make a snowman, watched Beth and Jacob lumbering hand in hand back up the hill. She was always watching, that child, always listening and storing information, big brown eyes and a translucently pale face. She was a strange companion for her son, who was as inconsistent and impassioned as his father. 'Delightful but hard work,' *her* mother had said briskly when she'd first met Jacob. Quite, thought Rachel, on top of a hill fifteen years later.

To her right, Dan was setting himself off with little grunts of exertion.

'D'you want a push?' she asked.

'No,' he said fiercely.

'All right,' she said mildly and watched him travel away – gathering pace past the trees, bumping over slight mounds in the snow, veering to the left, travelling smoothly, speedily down the slope – straight towards his father and Beth.

Rachel gasped and gave a laugh; it looked as if he were

heading straight for them. 'Watch out,' she shouted pointlessly, her voice disappearing above the slopes, 'you'll hit Dad.'

The potential collision looked comical. Jacob didn't seem to have noticed, eyes down on his feet, planting them steadily in the snow, pretending to be pulled up the hill by Beth.

'Dan,' Rachel shouted again, still half-laughing, 'go right, go right.'

Of course he couldn't hear her, and neither could Jacob. Only Beth noticed Dan heading for them at a frightening speed, metal runners pummelling fast over the compacted snow.

At that moment, when Dan had only twenty feet or so left to travel, Rachel suddenly thought that maybe this wasn't so funny and, leaving Greg suspiciously sniffing a snowball, she began to run and slither down the hill.

Beth was trying to remember Dan's dad's name. 'Look,' she kept saying, pulling on his hand. 'Mr, look. Dan's going to hit us.' But he wouldn't let go of her hand and continued to tune-lessly hum his way up the hill, gripping on to her.

'Dan, stop, stop,' said his mother, running and falling and scrambling her way down the slope, her arms flailing and coat edges dipped in white icing. She watched and with Dan's immin-ent collision with his father she stood still, open-mouthed, hands slightly raised as if perspective gave her the power to pick up the figures below her, wriggling like Lilliputians between two fingers. There was considerable determination in Dan's progress, his red jacket puffed out, his dark hair blown back, and he whizzed in a perfect diagonal, like a vengeful beetle, straight into Jacob's legs.

There was a muffled crunch, a roar and a high-pitched shout before she reached them but she was laughing again by the time she got there. Jacob seemed to have been up-ended, so the lower half of his body was now spreadeagled on top of the sledge. Dan had already picked himself up and was trudging off, keen to avoid explanations. Beth followed with a shocked expression. Rachel tried to stop laughing and pay attention to Jacob's ankle, which he was sure was broken. But he was such a noisy man that it sometimes did her good to see him up-ended.

Nevertheless, there were a few problems to resolve. Dan had gone into a dog-like sulk (unwilling to say sorry, fully able to realise what he'd done). And Jacob's ankle was too painful to drive, which left them unable to get home. Greg offered to drive, which was kind of him. But Jacob was cross, and something, perhaps the sight of Rachel still neat in her navy scarf, so dignified and useless like a Russian heroine, made him say, 'It would have been useful right now if you'd been able to drive.' Wisely Rachel said nothing, but piled all the children into the car for warmth and walked off to the nearest house to phone Beth's father for a lift.

When Roger arrived thirty minutes later they'd eaten all the travel sweets they could find. Jacob was sitting on a bench alone and Rachel was beginning to wonder if she were the only adult in Epsom. But they all cheered enormously at the sight of Roger, so tall and shy and gentle that he made an unlikely hero. Beth hugged him hard, Dan trailed round his legs and Jacob shook his hand ruefully. Roger, who didn't have the faculties for glibness, had a quickening, focusing effect on people. And thus he was often amazed at the vitality and cheer of others. He thought himself a rather dull and steady man. He and Lizzie, for instance, would never take all these children tobogganing. It just wouldn't happen, and that inability to picture it saddened him. He had to work quite hard all the way home to keep up with Jacob's chippy humour.

'Now then . . . why would a son try to capsize his father? Or, indeed, maim his father? Bit Freudian, really, isn't it? Maybe it's about his mother . . . or maybe it's because I took the favoured Beth on my toboggan. Maybe that's it . . .'

37

'Jacob,' said Rachel.

'Yes, sweetheart,' said Jacob with a flashy smile.

'Shut your mouth.'

Someone giggled in the back.

4. Frisk

Although she had new shoes with the frequency of a new moon Beth took growth with equanimity, until one Sunday in June, aged eleven and gangly, when she rang on Dan's doorbell. With that movement Beth realised she could now reach the buzzer and that the mark of adolescence was upon her. She found the idea of being a teenager terrifying. Obviously the concept of being an adult was beyond reach, but being thirteen was only a couple of years away. Time crept up so, years one on top of the other. It was frightening the way her childhood was accumulating.

Beth was relieved when Rachel answered the door. She didn't feel like trading snipey insults with acned Dave. Rachel was relaxed and conversational and Beth sought out her company more and more often. Rachel was distracted and ignored a lot of misbehaviour. She didn't seem to care much about mess or the amount of sweets they ate. Her children just seemed to be part of the house. Her companions rather than her captives. Beth liked that.

'They've gone to the shop,' said Rachel. 'I'm in the garden.' Beth followed her through the house and out into the scented greenness.

'Rachel?'

'Here, hold this.' Rachel handed her a ball of string. 'I need a piece about a foot long.' Beth cut a piece and held it out to her as she embraced a small shrub.

'Did you like being a teenager?' asked Beth. Rachel finished tying up the plant and then stopped still a moment.

'God, I don't know,' she said. 'Why?'

'I was just wondering,' said Beth, looking embarrassed. So Rachel thought and tried to answer her properly.

'I don't think I realised the potential of it, to be honest. I don't think we were meant to. We went from being too young to do certain things to being too old to behave like that. There wasn't any leeway . . . I remember being a little girl, and then I remember a lot of school, days and days of school, and then I met Jacob. And then I had Dave.'

Beth watched Rachel's tangled hair and wide-planted legs in tight blue jeans. Hearing someone talk about themselves with objectivity, analysis, was new to Beth. In her house things were what they were. Adulthood was sacrosanct and unnecessary discussion was like showing off.

'Then I had Dan,' Rachel continued. 'And to think I once planned to run away and be part of an Arabian harem . . .'

'What's a harem?'

'Umm. Good question.' Rachel looked at Beth as if assessing her age, her parameters, anew. 'It's a community of women kept hidden except to their children and husband,' she said instructively.

The description reminded Beth of someone. 'Like my mum, you mean. Women who don't go out much.'

'No, no,' Rachel laughed, 'not like your mum at all . . .' And then she stopped; what did she know? Jacob had told her more than once how Mrs Standing looked like she had hidden depths. Lizzie was certainly a strange mixture of shy and tough. The Standings' marriage at least seemed to have mystery.

'No,' Rachel went on, wanting to give Beth a boost – she looked so pinched in those silly flowered shorts – 'your mum is a private person, which is entirely different. And what about

40

you?' she continued, turning back to the bush. 'Where would you like to run away to?'

'To start a dog circus with Dan,' said Beth nonchalantly. It was a silly answer but less embarrassing than the truth, which was a little closer to home.

The orange blossom had landed. It bloomed in back gardens, bringing a whiff of Old England to Colliers Wood. Rachel's garden, ahead of its time in its sympathy to weeds and wildlife, grew and blossomed with a wild abandon. Peace roses grew greedily, fighting for air space with dog roses, nourished by soil that regurgitated broken china after rain. It was brightly, sweetly pretty and on days like these one was tempted to think that this terraced life was the best one. Breezy streets, where one might meet and comment on the day, windows and back doors open to the air, and then row upon row of differing gardens, mini-wildernesses through which you could see your own square patch of blue sky with neighbours and their windows kept at bay by green growth. Alleyways, not yet high with heat and cats, grew odd poppies and keen sycamore saplings.

Upstairs at number 22, Jacob did his teeth, his head fugged and parched with a booze and cigarette hangover. Last night, under the influence of a good deal of cheap Spanish wine, he had experienced an eye-wateringly optimistic vision of the future. Wholesome careers and happy family meals had flowed through his mind. Scenes of fresh starts in strangely American landscapes came back to him as he scrubbed too hard and spat blood into the basin. All things are possible with an excess of alcohol except, of course, sex. Jacob felt edgy and frustrated. He could hear his wife's voice in the garden. He'd have liked Sunday morning sex. No, he'd have liked Sunday all-day sex. He would have liked to lurch from bedroom to bathroom to kitchen to bedroom. He'd almost forgotten what sex smelled like. He considered going downstairs to the garden and approaching her from behind, pressing himself close to her, kissing the back of her neck, shuffling his hand upwards from her belly. God knows he still fancied her.

He had fallen for her way of standing more than anything else. What had struck him when he first saw Rachel was how unafraid she was of her own presence. For a man who had spent all his life in fear of discovery, who was as yet unreconciled to the man he actually was, as opposed to the one he wanted to be, Rachel was a revelation. She was a woman who knew how to use her height, never bowed or bent or slumped, who seemed to clear paths in crowds as she walked, her head high and voice low. He once said this to her and she seemed bemused.

'Serene,' he'd said.

'Oh please,' she'd said.

After a few years of marriage, among the many things he consciously learned – to try not to linger on a hurt where none was intended, to try not to provide an answer when none was actually wanted – was the need to keep his awe at her way of moving through life to himself. She made short shrift of his fitful ecstasies of adoration. His favourite mystery was her, but in a way it was a lonely worshipping, one that didn't need him, and sometimes, like this morning, he longed for someone to come alive in his presence only. Her unflappable peace grated him. He wondered how it would be to have a wife who lived for him, not just with him. The thought of going downstairs and putting his hand up her jumper seemed as unlikely as groping his mother. His penis had a tendency to deflate unless encouraged kindly these days. No, he decided wearily, no point in bothering, it would pass. All things come to pass. He splashed cold water on his face, but it was so chilling that he had to follow up quickly with warm water.

Rachel laughed below. He sighed and dripped into the basin.

42

So many things to wish for and so little movement to suggest their coming on a Sunday morning in suburbia.

He'd only been unfaithful to her twice in fifteen years of marriage. The first time had been many moons ago when he'd been in France, on his first job abroad. Afterwards he had been disgusted by himself and had been scared that with that one lapse of attention he had now put himself into a whole other category of person. Without meaning to, without thinking he was that kind of adulterous person, he had become just that. How had that happened? he'd wondered, shocked, on the ferry back. It was almost as if it had happened when he wasn't looking. Take your eyes off your life for one second and look what it goes and does.

If it had been as straightforward as guilt he might have been able to stop himself from the second brief encounter five years later. Or at least if guilt was as clear cut as regretting hurting someone else, Jacob might have been able to refrain from repeating his mistakes. But more than anything – one's own discomfort is inescapable – he regretted that he had proved himself capable of failure. That's what hurt most. And in his failure he sought comfort, affirmation that the mistake was valid, unavoidable, which could only be proved by mistaking again. There was an affirmation of importance, of existence, that came from his reflection in a girl's eyes. Spouses, he discovered, could be made to disappear, like thin women hidden behind trees, and in that dappled clearing lust's justification grew easy. Drama mistaken for importance.

As he dried his face he told himself, with typical, penitent severity, how lucky he'd been to get away with it all, how close he had come in that hotel in Birmingham the night before last. All that mini-bar vodka and flirtation. He sometimes wondered if he and Rachel hadn't married too early. He did love her a great deal, but on whose moral scale did two infidelities make

43

him a good husband or father? Jacob looked at himself in the mirror and thought, I am not a bad man but I might as well be.

And with that he felt a little redeemed, and his headache a little better.

Dissatisfaction, edgy aspirations and niggling frustrations were in the air. Perhaps they arrived with the orange blossom. The dogs in the park frisked and fornicated but in the corner shop Dan sighed at the selection of comics, echoing Jacob in his avocado suite of a bathroom. Next door, Jenny Garland's tortoise opened its ugly little eyes and began a month-long circuit of the garden. Inside the house, Jenny lay in bed, yawning. She'd come in later than she should have done the night before and had broken number one of *Cosmopolitan*'s Ten Beauty Commandments by going to bed still wearing blue mascara. Traces of frosted pink lipstick also remained in the corners of her mouth and she dug painfully at the spot on her chin as she thought about the night before in the pub, when Ian, a two-year obsession of hers, had looked at her long and promisingly hard, then said, 'You've got a sort of flat face, haven't you?' He had later been spotted outside the pub, snogging some cow in a bat-wing jumper.

Dave Frederick lay in bed and thought about Jenny. Jenny wearing the short black skirt he'd seen her leaving the house in the night before. He'd not been impressed by her legs, far too white and real, more like his mother's than Heather Locklear's. But the skirt plagued him, the critical black line above which anything and everything could happen. It seemed a very primitive piece of clothing, designed to torment him, remind him that real female genitalia lay next door. She might as well have been in Timbuktu.

Beth and Rachel worked companionably in the garden, weeding the trumpeting white bindweed out from between campanulas, sweetpeas and daisies. It was like an illustration in one of her old baby books, thought Beth. Over the road, half their garden had recently been patioed and potted.

Next door, she and Rachel could hear Mrs Garland and her sister Norma talking in their garden.

'I don't know,' said Mrs Garland, 'carrots, peas.' She paused. There must be more vegetables in the world. 'Beans?' she said irritably. 'Except I haven't got any.'

'Hasn't George been to the allotment? Aren't there broad beans?'

'I don't know. Would they be ready yet?'

'Well, *I* don't know,' said Norma.

Mrs Garland's unmarried sister came for lunch every Sunday. Presumably, thought Rachel, dead-heading a geranium, it's natural law that the one fortunate enough to have a husband has to pay for it with lunch.

'Mind that tortoise,' said Mrs Garland sharply, six feet away behind a fence.

Rachel was wondering about her own vegetables, whether the carrots would stretch if Beth stayed for lunch, when a wet-haired Jacob stepped through the back door. He was followed by the dog, who was stretching and wagging his tail in that 'Okay, I'm awake now, bring it on, let's play' way. He was a medium-sized, scruffy brown thing. A ubiquitous collie cross that they'd picked up from Battersea Dogs' Home three years ago.

It had been one of Jacob's impulsive family outings. Occasionally he would decide to lead his family head-first into a day of fun and learning. Which was endearing but demanding. The children, and adults too, would come back exhausted and easily upset, bodies splattered across the car seats.

The Saturday they arrived at the Dogs' Home had been a significant day in the family's expanding history. Dan had been begging for a dog for as long as he had been able to say it, but the possibility that he might within three hours be holding a lead with a dog of his own at the end of it had almost been too much to bear and his small face had gone white with shock. Dan had passed through the grey doors silently, into the strong smell of dog shit and sounds of dog purgatory. He and Jacob had found the noise and the need of the animals disturbing. They had walked up and down the alleyways, peering into the cages, Jacob with one hand on Dan's shoulder. So in the end the process of choosing his very own dog had been rather a joyless one, like choosing which drowning man to save out of a shipful. Dave had kept up a steady running commentary on the stink and Greg had quite reasonably demanded to know where they'd all come from, how they'd all got there, and why they were all talking to each other at once.

After twenty minutes they'd stopped in front of two alsatians who were scrapping in a desultory way. In the corner of the cage a mess of tufty brown fur was keeping a low profile. While they'd paused he'd sidled round the edge of the pen and licked Dan's outstretched hand through the wire. One lick and he was his. His notes had said 'Bad with cats, slight chest infection, HT', the latter meaning housetrained. All of which had proved wrong. He'd developed a chaste but time-consuming crush on next door's cat, had cost them a good hundred pounds in vet's bills with a very serious chest infection and was quite clearly totally un-housetrained. Every morning a warm odour would greet Rachel as she came down the stairs. For a year the first thing you'd notice on entering their house was the slight smell of pine disinfectant. Slowly, between them, Rachel and Dan had managed to knock him into some semblance of trained, but he hadn't ever really become a dog-dog. He was more like a slightly neurotic, very furry relative who was a little picky about proper food but would graze happily off everyone else's plates. Who was sent into noisy frenzies of fear by spiders and disliked men who carried golf clubs.

In the garden, Beth fell on the dog with joy. 'Morning,' said Jacob in his patriarch voice. His normal voice wasn't that deep. He walked up to Rachel and put his arm around her and kissed her neck.

'Did you know that dog was nearly called Dogger?' Jacob said to Beth. Using the girl's presence to reassert himself within his home. Showing off in front of a lonely eleven-year-old. Beth shook her head.

'Because Greg said if you say "Dog" fast enough it sounds like "Dogger". I was never sure myself. Anyway, we love his name, don't we, darling?' he said with jolly sarcasm to Rachel.

'You most of all,' she replied.

'Beaver is a fine name for a dog who is dark and wriggles and won't come when you want him to. But, as I said to Dan, don't ever, ever expect me to walk him.'

Beth saw Jacob squeeze his wife's bum and then laugh out loud as a branch of blossom Rachel was holding whipped back in his face. They were funny, Dan's parents, like something on telly.

Within an hour Dan, Beth and Beaver were in the park, on the lam from an invigorated Jacob who had declared it Helping-Your-Mother-Sunday. Beaver was having a fine time of it. He hustled his way round the Scotties and Jack Russells, displayed his virility by pissing on an Adidas sports bag by the goalposts and was now, sensing a good spread, hot-footing it towards the little hut by the green bowls pitch. Dan and Beth sloped resentfully after him. They knew he was after the bowls club lunch.

It was the first game of the summer season. Like a Persil advert, the men and women soft-shoed it in brilliant white at the base of the lawn which was the unnatural green of butcher's fake grass. There was a constant low murmur of chat but occasionally someone would make a ribald comment or another's shot would roll a little off target, clink another bowl slyly out of the way and throaty laughter would break out.

Beth noticed a spindly adolescent in among the pensioners, his white trousers a little too short.

'Look at him,' she said to Dan as they picked up speed towards the hut.

'Weird,' he said.

A little way up the path they heard a sudden cry – 'Oh my God, June, watch out for those sandwiches; there's a dog at them' – and Beth, unable to bear the embarrassment, ran the last twenty yards. She reached the hut and grabbed Beaver's collar just as he was finishing off a round of cheese and ham, paws on the table like a barrel-chested man at a bar.

'I'm really sorry, he's very greedy,' she said but they just laughed and said there's plenty more and doesn't he ever get fed? She dragged Beaver out, his tongue lolling, drooling white breadcrumb saliva, and they put him on the lead as a sort of punishment. If Beaver had been better behaved Dan would have always kept him off the lead and gone up the shops with him heeling all the way, waiting patiently outside the shops, watching his every movement.

'We could try and train him some more, you know,' said Beth helpfully. 'We kind of gave up on him.' Dan seemed to be in a funny mood and she'd learned by now that chatter could plug bad-day gaps in conversation.

'No point,' said Dan in a gloom, 'he's hopeless. He ran away again this morning, out the front door. I found him waiting to be let in to Jenny's house.'

Beth laughed. 'Stupid.'

'No, he's not stupid.' She'd made the wrong remark again. 'He got the right side of the road. It was only next door. He can't read numbers, can he?' They walked in silence for a few minutes.

'I think your brother fancies Jenny,' said Beth.

'Eughh.' Dan stuck his tongue out.

'I saw him looking out of the window at her yesterday.'

'She's got fat legs.'

'No, she hasn't,' said Beth, 'has she?' She looked worried and glanced down at her own jean-clad legs.

'Fat hairy legs,' Dan laughed, 'like you.'

Beth hit him. Rather too hard. She did that sometimes. 'Shut up.'

There was a pause. 'I haven't got fat legs,' she added aggressively.

'I'm the smallest in my class,' he said by way of compensation.

'So?' said Beth. A useless, useful word at that stage in life, the fallback of all young girls, carrying fear and superiority in equal measure.

'So nothing,' he said, giving up.

They were getting nowhere. It was only their second circuit and Beaver was straining heavily at the lead. Children hung on the swings, scuffing their feet in the gravel, and a young mother sat on a bench, smoking a cigarette. There was a sudden breeze and a burst of traffic beyond the railings and Dan felt the need for action.

'Let's do something.'

'Like what?'

'I dunno.' Why couldn't she think of something for a change? He had an urge to be destructive, to find somewhere and break it open, steal a horse and gallop it. 'We could go round to your house.'

Beth was surprised. They didn't do that often. 'What are we going to do there?'

'Something might be happening.'

'What, at my house?' It seemed unlikely. Silence fell again momentarily. 'I've got some new stickers,' she added shyly. Dan pulled a face. These days there were more than a few interests they didn't share. Stationery was one. Football was another.

In the end they did go round to Beth's. She and Dan and Beaver clattering into Lizzie's hallway, which always smelled of Pledge, and then into the small kitchen at the back for orange squash and a sandwich. Beaver padded back and forth, tracking the magnetic smells overhead.

Lizzie came down the stairs and looked very happy to see her kitchen being raided. 'Hello Dan, how nice to see you.'

'Hello, Mrs Standing.' Dan realised he was standing on her shiny floor and eating her bread without having been invited, so he clarified: 'We were a bit hungry.'

'That's all right. Do you want a biscuit? I bought some biscuits last week, I think; didn't I, Beth?'

Beth reached into a cupboard and silently took out a packet of custard creams and put them on the table.

'That's right,' said Lizzie, bending down and sliding back a glass cupboard door. 'I'll get you a plate for them.'

'Don't, we'll take them upstairs,' said Beth, picking up Beaver's trailing lead and adding 'Come on' to Dan.

'Don't go,' said Lizzie, and she gave a rather forced, anxious smile. 'I wanted to show you something.' Dan sat down at the small table while Beth hung back in the doorway, edging towards the stairs. 'Beth, I've asked you nicely, now will you just sit down?' Lizzie said, suddenly sharper.

But Beth said 'I've got to go to the toilet', dropped Beaver's lead on the floor and ran up the stairs.

Lizzie was silent, listening to her daughter's retreat, then shook her head slightly as if trying to break her irritation. 'Anyone would think I was about to beat her.' And she smiled again at Dan, pushing the packet of biscuits towards him. He smiled back and took one.

'How's school?' she asked.

'All right,' he said, 'thank you.'

'Any nice teachers this year?'

'Ummm.' Dan thought about them. It was hard to remember at the weekends. 'I like Mrs Briscoe, who does Biology; she doesn't give us any homework.' He looked at Beth's mother who was clearly hoping for a little bit more information. 'Miss Nightingale who teaches RE is okay, but I don't like Mr Williams. He does sport and he's rude.'

'Rude?'

'He shouts a lot and, well, it's really bad. If you do something wrong he makes jokes about you. He makes people laugh at you.'

'That's dreadful.' She looked very concerned. Dan was gratified.

'Last week, there's this boy called Ian who's a bit spast—' He stopped. 'He's kind of not very good at games and things and he went to kick the ball and he missed. It just rolled a little bit instead of even getting near the goal. And everyone went "Dur".' Dan bulged his tongue behind his lower lip and waved his right hand limply. 'But Mr Williams made everyone stop the game and went and made everyone stand round, and he had his hand on Ian's shoulder and started saying that it wasn't Ian's fault if he was crap at—' Dan stopped again and swallowed. 'Wasn't very good at games and that being disabled wasn't a funny thing and that if you were you needed lots of special attention and stuff. And Ian's really embarrassed and starts crying and it . . . well, it made everything worse.'

Mrs Standing was looking a little confused. 'And this boy, Ian, was he, is he, disabled?'

'No, that's the whole point,' said Dan, raising both hands in the air. 'He made it seem like he was, not just rubbish at football. Which he is.'

Mrs Standing looked sad. 'Well, no, you're right,' she said after a while, 'it doesn't seem a very good way of handling things.' She turned, hoping to hear Beth's footsteps down the stairs. 'Well . . . I wanted to show you both something.' She looked nervous and stopped. Dan wondered what on earth was coming next. He tried to look interested. 'I've spoken to your mother about it and she says she doesn't see why you shouldn't be able to come. It's a nice place, my friend told me about it. Lots of things for children to do she said, near the sea and a lovely café. And lots of pasties and ice cream. Sounds all right, doesn't it?'

'Oh,' said Dan, nodding vigorously. Then he stopped. 'Actually, I don't know what you mean.'

'Would you like to come on holiday with us this summer?'

'Can Beaver come?' First things first.

'Oh, I don't know.' Lizzie looked crestfallen. 'I hadn't thought about that.' Then, resolutely, 'Yes, I expect so.'

They heard Beth coming down the stairs and her mother saw her lingering at the end of the hallway.

'Well, now you're back, we've got some news. Dan's going to come on holiday with us this year,' she said to her daughter, a little triumphant. 'What d'you think about that?'

There was a pause and, though it was a bit difficult to see in the dimness of the hall, Dan thought Beth looked cross. 'Why?' she said.

'I thought you'd like it—' Lizzie stopped abruptly, trying to contain herself in front of Dan. She looked down at the brochure. 'I'll tell you what, I'll leave you to it. I've got to go to the corner shop. I'll put the leaflet here.' She got up and reached for her bag which was hanging on the back of the door. As she passed Beth she put her hand on her head. Beth flinched.

The front door clicked shut and Beth came into the kitchen. 'She's so annoying,' she muttered.

'Why? She's nice.' Dan thought Beth's mum might be the first and last person to ask him a question and let him finish the answer. 'Don't you want me to come on holiday?'

Beth picked up the leaflet and looked at it. Little houses with brightly coloured doors sitting on a cliff. She wasn't sure she did. Dan was – well, he was a boy, which she only seemed to have realised the full significance of recently. When she remembered it she sometimes found it a bit hard to know what to say. She went round to his to see Rachel as much as him these days. To be part of a different household. And if Dan came away with her he would get to see what it was really like at home with her mum and dad. Often babyish, dull and quiet, sometimes pierced with angry shouting, other days smothered in a pall of sad flatness. Compared to Dan's house, her template for normality, it was more than a bit weird. There were times, at night, when all the other houses on the street were quiet and she thought their home must shine in the dark with some strange incandescent light.

'You won't like it,' she said.

Dan looked at her. Sometimes she seemed very white and stubborn. He suddenly felt sorry for her but didn't know why.

'Show me your stupid stickers then.'

Lizzie came back to her kitchen to find it empty, the brochure about Swanage still on the table, opened out, face down. She made herself a cup of Nescafé and put two spoonfuls of the newly bought sugar in it. She sat down and listened to the sounds of the two children in the house. She wondered if they'd stay and have lunch. She doubted it; she'd got a little bit cross with Beth last night, who was still sulking. If she asked they might, but she only had three lamb chops in. Perhaps she should start shopping for more than one day at a time. She could go without lunch and roast lots of potatoes, but then Roger might think she was ill. He was out at a car boot sale and wouldn't be back until later. He was going to look for a spice rack for her, he'd said. She'd never asked for a spice rack, wasn't sure what she'd do with a spice rack, except, she supposed, put pots of spice in it. Hers wasn't really a spice rack type of kitchen she thought, looking round her. It was more like her mother's old kitchen in Harrogate than a London kitchen like Rachel's. It had hard, sharp edges, clinically blue formica surfaces and frosted sliding doors. The only decoration, frivolity, was a postcard slotted between the glass and wooden casing of one of the cupboards – a picture of a yellow beach in Yugoslavia from a work friend of Roger's. She took it down and looked at the small yellow people with blobs of brown hair lying on towels, and saw it had been sent over a year ago. She put it in the bin.

Even though Beth spent half her time at Dan's, Lizzie didn't go round to the more boisterous, male Frederick household often; she always thought Rachel must be terribly busy with three boys to cope with and a husband who travelled a lot. Also there was something about the little one, Greg, that reminded her particularly of Paul. Not just in the usual way, automatically averting your eyes from families in the street, from boys who have been allowed to grow and grow, holding hands with their mothers and fathers, laughing and loved. No, Greg reminded her of Paul in a distinct way. They had the same stocky stillness, a way of standing, open-mouthed, and watching a room revolve around them. Martin and Paul would have been teenagers now. Each year took her farther from them – as if they were living somewhere, with long legs and broken voices, without her. She felt a familiar wave of desolation. It hadn't been one of her better weeks she thought. She must have been hard to live with and last night when she'd shouted and shouted at Beth, who had rudely said that she didn't want her bloody dinner, Roger had just carried their eleven-year-old away.

She'd thought of the holiday idea during the night. It would be good; Beth would have someone to play with, which would relax Roger. People might see them walking along the sea front and think that they looked like a whole family. She was haunted by the idea of herself as the breaking point, the hairline fracture within her family. She felt she, Roger and Beth must be obvious in their damage. Beth might not have been told about her half-brothers but the child reflected her tension, Lizzie knew. It frustrated her badly. But here she was, trying to make Beth happy. Why was it so impossible for the child to try a bit harder too?

When she had popped round to Rachel's to suggest the holiday idea, their kitchen had seemed full of warmth and colour and Lizzie had thought how all sorts of family meals would be possible there. It was bigger, to start with; they had had an extension built, although Rachel had kindly pointed out where it was leaking in the corner. That meant they didn't have the same boxed-in grey square of yard outside the kitchen door which always seemed to collect earwigs. The sun had shone on to the table where they'd sat and had tea and Lizzie had thought how bright and up-to-date the yellow mugs looked on top of the pine table, a bunch of bluebells beside them, picked from the garden. That night, as they ate their dinner alone, she'd asked Roger whether he didn't think the house was a bit dowdy, a bit old-fashioned, which she supposed was the genesis of the spice rack.

There wasn't much Sunday traffic and Rachel, who had popped into the corner shop for some peas, crossed back over Boundary Road without looking. Even if there had been any traffic she wouldn't have heard it. She wondered whether she ought to turn left and walk a little further along to the park to check on Dan and Beth, but the thought of the footballs and dog shit in the sunshine put her off.

She let herself into the quiet house. The toilet flushed upstairs.

A radio mumbled behind someone's door. Jacob was probably unpacking, piling up dirty pants, carefully emptying his jacket pockets, sorting through the mini-bar receipts. She walked slowly through the kitchen to the garden and lay down on the grass. The big pear tree dropped a leaf and it spiralled down towards her. She put her hand out to catch it. One falling leaf caught equals a happy day. Odd, she thought, that her happiest moments were when alone in this fenced garden. Small sounds rustling around her.

There was suddenly a larger sound, Dan and Beth and Beaver scuffling to open the alley gate, then running into the garden.

'Where's the snorkels? I'm going on holiday with Beth,' Dan said urgently.

'Ask your father,' said Rachel. 'He says he's on duty today.' And then she added to Beth, hoping to get a smile, 'I'm glad about the holiday. You make sure you keep Dan in order while you're there.'

And they were gone. They needed a tunnel, those two. Except that when Dan came back she would be taking him away from Delia Street. And a tunnel would be pointless then. She was going to leave Jacob; indeed, she was already leaving by invisible increments, peeling herself away from him stealthily because staying would leave her terminally disappointed. She had loved him once but she didn't want to be his wife any more. Rachel wanted her own life (she even had a driving test next week) and she had as much right and as much responsibility to choose happiness as the next woman. Just because she'd got into it at the age of twenty didn't mean she couldn't get out. The children would have to come with her. She had a suspicion it would be the making of them.

Roger's happiest holiday moment came when surrounded by the others. They had been in Swanage five days. The sight of Beth and Dan running down to the waves made him think how precious this all was. The sound of Lizzie guffawing, a pasty in her hand, as she watched them jack-in-the-box right out of the icy cold sea, made him smile. He recognised the vital moment with a characteristic self-consciousness. A shudder of shyness. He put the back of his fingers to Lizzie's face and she turned towards him with a half-smile, mince and potato bulging inside one cheek.

For nearly a week the four of them had followed the same routine. Awake at eight in their small side-room with bunk beds (for which a tense Beth had apologised to Dan, saying with borrowed adult efficiency: 'It's quite hard to find places with lots of bedrooms in the summer'). Up at nine for breakfast, down to the beach by ten. The beach hours passed with a simplicity none of them would have suspected. They would stay and snack on ice creams and pasties and chips until five and then they would go back to the cottage for tea. It was a steep climb to the cottage and Dan and Beth would arrive back home gasping for breath, wet towels under their arms, plastic-weave beach bags banging against their legs, Beaver pulling on his lead and panting messily for his tin of Chum.

The intermittent sun was hot today. Dan lay flat on his back, his white chest, smelling too sweetly of Boots factor twenty-five suncream, bare to the sky, hopeful of a tan. He closed one eye against the glare and turned his head to the left. The perspective was odd. He could see columns of walkers far off and pebbles close to his nose. Huge pebbles, tiny people. He could see Beaver trying to eat the waves and Beth playing with him, crouched on her haunches, ready to leap like a grasshopper. Mr and Mrs Standing sat behind his head on deckchairs, reading things. Around Dan's towel, which he carefully straightened after each swim, then wrinkled immediately with a single seal-like turn, was a book, a walkman, a set of Travel Scrabble, a comic, a warm can of Tango, a lolly stick and a packet of crisps. He was hot and didn't know what he wanted so he lay still, one eye watching the seashore.

The columns grew slowly bigger. They finally drew level with Beth, just an ordinary family, no longer dignified by distance, a granny in a cardigan and flowery dress, a boy in a windcheater, a mother with a cooler bag. Beth hadn't moved at all. Still crouching, playing her hand in the water, watching Beaver in the sea. It was odd just being able to watch, not having to do anything. If his dad, Jacob, were here they'd be playing a game, he'd be catching them, grabbing them, manhandling them to laughter. Then they'd all eat at the same time, loud and squabbling, and then they'd be clearing up, moving off, getting in the car, going somewhere else.

His mum had given him twenty-five pounds before he came – twenty pounds for treats and a fiver for dog food. Mr Standing hadn't let him pay for anything so he and Beth were planning how they could spend the money before they went home. Mum would be cross if he *hadn't* spent all of it. He supposed he should buy Mrs Standing a present but he didn't really know what she'd want. His mum was always noticing things – saying things were lovely or revolting, always with humour, but Mrs Standing didn't seem to do that. She didn't organise the world as she went along like his mother did. She didn't pick things out of the view, name objects, claim them, question them. He had sometimes found himself taking over that role these last five days. Saying 'look at that' or 'what d'you think that is?'. Like he just wanted to hear someone point out the pieces. Like it wouldn't be a proper holiday without everyone saying what they could see. Beth only ever seemed to look straight in front of her, her head never swivelled in the back seat of the car, like a toy's, to catch a flying cow or a castle. 'You're not looking,' he'd say to her sometimes, hurt. 'So*rreee*,' she'd say huffily, like everything was a telling-off.

But she was okay, Beth; they had good games and she was rude and wicked sometimes in a clever way that impressed him. And when she went quiet, which she was quite often, he always wanted to know what she was thinking because he thought it might well be something good or new that he could put in his pocket and pull out to show someone else. They played at detectives on the beach most days. Taking notes about people, thinking up their secret lives, guessing their crimes. She had a scary imagination, but as his mother was always saying he and his brothers should use theirs he followed her story-telling leaps with breathless fidelity.

Beth was still crouching at the water's edge, her hair lifting in the breeze. She was wearing a black and white striped T-shirt, her 'prison' T-shirt, she called it. She had lots of T-shirts, all different colours, all different names; the brown and yellow stripes were Girl Guide Uniform, the red and white was the Ice Lolly, the plain navy was the Sensible Top, the white one was Bound To Get Grubby. It was all rather odd; Dan had never thought about clothes much before.

He propped himself upright so he could look straight at the sea. It was flat today, crescent-shaped ripples travelling into the distance, then rolls of grey working the other way, the two melding into low-breaking waves. The sun suddenly broke through the stretched cloud and a path, a broad, Roman road of silver-glinting water, stretched ahead, narrowing into the horizon to the line where the sky bends down to the sea. It was right at his feet, a straight line leading from him to an unimaginable point in the middle of an empty ocean. He knew that France was supposed to be out there somewhere, but to imagine the water and then a beach full of French boys, themselves squinting at the sky, imagining English boys, made his head feel stretched. From here the horizon looked very much like the edge of the world.

He looked over to Beth to see whether she'd seen his sun road. She was now upright, elongated, and so he sprang up, wiry and fast, to join her. He walked along the top edge of the pebble bank, then turned down to the shoreline, wobble-walking over the sharp stones. To his surprise he could see his path to the sun starting right at her feet. You took it with you, he realised; it just depended where you were standing. She heard him crunching towards her and turned round, her mouth open, tasting the soft salt on the air.

'Look,' she said.

'I know,' he said, 'it looks like you could walk on it.'

'But you can't,' she said, turning back.

'I *know*,' he said, 'but it *looks* like it, doesn't it?'

'Yes,' she said, smiling sideways at him again. 'Just imagine.'

They stood side by side, watching the great stream of shuddering light diminish into the distance. Time lay ahead, glittering with potential, clear and directed as a race.

Roger put his newspaper down on his lap once more and watched the two of them standing at the water's edge. They looked as though they were about to set off somewhere. Down the yellow brick road to find something. They made such lanky silhouettes in the bright light. It wasn't as if they didn't eat, but that was youth – all those crisps and sweets disappearing into hollow legs. Nothing seemed to mark them much – no indigestion or aching bones, just temporary grazes and scabs.

Bringing Dan had been a good idea of Lizzie's he thought; children needed other children. He hadn't been sure when she'd first suggested it. He hadn't known how they'd incorporate someone else, he was so used to it being just the three of them. Sometimes Beth struck him as a worryingly solemn child, but when he saw her play he would reassure himself that it was just the only child thing. And when he saw her laughing and running about he thought that since she hadn't got any siblings it was best that she never knew she'd ever had any. They would go out and eat fish and chips tonight in the Cauldron Café he decided. He reached out and took Lizzie's hand, bridging their two sturdy bodies. They sat in deckchairs that carried their weight low to the sand in striped hammock curves. Lizzie took his hand and patted it with the other, a comforting gesture acknowledging the status quo.

The hand pat said yes, she could see it was nice that none of them had to go anywhere or do anything. That Beth was standing looking at the sea rather than sitting in front of the telly, or with her head in a book, or both at once. That she had a friend with her all the time rather than sulking in her bedroom or hanging around the kitchen making silly comments. Good for the child to get out of herself. But, thought Lizzie with an uncomfortable urge for action, like needing a wee, a holiday was less different for her than for any of the others. It wasn't as if she were ever expected to arrive on time for school or a job. Perhaps, she thought, she should get one for herself. That's what Rachel Frederick would do, Lizzie had no doubt. Rachel would be up there splashing at the children, encouraging them to swim into the shifting path of sunlight that was as bright and illusionary as a new life.

5. The Dream of Wearing Shorts Forever

The clouds stayed mid-ocean for the next few hours. Dan and Beth pushed each other into the waves and swam doggy paddle in the shallows, then came back out, fussily shook and then relaid their towels, and lay down for no more than five minutes before getting up and splashing back in. Beaver had had a snooze, head under a deckchair, and was now after some attention. He came splashing up to Dan and Beth. It was sweet the way he lifted his glossy wet legs high in the shallow sea, like a show pony. He panted at them and then gave a single bark. 'I think he wants to go to the pier,' said Dan with a clumsy wink, so they set off with Beaver on the lead, Dan's twenty-five pounds in his shorts' pockets and instructions to be back in half an hour.

Dan felt giddy with freedom as they walked down the seafront, Beth's pink plastic jelly shoes making a wet smack. 'Look what I brought,' he said, pulling out his money to show Beth. Her eyes widened and she gripped his arm, saying, 'Ace. You're *brilliant*.' Dan felt rather pleased.

'I'd like to live by the sea,' he said, 'and be a surfer.'

'Surfing's not a job,' said Beth. 'It's a hobby.'

'Well then, I'd open a shop and surf after work and at the weekend.'

'You won't get rich,' she said. Sometimes she had a real knack of taking the edge off things.

'You were going to be a show-jumper last week and there's not much chance of that happening. You've only been on a horse three times.'

'Five times, and I haven't wanted to be that for ages.' They were nearly at the pier and the smell of frying food was mixed with that of cockles and whelks from the seafood stall. Beth watched a man walk past eating a mouthful of cockles from a polystyrene cup. The cockles looked like tiny unborn birds on a skewer. She turned to Dan as they stepped on to the pier and gave him a sweet, big smile and said, 'Please may I have an ice cream?' He sighed and pulled out his wad of money.

The pier, even this small-town one, early on in the summer holidays, had a dangerous, rakish air. Sounds of arcade games and loud sharp voices collided with the cries of seagulls. The water beneath the pier, glimpsed through slither-gaps in the boards, looked dark and polluted, not part of the grey-green sea around. Groups of teenagers hung together until some joke or insult sent one skittering outside the circle, pulled or pushed by another, laughter ringing as applause. Beth and Dan had to dodge them as they walked, knowing, now that they were both older and not old enough, not to get underfoot.

Families walked, small children racing ahead and then rolling back like footballs. Elderly couples sat in the shelter, making staccato comments, women bursting into laughter. But all this energy and movement was infectious and Beaver swung round their legs on his lead and Beth felt excited by the crowd and its lack of control. She could go on a game and win something to take home, or have her fortune read, or buy a useless huge red lollipop saying Swanage. Dan agreed. They could do anything. But since they had money to invest there was every possibility they might make a fortune on a slot machine, so they tied Beaver to the railings and went inside the strangely dark, carpeted arcade.

* * *

After three-quarters of an hour the tide turned and the water below the pier swelled. A bag of chips was dropped tantalisingly close to Beaver's nose and he strained and strained at the knot on his lead until he had to stop and cough a little before he could start again. But the seagulls found them first and carried the greasy potato soldiers away one by one. Down on the beach, the mini-living rooms created behind wind-breakers, flapping towels and umbrellas, were slowly dismantled and packed away. Swimming costumes and flippers were left behind to be taken by the next tide and regurgitated on another beach, another day. The sea becoming a watery junk shop – ordinary treasures hidden very deep.

The wind came up and the water in the bay simmered and swelled, its surface patched dark by passing clouds. After an hour someone took pity on the hungry dog and threw him half a burger, and a child, whose rabbits had all run away, petted him and set him free. Beaver stood still for a second, surprised to be loose from the pull of his lead. He was meant to be waiting for someone but he couldn't remember who. It would come to him with a walk. Most things did.

Beth and Dan were down to their last fiver and on their last warning. They'd been told twice that they weren't meant to be in here without a parent. They'd dodged round corners, small enough to be hidden by the machines. They had won something, a small stuffed frog, but that was all and Beth was worrying about the time. 'Come on,' she said, 'I'm bored and I'm sure we've been here more than half an hour. They'll be cross.'

'One more go,' Dan said and she leaned back against the slot machine, biting the skin around her little finger. His two-pence piece jangled down and out on to the shelf, good and far back from the edge where a ridge of copper coins balanced. The shelf moved backwards. 'Look,' he said, 'look, it's a good one.' Slowly the coin was shoved into the pile and the first two-pence fell below, then another, and another, then a great rush of them. Coins began to gurgle down the well and out into the pocket and Dan and Beth, caught by surprise, clapped and laughed. They'd won. Dan had won something for the first time ever – a whole galleon of coins. As he pocketed their winnings, his pockets bulging with change, Dan felt strangely adult. His dad's pockets were always bulging with change and sometimes Jacob would empty them and share out the proceeds. On a good day Dan and his brothers could end up with as much as a pound each. Dave would always hoard his, and Greg would just play with the coins, piling them up or pushing them round the table like a snaking train. Dan, on the other hand, would head straight for the corner shop, driving Nimesh crazy with his slow counting to pay for a *Dandy*, two Mars bars and seven fizzy cola bottles to take up the slack.

They left the arcade, stepping into a gust of chilly wind that jolted them back into their responsibilities as children. Beaver was gone and the beach stretching ahead of them had emptied. It was going to rain.

'He's gone,' said Dan, his voice high-pitched, his face scrunching into fear. Where had he gone? Dan didn't know where to start looking for an animal whose whole life purpose was moving fast in the wrong direction. He looked wildly from left to right and then to Beth. 'Where's he gone?'

'I don't know,' she said. She was more scared about being late. Beaver would be somewhere.

'Maybe he's been stolen,' Dan said.

'Don't be dumb. That's stupid,' she retorted and walked off up the pier shouting Beaver's name, thinking that if they found him quickly it'd only take four minutes to run back, and they couldn't have been gone more than three-quarters of an hour, and her mum and dad would have guessed they'd be a bit late. It would be all right – it was a holiday, people couldn't get cross on a holiday. She knew Dan shouldn't have come. She'd always known it would go wrong.

Dan turned the other way down the pier, asking strangers if they'd seen a small brown dog on the loose. But no one had so he turned left out on to the seafront. He was crying now, the tears blown diagonally down his cheeks and out into the wind. It had got darker with the clouds and the sea looked rougher. Beaver could have drowned. In fact, Dan wasn't sure Beaver could really swim. He'd never gone in properly, just paddled in the waves. Dan ran down the steps on to the beach, still calling Beaver's name, and turned left back under the pier, the shady look of it a magnet to his panic. It smelled damp and fishy underneath; there were bits of scary-looking litter, beer cans and plastic, but no wagging tail or even paw prints in the sand. He stopped on the other side and realised he didn't know where Beth was now. She was lost as well as Beaver. Or maybe he was lost. He hiccuped with tears. He should never have gone away with them.

He was too out of breath to keep running. He had a stitch burning inside him and he bent over, hands on knees, for a few seconds. When he stood up again he saw a young man jogging towards him. He was wearing big Doctor Marten boots and shouting 'Oi, you' and pointing at him. Dan stood still, his heart pounding. He was very tall, this man, but he was saying something to him and Dan was scared that if he ran away he'd run after him, back under the pier. The man beckoned him over.

'What?' Dan shouted. Then, on a desperate defensive, 'Piss off.' The man stopped jogging and laughed, but carried on walking over. Dan stepped backwards, his heart beating loudly. The man was only ten feet away. Dan backed away further still, thinking that this was what was meant to happen. Strange men coming up to you in empty places when there were no adults around. Maybe he'd seen him win all those two pences and could beat him up under the pier and leave him there for the tide and no one would ever know.

The man stopped a short distance away from Dan, but not close enough to start him running again, and smiled. Dan clenched his fist.

'You lost a dog?' he said.

Dan breathed out and could feel himself start to cry again. He nodded.

'He's up here with us, eating our burgers. Come on.'

Dan followed at a distance, wiping his face on his sleeve. There were loads of them sitting in a line against the wall. All dressed in dark clothes, some of them with long hair and T-shirts saying 'Motorhead'. Beaver was standing in front of one of them who had a beard, being fed bits of a bun by hand.

'Beaver,' Dan said angrily, embarrassed that his own dog hadn't noticed him. The dog stopped and then turned his head sharply, half a sesame-seed bun sticking out of his mouth. Beaver gulped it down and then came bounding over. All joy and tail. The men were laughing and Dan tried to join in but he felt very small and shy. He grabbed on to his dog's collar for comfort. 'Sorry,' he said. Then, thinking that he should, 'Thank you very much.'

'You called that dog Beaver?' said the one with the beard.

'Yes,' said Dan, smiling a bit. They all laughed. One of them laughed so much he dropped the can of lager he was opening and was left trying to grab it as it rolled down the shingle spraying like a Catherine wheel. 'How old are you?' he asked.

'Eleven,' Dan replied, not knowing why they needed to know.

'You don't know what that means, do you?' said the nice one.

'What d'you mean?' said Dan. Then: 'I've got to go.' He still didn't trust them. There were lots them, all wearing the same kind of thing, their heavy shoes in a row.

'Funny family to let you call a dog that.'

'Why?' Dan was curious now.

'Beaver means twat,' said the bearded one. Dan looked at him silently. He didn't understand.

'Leave him alone, he's only young,' said the nice one. 'Go and find your mum and dad.'

'Twat means fanny,' continued the Beard.

He started to walk away. 'Fanny means cunt,' he heard behind him.

Dan was starting to get the picture.

He walked slowly along the beach, cursing himself for being such a pathetic child. All this time. And he'd not known. He'd kill his mum and dad when he got home. He kicked at the pebbles as he walked, tugging so hard on Beaver's lead that the dog made a choking noise. He was taking it out on him, Dan realised, and it wasn't his fault. Dan stopped and bent down to stroke Beaver and apologise. 'I am very, very sorry about your name. We'll change it.' He took the scruff of Beaver's neck and mulched his furry skin between his hands. Beaver lifted up his head and panted in ecstasy.

Roger noticed they'd been gone a long time before Lizzie did. But he didn't draw her attention to it; it was so unusual for her to be this relaxed. He sat quietly pretending to read the paper, pretending not to notice that the sun had gone in and that it was no longer terribly nice here on the grey beach, in the late afternoon air, with everyone else packing up around them. It was 4.30, a time for movement, the sea growing and the air swirling round their heads, blowing up strands of Lizzie's hair and laying them down on the wrong side of her parting, stiff with salty humidity. Lizzie could feel her face being whipped but she sat still, thinking about what kind of a job she could do. The more she thought the more she was beginning to feel indefinably angry. All she'd been was a mother. And look how she'd failed at that.

She tried to rein in her thoughts, to ward herself from the familiar
spiral of bitterness and loss, but it was hard without the valium.
Roger had suggested she leave it at home and irritated by his
kind, patronising tone she'd done just that, just to prove she
could. Instead of hiding it, which would have been more sensible.
Challenges never brought the best out in her.

Roger stood up and stretched in a deliberately unhurried way.
'I think I'll just go and meet them on their way back. If we're
going out to The Cauldron tonight we'll all be needing a bath
and a change.' Lizzie watched him walk away with his long-
legged stride and straight back.

Yesterday they'd arrived at the beach to discover it was
Lifeboat Day. There were people selling raffle tickets, little stalls
displaying food and tombola prizes – jars of jam, a Jim Davidson
video, a bottle of perry. There had been an above-average current
of excitement on the beach. A fly-by was promised and a tannoy
announced that a child called Lindy, no sorry, Sindy, had lost
her mum. The deep, jovial Dorset voice promised to read out
any message for the sum of fifty pence, 'All in aid of those
brave men and their life-saving boats.' At about two in the afternoon the loudspeaker had crackled provincially into life.

'This one's from Dave,' the announcer had said, 'and it's for
his wife, Jeanette. He wants to say how much he loves you and
to say thank you for being a lovely wife and the most wonderful
mother to their three kids, Suzanne, Becky and Martin.' And
then the loudspeaker hum had disappeared. Lizzie had sat staring
at the sea, her mouth clamped, the hard mechanics of her jaw
pulsing below her skin. What woman was that – so blessed by
the air? What kind of fat cow was that with a doting husband
and nothing special to her family but luck?

She'd watched the other families on the beach clamber in and
around each other's space, big kids holding little ones in towels,
wiping their sticky ice lolly faces, and then had felt trapped by

her own past and the unstoppable future. Beth would make of life what she would, with no regard to what had come before – no respect of the hardships that had got her there. But she wasn't even an innocent, happy child. Sometimes, the way she looked at her mother, you'd have thought she carried the weight of the original sin around with her.

As Dan tried to teach his old dog a new name, his head swam with rebukes for his parents. He bet they thought it was funny. Roger found him crouching down on the beach. He called to him and together they went to find Beth. Roger didn't remonstrate, he was now worried about Beth, although it seemed odd to Dan that Roger should be so concerned. He'd forgotten his panic under the pier and now he personally presumed Beth would be fine. It was just a world out there. It didn't automatically get wickeder because there wasn't a parent around. In fact, Dan would decide when he returned home, parents caused more problems than anyone.

In the end they saw Beth walking disconsolately towards them. She'd given up searching the pier and had been crying. When she saw her dad and Dan she rushed over and hugged the dog – 'Where were you, you naughty dog? Naughty Beaver' – leaving Dan wincing at her innocence. She took her father's hand and walked along silently as he gave them many sensible, logical reasons why children shouldn't go to the pier by themselves, and especially why they shouldn't split up from each other. And even more importantly why they should go back to a grown-up at the first sign of trouble. The words were wasted on them. They came out of his mouth and were instantly airborne, lightweight with inevitability and kindness, floating upwards like a pink helium balloon that a child has absent-mindedly let go of.

Beth was scared. She knew Lizzie was going to be angry. She could feel it in her bones. Fear made it a certainty, fear had a strength that hope could never compete with. She could imagine how it would go. Lizzie would have a cross face but say nothing. Then she would ask Beth questions, hard questions that she didn't quite understand and knew she couldn't get right. 'What makes you think you can behave like this?' she'd say. No response. 'Do you understand what your father does for you, how he loves you, and how much you worry him in return?' No response. 'What's the matter with you?' Beth had no idea but clearly something was. 'Would you take that look off your face – I know you hate me at the moment.' There's no response to that either. What way to look? 'This is my face,' Beth would scream back, a dare to slap it if she cared. As if the mere amalgam of her parents' features was a challenge.

The three of them climbed down to the beach where Lizzie was still sitting surrounded by towels and holiday debris. 'We're back,' said Roger brightly, 'safe and sound.' Lizzie turned her head to see them, blinking as if she'd been asleep. She saw Beth's solemn face, blotched with concern, and she thought to herself, That's my little girl, with my mouth and her father's eyes, and she smiled at her a little sadly. Beth watched her expression anxiously, but she seemed defiant to Lizzie. 'Do you know people steal small children and do away with them?' she said to Beth. She couldn't be allowed to grow up thinking the world was an easy place. 'Do you think it's fair, then, to make your dad worry and go running after you?'

'I think it's time we got back,' said Roger, packing up.

'I think it's high time,' Lizzie agreed, raising her body slowly from the deckchair like it was a weight apart from her. They would go back, walking silent and a little apart through the tepid rain, to their created home and wickedly turn on the gas fire and run baths. Beth would disappear to the bedroom, avoiding a scene with her mother with such provocatively closed doors and short answers that within an hour of their return Lizzie would

71

feel herself needled to ask, 'And what's the matter with you now?' Then the scene would begin with such predictability – the sharp parries and senseless, belligerent retorts and smudged, girlish tears – that Roger knew how long to let it run and when to interrupt and how best to cajole the two of them to sit at the same table for tea.

While this plays itself out Dan sits in the bath. He sits listening to his friend behave like a baby, her mother being mean, and wishes he were in his bright bathroom at home, listening to his father singing along to the radio in the kitchen, his mother cooking her way round him.

6. Cut and Come Again

Shropshire, April 1985, four years later

Down in the yard Beaver was on the attack, growling and shaking the victim's limb violently, staying on his paws with a sinuous balance. A flurry of fur against the still, silent view. From the window of his attic bedroom Dan couldn't see what Beaver had in his mouth because of the angle of the porch. But he could hear some deep and traditional swearing. Perhaps Beaver had finally proved his worth and caught a burglar. Dan wondered, though, how a burglar would ever have found his way to the cottage. Everybody else had to be given lengthy and detailed directions to this last outpost before the mountains began. But never mind. Dan lived in hope of action. He loped out of the bedroom and ran down the narrow staircase, two at a time, jumping over the bottom two stairs that were decaying with a slow stoicism.

He landed karate-style on the lino and swiftly grabbed a spatula from a ceramic jar saying UTENSILS, then ran through the back door and out into the yard where a bearded man in a checked shirt was trying to shake off Beaver, who was hanging on to his leg like a leech. It was cold and Dan's hot morning breath hung ahead of him like a speech bubble. Dan grabbed hold of the bearded man's arms with the strength of surprise, propelling him round, face forwards to the wall.

Mike, only a few inches taller than Dan, nose to frozen lichen, his shin raw beneath his new elephant-coloured cords, felt this was more than he deserved.

'I'm a friend of—'

'What have you taken?' Dan shouted. He was enjoying himself. This was a soft, nicely dressed sort of burglar.

'Let go of me.' The man struggled a little, but not much as Beaver had finally let go at Dan's arrival.

'I'm not letting go, I'm getting the police. Mum,' Dan shouted up at the house, 'call the police.'

With sudden strength the man broke out of Dan's grip and turned round to face him, pinning Dan's arms to his sides like a straitjacket. He then proceeded to speak calmly and slowly.

'Dan . . . stop. I'm a friend of your mother's. I brought her home last night and stayed. Then I surprised the dog when I got up to make some tea. I am not a burglar. I am a tree surgeon.'

Dan looked at him and wrinkled his nose in disappointment. 'A tree surgeon?'

'Yes.'

He heard his mother laugh and come into the yard with messy hair, a red face and wearing pyjama bottoms, Wellies and a big jumper.

'Is this my birthday present? Two men fighting over me in the back yard.'

'He shouldn't go sneaking around our house. He could have been anyone.'

'*He* is called Mike, Dan,' said his mother, smiling mildly. 'I think it's time we found some plasters and some breakfast,' and she took Mike's arm and led him limping back into the kitchen.

Dan stood still and looked out over the uneven paved yard, over the wooden fence and the paddock into the green-blackness of the woods and hills beyond. From what he'd gathered of the world, stray men didn't just pitch up in the back of bloody beyond for no reason.

'Is someone going to tell me where he slept then?' he blus-
tered to cover his embarrassment. He struck out for the woods,
Beaver jogging ingratiatingly behind.

Dan wore a grey Fruit of the Loom sweatshirt. Every day. There
weren't that many clothes to choose from in Last Cottage and
the only way to ensure that things weren't stolen by his brothers
was to keep them on his back or about his person. His pockets
always bulged with small, usually grubby items he'd found,
thought useful and didn't want to chance leaving on an
unguarded table. They'd been here for over three years. The
deep, shifting displacement of the first year had shaken down
and settled. They were fifteen miles out of Oswestry, basically
Wales as his father always said bitchily from the safety of
London. The four of them had arrived one afternoon in July,
two days after Dan had been delivered back home by the
Standings after their holiday in Swanage. He hadn't even had
a chance to unpack his small suitcase.

Rachel had been brutally honest about their destination: 'We
shan't be coming back, ever.' They'd set off at 6 a.m., Rachel
thinking it would be nicer, less fugitive-like to arrive in the
daytime, and for a few days they'd ricocheted round the cottage
like trapped moths, returning every ten minutes to their mother's
side, baffled and angry. Dave was silent, Dan anxious, Greg
weeping at the strangeness of it all. All three boys had persisted
in thinking this was a holiday that would only last until she came
to her senses, or until their dad returned and came to get them.
And since the only thing they recognised in this strange terri-
tory was their own lopsided family, the brothers took more care
of each other than usual. It was a pattern that stuck as Jacob
fought to draw up the battle lines of loyalty between him and
Rachel. 'I'm sorry,' Jacob would say to Dan or whichever silent
boy happened to be at the end of the phone. 'I miss you. You

75

know I didn't want this. Don't you?' he'd say again and again until one of his sons was forced to admit that this was all their mother's fault.

The boys would visit Jacob every third weekend. Slowly they realised this was life's new pattern. Trips to Oxford Street, Lebanese take-aways and a rushed Sunday lunch before heading back to the train station. Jacob couldn't help himself, he wanted to know about their life with this strange Rachel of the Wilderness, and each snippet was swallowed with a grimace. Slowly Dan learned the value of hanging back, of tactically evasive answers, of the safety in ambiguity, of the potential disaster in enthusiasm. The three boys didn't discuss these things much but Dan was glad of his brothers as they trundled away from London on the train, packets of crisps in their duffel bags. Even their shrugging comments, 'You know what Dad's like' or 'Don't think we'll be telling Mum about that', helped to take the pressure off.

Dan swung between a longing for and a disappointment in his dad. The steamy warmth of his mother's kitchen inspired both homesickness and claustrophobia. Wherever he was he felt guilty at not being with the other parent, and if he enjoyed himself with his father it felt like a betrayal. Yet if he didn't think of his father for a whole day he would, in a wash of guilt, feel his father's wounds with a more lasting sensitivity than Jacob ever had.

Even after four years, with his Tigger-like qualities restored, his feet up on the kitchen table with an insouciance learned from his elder brother, an anxiety remained in Dan. What was left behind was a tendency to assess every situation, a tendency to notice too much, to flare up angrily in anticipation of failure or hurt to himself or his mother or brothers. He had an inability to let things go or let things go wrong. A fear of making choices, an expectation of disappointment. A child of divorce, he was blessed with a heightened awareness of other people's behaviour and emotions. For Dan it often created more trouble than it saved, as if he were an interfering time-traveller.

He stomped over the field. Distancing himself from the ridiculous appearance of the tree surgeon. In theory his mother was allowed a boyfriend; at fifteen he gave both lip-service and sporadic consideration to his mother's happiness. However, he'd thought she seemed pretty happy as she was. When he was little he remembered her going quiet for days but she didn't do that here. Perhaps there actually was a tree needing surgery. The chestnut at the end of the garden might want lopping he thought. It was quite possible.

He lifted up his head. The persuasion of the sun had come. He felt his small-world order being restored. Yes, there must be a tree in need. The light grew dazzling, bringing sharp definition to the outline of the landscape. The oak woods ahead were a dense mass, the round flourishes of the tree-tops paper-cut sharp. The black hills too seemed to have been stage-set against the blue horizon. Perspective skewed with stillness. Dan stopped and listened to the day. Nothing at first, then Beaver snuffling at his feet, snorting the warm air in search of a rabbity mystery tour, then a faint croaking crow. Beaver had kept his name in the end. It wasn't that Dan hadn't tried to re-educate him, just that the dog hadn't cared for it. After a while he'd almost found it funny, and he'd pre-empt comments when revealing the dog's name with a disarming grin and a raised eyebrow.

When they'd first arrived Dan hadn't believed that people actually lived in this place. How had these people got here? How did they stay here?

'Why did we come here?' he'd asked Rachel one morning.

'Because your father and I couldn't carry on living together. It would have made us all—'

77

'No, no, not that, I know that,' he'd said wearily. 'I mean, why here, why Shropshire? Why not near the sea or near Alton Towers, or . . .'

She'd stroked her petulant son's head. 'Because I used to come on holiday here when I was little. You know that.'

It seemed a flimsy reason to uproot your three children to a place whose main feature seemed to be mud. But Dan trusted his mother. Living without their father was soon only strange when they remembered that that's what they were doing. With practice, his gap was very quickly filled. Everyone expanded slightly to take up the space. Their mother became a little larger than life, capable of mending fuses, whitewashing walls. Dave carried more shopping bags and even, with stubborn relish, mended the gate and fences. Dan would stand by his mother and chat when they were in the shop or street. He would skitter from occasion to occasion, filling whatever space he spotted in conversation or attendance. And Greg provided entertainment, a talisman of innocence, unknowing, one presumed, of his importance in this new dynamic.

What they did sometimes miss, without even being able to articulate it, were Jacob's arrivals, the hiatus he provided in normal schoolday lives. On a dull Wednesday night when they'd had tea and the telly was on there was no one to arrive late from a strange city, carrying a new story like a present, hiding love like a game and then surprising them.

Rachel knew that they had as much time with their father as ever before, now that he was forced to dedicate one weekend in three to them, and tried not to feel guilty. But of course she did. Guilty that it wasn't normal, guilty that she felt so much happier out of her marriage, guilty that Jacob so plainly didn't. He was so bad at hiding his confusion from the children. When he asked them about her they had to say she was fine, that they didn't have much money, that their lives had been uprooted to suit hers.

But if she'd stayed it would have been to protect them from change and to protect herself from guilt. Either way they were subject to her decision. A childhood is a period of growing, nothing mystic about it. Precious, yes, but only in retrospect.

She encouraged the boys to keep in touch with their London friends so that there was less of an apocalyptic 'before and after'. But children are practical, dumping playmates out of convenience. They hadn't yet learned to shore up failing feeling with sentiment. Once the missing each other had passed, Dan wrote to Beth infrequently. Rachel would encourage him to ask her to stay but it seemed such an unlikely idea, neat Beth in her town shoes standing in their yard.

Dan needed to collect some more bits and pieces for his mother's birthday present. Part of him was unwilling to expend the energy on her, she who was probably nursing the tree surgeon's ankle this very minute. However, he guessed that the man would be gone by the time he got back and he was excited by the grandeur of his plan. He had something of his father in his need to dramatically punctuate special days.

Dan took the straightforward route into Cooper Woods. He'd learned at school that the trees within had been a source for coopers, makers of beer and cider casks. He'd liked learning that; it was as if he'd been given a secret. After a few minutes his eyes adjusted to the green underwater light and he turned off the main path, which was a few feet wide, on to a narrower one. Crouching at the base of a large oak tree he began to rip up clumps of live, green, moist moss. He brushed his thumb over the minute fronds, tiny drops of water sparking into the air.

His face was entirely concentrated. The flickering surveillance of his eyes stopped, his gaze and movements distilled into extreme deliberation. Around him the woods, stroked by the wind, reached, arched and settled with a sigh. The boy on his haunches mesmerised the air with the touch of his hands and the focus of his eyes. Trees shifted in time, flutes of sunlight stepping into the deep.

Then the dog barked and Dan's head jerked up. Beaver was chasing something unknown, perhaps something imagined, a fur-covered figment, skittling between the trees, unable to resist the thought of a bit of tail. Still a tart at heart.

The tree surgeon had slept on the sofa. Rachel knew he would rather have slept elsewhere but she thought it might have been a bit of a shock for Greg or Dan to find her in bed with a man after four years of walking unannounced into her bedroom. They had had sex on the sofa instead, her first time in four years. Imagine that, she'd said to herself each birthday. No sex for one, two, three years. Not this year though. Last night hadn't been entirely satisfactory but it was unlikely to have been after four years. Her desire had grown shy, unused to the presence of another, and so her body had felt a little unprepared.

She knew full well that Jacob, as is a victim's right, had initially sought solace in whatever female comfort he could find. She suspected that sex with women other than Rachel, always such an interesting proposition for him in the past, had quickly become too easy. He was a good-looking man. She'd probably never touch anyone so pleasing again. It was ironic that her grand new life had meant mud, celibacy and considerable financial constraints. But the knowledge that it was her life, without compromise, still gave a self-raising buoyancy to most days. Even after four years. She climbed the stairs feeling an unaccustomed and satisfying ache in her thighs.

The house had slowly developed into a whole. It wasn't coherently furnished or decorated. It had inherited and adapted to its new colours and random chairs. Rachel had never been a big fan of houses that looked themed, as if they'd all been purchased in one package. In Delia Street, with its logical, economic rooms, neatness had paid. Here, neatness made the house seem embarrassed, a woman in borrowed clothes. Here, clutter distracted from the cracks.

She opened the small window in the uncarpeted white bedroom. She hadn't actually had sex in here but it had a new air of potential. The bed looked rumpled rather than unmade and she picked a towel off a school-like wooden chair in the corner while singing a quiet Joan Armatrading verse.

She had sent an exaggeratedly limping Mike away, saying they'd speak later in the week and, yes, she might be able to get out for a drink soon. She wanted to have a bath, to get going quietly. Life couldn't just stop. She sat on the edge of the bath, without having turned the taps on, and thought how strange it was that she found herself sitting there at 10 a.m., the window of the green bathroom open, the sharp sounds of spring bringing the outside in, at the age of forty. She undressed and looked at her small breasts and full belly in the mirror. Whenever she looked at her stomach she thought of her three children. Huge boys that had fitted inside her.

'Jane, we have to go,' said Jacob from the bottom of the stairs.

'I know, I know, I know, I know,' she almost sang.

'I shall go and sit in the car and grow a beard,' Jacob said. Upstairs she made a face.

Dan wended his way back over the field and saw Greg sitting on the fence. He seemed to be doing something. As Dan drew closer he began to make out a white shape in front of Greg's face. He was eating cereal.

'Frosties,' he said cheerfully to Dan. He was wearing a very small T-shirt that said DENVER in felt letters and some shiny tracksuit bottoms that had once belonged to Dan. His hair was greasy, flattened on one side and spiky on the other.

'Greg,' said Dan, suddenly thinking that his brother looked a bit disgusting, 'have you had a bath this month?'

''Spect so,' said Greg, a little surprised. 'Why?' And he looked down at himself and smudged some spilled milk off the N of his T-shirt.

'When we give Mum her presents and stuff, you're going to change.'

Greg looked at him, wide-eyed. 'And I am too,' finished Dan. 'Why?'

'Because,' he said, exasperated, 'because it's her birthday and we're going to make her cake.' Greg's eyes opened even wider. 'You have bought her a present, haven't you?' asked Dan.

Greg thought for a while. 'No.'

'Have you got any money?'

Greg thought again. 'No.'

'God,' said Dan, 'you're crap.'

There was a pause and then Dan said, 'Come on, we're going to the shop. You're making the cake.'

Greg climbed off the fence and stood with his bowl, waiting to be led down the lane to the village.

'Bringing the Frosties too?' asked Dan.

'Yes,' said Greg.

'Are you sure about the M1? Even if there's roadworks the M40 might be safer.'

'I am quite capable of reading a map, Jacob.'

He turned his head to snatch a look at her. And smiled. She was sitting pert and tight-lipped.

'Sorry. Bit tense.' He moved into the fast lane. 'We'll stop after Birmingham, have some lunch. Little Chef sausages,' he said and squeezed her knee.

* * *

82

They got halfway down the lane when Dan realised he was still carrying all the moss he'd collected. He made Greg wipe out the bowl with grass and they packed the moss in and left it under a hedge. It seemed a reasonable solution and unencumbered they carried on.

'Pick some flowers,' said Dan to Greg.

'No.'

'Go on.'

'You do it.'

'You haven't bought a present.'

Greg sighed and stopped. He pulled some cow parsley out of the bank and held it out to Dan.

'Picking doesn't just mean picking, it means holding too.'

Greg looked sulky. 'We might meet someone and we'll be carrying,' he shook the cow parsley like some dead animal, 'this.'

'*You'll* be carrying it.'

'What do we buy for a cake, anyway?'

'Eggs, flour and things. Chocolate.'

'Oh.'

It was getting warmer and Dan took off his sweatshirt and tied it round his waist. The soft thud of their trainers took them past their nearest neighbour, John, on whose farm they lived and whose cottage they rented. Their monthly rent had meant John could update his milking system. Rachel had certainly improved the cottage over the last four years, what with the whitewash and the pretty garden. John was particularly friendly with Greg. They shared a fondness for Friesians. Greg looked towards the farmhouse wistfully and slowed his steps but Dan ploughed on towards the village.

Dawley, like most British villages, had expanded over the years, but not in a very cohesive way. Neat council houses brought regimented shapes to the straggling village. The pub, school (with only one hundred pupils) and shop sat on the very edge and the older houses, small redbrick cottages huddled together as if seeking warmth in company, were further up the one road that ran through the village. It was a functioning rather than picturesque place. While there were a few eighteenth-century cottages the remainder were early Victorian and stolid and small. The houses on the council estate were excitingly spacious (although somehow thinner) in comparison. In houses like that a man could come home and cross his own threshold without ever having to bow low his head.

A familiar-looking white Ford Transit passed by and pulled up in front of them as they reached the shop and post office. The door opened and Dan could hear something that sounded like country and western music before realising that the man gingerly pulling himself out of the driving seat was Mike, the tree surgeon. Dan had noticed this before – the way, when you discover something exists, you can't get through the day without it cropping up. Like manhole covers.

'All right,' he said to Dan and Greg, nodding rather grimly.

'Hello,' said Greg. Dan said nothing, only was rather glad he wasn't carrying the limp cow parsley. 'You were in our house before and now you're here,' said Greg. As if he were bloody Paul Daniels or something thought Dan, disappointed by his brother.

'Got work to do. Your mum sent you out shopping, has she?'

'Got to make a cake,' said Greg, sounding depressed. 'Her birthday cake.'

'Oh,' he said. 'Well,' he continued, moving towards the shop, 'I'll see you soon.'

Not if I see you first.

Rachel had driven to the supermarket in Oswestry, wondering why the boys were lingering in the kitchen in that disturbing way. Dan and Greg put Radio 1 on loud and found a recipe book.

'Chocolate Torte. What's that?'

'Cocoa, crème de . . . something. Can't do that.'

Greg stopped for a moment to perform a distractingly good imitation of George Michael.

'Let's make it up,' he said with enthusiasm.

'You can't make it up, it'll sink . . . or fry, or something.'

Dan started pulling bowls out of cupboards, rooting around for a tin of some sort. He found a loaf tin and a roasting tray and a pie dish and plumped for the last on the basis that it was at least round.

'What's she like?'

'Who?'

'Who d'you think? Your ex-wife. Rachel.'

'Are you sure you only want soup? I don't think it's their forte.'

'Yes. Are you sure she won't mind?'

'I'm having a full English.'

'Good for you. Do you? Think she'll mind?'

'I've no idea, Jane.'

'That's very reassuring.'

He sighed. 'You can stay in the car if you like.'

'Thanks very much. Some women might think you're ashamed of them.'

'Some women might not have insisted on coming.'

'You can't say that to me. You asked me to.'

'Then I said you didn't have to.'

'No, you were all for it, you forced me to say I'd come. Then you changed your mind.'

He sighed again.

'I'm sorry to be so troublesome.' She rearranged her knife and fork.

Jacob breathed in deeply. 'She's very . . . very rational. She won't mind. She's a sensible woman.'

'What does she look like?'

'Tall, long dark hair, attractive.'

Jane grimaced.

'Well, she is. I can't do anything about that.'

'You would if you could.'

Barbara the waitress arrived and Jane looked out at the grey forecourt and the smudge of fast-moving cars. Other people's journeys are always so mysterious.

'I keep checking it, Dan, and it's not growing.'

Dan got up from the table where he'd been simultaneously reading *The Hobbit* and sliding his grubby finger round the edge of the mixing bowl. He peered into the oven.

'I suppose if we don't split it in two, don't do the sandwich thing, it'll be all right. It'll taste the same.'

'Mum doesn't eat cake much anyway, does she?' Greg wandered round the kitchen, picking things up and putting them down. Dan sighed. He felt a bit tired and thought he might go and lie in front of the telly for a while.

'It's the thought, isn't it. She'll be pleased you tried.'

'When did you stop loving her?'

They were back on the road, taking the smell of a full English with them along with a lollipop she'd nicked off the counter.

'Pardon?'

'Or maybe you didn't.' She didn't believe he hadn't heard her. 'It's interesting, isn't it. I was reading a book about it, this really inspirational book by this guy back home. You know, where does love go? When the person's gone? Where does it collect?'

'I don't know what you mean.'

'Yes, you do. You know perfectly well. It's not complicated.'

She had a habit of saying that. Of saying things weren't complicated, a reductionist approach to life. It had the effect of making Jacob feel a bit woolly, a bit misshapen with the ten-year stretch between them. Everything was complicated as far as Jacob was concerned; it was all a matter of how you handled it.

'When Rachel left, you still loved her, yes?' She was speaking very slowly.

'Yes.'

'For quite some while.'

'Yes.' Small, slippy, stepping-stone words.

'And you'd say you carried on loving her?'

'Yes.'

'For how long?'

'A while.' He began to relax.

'So – does it collect inside you, until you have a huge well of it that can be given to someone else, or does it go out there and travel to the person so they know they're still loved? Or does it just go off; you know, grow manky and green and die?'

Bitch.

He turned and looked at her. She might have sounded challenging but she looked scared. He indicated and moved into the left-hand lane, began to slow down and pulled off on to the hard shoulder. He put on his warning lights and a slight tick filled the car after the roar of each passing lorry. It was exposed here on the hard shoulder, a small stationary car on the carved-out, bone-coloured strip of motorway. Quiet like the centre of a cyclone.

He leaned over and kissed her very gently on the forehead, his left hand at her face. He moved back, tracing the line of her eyebrow with his thumb, and said, 'What matters is that I'm here now, with you, risking our fucking lives on the M1 because you suddenly looked sad and,' he paused, 'you look so pretty when you're happy.'

She smiled slightly. He was so nearly there. For six whole

months he'd nearly been there. She knew she was pretty; it was the last thing she needed reassurance about. To make up for the disappointment she leaned over and kissed him instead. Kissing him gave her more faith in love than anything she'd ever known. Something about the taste of him.

'I wonder what his story is?' said Dan to Greg, the two of them sitting side by side on the kitchen table watching the alarm clock.

'What d'you mean?'

Oh good grief thought Dan. Today was proving to be exhausting. Nobody got anything. They were talking about Mike the tree surgeon. Greg had managed to miss the point – Mike had been there so early in the morning that he must have stayed the night.

'Everyone has a story,' persevered Dan. 'He must have come from somewhere and gone to school somewhere and had a girl-friend somewhere and live somewhere.'

'Oh. Like he might be a Secret Agent in secret.'

'Yeah, something like that.' A pause. 'I think we should take that cake out.'

The countryside had grown flatter and wilder. A green blaze that only held interest when the sun came out. Jacob played Steely Dan loudly on the stereo and sometimes turned to smile at Jane or squeeze her knee. She wanted to suggest they keep going, keep driving until they hit water. You never knew with Jacob, he might say yes. Except this time his children sat waiting. She refused to be intimidated by the thought of them sitting there with their suitcases, practising their scowls. At least now there was a rhythm to this journey, they were going some-where at speed, used to the idea at last. They both liked speed, a sense of getting away, import in anonymity. It was easy with a soundtrack, even if it were Steely Dan, to have a sense of occasion. She might have chosen Joni Mitchell or Madonna or Vivaldi if she'd thought to bring anything. But she'd been too busy worrying about the arrival to consider the journey.

Dan had made her a rock garden. He'd told her he was doing an experiment and not to come to the far right corner of the garden. Surprisingly, she'd obeyed.

It was a walled garden, about half an acre, with a small orchard of apple and plum trees in the far right quarter. It wasn't particularly well kept – the grass was always too long and everything needed pruning. The six-foot walls protected the vegetables and trees from the wind. Rachel loved it in a careless way. It was odd to enter your dim little house from the bright openness outside, then go through the kitchen and out into a boxed-off wilderness, over whose walls the skies and sounds of the countryside slid. It kept little except deer out. Seeds and birds and moles worked over or under the crumbling red brick. Now, in April, after the departure of daffodils and primroses, came bluebells and apple blossom, pure colours that arrived without being asked. By July, however, the garden was just a pool of different textured greens and Dan had planned the rock garden so as to give his mother flowers through the summer.

He'd bought campanulas, pansies, periwinkles, scabious and, on a whim, a small tomato plant from one of the houses in the village which had a rickety stall in their front garden. He'd planted them and then realised he'd run out of money – and there was still a lot of space to fill. Hence the moss.

The batch that he'd collected earlier in the morning was intended to fill the last of the big spaces. He'd had more confidence in choosing the rocks than the plants. There was one particularly beautiful one he'd found by the edge of the lane. It was smooth and tablet-like, seductively concave. If he'd been a tramp, thought Dan, he'd have chosen it as a pillow. He had tried it in the garden, lain down and rested it at the base of his skull. It had been cold. Properly cold, stone cold, the kind of cold that wouldn't ever warm up, and it had smelled cold too, sort of salty and damp. He had put it and the prettiest white creeping plant in the middle of the garden, mid-way up, the conversation piece of the whole thing.

It looked quite pretty, he supposed, once he'd squished down the last of the moss. He was a bit beyond telling. It might also look quite scrappy, like the cake which sat on the kitchen table next to the cow parsley in a vase. He frowned and began to think the whole birthday thing might have been a bad idea. He needed his mother to get back from the supermarket so that they could get it all out of the way before his father arrived. It needed to be kept separate.

Naturally Jacob arrived early, just as Rachel got back from the shops. She was lifting the plastic bags out of the boot when she heard another car coming up the lane, turned and saw her ex-husband driving a shiny new red BMW. Someone was sitting next to him. A woman with a blonde bob and a royal blue top. Rachel suddenly felt her gut tense, like someone anticipating a choppy channel crossing.

They parked and Rachel continued to take the bags out of the boot. Not many because she'd be spending the next seven days without the children, but enough to give them their favourites to take with them and enough to guarantee she needn't go to the supermarket all precious week.

It was quiet as they both stepped out of the car.

'Hello,' said Rachel. 'Good journey?'

Jacob walked forwards and stopped about ten feet away from her. He put his hands on his hips and pushed his shoulders back, stretching after the drive.

'Not too bad.' And smiled.

Rachel's hair had got longer and she was already a little brown. The wheaten colour of a biscuit. He ignored his sinking heart and turned and gestured towards Jane, who was standing uselessly a little way back by the open car door.

'This is Jane.'

'Hello Jane,' said Rachel.

'Jane's going to be coming to the Lake District with us,' said Jacob.

He'd wondered how that would sound. For quite some while. He hadn't gone so far as to practise it, try alternative wordings, but he was aware he could have done.

'Right,' said Rachel, smiling. She wanted to ask if he'd told the boys but she thought it would be too rude, too aggressive to say that in front of this Jane woman. She looked garish here in the yard with her yellow hair and blue blouse and neat slacks. This felt awkward. Somehow Rachel thought she'd have had more warning.

'Well,' she said, 'come in,' and she led the way.

They went through the front room to the kitchen, where Rachel put the shopping on the side and the kettle on. She turned round to look at Jacob and Jane, her guests, and saw them staring at the table. In the middle was a lowish, sloping brown cake. On the top were wobbly white icing letters which just about spelled MUM. Suddenly Rachel felt like crying. Next to it was a mug in which an overly tall stem of cow parsley leaned.

'I'd forgotten it was your birthday,' said Jacob, blasé with embarrassment.

'How sweet,' said Jane, speaking for the first time. She was Australian and high-pitched. No one said anything for a moment.

'I'll find the boys and we can all have a piece and then you'll probably want to get going.'

'No hurry,' said Jacob and Rachel went upstairs and shouted for the boys.

'You didn't tell me it was her birthday,' Jane whispered.

'I'd forgotten,' said Jacob, fiddling with a piece of hair at the back of his head.

'It's embarrassing. Wouldn't she rather her children were here for her birthday?'

'Then she should have said.' He stopped, picked up a cookery book and looked at the cover, adding, 'It's not as if they're ever there for my birthday.' Jane shot him a look of sympathy.

Greg came pounding down the stairs and ran across the room into his father's arms. He was only eleven. He hadn't seen him for a month. Jacob picked him up, saying, 'I can't pick you up, you're huge, you're ancient, you're like Giant Haystacks,' and he kissed the top of his son's head which made him wriggle out and down to the floor. Greg stood with one hand on his father's side, resting on his presence, and looked at the woman standing near the door.

'This is Jane. She's a friend of mine.' Jacob saw Rachel standing at the bottom of the staircase. 'She's going to come to the Lake District with us.'

Greg stared at her. Jane began to go red. But said nothing.

Greg sighed and Rachel came down the last step. 'Are you a vegetarian?' he asked and they all laughed and Jane shook her head to say no.

'Look at this lovely cake,' said Rachel. 'Did you make it?'

'Sort of, said Greg. 'Dan did most of it. Dan was a vegetarian last week,' he said to Jane, and then, turning to his mother, 'he's in the garden playing with your present. That's my present,' he said, pointing to the cake, 'but Dan did most of it.'

Dan was still standing and wondering whether it looked a mess when he heard his mother shouting that his father was here. That was another thing he'd begun to notice about life, that when you thought of a new potential problem it automatically arose. Antiwish fulfilment. He turned and walked reluctantly to the back door.

They'd sat down at the table and his mother was pouring tea by the time he got there. His mother at the head of the table, his father at the other end and Greg sitting next to a blonde woman, pointing out how the icing on the cake spelled Mum, telling her that they'd tried to squeeze it through paper like Dan had seen on TV but had ended up having to scrape it off and do it with a spoon instead.

He walked over to his dad, who stood up, banging his knee on the little table in the process, and gave him an awkward hug, bending down a little, embracing Dan's straight-armed body.

'Good journey?' asked Dan, wondering when someone was going to tell him who the blonde woman was.

'Fine, thanks. Dan, this is Jane; she's coming to the Lake District with us.'

Jane stood up and leaned over the table, stretching towards something. Dan wondered what she was doing. She was holding out her hand.

And then she wasn't holding out her hand, she was drawing it back, a cat slinking backwards, settling down again to lick its wounded pride. Her pointy face pursed. His father's face hopeful, his mother's concerned, his brother licking icing off his finger.

Clearly it was up to him to say the right thing. It usually was. He knew what the right words were but they lurked at the back of his throat. His parents and his brother and this Jane woman were all waiting and suddenly it occurred to him that he was in control – that his uncertainty equalled power.

He turned round and walked back into the garden. He simply couldn't be bothered to make all of it right.

'You told me you'd told them,' said Jane to Jacob after a moment's silence.

'I think,' said Rachel, 'he'll just need a bit of time to get used to the idea. He's not normally like this. He's a . . . a very sociable young man.'

'He's a child, Rachel.'

'They grow,' she replied concisely.

'Mostly when I'm not there, isn't that right?'

Rachel said, 'Oh don't,' like a sigh and got up slowly and left the kitchen after her son. Jacob fiddled with his ear, a concentrated look on his face, and then got up for a glass of water.

Rachel saw Dan leaning against the wall and went and took his hand.

'Show me my present.'

'No,' he said.

'Dan. Come on.' He was still silent. 'I know it's all a bit odd but you can handle this. Jane might be fun. Your dad's allowed to bring his girlfriends to meet you, you know.'

'Says who?'

'Well . . . he just is. He's bigger and older than you. And he's allowed to make his own mistakes.'

'No, who says? He says he's allowed so he is allowed. But it's our holiday. We're not just going so we can eat ice cream. It's supposed to be about us seeing him.'

'I want to see my present. It's my birthday, come on.' She pulled him down to the far end of the garden where she'd watched him trek back and forth over the last few weeks.

It was one of those days when tears linger, waiting in the far edges of your eyes, and at the sight of the sparsely decorated mound of earth in the corner of the red crumbling walls she wanted to cry again. It looked like a compost heap which had sprouted flowers and crazy paving.

'It's a rock garden. Like the one you said you liked at Mrs Drake's house. But it's stupid. It's ugly, it's all bitty, it looks all wrong. I made it too big and I tried to fill it but it doesn't fit together.' He was kicking at the base of it. 'Look, there's just earth, and not enough plants. The only good thing is the stone. It's a nice stone. And I had nothing to do with that.'

She kissed him on the cheek. He was only an inch or so smaller than her.

'If I tell you that this is the nicest present I've ever had you have to promise me you believe me.'

She had given him a choice, doubt or belief. Choose happiness Dan, she wanted to say, choose happiness.

He looked at the ground and turned and said, 'It's all right. It's not great but it's all right and it will get better, when things grow and get flowers and stuff. But nothing's gone right today.' There was a pause and he stubbed his trainer in the earth repeatedly. 'I'm fed up of trying to make things all right, I'm fed up of not wanting to upset Dad or you, of not telling people things, of being in between. It makes me feel funny, like I need to be sick, but I try to make things okay. Even Greg, you know, he's on another planet, but I think he's put himself there because he knows it's easier for everyone. I want it to be all right and I tried to make your birthday really good but other people muck things up, tree surgeons and Australians . . .'

Rachel turned him round and held him by the arms. 'It's not up to you to make everything work.' He said nothing and she thought to herself, How can I explain your life to you in a moment? How can I explain that it's yours for the taking? 'I don't want you to have to feel sick or responsible for people being happy,' she tried. 'It's hard not to say to you, "You'll understand when you're older". I don't want to say that because I know how much I hated it when *my* mother said it, but when you're older you will see how easy it is to get selfish and you'll see how much it isn't a fourteen-year-old's responsibility.' I knew this, she thought, if I'd just allowed myself to think it. They've grown old too early. And she hugged him again.

95

Dan withstood the hug and then wriggled out. His mother was talking about his life as though he had a choice about it. When in actual fact they both knew he had to go on holiday with his dad, then come back and go to school. Anything else would be disruptively radical. And radical he did not want. Besides, as he would recognise only much later, it was easier for him to be told what to do, safer to obey and then blamelessly sulk, than disobey and take it alone.

'We'd better get back to the kitchen,' he said, almost perky-sounding. Dad would want to get going soon.

7. Hanker

South London, 1986

The Tooting branch of B&Q was a corrugated orange aircraft hangar nestling in an estate of twenty other retail behemoths. Out on the shop floor there was the smell of construction, of woods, metals and plastics. Out back there was the smell of frying food, which rose fresh from the canteen at 7 a.m. and lingered stale through the day. B&Q gave their canteen staff half an hour's coffee break. At 10 a.m., between finishing the breakfast shift and starting the bulk of the lunch prep, they were told to collect one beverage and one piece of confectionery and take no more than thirty minutes. They weren't paid for the pleasure of resting their bums on the red moulded plastic chairs, so naturally they always took the full half hour.

Beth took her coffee and biscuit and an abandoned copy of the *Sun* and sat three seats further down the refectory table from everyone else. She always made sure she sat at the same table as the permanent staff because sitting at a different table made them think you were posh, too up yourself to share their space. She crossed her legs, laid open a copy of the *Sun*, quickly turned over page three and then surreptitiously began to reread a letter from Dan.

She was sixteen – an underdeveloped sixteen rather than a hurrying one. She was skinny, pale and her face, with its brown eyes, thick brows and full cheeks, could have belonged to a ten-year-old. She didn't have pierced ears and during the day, when she had no make-up on and her hair was pulled back into a low-lying ponytail, she had an inviting innocence to her. Men said 'Cheer up, love' to her on the street, which was nothing new, but it was true that her eyes and mouth would settle downwards when she was left alone. And then when the men on the street spoke to her she would look up, round-eyed and timid for a moment, before there was a shift in her attitude and her face, her pride connecting with her jawline, and she would suddenly look a little tougher and more brittle, peculiarly like a disappointed woman.

The B&Q bunch, however, were pleased by the propriety of her silence (there's nothing worse than a temp who attempts to join in). Janet, who'd been there five years, leaned down the table and said, 'Come on, budge up here. We don't bite.' Beth smiled, reluctantly put away her letter and moved up, slopping her coffee on the table.

Janet asked her if she was still at school and, after hearing that Beth was in the first year of her A levels, told her about her sons, one of whom, Ray, was as good as gold and wanted to be a vet (he had six pet rats in his bedroom), and two of whom were lazy buggers and on the dole. Lesley, who had a big perm, said Ray could always work for Rentokil if he didn't get the exams. They all laughed and began to talk about the kitchen rats they had known. Beth, emboldened by the caffeine and a Club biscuit, told a story that Mr Garland from Delia Street had told her about killer rats in Borneo. She meant well but it was a bit too *National Geographic* to be of real interest.

The conversations fragmented again. The wittering radio could be heard, a cipher for silence. Janet looked at Beth with some-thing approaching weariness (it was always her that ended up being nice). She fell back on the inevitable, 'You got a boyfriend then?' It tended to make the temps coy or confessional. Which could be funny either way.

Beth was both shy and polite, which was a problematic combination. Shy and sullen would have been an answer in itself, but shy and polite meant she was her own worst enemy. This particular question was a spectator sport and she had learned to outwit it, in other words lie, because the alternative was too embarrassing. 'Yes,' she said with a smile, 'he's called Dan but his family just moved away.'

It wasn't that much of a lie she thought to herself as she finished her shift. He was a boy who had been a friend. Who had indeed moved (time was very subjective) and did indeed write letters. A chronological lie but also a lie of content, since his letters conveyed information, with an adolescent jocularity, rather than anything else. It was pathetic, but at least a lie was a private humiliation.

Beth worked Saturdays and holidays with the Regina Catering Agency for extra pocket money. Sometimes she got to serve stodgy public school puddings and blush at poor innuendo in wood-panelled rooms in golf clubs on Wimbledon Common. But mostly she washed up or made sandwiches in industrial canteens. Stirring great tureens of Smash, slopping peeled red tomatoes, lung-like ballons, on to plates, scraping beige gunk and carrots off again. She had become a veteran of temporary catering, a money-earning process only slightly higher than cleaning toilets in the depression stakes. When Beth had started she'd had visions of gracious Silver-Service Saturdays but then she'd discovered that drunken men in dinner suits are filthy-tongued if missing their *pommes fondants*. She discovered that people were at their most aggressive when trying to enjoy themselves.

She walked down Acacia Avenue to the bus stop on the main road. The name was deceptive. There were straggling fence-weeds and dumped prams and cookers and crossing the estate on foot was like walking over an airfield. Beth was a pedestrian freak in an urban landscape that had been designed for wheels alone. Just occasionally she would spot another two-legged creature, flickering in and out of sight between silvery saloons in the still, dense car parks.

It was easy to feel lonely on those walks, up too early, finishing before everyone else, catching early afternoon buses with old ladies in wet raincoats that steamed up the downstairs windows. Her journey home always lasted a good thirty minutes so, hunched against a top deck window that had been thickly smeared by a head of oily hair, Beth got out her letter from Dan once more.

Dan's letters would usually begin with an elaborate conceit:

The third day of the tenth month in the year of Nineteen Eighty-Six
Nine twenty-three p.m.
My new bedroom
The Attic, The Last Cottage, The Last Village in England

And continue with expressions of general interest:

Dear Beth
How are you? How are your mum and dad? Do you see Jenny Garland ever? Is she still fat?

Then move swiftly to the meat of the matter:

I have a new bedroom. It was Dave's until he decided he was too much of an adult to ever want to come to Shropshire again. He has a punk girlfriend. Swansea probably still thinks neon pink hair is cool. She came to visit and even Dave must have thought neon pink looked rubbish in Dawley daylight.

100

His burgeoning personality became clearer each year:

I've stuck posters all over the walls. All my favourite ones. I've got lots of Warhol and Dali pictures and this weird Magritte one too. Mum buys them for me in Hay-on-Wye; they've got lots of dusty shops there. They are full of crusty gardening tools and second-hand books. That's what Greg and I always say to her: 'Going to your dusty shops?'

While his inherited wit peppered the pages:

Mum's got a new boyfriend. The tree surgeon won't speak to her still, even though that was ages ago, and now the local doctor keeps coming round for a glass of wine. He's a prat. He has a moustache but he's better than Mike was. At least he brings his own wine, Mum says. Anyway, I've got to go. Mum's made her 'bog standard spag bol' and is dishing up. It's my favourite thing for tea and I want a good plate full. Have fun. Dan.

It was strange, Beth supposed, that she and Dan had never managed to meet up since he'd moved. They'd tried once but they had had to cancel it at the last minute when Beth was already dressed for the trip to the movies in Leicester Square with Dan and his dad. Only, Jacob had explained on the telephone, he and Dan and Greg had been out all day and Greg was knackered and wanted to go home, and Beth didn't mind, did she, and they'd do it some other time. And Roger had felt so sorry for his daughter that he'd taken her up the road to see *Top Gun* for the third time.

The letters were few and far between. And getting fewer. Beth was too self-conscious to reply any quicker than Dan. Dan was too absent-minded to do it unless his mother reminded him. But at the age of sixteen they could both feel themselves outgrowing the medium. Beth's patience was now invested in her diary, and as soon as she got home she headed up the stairs for the privacy of her room and her faint-ruled A5 notebook.

It wasn't so much a diary as an occasional book. She'd not write in it for ages and then pick it up again and start with a breathless, scrawling apology: 'I'm so sorry I haven't written for weeks, it's been so busy.' She wasn't sure who she was writing to. It was a bit like a religion, summoning a faceless force for confessions, her honesty varying, once again, according to the subject matter. There were too many exclamation marks on the pages and she knew this. The trouble was there wasn't a punctuation mark to express a knowing despair that's trying to be jolly. There is only one kind of mark to use at the end of a sentence to say 'See my joke, I know it's kind of lame'.

She hadn't been kissed, let alone been out with a boy, and it was a problem because everyone else she knew had. It seemed to have happened magically to all the others at her all-girls' school. Sometimes as early as thirteen, perhaps beside a pool with a French boy called Jean-Paul. She read so many problem pages in *Mizz* magazine and *Just Seventeen* that she knew the next stage would be for someone to start calling her frigid. She knew this would be unfair since she'd not yet had a chance to have a go at it, but even the fact that you could be good or bad at kissing and sex terrified her. She'd always thought it was something that just happened, like breathing or sneezing, and then one day, while watching *The Thorn Birds* on telly, Rachel Ward had taunted a man about being bad at making love. She'd thought to herself, horrified, Why did no one tell me? So she was honest about that in her diary – her toadstool bedside lamp shafting light on to her posters of Bruce Willis and Arab stallions stampeding in dust clouds through the mid-west of America.

* * *

It was late in the afternoon and Beth was stuck between various tasks: rereading her diary and thinking how childish she had sounded a year ago; revising; making a tape; rearranging the postcards above her bed. The mushroom-coloured carpet was covered with books, tapes and pieces of paper. So much mess and stuff for a person of only sixteen. But then there was so much cutting-out of pictures and copying of words to be done before Beth could choose what she liked and how she wanted to be. She sat cross-legged on the floor and reached up to her bed for the scissors when she suddenly started at the sight of her mother at the door.

'Mum. Jesus. I didn't hear you.'

'Gosh. Should I be knocking these days?'

Yes. But she says instead, 'What is it?'

'Nothing . . . just saying hello. I haven't seen you since you came in.'

'Hello.'

'How were the postmen this morning?'

'B&Q. It was B&Q today, not the post office.'

'Oh right. Good.'

'Why?'

'Why what?'

'Why good?' Beth thought her mother talked nonsense. She thought that Lizzie made pat responses half the time and wasn't listening at all for the rest. She thought she was vague and vacant and yet like a pit bull when she wanted to criticise. She thought a lot about this.

'Oh Beth. I don't know,' Lizzie said with a snap. 'I'm just trying to have a conversation.'

'I'm quite tired.'

'Then you shouldn't be going out tonight, should you?'

'It's just one evening out with my friends.' Beth looked nervous.

'Oh honestly.' Lizzie was exasperated. 'Who d'you think you are? Cinderella? It was your decision to work in those kitchens. There's no reason why your dad should be giving you money to go and spend on daft clothes.'

'I never said he should. I don't care what I get. I don't ask for stuff.'

'You don't have to. I can read you like a book,' Lizzie retorted, which Beth found threatening even though it wasn't the first time it had been said. If that were true then Lizzie would know just how pointless and yet terrifying Beth thought she was.

'Why d'you always have to go on at me? I was just sitting here revising. What have I done now?'

Lizzie sighed. Her daughter looked almost scared, which was fancifulness on her own part, of course. She never shouted at her. Not any more, not now she was a bit better these days. It was surely just sullenness that blanketed Beth's white face. 'You haven't done anything. I just wish you could find a bit more to do with yourself than moping up here and hanging around on street corners all night like a load of no-hopers.'

'What else am I supposed to do? I'm not allowed to do anything else anyway.'

'Your life isn't that dreary.' They looked at each other, stony-eyed, stalemate. 'If you could just perk up sometimes it would make all the difference to this bloody house.' Lizzie sounded exasperated.

There was more than a generation missing between Lizzie and her daughter. If only she would just show a bit of life thought Lizzie, returning to her own bedroom. If only she would get going instead of dragging her heels through school, through each day, then they'd let her do anything she wanted. She was so stubborn, so flailing against the world, so unaware said Lizzie to herself as she drew the curtains in their bedroom. She fiddled with them, getting the meeting of the two halves right.

Lizzie wondered what to do now. The house was more than clean. Sometimes her days felt like one long gap in a stilted conversation. She opened one of the fitted cupboards, inviting her possessions to direct her to a task, and pulled out an old Fyffes banana box. It said Summer Clothes in black marker pen. It hadn't been opened for several years. She would sort through them and take them to Oxfam on Monday. Under the cardboard flaps the striped shirts and flowered skirts were folded neatly, and although they didn't yet carry the sour smell of age she thought they could probably still do with a rinse. She placed the box by the door, ready to take downstairs, and returned to the open cupboard. But instead of closing it she stood looking at another box on the shelf. It was the box of things Roger had rescued from her house in Leicester.

In the end Roger had only waited a few weeks before rescuing her. She'd spent days just sitting, as if waiting for an invasion. She was so clearly unable to look after herself that when he'd said 'Shall I take you with me?' she'd just shrugged. So he'd packed her a suitcase, with some framed photos of the boys and Gavin, a toy, a toothbrush, underwear, some skirts and jumpers and a change of shoes. Upstairs, the door to the boys' bedroom was open and their beds made. She'd caught sight of a drawing on the wall as she'd made her last trip to the toilet and she'd pulled it off. They couldn't take everything, he'd said. Better to take hardly anything, she'd said, shutting the door on the perfectly tidy room, just a scrap of paper in her hand.

The house had been sold and Lizzie had received £1500 a year later, along with her mother's best teaset – by which time she was living in London. Gavin's parents had organised for the house clearance, for Lizzie's one good teaset to be delivered, and for the house sale. Lizzie had given them half the money and had never seen them again. And it was probably best. They blamed her in a confused way. Her moving away, her new pregnancy – all of it threw shadows on her role as a wife and mother in the past. The money had been spent on moving Lizzie's senile mother to a new home, where Lizzie had visited her twice before she died.

She pulled the box down. She'd never opened it since they'd moved to Delia Street, and with defiance rather than anything more tender in the midst of this long, unsatisfactory day, she opened it now. Photos in plastic frames, a toy and a curl of yellowing paper. She pulled out the paper; it was a picture of a dog, a smudged black thing, with five stick legs in strange places. The word DOG was written at the top in an adult's hand.

She heard the gentle stroke of the door opening on carpet and turned to see Beth in the doorway. They watched each other silently, Lizzie still holding the picture, frozen by the combination of people now in the room. Beth hovered on one leg in the doorway, the other foot curled under as if it were deformed.

She'd done this as a very small child. Crept into a room after a tantrum, holding a bear, hoping to appeal with her sweetness. Waiting for her dad to scoop her up in the static nightie that sparked fairies under the sheets.

'Mum?'

Lizzie nodded.

'That's a funny drawing.' Beth exhaled, risking a little humour. 'Was that me?'

'No,' Lizzie said to her.

'Was it you?' Beth asked, glad that her mum was still talking to her.

Lizzie felt the potential of the truth as if she had the demolition of an entire tower block at her fingertips. How odd that just the saying of a few words would change everything so. What was stopping her? No physical impossibility in speaking the words, not even protective kindness at work, just an unwillingness to open herself up once more. She could no more handle the destruction a second time than she had the first.

Beth's strangely sweet patience, as she waited with trust for the answer, made Lizzie feel closer to her child than ever before. And she wasn't sure she could take it at all.

'No, a child I used to know did it.'

'Who?'

'No one you'd know, before you were born.' Lizzie began to close the box. 'Would you go and check on the tea for me? You'll have to eat before you go out.'

A half-life is not no life, thinks Lizzie. It is something.

Beth put the potatoes on to boil and went back to her room to finish lying to her diary. She was never honest about her parents on paper. She didn't like to examine whether it was because she thought her diaries might one day be read by someone else. Or whether it was because she thought that anger committed to paper would be a permanent black mark in the larger ledger. She had a sense of the rest of her life as the far-away hills that you could sometimes see on vantage points in public parks in south London. She knew at some point she would be there, staring back at her former self, thinking what strange child was that, nothing of me in her, and in a way her dishonesty about the adult world around her was in order to try and live up to that grown-up vision, not to let her older self down. So her book was full of expressions like 'Dad really funny today' and 'Something very awful happened in a place called Chernobyl in Russia yesterday, which is really much more important than anything I could have to say about my day at Colliers Wood High'.

She stood up, treading on a tape and some photos, and looked out of the window. It was six-thirty at the very beginning of

107

October and it was beginning to get dark. It looked cold out there. The brickwork of city houses exposed, neighbours revealed to each other after leafy, closeted summers. Fences and boundaries visible from high windows, the private parts of the street exposed – alleyways, lean-to toilets, dustbins, sheds – the back gardens stepping northwards like a ladder. She would go to this party tonight and she would look wonderful and be funny and sleek, play pool and recite poetry. All things to all teenagers. She would go downstairs for a little while, in a minute, and be nice to her dad to make up for the fact that she so wanted to leave the house.

Tomorrow her father would go with her to the Museum of Mankind in town which would be a calm treat – out of the house, keeping pace with his neat, swift walk, and peace, allowing time for daydreaming and cake and tentative observations shared between the two.

There was the sharp sound of a crow or a rook, or some dark bird, and she saw that in the last two minutes darkness had fallen without her noticing. She supposed if she'd paid attention it might not have struck her as dark. But she wasn't paying attention – as with everything else her mind flittered from alternatives to the future. There was always that, she thought, nose pressed to the cold window, breathing in moist air off chill glass, always that to hold on to. There was one thing that was certain – she would grow, leave home, become an adult. It was just a matter of waiting. Life would begin at some point, that was for sure. The trick was just to know when.

At seven thirty-five Beth took a deep breath and stepped into the loud brightness of the train station. A big night out like this one was an assault course, every little element, every arrival and move taking such courage. The station and the local McDonald's were their main social venues. (Central London was only for very special occasions, and required much planning and alcohol which invariably cancelled each other out.) Logically Beth knew that this might be another average evening, that there would be more parties in her life. But who knew what could happen in one evening? Missing out was a risk you had to be much older, much more confident or much less hopeful to take. She searched for familiar faces among the loud, excitable groups.

Beth's friends would be carrying bottles of cider and beer and fortified wine in blue plastic bags. They would all be wearing jeans, the boys' baggy, the girls' tight. The Goths, who also gathered at the station before a night in the damp darkness of the William Morris club listening to bands whose names and guitarists changed each week, were tightly cut and glittering in comparison, with their white-powdered skin and pointed boots, silver rings and flashing insets of purple velvet. But they were weird. The boys wore make-up.

Beth's gang looked like their mothers and fathers in tight skirts and jeans and sweaters, only they were less lined. In fact, some of the boys wouldn't have minded a night out with one or two of their mates' mothers. Pete's mother in particular – a jolly, buxom, blue-eyed woman with a blonde bob and a twinkling face. The boys loved her, happy to boast of her mumsy sex appeal in a way that the girls found disturbing and threatening. They didn't go on about Pete's father, for fuck's sake. But then the boys had discovered more about what they found interesting, what gave rise to those urgent sensations. Beth and many of her girlfriends were slow to imagine sex with older men because it carried dangerous connotations, ones similar to the odd incidents they'd all had, men in the street offering a hold of it, men in the park giving you a sight of it, middle-aged men who accidentally come into your room when there's a grown-up party below and don't leave fast enough. None of that was sexy – it was frightening, snippets of a dark world you didn't ever want to go to, a dark world where you'd disappear and your smiley photo would flash up on the *Nine o'Clock News* and they'd hunt for you and you'd never be found until your shoe and your blouse were finally discovered under a tree.

It was easier for the boys she thought; they didn't suffer the swilling doubt that sex could bring to a girl. Fancying Pete's mother was a pleasant way of passing the time. And Pete's mum liked it. The girls could see that. She liked the way all the boys were so nice and said thank you for their tea and vied with each other to pull on the blue rubber gloves to help with the washing up. But then Beth and her mates agreed there was something a bit pathetic about the way Andy put on her frilly apron last time they were round there. That was never going to get him what they all knew he wanted. The girls understood full well that they, not a mother, were his best chance of a sniff at it. They had what the boys wanted and that was power, in a way.

Beth and her friends, aware of their prized potential, dressed with a mixture of bravado and puritanism. Beth wore a short black skirt, black tights, black ankle socks and lace-up shoes. 'Minnie Mouse feet' her dad called them. Her tight top was a gesture to sexy but Beth knew it was better that all emphasis was cast on her legs, made thinner and longer by so much tight blackness, like sticks of charcoal. She was wearing gold dangling earrings, brown mascara and grey eyeliner and a lipstick called Bon-Bon. The make-up sat on top of her face, bright coloured stripes like felt-tip pen on a white page. She had a full mouth with lazily designed lips, as if someone had used a flourish of a thumb to create the flat curve of her lower lip and the seagull span of her upper. Her donkey jacket jangled with keys, money and lipstick as she walked. She and her girlfriends might have been old enough to have sex but they weren't old enough to wear handbags.

Beth made her way across the forecourt towards her friend Ruth, who was screaming with laughter beside the ticket machines. She saw a tall, broad boy in jeans and a navy jumper, his head thrown back in laughter. She had seen him about before, he was a mate of Ruth's brother. He had clear skin, sports appeal and popularity. The only boys Beth liked were the ones who didn't talk to her. They ignored her and the insecurity that brought was an intense, anxious emotion that she took to well and confused with desire.

Halfway across the forecourt, self-conscious of her legs, she saw him see her. He looked at her for a few short, appraising seconds and then flickered away again. She felt a sharp, wicked moment of triumph.

It was nine o'clock and Lizzie and Roger were watching the news. Lizzie was restless. 'Anything I can get you?' asked her husband.

'I don't know,' said Lizzie, 'I think it's indigestion, maybe.' Roger squinted at the telly. A man got punched by a policeman and Roger winced. He'd always been one of those men whose reactions showed with comic clarity on their face. If you saw him look at his watch you could tell what he thought of the time, whether it was pushing it or taking it slowly that day. You could tell what he thought of a new smell by the way his eyebrows would rise and his head would tilt slightly to the right. It was endearing, puppy-like. He'd take a bite out of a chocolate bar and nod to himself that it was a good taste. You'd know his politics at a glance by the way he would grimace and suck air through his molars at the headlines. This evening a certain state of agitation was clear in him too. Both hands on his thighs, his fingers running fast in the dip at the top of his knees. He turned to Lizzie and opened his eyes wide. 'She's growing up, isn't she?' He said it like it was a long-hidden truth, like an illness that could no longer be denied. Lizzie felt a wave of affectionate irritation.

'She always was, you silly man.' He pressed his lips together and nodded seriously. There was silence, coinciding for a moment with suspense on the telly.

Beth had drunk half a bottle of warm white wine since they'd arrived at the party in the Methodist Hall near the industrial estate where she'd been working that morning. Things were beginning to look up. She and Ruth had already given in to temptation and performed the whole of a Five Star routine to each other, breathless with laughter as they made windmills with their arms. She'd had her bum pinched twice and someone had told her she had the best legs in south London. She went to the toilet for the fifth time to check her make-up and was surprised by the sight of herself, flushed with drink, eyes smudged dark with the heat of dancing, hair big with sticky spray and the rain and flicked carefully to the right-hand side. She looked quite good. And she looked a moment longer than necessary, her mouth a little open, her chin slightly raised – gazing at the mirror as if it had just said something saucy.

She walked back into the hall, which was dark and humid, and thought how fantastic it was, literally fantastic, almost like magic, that she could be this larger, louder person, taking a drink, having a laugh, noticing the winks, two hours after leaving the politeness of her home. It was like being two people, like Superwoman or Jekyll and Hyde. Right now she could do anything she liked and to prove it she nicked a plastic glass of cider as she walked round the side of the room, swinging her shoulders and minxing away as someone shouted 'Oi' after their pint.

Ruth was sitting on Andy's knee at a wobbling table in the corner. She leaped up when she saw Beth and grabbed her by the arm, pulling her away. The boys watched them huddle into each other, whispering, giggling, long-legged and hunch-shouldered, bodies just a little beyond their own control.

Beth's reaction to Ruth's secret was exaggerated and excited. 'Oh fuck off,' she was saying to Ruth, but laughing too.

'No, he does,' Ruth was saying excitedly. 'He means it. He says he can't decide. You won't though, will you?'

Chris, the boy in the navy jumper at the station, had pronounced – the best-looking boy in the group always laid down the ground rules – he didn't know whether he should like to kiss Ruth or Beth so he intended to toss a coin.

'Fuck off,' said Beth again, all high-pitched mock outrage and womanliness. 'Of course I won't – he's awful. He's really rude and up himself. He's not even that good-looking.'

'Good,' said Ruth, pleased, 'I knew you wouldn't.' Sisterhood established, they returned to the table, Ruth leading the lesser-known Beth by her hand. She stood in between Chris and Andy, all the while holding Beth's hand as if they were five.

'She says she won't,' announced Ruth to Chris, sounding missy.

Chris looked at Ruth and smiled slyly at her. One of his teeth was broken and he had glinting eyes. They were small like his mouth, muscle crowding out expression. 'Yes, she will,' he said.

Ruth shrieked, her gob open very wide: 'Chris, you're a pig. Neither of us would kiss you if you were the only fucking boy in the world.'

Ruth sat down again on Andy's knee with just the right level of flourish. But what she didn't know was that Chris's right hand was slowly crawling up Beth's leg. He was moving with stealth up her thick opaque tights. His big fat fingertips were surprisingly light and she stood there like a still tree. He reached the back of her knee and for a second she thought her legs were going to give way with the sweet tickling pain. Ruth, still holding Beth's hand, wriggled about on Andy's knee, making him complain about her bony ass. She was having a fine time, a friend within reach and a boy underneath her.

Beth, meanwhile, was looking rather odd, making an introverted sort of face. The same look she used to have as a small child when she was concentrating on the potty. His hand was still travelling but her legs seemed interminably long, and unlike her he was in no hurry. He was smoking with his left hand and watching the small tremor in her back. Then someone called him and he looked away from her and for one second she thought he was going to stop. She wasn't sure if she'd be able to stand up if he did. She'd never felt anything like this before but she recognised the need for him to reach the top of her legs and touch her there as desire. How she recognised it was a mystery, but she just knew that if he didn't get there she'd want to bust. His hand was trembling a little now with the effort of the clandestine creep up her leg. His hand spread out to get the feel of her thigh, to catch the curve where her leg became bum. He shifted his chair a little closer to her and said 'Lean on me', so she did and spread her legs a little so that his hand could travel up between her and then slide down the front of her so that his hand cupped the warm, curved swell of her crotch, enclosed in her white pants and impenetrable tights.

'Go on,' continued Andy to Chris, 'you can't back out now. You said you'd toss for them. Beth . . . heads or tails?' And Beth, anxious to keep Chris where he was, said 'Heads,' and Ruth went, 'Beeeeth. Jesus.'

Chris was laughing, and when Andy tossed the coin and called 'heads' Chris said, just to be greedy, 'You know, I think I'd rather give Ruth head.' He leaned forward in front of Beth to stick his tongue down Ruth's throat.

But Beth didn't care that she'd been spurned in public. Because his hand was gripping her arm like he didn't intend ever to let go. And she looked at Ruth slobbering in public and thought how vulgar she was, how much more interesting it was to be felt in secret.

'I've been thinking,' Lizzie said as Roger turned off the telly for the night. 'I was thinking that since she's so rarely here now, I mean, as you said, she's on her way, I thought maybe I could get a bit of a job, a couple of days in the Oxfam up the road. There's a sign saying they need volunteers.' I've been waiting for life to come back to me and gather me up and set me in the right direction she thought. And it doesn't seem to be happening. In which case she needed to get out of this damn house. When she walked into Tooting to the shops the rest of the world seemed to be moving to a faster beat.

'Why not? I think that's a very good idea.' Roger turned and smiled at her. He'd never quite understood how she'd filled her spare days anyway. But it wasn't something you could really ask your wife. It was odd though, he thought, the way she talked about Beth as though she was emigrating, not just growing up. Was that it? Was that the end of his child? He'd been counting on the years to come as the time to convey all that mattered to his daughter. He'd had clear visions of the three of them in *Golden Age* settings, leaning in to each other slowly with a trust as nourishing as the sun. Would those never now be fleshed out? Her littleness was long gone, and although Roger was the first to admit he didn't know much about teenagers, he thought perhaps Beth was unlikely to lean on them for anything.

He had been wondering for years whether they hadn't made a mistake in not telling Beth about her half-brothers. Hadn't it come between Lizzie and her daughter? But once again it wasn't something you could really do – ask your wife whether they'd made a seventeen-year-long mistake. All this *not* doing he thought with an uncharacteristic flash of anger. All those years ago, when he'd first met Lizzie, it had begun in the very *losing* of inhibitions. Suddenly Roger, his eyes still on the dying star of the television screen, said quietly, 'I'd like to go to bed with you. Now,' to his wife.

Lizzie coloured pink and laughed. Pleased. Here was a start.

PART TWO

8. Lovers' Backs

2000

The evening of Jacob Frederick's fifty-fifth birthday party brought heat so strong the pavements began to crack under a heavy, storm-grey sky. Until that night Beth's adult life had felt safely constructed. Yet on the way home, as the storm broke, she felt the husks of dried memories plump and colour with the sudden London rain.

The snakes and ladders of her twenties had been assimilated. She felt, what with her job, her home, her friends and her un-challenged liberal views, on solid ground. The only uncertainty was whether the future would be any different, and it was that that made her suggestible enough to hold out her hand and take from Dan a flimsy grey clipping. A gift of print is always worth examining and she had to admit the oddness of it all appealed. The symmetry of boy turned to man, girl grown woman, and the framework of childhood used to very much more adult intent had sexual potential too. Even Beth, or perhaps especially Beth with her stylised and stylish pessimism, hoped some things happened for a reason.

The venue for Jacob's birthday party was not a promising one: a 1950s Methodist Hall that Beth remembered visiting as a teenager. As far as she could remember she'd drunk too much and been groped by a boy in a sweater. She'd enjoyed herself enormously;

119

a secretive, fumbled epiphany. In fact, she thought to herself as she followed Lizzie into the orange dim of the hall, it had happened right there, in the far left-hand corner beside the stage with its looped-up curtains of mangy red velvet. They'd hired some coloured lights, giving the fifty-odd guests a blue then orange tint. It was only 8.30 and the hall was still too big for its party. People stood in corners, frightened by the clear statement of space.

Lizzie and Beth came to a tentative halt a couple of yards in, their feet just inside the goal-shooter's circle of the indoor netball court. Beth could hear her mother take a deep breath as if she were about to tumble backwards into the sea.

'I think we need a drink,' Beth said, leaving Lizzie adrift on the edge of the party like a child.

Trestle tables covered with food and booze lined the left-hand side of the hall. Bowls of sticky rice salad and cold pasta with specks of red pepper sat beside beef the colour of old insoles, a reconstructed salmon and baskets of sliced baguette. She helped herself to a sausage roll and two glasses of white Chardonnay. She didn't like cheap Chardonnay but equally didn't fancy being caught examining alternative bottles. She took a large swallow of wine, the shortcrust pastry and sharp alcohol mingling in her mouth, and wondered which of the family she'd see first. Wondered what they'd do when they saw her.

Bang on cue, with a timeliness that disturbed her more than it should (it was his own birthday party, after all), a voice said 'Hello Beth'. She turned round. It was Jacob. She swallowed and then coughed as the pastry clumped in her gullet. He waited, an almost avuncular look on his face.

'Hello Jacob.' There was a pause while they looked at each other. 'Happy birthday.' They smiled formally at each other. He looked just the same.

'Well, it comes to us all,' he said, scratching his head. She was momentarily confused.

120

'What does?'

'Age. Getting old.'

'Oh yes,' she sort of laughed, 'even you.'

'Not you though,' and he smiled again without opening his mouth, a flat, wide smile.

'No, not me,' and she smiled flat as Norfolk right back.

It must have been at least eight years. He and his third wife had recently moved back into the house in Delia Street but she hadn't seen him until now. She could see that he did look older – the plentiful, soft, straight dark hair was shorter with a lot of grey and deep grooves branched from his nose to his mouth. But the skin over his high cheekbones was still flat and smooth, and his brown eyes still sat inside dark rimmed spaces like a quiet child's. He was wearing an orange silk shirt. It was a mistake since he was naturally yellowish, and a disappointment. He had been such a vital, impulsive figure. This bad shirt seemed a parody of the young-at-heart. Like wearing a badge saying you're only as old as the woman you feel. She always remembered him as wearing denim shirts rolled at the sleeves and brown lace-ups but, then, that was in a previous decade.

He was smiling at her. 'Are you well?' he said. 'Are you . . .' She could have sworn he was going to say happy but he stopped with the arrival of a woman who took Jacob's arm.

'It's Beth, isn't it?' She was wearing an emerald green dress and she held out her hand. They looked like little squares from a paint chart standing next to each other. 'I'm Laura. We've never met but I've seen your photo at your parents'. It's lovely that you and your mother could come.'

Beth silently acknowledged the woman's proper manners. Jacob's third wife (they'd married five years ago) didn't have to come and talk to her. Yet although Beth had a strong sense of pointlessness, an urge not to bother with polite conversation, Laura took her by surprise. She gave her a soft smile and said,

'You should talk to Dan, you probably haven't seen him for . . . ohhh, ages. He's about somewhere.' Then she turned to her husband and said, 'Will you come and sort the music out? I want people to dance.' And then they left her – feeling exposed and a bit silly with her handbag slipping and a glass of Chardonnay in each hand.

Beth stood a moment, feeling with her tongue for compacted sausage roll. Allowing her stance a few moments longer for authenticity's sake. She tipped half the small glass of wine inside her, then turned to look for her mother. Beth saw Lizzie sitting at a table with Mr and Mrs Garland, their old neighbours from Delia Street, typically perched at the edge of her chair, bag on lap, a transitory look about her. Beth thought to herself that surely at some point in the past, maybe to her father, she must have seemed more of a person and less of a shadow? She'd been watching life from the oblique angle of a recluse since Beth had been able to recognise her. It seemed inconceivable that Lizzie had managed anything as dramatic, as optimistic, as marrying a man. She looked smart tonight though; she had made herself a new dress out of a thinly striped fabric and looked younger than usual. Beth would give her that.

The flick-flack smash of her shoes was loud on the lacquered floor and as she walked across the empty space back to the table where her mother sat she kept her eyes down. Beth said her hellos to the Garlands and they all had a static chat about home improvements and skips on Delia Street while waiting for things to begin. And, sure enough, with the soft-focus effect of the wine and the loosening arrival of Dionne Warwick, the guests began to inhabit and warm the hall. People grouped and regrouped, gaggles of men breaking off from circles of women as if the hall reminded them of school dances, of a period in their youth when the fact that women were women was not just a truth but an insurmountable one. There were young boys in khaki trousers and ironed shirts, hands in pockets, older women laughing and surreptitiously slipping feet out of tight court shoes, Jacob's colleagues in leather jackets, middle-youth and middle-age seeming to blend indeterminately into each other.

Lizzie watched the men and wished Roger hadn't been on a course for his new role as an administration manager at the local comprehensive and had been able to come with them and see her in her new outfit. They could have danced together. What would Beth have made of that? She smiled slightly and tipped to the right like a heavy-bottomed buoy. 'It's nice,' she said to no one in particular, 'you used to be able to tell how old someone was by what they were wearing. It doesn't seem to matter much any more.'

Twenty minutes later the floor had filled and Beth was standing up watching Jacob and Laura dance closely, their barely moving foreheads bowed to each other, backs to their guests. Beth's arm was wrapped around her waist, supporting the elbow of the other arm. She was wearing a dress the colour of dried lavender. From the front it appeared to be a plain, sleeveless shift dress. But from behind it draped low to reveal her back. Her shoulder strap was slipping slightly, revealing more of her shape and the indent of her waist than was perhaps intended. More shiftless than shift dress. Less a dress than a drape.

A dark-haired man who had just come back from the chilly, childishly pink toilets saw her standing there and stopped. They were playing Frank Sinatra. Beth moved her weight from one foot to the other. The fabric moved with her and the muscles in her back rose and slid. The steps of her spine were just visible, their concave curve, before her form gathered to the mound of her bum, giving her lower back a darker-grey marble shade. She was very still, standing in her own circle of space like a statue.

Dan, who had made a preparatory trip to the pub before his

father's party, thought her back was possibly one of the most perfect things he'd ever seen. The woman was facing the other way with no knowledge of him watching her. The coloured discs of light slid around the wooden floor and she stood a little apart, made of a different matter. Her stillness was mesmeric. Her off-white flesh moulded smooth to her skeleton, her hair a blunt fall of darkness between her shoulder blades. His urge was to place both hands at her side, in between fabric and skin, and follow her below.

He walked right up behind her. Beth, whose head had been somewhere else, sometime past, sensed she was sharing her air with someone. Once again she heard a man's voice at her back and for a moment the interruption to her solitary watching seemed God-given.

'I like your dress,' a voice said to her.

Unwilling to turn around, to change her view, she simply said, 'Thank you.'

'You look like you've been made very carefully,' said Dan, which of course did make her turn around, laughing and questioning.

They looked at each other. Something about his eyes and mouth was more than familiar. There he was.

'Dan,' she said.

'Beth?' he said.

He wasn't much taller than her, compact rather than lean, and afterwards she had problems describing him in detail. She remembered the fact that he stood quite close, that he looked straight at her, that he was wearing a blue shirt made out of something soft, that his neck was brown, and that when he smiled a repeat of curved lines spread across his cheeks which reminded Beth of Rachel's loose laugh and easy humour. How odd to want to stand so close to him, as if she were trying to smell him. How odd that he'd grown up, had a whole life, existed outside of her head. His physicality and his brown skin took her by surprise. If he looked so convincingly adult then she must do too.

'You remember me,' was the first thing he said.

'Of course I do,' she said. 'You've not changed that much, have you? Better dressed, maybe.'

His clear eyes looked hard at her. 'So, tell me about you. What are you doing?'

'Working, living in London, you know.'

'And how are your parents?' He gestured towards her mother. 'Are they all right?'

'Fine. I think. How about your mother?' They watched each other, their mouths of more interest than the words they shaped.

'She's okay, really okay, it's good,' he said. 'She's got lots of time now for herself, which is what she always wanted really. And she likes being our friend more than a parent, I think.'

'I'm glad,' she said and thought how she'd like to see Rachel, who had always seemed so rich in experience, love and certainty. As if, in her relaxation, in her green garden, she would have given Beth the answer to anything she needed to know. But she didn't say it and, momentarily distracted, her eyes cast around the room for another comment. Dan's father and Laura were laughing with another couple, arms around each other's waists.

'They seem happy,' she said.

'Who?'

'Jacob and . . . Laura, is it?'

'Oh, Dad . . . yes, I suppose so. He still works too hard. Not abroad any more but still as frantic as ever.'

'Nothing changes much, does it?' Beth said quickly, smiling and exhaling at the same time.

'Oh but it does,' he said, suddenly earnest. 'Look at Mr Garland. He's in a wheelchair. Did you know he was in a wheel-chair?' For the second time in the evening Beth was shocked. She hadn't noticed the wheelchair and felt ashamed. 'He used to take us to the swings with, what was she called . . . Jenny,' he continued. 'And d'you remember all those volcanos?'

'God, yes,' she said, grateful for the easy subject. 'We must have been the only children of the seventies who dreamed of earthquakes rather than bombs.'

'Earthquakes and cyclones and floods and tigers and sharks.' Dan looked delighted, and the memory of his energy, the energy that had pushed her every day to faster races and higher swings, the child that had enticed and exhausted her out of stolidity, flooded back. There was silence and he added, with child-like mock bravado, 'I won a pub quiz the other day because I knew that all the eels in the world came from the Sargasso Sea.'

She was amused. 'Everyone we knew came from the same place, though; it must have seemed quite reasonable then.'

'We spent our whole time together,' he said suddenly. 'That's odd, isn't it?'

'We did,' she said at last.

'All the time,' he said. 'I loved your house. It was quiet, no one shouted at you. Ours was so chaotic; I don't ever remember a time when all of us were sitting down.'

'You didn't much. Your mother was so calm that you were all totally free to race around and to bounce off the walls. I remember being amazed that none of you realised how much you risked breaking.'

'So go on then,' he asked, changing the tone. 'Why didn't you answer that last letter I wrote you?'

She laughed and then asked, 'How old were we?'

'Sixteen?'

'In that case it was the year I discovered boys.' Before the conversation could get any more intimate she added, 'We did have lots of fights, you know, when we were little. You sulked a lot.'

'I did not.'

'You did.'

'I didn't.' Dan camping it up.

'You did, you were very changeable.'

He shrugged, bored now of the glib parry, feeling confessional with all these memories. 'We hated it in Shropshire, you know. At first. It felt odd for ages. We didn't really settle in, we didn't really know how to do it. I got in lots of fights and hated everyone and everything. I think if we grew up at all it was defensively, not naturally.' What would Rachel think to that? Beth wondered. She certainly didn't know what to say, so said nothing. It seemed a long time ago, like talking about two characters in a novel.

'Funny how it's so long ago,' he said, his thoughts clearly also struggling with sentimentality and reality. 'And not funny, I suppose, quite ordinary really, time passing and everything. Funny, I mean, how really obvious things like your parents getting older seem strange, don't you think?'

'Yes,' she said, smiling without meaning to, 'I think I do think.'

His sentences rambled and fell, as unconstrained as his family had been to her as a child. He smiled back and their stances relaxed and things seemed a little more natural. He had the same springy hair. It was disturbing how a sense of his physical potential was seeping through her. She thought this might be how aunts felt about manly nephews.

'Mum said that you paint,' she said.

He made a 'Hum' noise and then said, 'When I can't put it off any longer or if I can't make getting up last all day. And when I'm not working in a bar to pay for the paint. Mixing stupid cocktails, making the rocket salads stretch, giving tossers brunch. I hate the word brunch.' He suddenly looked a bit miserable.

'Do you like your paintings?'

He looked at her sharply and said after a few seconds, 'No one ever asks that. They always say "What d'you paint?" or

"D'you make any money?", or my friends from college say "What are you doing now then?" in an aggressive way.' Then his eyes flickered to the back of the room and he reverted to a more artless rhythm, 'Umm, God, I don't know . . . usually but not always. I'm not sure you should, necessarily. I certainly don't want to look at some of them every day, and that goes for the ones I'm quite pleased with as well as the ones I know are really bad.'

'Would I like them?' She didn't know why she'd asked that, she must have wanted to be in the equation somehow.

'I've no idea.' They looked at each other. 'Or at least I've an idea, but I could be wrong. I'm quite easily surprised.'

'No, you're not, you just pretend you are because it gives you more to say.'

His eyebrows rose as if he were taking a look at her over a pair of spectacles. 'You've lost none of your edge.'

'Well, you always had a mouth on you.'

'Yup, I always did.' There was a pause. 'You were a sulky little cow though.'

She was shocked; that wasn't quite true. She'd been unhappy. She'd worked that out several years ago. And she knew whose fault it was. But she liked Dan's directness. 'I had to take it out on someone,' she said, her lower lip loose. 'You had a younger brother to bully.'

'Greg's just joined the Territorial Army. It's a bit worrying.'

She snorted with laughter.

'Who do you boss around now then?' he asked. 'Are you living with someone?'

'I'm not quite as bossy as I used to be,' she replied, not answering the question, playing at petulance. She wondered whether this conversation didn't have the provocative rhythm of a flirtation. She was conscious of her body and the dress that didn't really fit, and the fact that she was standing with one arm around her waist and her pelvis ahead of itself. She remembered an early ballet teacher shouting, 'Bottom in, pelvis out.' Lessons in life for seven-year-olds.

He was looking at her with intent. 'I think we should go out sometime.'

Oh God, she thought. 'Yes. No, we should definitely meet up sometime.'

'No, I mean I'd like to take you out. On a date,' he said slowly.

'I know you do,' she said, suddenly honest. 'I just don't know if it's appropriate.'

'Why not? It'd be fun.' Less sure of himself now.

'Just not.' They waited. Oh this felt familiar to Beth, she was good at this, the seductive evasions. He looked at her intently, unperturbed. Knowing again.

'I'll tell you what, I'm going to go now but I'll give you my number and then you can change your mind and ring me.'

She was surprised. She was never surprised three times in a single evening. She made a point of it.

'Optimism is a very underrated quality,' he said, grinning. 'Wait here.'

She did wait, and while she waited she wondered what she thought she was up to, her eyes casting around the room. In Dan's absence this suddenly felt unnecessary. There had to be more to life than this, something a little larger, something a little more urgent than whether or not to say yes to a drink with this person. It was foolish.

He returned with a pen and a piece of newspaper. 'Read this,' he said after writing his telephone number at the top. 'I read it on the way here and then saw you. It seems,' he smiled slightly, 'apt.' She looked into his eyes and he smiled and she felt a familiar tug of illicit desire. The recognition of his mouth – wide like his father's – made her stomach lurch. She might have shaken her head and refused the gesture if she hadn't been distracted by that fault-line shift within her. A slide that happened with his smile. Oh, he was endearing enough, had grown beautiful enough, and yes, the gift and the promise within it was suggestive enough for a respectable pass on an average kind of a night. But with it came urges and questions she had been running to outpace for years. He felt like a temptation – not just a romantic one, something much more dangerous. A temptation to go back, unpiece and make sense.

And yet when he handed her the piece of newspaper there was a quiet demand in his voice that she could imagine obeying, and when she read the article under a flickering street lamp, with the first thunder growls in the sky above her, she laughed at his technique and her seduction. For she was indeed seduced by the first gift, and its promise.

Rodin's famously erotic sculpture, 'The Kiss', has finally been honoured by its hometown, Lewes, Sussex, with a celebratory exhibition. For forty years it was just a piece of municipal decoration in the Town Hall, witnessing meetings, lectures and, most interestingly, annual boxing matches. Legend has it that, as the fight heated up and the crowds grew drunker and louder, condensation, like sweat, could be seen trickling down the lovers' backs.

It was a promise of passion. A misguided promise she thought as she re-read it one hazy hour later in her old childhood bedroom, a little drunk on the mix of wine and remembering. But still, it was something to allow herself to be promised anything.

9. Sleeping Dogs

Beth awoke to the sound of her mother hoovering. It was Sunday. Beth got up and went downstairs.

'You're hoovering,' she shouted at the noise.

'What?' said Lizzie, screwing her face up to try and hear.

Beth pulled the plug out. 'You're hoovering.'

'Well, I was. Yes.'

'It's Sunday.'

'I know that. I've laid your breakfast. Go and sit down.'

Beth sighed and sloped through to the kitchen in her old T-shirt and tracksuit bottoms. Lizzie made a 'Well, excuse me' face back, but only after Beth had gone.

Beth rarely went back to Delia Street to stay. She had her own home just a few postcodes away. But it had made sense to go back after Jacob's party, and Roger had specifically asked her to stay the one night he was away. Beth had arranged to meet her friend Sarah at lunchtime so she'd be on her way soon. She felt too big for this house now. Overgrown. Bully big. She wondered how her six foot one dad could bear it. Everything was too tidy, too familiar for Beth to be able to breathe freely.

Lizzie made them both a poached egg, cooked at diagonals in a neat palette of four, and placed it in the centre of a piece of white toast. They ate silently, the warm smell of egg yolk making Beth feel a little sick. She wondered whether she'd drunk too much last night, whether she'd made a fool of herself. That she'd gone at all, back to Merton Methodist Hall on a Saturday night with her mother in tow, was in itself a little demeaning.

'Strange to see Dan, I expect,' said Lizzie. 'He's turned into a nice-looking man. Makes me feel old. I remember him when he was so young. Just a funny little boy, fizzing round the streets.' Beth thought her mother was strangely talkative this morning and she stood up to leave the table for a bath when Lizzie suddenly said, 'I thought you might like those cups.'

'What cups?'

'Those cups, your grandmother's cups.'

'Why?'

'You always liked them as a child and we don't use them, and you've got your own home now. You're very settled and independent. I'm sure you have people round for tea sometimes. Or coffee. You could use them for coffee too, you know. People don't hold with using different cups any more, I'm sure.'

'Oh.' Beth sat down, feeling inappropriately worn out as if she were being invited to adopt an orphan. 'All right. But not today; I'm meeting Sarah at one. I wasn't going to go home first.'

'But I've sorted them out and cleaned them. I just need to get them down from the bedroom.'

'But I don't want to carry them round the bloody gallery, do I?' Beth's voice grew loud at the end of the sentence. Lizzie looked hurt. She turned to the washing up.

'Fine,' she said.

Beth lay in the bath. As a child she had thought those tea cups beautiful, the epitome of gracious adult living. They were small with handles as milkily transparent as a child's ear and saucers that were practically flat. The insides of the cups were decorated with three bands of green, increasing in thickness; a pale aquamarine, a faded smoky green that ought to be called apple wood and then a sharp olive green, a colour that seemed to belong to

132

an era that, like peculiar faces in Edwardian group photographs, surely couldn't be found now.

Lizzie had always said how much her own mother, Moira, had loved the cups, and it was one of the only personal items, things with a bit of her own history, that Lizzie had ever shown to Beth.

Beth felt disturbed by their spat in the kitchen. She resented the way Lizzie still made her feel guilty when she herself had been a peculiarly remote mother. However, it had recently struck Beth that for every role there was a potential judgement. That someone might feasibly ask her how good a daughter she was. But being a good daughter sounded a strangely old-fashioned notion. And relied, surely, on there being a demand.

Still, she did feel unsettled, she didn't want to be disapproved of this Sunday morning. She had enough on her plate without that. So, wrapped in her towel, she went in to her parents' bedroom and, seeing the cupboard door open and not noticing the box on the bed, reached in and took out the one box on the shelf.

It was light – the cups were very thin, fragile things. She kneeled on the floor and opened it up. But inside there was no china. Instead there were three photos in frames, a toy . . . toy horse maybe, and a child's drawing. She looked at the photos. They were black and white. The first was of two small boys in old-fashioned white jumpers. She thought they might be the same children that sat at the back of the mantelpiece in the sitting room. Second cousins or something, Lizzie'd always said. In the second photo they were sitting on a sofa with a dark-haired man. Finally there was a photo of a young woman with dark, dark wavy hair, in a park with one child on a tricycle. It could have been Lizzie but it was difficult to tell, the woman was small, pin-headish, and her face was scrunched up against the sun. Beth unrolled the piece of paper. She knew she was prying, knew from experience that Lizzie would freak at this level of interference. It was a child's drawing of a dog. Perhaps it had been done by her. Should she be able to recognise her own early alphabet she wondered? Worse still, she should probably be able to recognise her mother in a photo. But then who knew about photos, about people's faces in the past? And who knew about children's pictures? She would never know if it was her own because they all looked the same. Always a primary animal or a house with four windows, never the sky underneath. But then the more she thought about it the more she thought that she did recognise it, that she had seen this years ago, in here, in the bedroom. Who'd done it? Her mum had told her. Beth couldn't remember, something about some kids she'd once known. The cousin's children, obviously, the ones in the photos. She put it all back in the box and then back on the shelf.

So what was wrong with that bit of the family then? Beth had decided long ago that there must have been some falling out between her mother and her grandmother to alienate Lizzie so, down in the south of England without mother or relatives. But she'd never actually asked. It wasn't the kind of question you asked Lizzie. She headed off those questions long before they came to pass with a lowering of her eyes, a losing of company, a retreat inside.

She shut the cupboard door and moved away before Lizzie could catch her snooping. How extraordinary; half an hour ago Beth would never have imagined herself ferreting in her mother's cupboards. Let alone finding something. It was weird the way it was all in a box. Like the way love letters are meant to be kept. Secretively. If it had been someone else Beth would have wondered whether this wasn't a boyfriend Lizzie had had before Roger, a boyfriend and his children, whether this wasn't a past love affair she'd stumbled on. She knew anything was possible, she'd seen quite enough television to understand how much deception was practised in families. But Lizzie, whatever else Beth may have thought of her, was most certainly a one-man woman.

She saw a second box on the bed and with some trepidation opened this one up. There really might be old letters in this one – perhaps between her parents – and then, faced with true intimacy, real passion, what would she do? But inside there were six fine bone china cups and saucers, and Beth carried them downstairs, making a detour via the sitting room.

Lizzie smiled to see her with the box and began to say something when Beth said carefully, placing the cups on the kitchen table, holding out the photo from the mantelpiece, 'I've been meaning to ask, I can't remember, who are these two?' Lizzie's face stilled.

'I've told you before. My cousin's children. Why do you ask?'

'Just noticed them this morning.'

'They're my cousin's children. I used to see them before I moved here with your dad.'

'In Harrogate?'

'No, well, yes . . . yes, in Harrogate.'

'No?'

'Yes,' said Lizzie, 'yes . . . a bit outside Harrogate.'

'What were they called?' There was a beat. 'Can't you remember?' Beth said unkindly.

'Yes, I can remember, they were called Martin and Paul.'

'Why don't you keep in touch?'

'Because it's difficult, particularly with children. You never find the time . . . you just move on. So . . . have you decided to take those cups after all?'

At that moment the phone rang. Beth moved to answer it but Lizzie lifted her finger sharply, as if the sudden ring had broken her pose, and said, 'This is my house and my phone. You have your own now.'

Except it wasn't for Lizzie at all. 'She's here,' she said and handed the phone over to Beth, shutting the door quietly as she left the kitchen.

'Hello,' said someone Beth didn't recognise. 'It's Dan.' And then he added, 'Frederick,' just in case.

'Hello,' she replied with a frown. Wondering still quite what had been happening in that exchange with her mother.

'You don't sound very surprised.'

'Don't I? Well, I suppose I am a bit. I thought I was supposed to phone you.'

'I thought bugger that. I only rang your mum to get your number, didn't realise you'd be there.' There was a pause. 'What are you up to?'

She hesitated. 'Arguing.'

He laughed. Did he think it was a joke? she wondered. There was another pause.

'D'you want to go out for a coffee?' he chanced.

'No,' she said. And she had to laugh, even if it did come out a bit indignant.

'Never mind, I'm supposed to be working anyway. What about a drink later in the week?'

Beth, now distanced by daylight from the unsettling but creeping pleasure his presence had given her, felt like asking him what exactly he was up to and where his sense of propriety was. She felt like saying that, quite apart from anything else, he couldn't just ask her out as if they'd never known each other, and equally that he couldn't just presume they ought to try a meeting-stroke-date because they'd liked each other as ten-year-olds. They were now adults who were known to have sex occasionally. But then again that would all be a little heavy-handed at noon on a Sunday with someone she didn't know very well any more. All in all it was easier to give in and say, 'Okay then, Thursday?', to which he responded, 'Fine.'

Beth left without either of them saying much more, kissing her mother on the cheek from a distance, and took the tube back to her flat in Camberwell. Her existence these days was a very urban one. She still found it hard to think why anyone would live anywhere other than the inner zone of a city or the furthest, wildest reaches of countryside. Anything in between was surely just settling for mundanity. She was a freelance TV editor, working mostly on documentaries and reality TV series. The editing studios depended on the job in hand, but they were often around Soho or the west of London, which meant journeys up round the Oval, Vauxhall's tangled multi-lanes, Victoria's one-way system, streets seedy with train station spillover, into the sudden grandeur of Hyde Park Corner, with cars circling at Parisian speeds, magical silver gates and Peter Pan connotations. Only SW1, Beth thought, could still afford to support such romance.

Beth's flat was made up of two floors in a grimy Victorian redbrick, easily reached by bus or juggernaut. It was a busy yet empty area; broad, jammed roads and pavements that were bare. On the ground floor was a florist's that specialised in wreaths and floral words. Beth and the florist shared a small yard out the back, which she accessed by climbing down narrow, dark stairs and past sooty windowpanes.

But it was cheap to rent, then cheap to buy, and safe in its hemmed-in height and unpromising location. And she liked feeling as if she were in the midst of an electrical circuit. She lived in the palely decorated interior alone and at night she could lie awake counting shuddering buses, the traffic sighing to a halt at the lights outside her window. Often she'd hear sirens approaching and ambulances screeching past and would then listen to cars speeding behind in the slipstream, like surfers catching a big wave. Below her the florist would work until midnight in the back of the shop to finish a big order, the proper decoration for a matriarch's funeral, while outside police cars would yelp and a helicopter would try and shine out something dangerous lurking in the wasteland behind the house. Beams of light would penetrate the curtains and Beth would have the strange, almost exhilarating sense of a city fuelled by crisis, human traffic freewheeling on tragedy.

Delia Street had very little traffic. It had always been a place of silence and sudden, sharp hiccups of sound, a land of small trees and domestic arguments, half-drawn curtains and murderous cat fights, matching bedside lights and strange faces at windows. Crime, when it appeared, was more silent but also more devastating. A woman murdered on the allotments, her scream heard in the dusk and dismissed by two boys rumbling by on skateboards; a man neatly turned out in black levering a window, climbing in while an old woman sleeps.

In contrast, the grimed streets around Beth's flat came alive after dark and by night they emitted a saucy lullaby of drunks and tarts. Perky, staccato tunes with undertones of plague and abandonment floated up through the windows. Silence had always come so easy to Beth that she loved the access to other people's music, loud in their cars, booming from flats over the road. She liked the way hardcore pirate stations cut in and out of Radio 1. There was a subversiveness in the air, a need for noise.

It was nearly 1 p.m. and she bought milk in the local 7–11 and dropped it and the box of china off at the flat. It was airless inside, the curtains closed, but she left immediately and went on to meet Sarah at the Tate Gallery. She and Beth had been at university together, neighbours in their first hall of residence, and Sarah was one of the few people Beth had met in Birmingham that she continued to see. Beth liked her more and more as the years went by for her tenacious surprise at luck's twists and people's behaviour. She was too busy laughing to develop much cynicism.

But Sarah's boyfriend had recently left and her laughter had a desperate edge to it at the moment. She was fairly one-track company at times like this but she did at least want conversation and to take advice and hold it to the light, which gave Beth something to do. She knew that Sarah was still on the break-up wheel: 'I am now free to cultivate my interests on Sundays and must go to exhibitions and go swimming regularly.'

The heat had broken with the storm the night before, the sky still churning. Beth and Sarah met on the windy steps and kissed mouthfuls of hair hello. They fought the urge to drink coffee and eat cake first and meandered through the busy rooms with rumbling stomachs. Wandering past the careful groupings of paintings, moving slowly, leaning into each other's words, dividing and circling around sculptures, they talked brokenly of recent events, of who had said what to whom, of Beth's scene over the 'coffee cups', of the secrecy of cupboards, of the impenetrability of parents' pasts. Beth felt better as soon as she had aired her head, expressed her irritation and then reduced Lizzie to a generalisation. She didn't actually want to puzzle over her mother any more than she would want a father who still kissed her on the lips.

They stopped longer in front of certain paintings when a colour or shape, or the real version of a familiar reproduction – less glossy, less unassailable than a postcard or poster – struck them. Beth liked the figurative paintings more than the abstract or conceptual art. She liked the framed windows into other worlds. They were potent, mysterious. Much more so than sculpture which revealed all its sides. She stopped in front of a large Chagall, little voodoo dolls of people free-falling through night-blue skies.

All around her people performed the gallery shuffle; an intricate dance for the self-conscious, where visitors avoid physical contact as they stand around a painting smaller than a bathroom mirror. On the opposite side of the room a large lady in a waistcoat was hogging the dog in the lower left-hand corner of a family portrait, and the tall man behind her, stubbornly unmoving, serenely observed structure over their scalps. Beth found human behaviour in the face of art irresistible; all of them, including herself, offering up such hopeful, personal, bumptious banalities.

'That blue, it's so intense . . . what would you say it was? Midnight blue, velvet blue . . .'

'I do like the way he's done that dog, very life-like.'

Or, as she crab-stepped to the portrait of a nude inside a dusty room: 'Looks like the sitting room in that house we stayed in in France. Year before last.'

'Yes, you're right. Still, it's a bit odd, isn't it? Doesn't look very comfortable to me.'

'Nude three, 1923, loaned by Mr and Mrs Kirkpatrick of Westchester, USA,' a man intoned. Some things are better left read thought Beth. And his companion nodded sagely as if this was of enormous help in unlocking the key to what was, essentially, a purely beautiful nude. A purely beautiful nude who yet looked saddened by the puce revelry in her body. Who looked – the man in the hat and anorak had been right – highly uncomfortable, turning her head over her right, doughily soft, reclining shoulder. She struck Beth as a woman unhappy in adoration. She was naked yet she might just as well have been clothed in an inappropriate fancy-dress – a modest mother dressed like Little Bo-Peep.

The loudly, self-consciously knowledgeable ones also annoyed Beth, the people who employed words that she couldn't quite have defined like bravura and chiaroscuro. She did try to curb this petulant dislike of displayed knowledge but she still felt for the dog-spotter more than the connoisseur.

She had once seen a blind man being taken round an exhibition of Russian drawings. Lingering surreptitiously she'd listened as the seeing friend embarked on the revelation of each new picture. He'd had a low, melodious voice and he began the recreation of each work with the conspiratorial tone and cumulative language of a fairytale. The blind man had listened low and close as they'd moved slowly along the rows of brown pen-and-ink sketches, his mouth registering his reactions with small movements and twitches. Beth had closed her eyes and listened to the picture painted, until she'd got too close and the blind man had stepped back on to her toes. She wasn't sure she'd ever seen a picture quite so moving as those two men. She'd never seen anyone cry in front of a painting. But then she only ever cried in front of bad television. Art did something else. The work's intent to be viewed, the artist's intent to be seen, provoked admiration, even awe in her. And that sensation of respect was unusual.

Sarah was standing in front of a painting by Bonnard. It was of a dimly lit dining room with a checked tablecloth, where a young girl bent her head in study, a brown puddle of dog in a chair beside her. One could imagine the squally weather outside. Something in the enduring domesticity of the picture reminded Beth of her mother's kitchen, condensation trickling down the window from the heat of the oven. The painting emanated warmth in this chilly white room and Beth felt suddenly sad for Lizzie, back there alone, brooding over this morning, waiting for Roger to get home.

Beth wondered why more men and women didn't trawl for love in art galleries. They were full of people in search of sensation. Paintings might be static in form but they were so sensuous, even the abstracts created from tyre-skids of thick, glistening oils. Beth saw people's fingers hover lasciviously over the canvases and she dared them in her head to break the invisible force field, to go ahead and touch the priceless surfaces.

Dan does this she thought to herself as she walked around. He's probably rubbish but, still, he puts colours on a surface to form a shape. A strange way to spend your time, offering up pictures to other people. It was almost generous. But then, she remembered, he always was a show-off. Like his father. Unlike her. And her mother. But if that was all it was, why then did she feel so envious?

'Because his family are dynamic; they know how to live and be happy. And yours don't,' said Sarah while trying to work the coffee machine a little later.

'Thanks,' said Beth dryly, wishing Sarah didn't always dispense her wisdom so loudly in public places.

The underground café was busy. Tourists looked joylessly at guide books, women pored over their postcards, children drank their enforced fruit juices while the odd parent tried to engage them in healthy discussion of the things they'd just seen: 'Which was your favourite, Jack?' 'The one with the boat.' 'Which one with the boat, Jack? There were lots, weren't there?' In the corner a group of at least seventeen French teenagers whispered saucily, laughing and play-fighting over their two Diet Cokes.

Sarah was complaining about not being able to smoke. She always complained about not being able to smoke, surprised afresh each time. 'It's an infringement of my civil rights,' she said indignantly, 'they only do it so you eat more cake, I'm sure.' From Sarah's impatient and brittle tone Beth knew that she had a story to tell, the latest instalment in a romantic saga that had involved all the passion and suspense of *Wuthering Heights*.

'So,' she launched in, 'I went round to Andy's to pick up my stuff on Thursday.'

'Ah,' said Beth, her mouth full of chocolate cake. She decided she should have gone for the carrot cake instead and helped herself to a bit of Sarah's icing.

'I went round while he was at his creative writing class.' There was a sneer in Sarah's voice that made Beth suddenly feel for Andy. He hadn't asked to be cast as Heathcliff in Sarah's dramatic

142

world and the dangerous extremes that Sarah had explained to him their relationship involved had rather taken him by surprise. He just thought he'd started seeing a bright new blonde from his office. In a rash, Rioja-induced moment he'd said he'd wanted to be a screenplay writer before he got sucked into the remarkably comfortable world of Information Technology, and Sarah had suggested he start going to creative writing classes. But when Andy had started to enjoy the classes and begun drinking with his new-found friends, and peppering their conversations with, 'It's like Miranda said last Thursday,' Sarah had suddenly wondered whether adult education was such a hot idea after all.

Sarah noticed her icing disappearing. 'Eat it, go on, I haven't been able to eat properly for weeks. I've lost so much weight it's the one good thing in my life. I think I want food, then I look at it on the plate and think, oh fuck that for a laugh, life's too short to chew. Or too long. Whichever.' She *was* looking rather thin thought Beth, pulling Sarah's plate towards her. Sarah sighed and looked as though she was going to burst into tears.

'I feel appalling. He's got someone else, Beth.'

Beth stopped chewing for two seconds. 'Oh God.' She looked at Sarah, grimacing empathetically, 'How d'you know?'

'I let myself into the flat with my keys when he wasn't there. I was meant to post them back through the letterbox and, oh, it was awful. I walked in and it all just felt so familiar, even the smell of it. I had to sit down, it was so . . . so deflating and sad.' She talked fast, with a hunger the cake hadn't warranted. 'There was the stain where I'd spilt tea the first time we slept together, and this sweatshirt he always used to wear and the West Ham egg cup I'd bought him. And then, on the side in the kitchen, there was this milk bottle with a yellow rose in it.' There was a moment's respectful silence.

'Coward's colour,' Beth added. Sarah looked at her, wondered

143

if there was anything she could do with that comment, decided not and moved on.

'I just felt sick. I went all weak. How could he, it's only been two weeks. Stupid fucker.'

'You don't know what the story is. It might have been from a friend.' Beth was entirely unconvinced by her own suggestion. Sarah jumped at it, though, like a kitten after crumpled paper. 'D'you think so? It could have been.' But looking at Beth's doubting face she took the failure of the suggestion on her own shoulders. 'No, you're right. Wanker,' she added emphatically. The French teenagers burst into a peal of laughter behind them.

'You'll feel better, you know. Honestly.' Beth was worried; Sarah was usually a little feistier in the face of rejection.

'Oh, I felt better by the time I left,' she said with a slight smile.

'What did you do?' said Beth, also smiling.

And with the satisfaction of the avenged Sarah said, 'I microwaved the rose. On full power for three minutes. And left a nasty putrefying smell for him to come home to.'

Beth hadn't wanted to embark directly on her own news items. She felt she should leave a respectful gap between Sarah's loss and her own complications, like distracting a woman who's just miscarried from the sight of a Baby Gap, but Sarah wasn't going to let her get away with any evasions.

'So. Did you talk to him at the birthday party?'

Beth grimaced.

'You are strange,' continued Sarah, 'you didn't *have* to go, you know.'

Beth shrugged; why did people always presume passive wasn't its own kind of proactive?

'And did you talk to him?'

Beth shook her head.

'Beth . . . talk to me,' Sarah wheedled.

There was a pause and Beth opened her mouth, stopped, smiled lopsidedly and a little ruefully and said, 'Dan asked me out. He rang me up this morning. Ironic, isn't it?'

Beth had forgotten irony wasn't Sarah's strong point. She looked shocked and was silent for a minute. 'It's not ironic, it's sick.' Sarah was right of course thought Beth; why on earth did she feel so brimming and tense as if she was hatching something nice, not something peverse. Beth looked doleful, like a dog keen to get the beating and forgiving out of the way.

'You are *not* going out with the son of a man you had a two-year affair with,' said Sarah. 'Oh Beth. What are you doing?'

10. Unique Experiments

It was just over a year ago that Lizzie had finished her Beginners Stage One Dressmaking course with flying colours. Mrs Amrati, their teacher, had told Lizzie, 'You have an artist's eye for fabrics,' which was such a fulsome, exotic compliment that she was too embarrassed to repeat it to anyone. She'd told Roger that Mrs Amrati had said she was very good on the details. Where she came from people used the word artist as an insult, as in 'What do you think you are, an artist?' to anyone who had got above themselves. Either way, Lizzie thought it was all a bit of fun and that was why it had taken her the last twelve months to work out that Beginners Stage One wasn't actually the end of it.

She found it very hard – working out what she wanted. It wasn't the sort of question they'd asked her much while she was growing up. She had gone to school until she didn't have to, in a grey, lichened building on the outskirts of Harrogate. She had been born in the early forties and her daddy had died in a jungle in Borneo sometime in March 1946. After the war was supposed to be over. She still couldn't understand the historical anomaly of it and she still couldn't remember him. After leaving school Lizzie had gone to work in Taylor's, Harrogate's main department store, in the men's department. Lots of socks. Socks, suspenders and ties. Some customers with only one leg, making jokes about selling them in singles. Most of them were old, scratchy-looking types except Gavin, who was working on the electrics in the store and came looking for a suit for a family wedding in a dirty pair of trousers and rolled up shirt. He looked like Ben Hur compared to that lot. They were married after a year and moved down to Leicester, where Gavin's family lived, soon after that.

On Monday, Thursday and Friday afternoons during the dress-making course Lizzie worked at the kitchen table. She surrounded herself with magazines and swatches of fabric, humming over her new Singer sewing machine. She liked rich, dark colours – clarets and mossy greens. She'd finger the fabrics, rearranging patterns, paisley and floral. One day Mrs Amrati suggested a field trip up to Soho, to the fabric shops on Broadwick market. Mrs Amrati knew the shops well because she bought fabric for her range of saris round there. That Thursday, what with the noise of the fruit, vegetable, fancy bread and sausage stalls and the flirtatious, stocky men lifting down bolsters of damasks, Lizzie could suddenly see the point of London. It reminded her of the Christmas markets in Harrogate, none of the noise control and cold politeness of suburban south London. Real people living their lives out loud. Not passing each other like lonely ships in the icy supermarket lanes.

On the other days, Tuesdays and Wednesdays, Lizzie worked in the Colliers Wood branch of Oxfam. She'd been a volunteer for over ten years now. In the mornings they gathered up the bin-bags of clothes from the doorway – split by the homeless and the foxes who sniffed through the wardrobe rubbish over-night. They sorted through the smelly trousers and T-shirts, hooting with laughter as Maureen tried to work the till.

'You've got quite an eye,' the new manager Jill had said one day a couple of years ago, and she'd let Lizzie dress the window dummies from then on. And even Roger, who made a special trip up to the shop, agreed they looked better.

She'd known the Oxfam lot so long that they'd had every

party imaginable, wedding parties, leaving parties, Christmas parties. They'd even been to France on a ferry once. She was one of the less eccentric figures. But then some of them were so old that frankly they'd forgotten their manners, and would bang on for hours, telling the same stories week after week. It was hard asking those old ones to leave. Funnily enough Jill began to ask her to do that too. And Lizzie discovered with pride that she could be quite tough with people outside of her kitchen too.

She could have had a very good career, Lizzie. She was intuitive, quick and, at heart, curious. And she was just beginning, as she watched Beth acquire credits, both literal and metaphorical, to work out that she might have liked it. That it might have exorcised some of her frustration, given outlets for a polite form of power, and released her temper somewhere other than the home.

It was Jill who had made her really think about doing something with her dressmaking. Finding your vocation, she pronounced it. Just last Thursday Jill had said that as Lizzie had seen her daughter through college and her twenties it was now her own turn. Her turn for some attention. Lizzie had blushed, then snorted and busied herself tucking strands of her brown-grey bob behind her ears.

Last night Roger had told her off for being diffident about the subject. 'You should know, you're a war baby too, we just took what we could,' she'd said defensively. We made the most of the direction we were already headed, she'd added. Most of them had had children and lives as full of the minute logistics of life as a Lowry painting from their early twenties. They had been too busy getting through that to think of achieving any of the other things it later transpired would have been possible. (Sometimes she felt the need to give Roger a few hard truths, because he'd been to grammar school and had qualifications,

148

and his dad had owned a whole shop, and he'd grown up in a semi-detached house with a new bathroom.)

'You shouldn't keep brushing people off. It makes it difficult,' he ploughed on, but softly, 'for others to be involved.' He said he still wanted to be involved. He said that they might have been married for thirty years but she was still the great love of his life, and that he thought she deserved her own story, deserved to accumulate some things for herself. He didn't say that she'd only ever given things away so far but she knew that was what he meant.

She had suddenly felt so flush with attention, almost importance, that she'd felt bold enough to plan some happiness for herself. Suddenly she had a new urgency. After three decades her grief had shrunk to a no longer overwhelming black spot within and she had energy in her bones unknown since she'd first met Roger. She realised she wanted very badly that his gift, the silver locket given in admiration all those years ago in Betty's Tea Room, might not go undeserved.

It was the Monday after Jacob Frederick's birthday party. Monday after Beth and the business with the cups and the questions. The wrong questions Lizzie had thought to herself later. If Beth really wanted the truth, those weren't the right ones to ask. Maybe her daughter should concentrate first on getting a proper life for herself. A boyfriend and a baby of her own. Then they might have some common ground.

Today was the first day Lizzie could register for her intermediary course at the adult education centre in Merton Park. She got there half an hour after opening and had to fill in the form against a wall (a large woman stood blocking reception, complaining that there were never any yoga classes on a Friday). Lizzie did it quickly, childishly pleased to be ticking the 'Stage Two' box, and cheekily handed it to the receptionist round the side of the fat woman. Lizzie smiled, almost happy. Her life was just awakening and right now, she thought with defiance, buttoning up her summer mac, it had strangely little to do with any of her children.

A black man slowly polished the lino ahead with a hovering machine and Lizzie stopped to put her pen away in her handbag. Beside her, above a row of blue chairs, was a notice board that caught her eye.

The suburban marketplace – discussion groups, bulbs for sale, masseurs, wedding dresses (unused, half-price for quick sale), childminders, kittens and a noticeably professional piece of yellow A4 saying: Have you ever suffered a sudden bereavement? Have you lost loved ones through an accident or a crime? Would it help to talk to someone? Would you like to take part in a unique television experiment to help our understanding of grief and the benefit of therapy? If so, contact Jeanette at Freefall Productions on 020 8669 3275 and quote *Carrying On*.

So, thought Lizzie, just in case I was in danger of forgetting my sons for a moment God sends me a little reminder. She was disturbed by the coincidence of her having been so bereaved and now making some progress and then seeing this sign today. Very few had been as bereaved as her, she reminded herself. She felt cross at the way people tried to muscle into her privacy, into her head. The way life refused to leave you alone, to let you be to achieve one or two things. Someone up there had a very sick sense of humour.

As if she would. As if she, or anyone in their right mind, would go on to television, have therapy on television, going on about people who had died, who were now (at long last) quietly dead and beyond chatter like that. Therapy! She'd not had therapy. She'd not been offered it, let alone taken it. You had to get on with things. She had. Sort of. Christ. No one had offered to help her with her grief. Except Roger, of course. She'd had

150

her new baby and she'd got on with it the best she could. And having to get on with it, having to live and make sure a baby got fed, had saved her.

It was a *private* thing, loss. Private; something too precious to make vulgar with chat and cameras. Christ, she'd not even told her own daughter. She could have blurted all this out to Beth at the weekend, passed on the sadness of it, watched her try and work it out as some kind of 'therapy' for herself. Instead of making up ridiculous excuses which had left her sons seemingly debased. No, instead she continued to let her daughter think she was nothing, rather than a survivor, just so she shouldn't have to suffer the past. It was that private. And there were only the three of them. Three left in her whole family. And only one person to talk to about her boys. One other person who knew they'd ever existed. And after all the heightened excitement of the morning, she began to feel very hurt by the smallness of her world.

11. Happiness

Dan opened the door to his flat, dumped the plastic bag with Nurofen and other essentials on the one empty chair near the door and scrabbled at the back of his jumper, pulling it off hurriedly and awkwardly. He was having a hot flush, a hangover flush, as if the walk in the morning's warmth and then the climb up three lengthy flights of stairs had stirred up last night's alcohol and started some home-brewing system within him. He felt awful.

He wasn't meant to be feeling awful because today was Thursday, five days after his dad's party, and he was going out with Beth. Since this was his only day off this week he was also meant to be working hard. Today was supposed to be a fresh day, a concentrated eight hours to set him up for the evening. (He wasn't overly worried that Beth hadn't returned his call yet.)

After the wet pavement smell of Southwark his flat smelled closely human – of old food and oil paint – so Dan began to open windows, each one flaking white paint as he pushed at them. It was a big, light flat in an old 1930s factory in Southwark. The main room was lined with three huge windows, each one divided into smaller panes, only a few of which actually opened. It had once been a clothes factory so the access of daylight had been essential, but fresh air for the machinists had clearly been less of a priority. Dan found the deluge of light in this place both inspirational and overpowering. He had never seen colours more clearly than here; they took on elemental qualities as he laid them in slugs on the canvas, glistening thickly like pastes of beetles' shells and fat crushed fruits. But daylight isn't necessarily natural. Surrounded by glass he witnessed strange showy changes in the weather and the light. Winter rain would be heralded by an ecliptic low light which would give his room and his sundry possessions, even his daubed hands, the lugubrious green-glass filter of river water. And then the bright morning sun brought the smell of daffodils.

Dan, as he travelled between his flat and the basement bar where he worked, was also all too aware that most people avoided bright light. At closing time he would turn the lights on full blast, scaring the punters away. The women yelping and putting their hands to their eyes, covering up the years they'd suddenly reacquired like vain badgers under a torch.

He'd been living here for nearly a year. A regular in the bar called George had bought this factory in the mid nineties for much too much money and had begun to renovate it. But his business partner had gone AWOL, clearing the bank accounts, so George and his luxury flats were in limbo. In the meantime he had given Dan cheap rent on the flat as long as he paid it in cash. It felt temporary, like a show home invaded by squatters. There was a lopsided double bed in the far right corner of the room, the corner furthest from the window. The daylight would reach out and wake him at seven in the morning, pushing for action like a wide awake child.

Dan seemed to remember the business of the bed had come up in conversation last night when he was unintentionally getting pissed with his Scottish friend from the bar, Steve.

'Face it,' Steve'd said, 'you have a fucking awful track record with women.'

'No, I don't,' Dan had replied, 'it's just none of them have been right yet.'

'Bollocks. You've a nose for trouble; you see a woman and

you think "She looks like a whole heap of trouble, I'll try that one". Look at you, you're not bad looking, and the painting thing is a fucking gift apart from the fact you're always broke, but you're twenty-nine and you've not had a girlfriend for years who's been sane or single or who's stuck around for longer than a few weeks.'

'All right,' Dan had said, bridling. The couple at the next table had been listening and looking at Dan in what he thought was an assessing kind of way. 'And you of course have it all completely worked out.'

'Ah, fuck off,' Steve had retorted, 'I like it better bad. But you don't. I think you should get rid of that flat for a start. No woman will ever be able to sleep in that aircraft hangar. It's like sleeping in a field. And women think not being able to sleep is a bad sign – it freaks them out.'

Dan had taken a mouthful of beer and made a face at Steve. 'Thank you for the suggestions. Can we change the subject now?'

'Only trying to be helpful.'

'Thank you, but I'm going out with someone very nice tomorrow.'

'Oooohh,' Steve had said mincingly.

He put on a filthy T-shirt and took a bite out of the Ginster's sausage roll he'd bought on an impulse. Then he swallowed three Nurofen with milk and went into the main room and looked at the large canvas hung at the far end of the room. Tilting his head to one side he was realistic; it was certainly big. He should, he thought, develop a more economic style. Thin washes of watercolour would be cheaper than the acres of oil paint, but then he might find himself doing subtle landscapes and he couldn't think of a fate much worse. As Steve would say, he'd rather be Bernard Manning's best man.

It was to be the first in a new series of works, although he'd done many preparatory four-foot square sketches on paper, building up to the main attraction. He took his shoes off; it was easier that way. He figured he probably walked miles each day. Up the stepladder to work on a section, down again, no looking back as he retreated to the end of the room, and then turn. Sometimes he played music and he had been known to shimmy around the large white sheets that covered the floor. He was a good mover, Dan, neat-footed.

In the centre of the painting was a large blue circle. A thick-textured boiling pot. Dan moved up close. The circle was flecked with pink, white and green but the centre was a purer, darker blue. A negative sun. Dan coughed, then removed a piece of Ginster's plastic from his mouth. The background was the colour of pale sand and he'd pricked and dragged at the paint like a rain-needled sea.

Outside the clouds smudged and shifted, grey like dirt moved around a window pane. Dan went up and down his ladder, back and forth to the end of the room. His mind flicked between detail and impact, no middle ground. When you got close it was all paint manipulated, paint nudged into miniature completeness, one circumflex stroke suggesting a hundred other sources. But when he reached the back of the room and saw it afresh, an ambitious architect, he was pleased with the scale, with the balance of colours, with the first-sight symmetry, the lack of ambiguity in an object made of a thousand slight strokes.

Dan specialised in structuring the unstructured, whether it was a family lunch or a painting on a subject as nebulous, as grandiose as happiness.

This was to be the first of seven wonders. Real wonders. His wonders. Number One: 'Happiness'. The colours of cold flesh, deep water, indigo, a live wire, blue blood, a fresh girl's eyes.

The sun turned to the perfect colour of night. A bold blue sun – a massive, new illumination. That, he thought, is how happiness comes.

Painting – like falling into happiness or love would – gave shape to all the pieces of his world. He had such power in paint; all the complicated imperfections corralled into his own large, primary coloured statement. Since he was a child he'd been trying to bring some order into the adult mess around, never settling until something was fixed. Happy. He'd fiddle and fiddle with a bad television picture so that a Saturday evening movie would be as sharp as 007 himself – until he broke the set. And now, even when he knew he was done, he still climbed the stepladder with a smallish brush to dabble with the far left-hand corner. It needed work, this corner; you had to be careful of wasting your endings.

Last night Steve had said to him, 'D'you know what the last word said on the moon was?'

'Is this one of your routines?' Dan had said dubiously.

'No, seriously. What d'you think it was?' He paused. '"Yup." It was "yup".'

'"Yup"?'

'Isn't that fantastic? You spend decades racing to get there, build the best toy man's ever known, become icons, and the last word to echo round the Sea of sodding Chaos, or whatever it's called, is "yup".'

You could plan and plan all you liked but you could never stop banality creeping in. It worried Dan. Even geniuses said cool. Rothko probably loved his slippers, Tom Stoppard the Byrds, Shakespeare played innuendo and DNA discoverers golf. Humanity was careless sometimes.

At about two, when the sun in the sky was strong and his hangover was going through a trough, he was forced to admit

156

he'd finished. Finished the top left-hand corner and all the others. He didn't want to let it rest and felt edgy rather than celebratory. It was no more at an end than any product of the imagination, an engine that never recognises its limits. He wondered what else it was that was working at his gut and remembered Beth, who hadn't phoned. He made coffee and thought of her clear eyes and round face. Her jaw set. He'd noticed that she still did that when put under pressure, jutting her jaw forwards, mindful of her ability to say no, aware of her power to make things change the way she wanted them. Stroppy. Something about her now made him want to struggle with that, overcome her, make her admit basic things in a filthy language. But she was also the first woman in a long time that he had wanted to unscrew. He thought that he'd like to take all her components out into the clear light, to see how she works, see connections flicker in her head, watch her thought patterns wander.

He was shocked by the lack of tenderness in his thoughts. Perhaps he was just tired. He'd have a sleep and then he'd feel better.

He slept on top of the duvet as the room warmed. A wasp head-butted the window. Dan's head lay unmoving, eyelids flickering slightly, raw-red and veined in the direct light. He had a broad, slightly freckled forehead. His nose snuffled slightly. His ears were pink with sleep like a child's and under his head one was folded over itself. In the kitchen the phone rang four times. His eyes moved faster under their lids but he didn't wake up.

'Leave a message,' the machine instructed, so Beth did.

'Dan, hello, it's Beth. Listen, I'm really sorry but I'm not going to be able to make this evening, I've got to work late. So, well, I expect I'll see you around. Okay . . . well . . . bye then.'

Dan turned over, rustling up waves of duvet around him,

157

swaddled in Technicolor dreams, and continued to snore lightly until 4 p.m.

Beth put the phone down and breathed a sigh. She was sitting in an editing suite in a basement in Soho. After her conversation with Sarah at the weekend she had decided to get out of Thursday evening and get on with things. Four days of self-obsession had made her feel stuck, as if the wind might change and she'd be left there, one of those women who did nothing but gnaw at relationships. She wanted to put the taste of nervous emotion, both sweet and sharp, behind her and feel composed once more. She had had this churning sleeplessness before, over his father, ten whole years ago. She couldn't even begin to try to separate Dan and who he was from what he represented.

She had shied away from considering what the temptation of Jacob's son implied, the biblical connotations of genealogy and lust, and had played instead with the possibility of meeting him in a dim place and drinking wine, flirting with the past, feeding off Jacob's son, toying with this boy who disturbed her with his dark eyes and boldness, whose neat body, standing behind her, had for one small second made perfect sense.

But there was no point in it, Sarah was right. Intoxication could only lead to trouble. So she made the call and put down the phone with a heavy sigh. She reached for her expensive sandwich, created out of things that were never meant to sit between bread.

'Pesto and rocket,' Mike, her colleague and chief editor, said, looking at the wrapper. 'What's that all about then? What happened to ham?' She shrugged. On a roll of sorts he began a long commentary about the overlooked pleasures of corned beef and Toast Toppers. Beth didn't respond. 'What's the matter with you then?' She shook her head, unable to talk, her mouth too full of dry bread to speak.

'This film *is* blindingly depressing,' he said and took off his glasses and rubbed his indoor eyes. They were working on a television documentary about bereavement for Freefall Productions. Volunteers were being interviewed about their experiences of grief and therapy and a few actually underwent therapy in front of the camera. Until she had become numb with familiarity, Beth had found the material disturbing, almost distasteful. She'd wondered if some of these things weren't better left unsaid, if some of the old souls weren't better left to rest instead of being raised, ghostly, in a photo before the camera.

Mike and Beth had been through love, death, divorce, disaster and gender-swapping between them. It was, as Mike said, enough to put you off life for ever.

'I think,' he continued flamboyantly, 'I'm going to get a bit of wildlife in my life. That's what I need instead of this stuff – some pink flamingoes and mangy lions.'

Beth nodded, still chewing slowly, one foot up on a chair, her hair, heavy and unshiny in the not-light of the basement, tucked behind her ears.

'You're no fun.' He tried a new tack. 'What happened to the chef then?'

Beth coughed and then laughed. 'That was ages ago.'

'Well, you never told me what happened. I was there when he asked you out, remember?'

'We need some secrets, you and I. We spend too much time together as it is.'

'I thought you'd like a chef, with your appetite,' Mike needled.

Beth picked up a napkin to wipe her hands and said, 'Okay. We went out and ate crab, which, quite frankly, wasn't a full meal. I met some of his friends and we got drunk and I went back to his flat and we had sex.' She watched Mike, enjoying his wide eyes. 'And then we fell asleep and, ohhh, at about three we woke up and had sex again, and then we went back to sleep

159

and woke up feeling awful and *thought* about having sex but couldn't quite make it, and then I had to find my underwear and my skirt and went home in a minicab. And eight days later he rang again, so I didn't ring him back.'

'Blimey,' said Mike.

'You did ask,' she said. And then laughed and patted his knee.

Dan was stuck holding a bloody great tree underneath Beth's window when he was woken up. Dumb and claggy-mouthed with sleep he shambled into the kitchen, picked up the phone and grunted hello.

There was the crackle of a mobile and then, 'Is that you, Dan? It's your dad.'

'Hello,' said Dan, surprised.

'What are you doing? I'm just round the corner and it's pissing with rain so I thought I'd drop by.'

'Oh.' There was a mixed compliment in there but Dan said, 'Sure, come round.'

He sat down at the kitchen table and wondered what the time was. It felt like late afternoon. His eyes were beginning to close again when he remembered the dream and Beth and, on the surface beside him, noticed the flashing red answerphone light. He was about to press play when the buzzer for the street door sounded. Dan went out into the sitting room, pressed the button to open it and left the flat door ajar. He heard Jacob's rapid tread up the stone steps as he returned to the kitchen and played the message.

Jacob came into the kitchen and saw his son standing alone, leaning against a cluttered white surface.

'Thought you had company,' he said brightly, 'I heard voices. Any chance of a coffee?'

He seemed to Jacob in need of the kind of embrace you rarely get as a young man. A big enveloping hug. They made coffee

160

and Jacob turned on the kitchen lights. It was only four but the clouds and rain muffled the flat in greyness. It struck Jacob that at Dan's age he'd had a house, a wife, two children – reasons for existing. It was an unusual thought for Jacob who rarely contrasted his and his sons' lives, never normally laid them out alongside each other, measure for measure. Perhaps that was because he hadn't been there for a large part of his sons' lives. Perhaps that was because his father hadn't either.

Dan and Jacob usually spoke about once a month, arranging to meet periodically in the King's Head pub in Clapham, somewhere between the two of them. They'd been doing this since Dan had moved to London aged eighteen and it was a relationship that a lot of Dan's friends envied. There had been no great surprises, no big issues. That Dan was a fully grown man never took Jacob by force on a particular day. His children had grown so much in between each childhood visit, arriving at Euston rumpled, initially hugely silent but soon feisty with chips and city lights, that it sometimes seemed as if they'd never stop getting bigger. Through the years he'd watched each one step off the train, stepping slowly out of crushing teenage uncertainty. One by one they'd become a little more vocal as to what they were and what they liked. Determinedly resilient, bright-faced but brittle children of divorce. As time had passed Jacob had credited Rachel more and more for her gift of independence to her children. He knew she'd always been suspicious of the time-consuming and, she felt, sentimental cord between him and his mother.

They walked back into the main room, hot mugs in hand. The huge blue circle seemed ominous in the gloom.

'What's it called?' asked Jacob.

'"Happiness",' said Dan.

Jacob laughed. A loud bark of a laugh. He couldn't help himself. He hadn't seen anything so oppressive in ages. They stood in the doorway looking at it, maintaining a respectful distance, Jacob's face frowning, Dan's blank.

'D'you mind if I ask why?'

'No. I don't mind, but it kind of defeats the purpose, doesn't it?'

They'd been down this road before. Jacob was always amazed at how such simple shapes could be so complicated to understand. He could see the purpose of abstract art and even of modern installations that were called art in their provocativeness. The crystallisation of many sketches or sparking impulses or personal epiphanies into suitably obtuse lines, important colours, enclosed spaces, arranged piles – confusing, constructed mini-worlds. But what he had tried to explain to Dan was that he resented the fact that the onlooker arrived at the end of the trail. That the onlooker had to just take the creation at final value, with no knowledge of the artist's journey. From a usually damnedly unhelpful title he was meant to be able to recreate the trail. It seemed to Jacob curious that the artist was prepared to risk the viewer getting the trail wrong (he presumed there was a wrong and a right). If the work were that seminal you'd have thought they'd mind.

Jacob liked journeys – there was a progress to be traced in almost every art form, in a song, a film, a novel. The resounding stillness of art worried him. Even the videos, the moving installations, seemed to him to be about as progressive as a plastic snowstorm, just trapped flurries of activity.

'It's very beautiful, very strong, Dan. No compromise there.' He had wanted to say something proper, something positive. Dan turned his head to look at his father in surprise and was moved to reciprocate with something he'd told no one else.

'It's the first of seven. The seven wonders of the world. It could be a bit wanky, maybe . . .'

'Yup,' said Jacob too soon.

'. . . but I felt like doing something over-ambitious. Something big that defines everything.'

Jacob smiled. Oversimplification was the prerogative of youth. Let him live awhile. Then let him try and fit it all into seven frames. Still, he had chutzpah. Jacob gave him that. 'I seem to remember that all artists are meant to do that, state a . . . a creed.'

Dan made a face. 'I think that's just what we're not meant to do any more. I think I'm a bit out of step.' There was a pause. 'Never mind, I never wanted to be fashionable.'

And suddenly it did strike Jacob that Dan might be a little old-fashioned, and he in turn suddenly felt something rather old-fashioned like paternalism for him.

'D'you want to go out and have a drink? Or are you busy? You're probably going out.'

'I was, but I just got blown out,' Dan said dryly.

'Irredeemably?'

'Fairly; she said she was working and she'd see me around.'

'D'you like her?'

'Yes.' He stopped, not wondering whether to explain to his father who she was but wondering how best to describe the hold that the memory of the shape of her standing alone at the back of a church hall had over him. 'I'm curious about her.'

'It's a good start.' He looked at Dan, scuffing at the white sheet on the floor, and said emphatically, 'In that case, find out where she works and go and meet her, bring her a take-away . . . turn up, risk it. Go on. Live a little, for Christ's sake. What have you got to lose?'

Dan sat on a bar stool and stared out at the street. He was dressed in his new trainers and a stained jumper. He looked down at his trousers. They were Steve's and they were green and they could quite possibly be fashionable. But he wouldn't put money on it. He drank his pint and wished it were dark. There was something about taking a woman by surprise in the daylight that didn't seem quite right.

It was mid-evening and the streets of Soho were busy. He watched groups scatter past, women rushing late to bars. They had the air of people for whom socialising was a serious business. Deserving of fun, drunkenness a right. This was, after all, the media centre of the world, and hadn't they all talked it and earned it? Within the pub the urgency, the purposefulness of their social lives created miniature inebriated families for the night. The fat, friendly man from accounts balancing little women on his knees.

Dan looked down at his watch. Seven-thirty. He was expecting to have to wait a good while yet. After all, she'd said she would have to work late. A cab drove past, stopped and a businessman on a mobile got out, handing the driver a note, waving away change. The cab moved off and he suddenly saw her standing in the doorway opposite. She looked up at the sky. It was beginning to sieve rain once more. Her hair was loose and thick and she moved impatiently as she put her bag over her shoulder. For a small minute it was enough just to watch her. To wonder how the light water felt on her skin, whether she could feel the loose, dark weight of her hair on her shoulders, brushing her cheek. Then almost reluctantly he left the anonymous, beery society of the pub and followed her up the street. Dodging two women arm-in-arm, he saw her turn a corner and so he broke into a run, covering her footsteps, depleting the distance between them. And then, when he'd caught up, he reached for her arm.

Again he was faced with her back, again he saw the turning around, her surprise, her hair in the way. He thought how he was behind her again, on the back foot again, needing to convince her once more. But, he thought to himself, this was a verbal game he could play standing on his head.

They stood in the street like any other couple untangling a

few wires. But we're nowhere yet, said Dan, so why not have a drink first before deciding whether there is a purpose to this? And Beth, softened again by the feel of him near her, his child-charm, and enticed by the need for secrecy, allowed herself to be seduced into a bar called Red.

He ordered two vodka and tonics and they found a forgotten, smeared table in the corner. Beth looked plain uncomfortable now that the movement was over, now that they were just left facing each other.

'Cheers,' he said and drank half the glass with one big swallow. 'I don't normally wait and pounce on people, you know.'

'Don't you?'

'No, sometimes I just use binoculars and watch them in their house.' She didn't laugh. 'I feel like I've kidnapped you.' She was still silent. He could see the spell fading from her eyes. He took a deep breath. 'Maybe I should have been a bit more subtle and pretended I just wanted to hang out like when we were ten. It's just that you've, well, you've got rather beautiful and I thought I could skip the pretending bit because we already knew each other.'

'Except that we don't, do we? I don't know anyone I knew when I was ten. People just don't. We were children.'

'Obviously I wasn't harbouring sexual fantasies about you then . . .' He stopped. 'Let's have a drink and then we can go home if it's awful. Okay?' He looked at her. He was trying to make her feel happy, trying to persuade her something was fun, as he'd done when she was just a child. She'd always needed to be coaxed out to play. So she said okay.

'So,' he said, taking a deep breath, 'tell me everything you did today, from the beginning.'

She told him about Mike and the incessant bereavement, about how they'd been working together on and off for four years and how she'd never met his wife or family but they spent a lot of

their lives in the dark together. About how freelancing sometimes left her with so much spare time that she stopped using it
usefully, but that she read a lot and went to look at pictures and
went to the cinema and often came out while it was still light
outside. And that rather too many of her friends had said to her
recently, 'But Beth, you're so good at being alone', as if it were
a skill like baking. That she still found her mother tricky, her
father sweetly old-fashioned, her upbringing lacking. That she
still held Rachel's family home as an ideal in her head.

It wasn't that she said anything extraordinary, it was the turn
of the words which made him lean and focus. She was blunt
and unflirtatious, with a low laugh, and she reeled him into her
carefully worded phrases.

Dan told her about his day – Steve, the hangover and the big
white sheets on the floor of the flat that wasn't his. He missed
out the bit about his father because he didn't want to come close
to explaining the part he'd had in getting Dan there, but told her
instead about the small blonde child he'd seen leaning out of
the top window of a small house, flying, or rather flapping, a
home-made kite in the evening air.

She asked him about Beaver and his sad end and, laughing,
asked when he'd given up trying to rename him. Dan talked about
how much he still blamed his dad for the whole thing, never his
mother, and then at a tangent reminded her of the time Jacob had
placed a supermarket egg under Jenny Garland's escaped tortoise
and they had both run around the street in delirious excitement
saying, 'She's eyed a leg, she's eyed a leg.' And then Beth quickly
offered to go and get them their third drink.

Dan couldn't remember having eaten anything all day. But
knew, as he watched Beth at the bar with an alcohol-heightened
sense of drama, that he wouldn't suggest going to find somewhere to eat for fear of interrupting the flow. That and the fact
he was broke.

But when she came back with a bottle of wine, saying that it was actually cheaper, she set a new tone and asked: 'Tell me about your paintings; what are they like?'

'I'm not sure if you want me to do that,' he said. 'I can go a bit self-conscious and coy. Disgusting, really. I don't like talking about them much because it's easy to sound like a tosser.'

'All right. Are they big or small?'

'Big, mostly.'

'Acrylic or oil or charcoal or faeces?' Beth spoke rapidly.

'Oil.'

'Have you ever been known to use pastels?' Deadpan.

'Yes, but they do funny things to a man.'

'Do you think you paint like a man or are you just a person?'

'Can't answer that one. Too close to tell.'

'Try.'

'A man of sorts.'

'That'll do. Would you object to someone buying one because it matched their sofa?'

'No, but I'd rather not know.'

'Do you buy other people's pictures?'

'You need money for that.'

'You should barter.'

'Barter?'

'Barter.'

'Barter? In Southwark?'

She tutted. 'What's the one you finished today?'

'It's called "Happiness".'

'Is it?'

'What?'

'Happy?'

'It is if I say so.'

'Why?' she said, in two syllables like a child. 'What if others disagree?' He frowned for a while before speaking; it was hard to explain how painting was his universe to control.

'I want them to know I've tried to create a . . . a symbol of happiness. Its beginnings were in the sky, in the place people look to for comfort, to celebrate feeling good or look to find something they've lost. It's a big blue circle on white; it's like a surprising sun.'

'Need you tell them what it represents at all?'

'I want them to get it right.'

'Why can't you let them be?'

'Why should I? It's my painting.'

'You should call it "Sky" or something and let them make of it what they want. People think about pictures in a very selfish way. I just like the way they hang there, full of life, like windows. Why can't other people find it depressing if they want?'

'Because they're not meant to.' He thought for a moment, focused on her face, then said, 'Much more happens to you when you're an adult than a child. All sorts of busyness. But very little of it has as much resonance as childhood. I remember days with you much better than endless arsing around at college, or being in London over the last ten years. There's a clarity, a boldness to life when you're young. We're scared of taking life and living it the way we want to. So this is part of a series celebrating things. I want them to be taken at face value, I don't want them muddied with the mysterious, dark side that people always want to see. So it's kind of in your face, childish I suppose, a clear thing meant to . . . encourage good associations.'

'You've really not thought through the potential for irony here, have you?' She was smiling at him with the amused reprimand of a teacher. It had the same effect on him as a brake.

'Sorry,' he said. 'I warned you.'

'No, don't be.'

They said nothing for a minute and he was a little embarrassed.

'I hope no one can hear us. I think I'm a bit drunk. It's not even ten yet.'

'I certainly am,' she said.

'I did something for you,' he said and out of his book he pulled a piece of thick paper.

'More bits of paper,' she replied, holding out her hand. 'You don't give an average gift.' She looked carefully at the smudged charcoal picture of her back, softly angular, her head bent and the ridges of her spine clear. A promise of adoration.

'So . . .' he said, wondering what he was building up to. He knew what *he* wanted.

'I'd like to see more pictures,' she said.

They sat in the cab, accidentally touching but not moving apart. She wanted him to stay there, his leg alongside hers, shoulders joined, almost as if she needed the warmth on this damp evening. London flickered past; snatches of conversations between brightly dressed people leaped through the open window, red car lights ahead, yellow-lit shops, framed restaurant lives, the surprised O-face of a late-up child, raindrops dragging silver down the windows. Beth's hair fussed in the wind but they sat quiet and concentrated, looking intently out the same side of the taxi. Concentrating on their co-joined warmth. Something came on the radio that took the driver's fancy and he turned it up, and it occurred to Beth that right now she was where she'd always wanted to be, less a watcher than a player. A woman with a soundtrack.

She began to sing quietly, a little bit drunkenly. Dan recognised the song as the one crowd-pleaser in *The Deer Hunter* and laughed.

They were rumbling down narrower streets and getting closer to his flat when Dan leaned forward and said, 'Just here's great,' then 'The scenic route,' by way of explanation. They climbed out and walked down a cobbled, empty side street. It was darker now they'd turned into this alley, no street lamps. The buildings faced each other closely; above their heads ledges and roofs were stacked, brickwork tangling like an untended creeper. 'Some of these have been done up but some are only just beginning,' he said, taking her hand. Silence came near again – just a dripping sound and the soft slap of their footsteps. 'This one,' he said, stopping after a few minutes at a deeply set square entrance. 'It's not my flat, it's another of George's, just left empty. Can I show you something?' he asked. She nodded and he pushed open a door that had clearly been made in an emergency, a thick slab of plywood with a large but broken padlock.

They paused inside, getting used to the blackness, Dan still holding her hand tightly. It smelled of damp stone and Beth shivered, imagining unknown wet things underfoot, but as her sight adjusted she realised the floor was clear and the walls stripped down to clean, bare bricks. It was a huge, pure space, the size of a small supermarket but completely empty. Dim light in a stone box.

Large windows faced out on to the street. In the left-hand corner there were open stairs and Dan led her towards them. They climbed hesitantly, rounding corners with their spare arms outstretched as if the darkness were a tightrope. They climbed three more flights until they reached the top. The light was just strong enough to make out solid shapes but not enough to illuminate the ceiling corners or the outside edges of each floor. She imagined heavy particles of stone dust eddying unseen, settling softly on to grey, the air disturbed for the first time in years. The two of them breaking into abandoned aspirations.

'Close your eyes,' he said as they stopped on the fourth floor.

'Why?' she said. 'Are you sure we're not going to get arrested?'

'The view,' he said. 'It needs to be a surprise.' So she did as he asked and, standing behind her, holding her arms, he slowly steered her across the concrete towards the back windows.

'Now open them.' There was no glass in the frames so she stood as if on a ledge, the wind coming towards her and dividing around her. She saw a dark scramble of yards and wire and low buildings, a block of warehouse to the left and to the right, and then, in between, in a surreally neat section, the black flow of the Thames. Beyond, lights swayed and jostled on the north bank of the river, stringing upwards, ever smaller, into the City. Beth took a deep breath and smiled. Dan stood behind her, hands on her arms still, holding her to the view. They looked outwards in silence, conscious of the sliver of strangely tangible air between them, the space at her back, his body an inch beyond.

He turned her round and Beth's body became taut. She was fleetingly surprised at the way these things happen. How two people who know nothing can make each other's breath quicken. She felt suspended and waited, tense, holding on to her breath, to see what would happen. How it would happen. His grip on her arms tightened and they looked straight at each other. She could see nothing in his eyes but the muscles around them worked with concentration. Their only contact was his hands on her arms. She could hear him breathing and see him breathing, and she opened her mouth as if to start something or stop something or to say 'Please . . .' when he leaned forward very slightly and put his lips on hers.

They rested there, the softness and fit of their mouths together shockingly intimate. His head moved back a little and waited again, before kissing again, carrying her upper lip on his. Soon he pushed her backwards so she could feel the ledge pushing into her lower back, and he put one hand to her face. She felt surrounded by him and yet exposed, her back to the city. The uncertainty quickened her blood. His fingers moved slowly down her neck, down the centre of her chest, the join of her shirt, the middle of her stomach, tracing a line between her two halves. She wanted to catch her breath and moved her body forwards, trying to create some space, but he stayed still so that they felt, through fabric, the full pressure of each other's bodies. His hand moved up her body and her back arched instinctively. She suddenly wanted him to undo her shirt, to see her own flesh in this half-light, to be exposed, streets and people behind her.

He began to unbutton her, their hips still ground in, and unfolded the fabric leaving her skin stark, cold and perfect. He bent his head to kiss her and she felt the warmth of his red mouth on her white skin. Eyes wide, lips apart, she looked over his head into the cavernous, colour-drained space, focused purely on the movement of his tongue and the creep of his hand on her legs. Just as she willed it, he brought his hand up hard between her thighs. Beth breathed in sharply and her head went back, eyes still wide, blood moving lower. He began to unbutton her trousers and, like a child engaged in something complicit, she bent her head to watch him peel her away, layer by layer. He had his hand within her skin, between her thighs, and Beth, trapped and liberated, felt the pulse of her body's concentration. With the push of his fingers she gave a cracked cry.

It was like being found for the first time and, with the feel of Dan's face against hers, her hand in his hair, the quiet constricted urgency, so much desire that their tangled limbs were obstacles to a full embrace, she remembered the way sex worked with love. Once, years ago, she had had both familiarity and desire as her bed-partner had shunted in love and lust from predictable to essential. She had rarely felt this combination of emotion and wanting and in the distance she sensed a memory of Jacob and the way he would hold her, carrying her weight through the air, rescuing her burden in bed. She felt tears come to her eyes and, confused, memory's arms intervening, suddenly feeling Dan's hand rather than her reaction to it, she said 'Stop' quietly. He did, freezing for a second, someone caught somewhere doing something wrong.

'Oh Christ, I'm sorry,' he said, pulling back, his face contorting as he saw her watery eyes. 'Was I too . . . ? I'm so sorry, I didn't mean to . . . I just wanted you so much,' he stumbled, trying to piece her shirt back together.

'It's fine; really, it's fine,' she said, doing up her trousers. 'It's just not a good idea.' She tried to smile and saw his face so concerned that tears washed her eyes again. She had a heart-clutching feeling of being in the worst kind of control, reducing him to fumbling with her shirt buttons, and wanted to distance herself from his furrowed face.

'It's my fault, I've got to go.' She grabbed her bag from the floor and moved towards the stairs. He followed, saying, 'Wait, wait, we'll find you a cab home,' but he tripped and stumbled in the semi-darkness and by the time he got out into the street he could just see her bag, like a tail, disappearing down what he knew for a fact to be a cul-de-sac.

12. On Wanting to be Wanted

'Fuck,' Beth muttered to herself, wiping a snotty nose on her sleeve, 'fuck, fuck, fuck.' Her mother would be horrified by all this fuss, this over-reaching drama. Beth could imagine her slight stutter and glaze and then the way she would just remove herself to a different place without even moving from the sofa. Beth thought, with a burst of self-pity, how she just wanted to be wrapped up and held. Not flickering alone like a wandering target on a radar.

Of course she rarely cried properly. That's why it felt unfamiliar and messy. She tried to stop, sniffed and swallowed, but a rush inside and she couldn't tell if she needed to weep or cough. She spluttered and tried to breathe deeply. Am I really doing this? she thought, watching herself stumble down a dark street, wrapping herself tighter into her jacket. She wanted to stop and curl up in a doorway, cry into her knees. This was awful; she was being awful. She had a talent for it sometimes.

Beth hiccupped. And how was she going to explain this to Dan? That one moment she was watching the way his hands followed his words, the next she was clutching at his hair, and the next she was running away. She had so loved his blatant desire.

And then explain this: the reappearance of his father in her imagination. Someone she had loved, whose parting gift had been a swift lesson in life. Something that had made her older and wiser and beyond naive romantic fantasy. Someone who, in the end, had taught her that the disturbing beauty of an unspoken connection isn't to be trusted.

The problem, she now realised without wanting to, was that no one until his son had proved subversive to this education. No one until Dan had taken her back to that intrinsic excitement, that unassailable feeling of being uncovered and understood. The temptation – to decide their meeting was pivotal, to fall into his way – was so strong that she couldn't work out whether it was him that was so magnetic or the fact that he was Jacob's son.

She'd kept that desire to be held, enclosed and protected hidden since Jacob. But even after all this time, after ten whole years, she could still plunder that store of physical sensations. The warmth and height and smell of him when in his arms. The feel of his looseish skin, the proddable, comfortable quality of his body, like a bean-bag toy. For years she had dreamed of Jacob and then woken up cross and depressed that he was as persistent a figure in her nocturnal source bank as some childhood bogeyman. But that hadn't lasted for ever. She didn't miss him, she didn't love him, she didn't want him. She had seen him that night at his birthday party as a different being altogether. But she *had* been dangerously curious to see him, and she seized on passing information of his life with the perverse ferocity of a wayward child. Try as she might he had stuck limpet-hard to her idea of love, that sense of an unending future.

Oh, he had loved her. She had been loved, held iconic in his gaze, owned by his arms. And this warmed her a little. Calmed her. It is to be found, she said to herself, there are places you will be taken to, that will transport you, streets that are best crossed hand in hand. I want so much not to be unexplored. And

175

yet, am I not meant to be beyond wanting to be wanted? Am I not supposed to count my life satisfactory, even if alone?

Suddenly she was aware of a looming darkness. As if something were going to strike her in the face. Ahead there was a wall. She'd reached a dead end.

Slowly, resignedly, not crying now, she turned around. Some two hundred feet away, halfway up the road she had just walked alone, stood Dan. They watched each other.

'You followed me,' she said.

He shook his head. 'Looked for you.'

Neither of them moved. 'What did I do?' he asked.

With what seemed like an extreme act of strength she walked slowly towards him, stopping about five paces away.

'You didn't do anything. It's me. I'm sorry, I shouldn't have let it get to this.'

'Won't you talk to me about it?'

She clenched her keys in her jacket pocket over and over again. 'No. We shouldn't do this. You can see . . . you know I want to but we—'

He interrupted, 'I don't see why us knowing each other already is such a problem. Is that it? Or is there something else? Someone else? Talk to me.'

'It just *is* a problem. The whole thing.' She could tell him, she thought, she could just let him know, solve the problem. And create a thousand others. She couldn't tell him; if anyone was to tell him it should be Jacob. No one knew and Dan was the last person who should discover that she was if not responsible then involved in the second divorce of his childhood. One loose end and everything would begin to unravel. It had been tightly packed away into the past, and secrets awoken would rise like dragons from green blankets of hills, shaking themselves to see who or what would fall. Telling wasn't an option.

'I don't believe you,' he said softly, simply. 'If you just said "I'm not interested in you" then I'd have to believe you, but it's not that, it's something else. I can tell.'

'I'm not interested, then. Please, Dan, just say I'm not. Okay? This isn't a love affair, Dan; we've seen each other twice in the last eighteen or nineteen years, it doesn't constitute a . . .' She flailed slightly. There was a word to describe what it wasn't and she needed to get it right – it needed, in effect, to describe what it could easily be. 'A relationship.' She was almost convincing. But how could a connection between two interested parties be anything but?

'But this is extraordinary, Beth; it's magic, it's more than coincidence, it's more than just lust.'

'Dan, Christ, don't. Stop it. I need to go home.'

'I won't stop.' He looked at her; she was tired, the bruised grey colour of a negative. 'But I'll take you home,' and he held out a hand which she didn't take but slowly, walked around, an old-fashioned movement that made her seem, for a moment, part of some slow, stately dance.

Dan eyed her as she skirted around him. He put his hands in his pockets and stood watching her walk up the street, frustration grinding like indigestion in his chest. There was usually a way to make things come together, persuade people to go where he wanted them, but this time it would be harder. He had a faint suspicion that he was not in control.

13. Palace

London, 1988

Jacob kissed her. By surprise, when she was glancing down to button up her white denim jacket. She looked up, her mouth open with shock, her lower lip full, red and slack. He took it between his, sucked at her, while his bulk moved in closer. She had never been kissed in this way before. In daylight, within the sound of birdsong and traffic. By someone older in proper shoes and a leather jacket.

It was a fussy, wet Friday evening and they had been walking back to his car through Kensington Gardens. Past the redbrick palace and dainty poodles that picked their way round puddles towards the scrum of ear-piercers and black denim inside Kensington Market. She was on a week's work placement after finishing her A Levels and they'd spent the full week together as he filmed the remaining scenes for a piece of prime-time period drama around London.

It had been Roger's idea to ask Jacob to give Beth a placement. He saw her endless hours in front of the box as an interest. Which was generous of him, and perhaps naive. Lizzie knew it was escapism, which was not something she approved of. She of all people knew evasion didn't work. Either way Beth did love television. She was an electronic synaesthete; TV shaped, coloured and numbered her days. Television dramas and characters all contained possible futures of her own.

Jacob, who had recently been doing up the house on Delia Street for new tenants, was happy to oblige. He liked having apprentices and had always thought cross-generational friends, mentors even, to be healthy things. It suggested a meeting of minds that was based on something other than circumstance. It put the romance back into acquaintanceship, if you like. And romance was something he looked for in all sorts of places, not just women but in the streets and overheard conversations, in exchanges with shop assistants and suddenly vivid sunsets.

It was, she knew, a very superior week of work experience. Julia was working for the *Tooting Times* and had only been allowed to do the filing, and Rebecca, who lacked imagination, had been given a week learning how to manage B&Q. So it was that five days before the kiss Beth was handed over from one greying man to another, a door-step event which rendered her silent with embarrassment for half a day. Jacob then took his eighteen-year-old helper off to the set of *Three Men in a Boat*. He told Beth she was to be his shadow and that shadows were good because 'they proved you weren't invisible'.

Jacob was hostage to the changeable weather all week. During the rainy hours he took her to catering and talked her through the processes, let her film a tree and a child with a ball. The rest of the time she concentrated on not being trodden on or shouted at. She read scripts and talked to the caterers and watched other people in the street watching them, a unit in the business of producing a different world. He took her to see the rushes in Soho and gave her strong Italian coffee and bought her a pizza. She was intoxicated; it was like doing a school play, only better because it was real, or at least real fakery. They dropped into pubs at the end of the day where she drank gin and tonic and he drank Guinness. He ate a lot of crisps. He said savoury snacks were probably the best thing in the world and that he would have moved to America for the crisps if it hadn't been for his children.

He'd said 'my children' like they were much younger than Beth, as if she hadn't hung out in his own house with his own son every day for years. Beth figured that Jacob hardly remembered her as a child, that she was just one of many who had passed through their kitchen, spilling squash on the floor. And so she just nodded understandingly as Jacob spoke, assuming an older persona. Which was easy because anyone, whatever age you were, could see you couldn't just leave the country when you had three sons. He hadn't said, though, which she'd also noticed, 'If it hadn't been for Jane'. In fact he didn't mention Jane at all, ever, but talked about how hard it was being so far away from the boys. He didn't do it in a whiny way but in a matter-of-fact tone and she'd encouraged with noises and smiles. Then, suddenly, because she was genuinely interested, she asked, 'What was your dad like?' And he told her what he knew of his parents' past, which wasn't very much, even less than she knew of hers.

On the Thursday night he took her to the wrap party for a couple of hours, putting her in a cab before the drugs came out. She stood with a drink in her hand, bright eyes and shiny hair, a pink rucksack on her back, speaking when she was spoken to. Jacob looked at the pouchy faces around the room, thought of what he knew of all of them, what cumulative experience they had of him, in strange locations, different rooms, paid work weaving spidery connections between them, sex, and sometimes love, entangling things, breaking things, spectator sports within the spectator industry. He looked at her drinking it up; hard-nosed, red-nosed adults with no more intelligence than her, just more years. He vaguely remembered being eighteen, awaiting the arrival of his life, expecting it to plop on to the doormat like his photography club newsletter. How lovely, he thought with a rush, to be at an age when you presume you'll get it right.

She saw him watching her and smiled and whispered something in his ear. It was that sentence that moved her into his realm of possible endings.

'D'you ever want to run away?' she said, only because she saw everyone speaking and no one listening and thought Jacob, who so liked being listened to, must find it a shallow place to be in.

'Oh yes,' he said. 'And I do, often.'

That Thursday night when he walked her to the minicab he'd booked they didn't say anything, Jacob's self-amused week-long commentary on the world of TV no longer of interest to either of them. 'Thank you for a lovely evening,' she said with no side, and he put his lips lightly to her forehead, like she was a fragile, rare thing. He shut her in and watched the car take her away, and thought that tomorrow he'd pick her up even though, really, there was nothing left to show her.

The next day Beth was astonished to find that what she'd wondered about in bed was right – the grounds had shifted. Conversation was harder, sparser. The warm summer air was resistant, slowing down their looks, making her head heavy on her twisting neck as she followed his figure with her eyes. And after the tension of the day, when he first kissed her in the park she felt as if this was what she'd been waiting for all those slow afternoons in her bedroom.

She felt her legs give way beneath her and as he kissed her again he held her shoulder tight in his hand. Her stomach surged. She stepped back in shock at her body's reaction. Twenty-four hours of imagining and eighteen years of three TV channels hadn't prepared her for this purposefulness, the adult strength of his movements, the blood rush to her senses so that she felt the wind on her skin and heard the creak of the trees. And when he kissed her again, for the third time, she had a sense of the world spiralling and she opened her eyes to better see the cinema of the moment. The grey, darkening sky whirling, she and he on the grass in the park, at the centre of the growing wind. He pushed her into his pelvis and then said into her ear, 'Can you feel me?', which shocked her, although she'd heard and watched much stronger, much more graphic scenes on a flickering TV screen. She stuttered, wide-eyed. He pulled her head down to his chest, put his lips to the top of her head and said, 'Come on, I'll take you back to the car, you're cold.'

They sat in the fading light, rain spotting the windscreen.

'Were you expecting me to do that?' he asked.

He seemed suddenly uncertain. Beth felt powerful with the ability to seduce and comfort. She had the feeling of a suspicion confirmed – this was what being a woman was about, enticing and forgiving. The eroticism of rescue. She thought of Dan fleetingly, stuck in the aspic of childhood memories, and felt all the more adult.

She turned to look at him and smiled. 'Sort of, but not right there, then.'

He looked pleased. 'Can we go and have another drink? Or should I take you home?'

She said quickly, 'You don't have to take me home.' She was supposed to be staying at Julia's, who was having a party that night, but she didn't tell him this. Beth was so young that she was embarrassed by the very fact that she had a mother. What would Lizzie think, thought Beth with triumph trumpeting in her head, if she could see her now?

It was quiet in the car apart from the traffic and rain. Beth waited to see what would happen. There was the moment when things would fall – a cumulation of little weights, one ounce of movement, a half-pound word that would bring things wobbling to the crux and dip of an event. The word didn't matter so much as what went before. I have, she thought, been

182

well-behaved all my long, long life. And with the speed of a grab she leaned over to Jacob and kissed him back.

'I wish it wasn't a hotel,' he said to her two hours later in the lift of the Palace Hotel.

'Why?' she asked.

'Because it's a bit of a cliché. But it doesn't matter, does it?'

He needed her to agree and she was happy to say, 'It doesn't matter where we are.'

Of course Jacob could picture Lizzie at home thinking of her daughter, but he didn't linger on it. He chose not to imagine Lizzie on the sofa, hoping her daughter was having a nice time dancing around with her overgrown girlfriends, flirting with some good-looking boy who wouldn't upset her, wondering if she was as quiet and moody with her friends as she was at home. Or her father, changing the light bulb on the landing, looking through the open door of her room and realising that now the posters of ponies and pop stars were gone her room could do with a lick of paint.

Of course Beth was young. But her youth was a connection, rather than an obstacle, for Jacob. In their own ways they were both lost, waiting to feel valid in an adult world. She wasn't a child and the only time he had seen a red flag of propriety before his eyes he'd asked, fair and square, whether this was what she had been expecting. And she, he felt, had understood, had moved things an inch further by her acknowledgement of their attract-ion, by her acquiescence on the path to bed.

Jacob looked at her and touched her again, in the area of her belly button, as if his thumb were wiping a smudge from her skin here in the lift of the Palace Hotel. He kept hold of her all the way down the corridor, as he unlocked the door and slammed it and then as he pushed her up against the wooden wardrobe. She was so young, so unlined, so wide-eyed. When he looked at her like this, fragmented with focus, it wasn't her beauty he wanted to consume, it was her life. He heard her breathe fast and he suddenly felt so fucking desperate that he knew that if he could just be inside her then he would be all right. Then he would be vital again; a transfusion as much as an act of lust.

He pulled her jumper over her head and stopped to see how white she was. With the flat of his hand he grazed her breasts, wanting to climb inside the skin of her but holding, waiting as long as he could. Her back arched and he placed one hand in the small of it, as if to carry her through. Her arms hung unmoving by her sides and he thought how much she must be enjoying being adored.

Then she reached up for his shirt, neatly unbuttoning him until she could pass her hovering, curious hand over his chest and then down lower to the diagonal from straight hip to groin. She stopped there and stroked him with the back of her hand, fascinated, feeling the stretch of his skin, his flat, smooth body hair. He was so real.

Her entrancement was rare. Never to be quite repeated.

'Am I . . . I'm not the first, am I?' It had only just occurred to him.

'No,' she said truthfully.

But with that reference she suddenly felt aware of her lack of voluptuousness and experience, of her small breasts and birthmark on her thigh, of her speckled red legs from overuse of Lady Care razors, of the spot which showed, like a little molehill, in profile. He was watching her, holding her waist.

'Don't stop. I don't want you to stop.' She thought she might cry from the failure of it if he did.

He hadn't thought about stopping. He'd been watching her breathe, watching her find this extraordinary; the undressing, his form, the fact it was happening. He was thinking how this was actually momentous, her youth, their connection, lost in romantic lust.

He led her, half-dressed, to the bed where he sat her down and took off her shoes and skirt, then undressed himself. He stood over her, basic and representative, greying. A man with a hard-on. More unashamed than anything she'd ever seen. It was very quiet in the room. Beth couldn't believe this was her, here. She could hear their breath, hers shallow and quickening as he pulled down her knickers. He pushed her back with authority, took her legs in his hands and spread them.

She looked at the ceiling, pebbly white, and forgot about her shaving cuts as he licked his way up from her knees, moving into her crotch with a stubbled chin and hot mouth. 'Oh God,' she said, serious-sounding, as if she'd lost something, her voice loud in her own ears. She clutched his hair hard, forgetting to be amazed that she was here, naked, on a hotel bed with Jacob Frederick.

The next morning she was woken by the sound of a lorry screeching to a halt just below the windows of their room. Her eyelids flipped open and she stared at her morning landscape. Jacob's arm trailed over her torso, heavy and freckled, dark hairs ruffled. Bodies lumber and lank after a tightly held night. The white duvet rucked up to her face, tickled her nose and she discovered an ache in her stomach. She tried to concentrate again. The edge of the bed slid with bedclothes to the floor, where sunlight had slipped under the curtains and turned to spilled pools on the carpet. Here she was, all alone in Kensington, desperate for the loo but with no idea how to make the journey out from under his arm, round the edge of the bed, over the hurried heaps of clothes to the stiff bathroom door and noisy flush. She closed her eyes again.

Jacob was half asleep and rounding fake corners in his head. He took a left, a right, another left and ended up where he'd been before. He opened an eye and saw a back and a wall with windows. If, he thought, we can just get round the wall there may be a door to the left, and then through that the room, but here . . . no door. He stepped backwards, closing his own curtains.

Something will happen, she thought. He would wake up soon, surely, and then she could get up without moving him. She needed to go home at some point before it looked odd. She wanted to be back on time because she thought she'd cry if there was an argument. But she was wearing nothing and she'd rather have got up before he was awake to see her. She blew upwards, the duvet was still tickling her nose. It was getting quite hot in here, under Jacob's arm, the sunshine encroaching into the room. Beth desperately needed the loo now and it was a mean, basic way to show an eighteen-year-old that just because she was old enough to seduce didn't mean she knew how to deal with the fall-out.

There was a strange ticking sound in his head. It felt like insects and he wanted to scratch all over. They might have been in the room, coming from an air vent, and then what was he to do? How would he block it? He could see what it would come to, see them both covered in black, moving specks, feel them crawling into his nostrils, up his legs, into his pubic hair, fiddling through his body . . . Suddenly, to Beth's relief, he sat upright, swatting the air.

She bolted to the bathroom.

They showered and politely negotiated the limited space, re-clothing themselves around the perimeters of the bed. They didn't speak much. Beth was shocked by what had happened (how could the fact that he was married not have worried her last night?) and Jacob seemed to need her input less this morning now that the deed was done. They travelled down in the lift, an odd couple, and he squeezed her hand briefly as a quick acknowledgement of their new status. Generally he had found the best way through a new situation was not to think about it much.

He walked away from her quickly, towards the front desk. The receptionist took his credit card, noticed his wedding ring and while filling in the Visa slip looked at the girl lingering near the pot plant at the back of the lobby. She had long, wet hair and a denim jacket and looked around her with the wobbly defi- ance of a woman last spotted weeping on a bus. The receptionist wondered why the girl thought anyone would care. Why didn't she enjoy her last minute of triumph? She only had until she walked down the steps of the hotel and back on to the street.

'Hope to see you again, sir,' said the receptionist with a smile and a flourish of paper bills.

14. Saturday Night, Sunday Morning

Roger was listening to the *St Matthew B Minor Mass* on Classic FM as he moved things around inside his shed. He jabbed into the air with his chisel at the opening bars and sung and then hummed, 'Cum sancto spiritu, dah, dah, da, da, da.' With the trumpets he got louder: 'Pom, pom, pom, pom, pah, pah, pah, pah.' He huh, huhuh'ed with the altos, whistled with the sopranos and then turned the sound up even louder so that his wooden Tardis emanated a choral blast. In a cartoonist's hands the shed would have lifted off and flown with wings as light as balsa wood. It could be heard out the front by a bloke walking back from the off licence, six-pack in hand. Visiting angels somersaulting around the privet. Lizzie could hear it inside the house as she washed up their light Saturday lunch.

'Pom, papapapapapap, pom, aaahaaahaaahaaahaah.' Such noise a choir could make, such a glorious sound . . . His enthusiasm outstripped his voice and whistles so that he was left almost shouting the notes in chesty exhalations. He so loved the give and take of the male and female voices, its marriage of growl and lullaby. He conducted to the final chords, the tremendous climax, the final drum pulse, seized by a ferocious energy in his reverberating box.

There was a moment of silence, a physical feeling of lightness as if it were he who might now take off, as if the voices had pressed his flesh like massaging hands and their sudden absence now left him unconnected to land. And then the station's jingle began and he quickly reached for the on/off knob and sat down on the stool in the corner of the shed.

They'd heard the Mass in B Minor once in Battersea Park, an open air concert last year. Not a grand affair – you took a picnic and sat on the lawn. They'd lent a young family a corkscrew and had all laughed at their grass-stained knees, and Lizzie had looked incredibly young, incredibly twinkling that evening. She'd worn a skirt she'd made herself and he'd thought how proud he was of his wife. He found her mixture of bravery and pleasure very moving. No, more than that, very erotic. She was a true woman. She'd seen everything and yet she was his.

He still felt rather strange, unsurprisingly. Even more puffed-out than ever but conversely a little better. Not so cooped up. He could get back inside now and give Lizzie a hand with the shopping. There'd be more bags than usual because he'd spoken to Beth earlier and asked her to come for supper tomorrow. She'd mentioned the photo of Martin and Paul on the phone. He'd have to tell Lizzie.

All those years of hum-drum, he thought. All those years of quiet and then it was all let loose at once. Just, paradoxically, when they were all learning how to live.

'Even if I give her the benefit of the doubt, and even if you assume that she has a broken heart and is clearly taking her life very seriously right now, she sounds like a real neurotic cow,' Steve said to Dan.

'No, she's not neurotic.'

'Oh come on . . . you take her to a nice romantic warehouse, remove various items of clothing with her full consent, and then she runs, not walks but runs, away.'

'She—'

'No, come on. Then you find her down some alleyway, crying

189

like a baby, waiting to be found, and you get her a taxi and she says not to ever phone her again, all the while knowing that if there's anything bound to make you phone her again it's that.'

'She doesn't know—'

'And now you're sitting here thinking –' Steve mimed a puzzled man – '"Where's the loophole in never?"' Steve dragged on his cigarette, then pointed it at Dan, a smoky wand, and continued, 'There's no loophole, Dan, just some great bloody pit. Try taking the woman at her word. She said it, it's her fault, there's no chalice. Unrequited lust is the most banal thing in the world.'

'It wasn't unrequited.'

'You're sure about that? I was beginning to think the problem was just that you were shite with your hands.'

Dan looked at Steve and for a moment he wanted to hit him. Instead he laughed, put his tea towel over his shoulder and went to serve his last customer of the shift.

'So am I right in thinking you'll be phoning her soon?' said Steve loudly from his end of the bar. 'That you've picked up the phone twenty times and can't stop thinking about her, which over a week later is fucking drastic.' Dan returned to his post, leaning into the corner of the end of the bar, next to the glass bowl of oily peanuts. 'That you'll come to this party with me tonight and instead of getting the drinks in while I try and pull the lovely Sarah you'll slope about in a corner and then leave early.'

'Might do.'

'Give me three beyond-good, totally unanswerable reasons why you should see her again.'

Dan leaned down and fetched himself a bottle of beer. 'One: I am desperate enough to spend an evening talking about her that I'll even do it to you. Two: she's very . . . attractive, I suppose. You know sometimes when you go into a place and it's full of people and there's a woman there that you keep looking at, not necessarily because she's the best looking, just that she seems to have a spotlight on her and a way of holding herself. She's not hunched in a corner or tarting about all over the place. She just holds herself right.'

'And three?' Steve asked, bored. He thought Dan was a great big drama queen and was frequently irritated by his over-emotional gestures. Like the time when they'd been really, really drunk and Dan had told him he'd cried on the underground that day. On the platform at Kilburn Dan had seen a Sunday father sitting alone with his two kids, saying with fake jollity, 'And whose dad am I?', like he just wanted to hear the two solemn little creatures say it. Like he wasn't quite sure they'd remembered. And Steve had punched Dan in the arm for being self-indulgent and for being exposed and for telling him such things that were better kept hidden, hardly ever articulated, inside your head.

Dan ran on oblivious. 'Three: despite the fact, or maybe because of the fact that she's been known to run away, it's interesting, it feels like it matters. That it's all important.'

'That you're important.'

'Both. I know it sounds inflated. But the whole thing feels different.'

'She's not exactly being open with you though, is she? All this playing hard to get.'

'No, but you could probably say the same about me. At the start I just fancied her. And now I think her complications make it more . . . interesting.'

Steve was silent and Dan wiped a puddle off the wooden surface.

'Well, there's a thing,' Steve said flatly, at last.

The tatty train was drawing closer to the city – any moment now they would pass the tethered hot-air balloon that bobbed pointlessly in a park by Vauxhall station. They had left behind hills, fields, a castle, ducks, gardens with swings and homes with rooms for dining in. They had left behind their mutual friend Kate in her two-storey home in Winnersh Triangle (or The Bermuda Triangle as Sarah usually called it), near Reading. Or Ascot, depending on who you were talking to. Kate had a small child called Daisy. And Sarah and Beth were fascinated by her. Most of their friends were only just beginning to have or think about having children. They didn't know any small girls. Neither of them came from overly fertile or large families that spread ages between scratchy generations like honey. So they were struck by Daisy's small completeness, by her undeniably female tactics, by her pure delights and displeasure. This was the closest they'd been to a three-year-old since they'd been at nursery school themselves, and her growth between visits and her broken sentences struck them as extraordinary.

Although Daisy's placid nature, mini wardrobe and stuffed toy collection encouraged them to play with the idea of themselves as mothers, Sarah and Beth were humbled by Kate. She had so much more resonance and purpose than them. The fact that she took their lives seriously, listened over and above the chatter of her little girl, only served to increase their sense of inferiority. A woman with a child has power.

But, then, women on their way back to London have places to go and bright lights in their eyes. Beth and Sarah adjusted quickly, forgetting the humid warmth of damp clothes on the radiator, and convinced themselves that such a lifestyle took more certainty than they had to offer.

'I want her skirt. And her scarf.'

'The pink one?'

'Pink and red stripes.'

'They're much nicer than adult clothes.'

'Daisy's much nicer than an adult.'

192

'And prettier.'

'She'll probably be your babysitter in sixteen years' time and run off with your husband.'

'Thank you.' Beth took this historically and personally.

'Oh, sorry.' Sarah made a dreary face and then, after a pause, said, 'My mum had had two children by our age.'

'Then you can hardly blame her for being loopy by now, can you?'

'Why do you think your parents never had another child?'

'I don't know. Age? Dad's older than my mother, you know. Can I borrow something to wear this evening?'

'I love your dad. He's so sweet.'

'I know you do.' And Beth smiled; the same slow smile as her father.

'Omni Dad,' said her friend.

'*And* your mum, you know.' Sarah was thinking how peculiar Beth had seemed in the Tate the last time they'd met. She wanted to try and make Beth look at things a bit more calmly instead of always ploughing on just as she wanted, blinkered and stubborn as a pony. 'I know she's problematic but I think she's interesting, you know. There's something dignified about her, sort of elegant and wise. I know she's got a temper and I know she's very private,' Sarah continued, a little nervous, 'but so are you.'

Beth snorted, an embarrassed laugh, and looked out of the window. 'Can I borrow that black wraparound top?'

Sarah looked pained at the evasion, then gave up. 'Yes, if you tell me what I should wear.' There was a long pause in which Sarah began to hope that Beth might offer a small corner of honesty.

'What's Steve like?' Beth asked instead.

'He's a barman. That's where I met him, in his bar near London Bridge. He does stand-up comedy on the side, he's got a Scottish

accent and he's got a nice dark barman friend you can talk to.
I think the pub's in Islington.'

'Red shirt. You look nice in red,' Beth said and bit a stray
piece of skin off her finger.

It was eight in the evening and Beth stood in front of a mirror
in a flat in the north of the city, painting herself together. Making-
up, her mind and her face, to forget about Dan, to forget about
the fact that she had to go back home again tomorrow, that she
had been asked for supper which was so rare that it was close
to a summons in her book. In search of distraction, she overdid
it on the blusher. With each small speckled egg of colour she
broke and smudged on her skin she became more replete with
life. She willed herself to ignore the multiple possible reasons
for the invite (to make up for the argument over the sodding tea
cups, to prolong the argument, to announce something – a
divorce, a love affair, a skeleton from the cupboard). Her pale
cheeks with their threadworm broken veins became plump and
rose-beige with foundation. Little smooth buttocks blushing to
order. Black eyeliner went in close to the upper lashes to make
her whites whiter, her browns browner. Dark eyebrows, messy
slug shapes combed to neatness. Sneakily her thoughts kept
returning to her phone conversation with her father that morning.
'I wonder,' she'd said out of the blue, clunky as falling masonry,
'why Mum never kept in touch with her cousins and their children, those two boys.' There'd been a pause from Roger and to
remind him of whom she meant she'd said, 'The ones in the photo
on the mantelpiece. You know, they lived in—' He'd interrupted
and said, 'Yes, yes, I know, from Leicester. I'm not sure really,
you'll have to ask your mother.' The thing that was odd was that
her mother had said the cousins were from Harrogate. But her
father was probably wrong. Family clearly wasn't either of their
strong points. And she didn't want to wonder too much. Didn't

want to be too full of wonder. It would not be wonderful to wonder, and she began to sing the Wombles theme tune, heroic, she thought, in her skills of repression. She didn't put on lipstick, it felt too much like make-up, too obvious, while the rest felt like maintenance. But she had shiny lipgloss which she applied before leaving the house and that lasted exactly six minutes into her journey before dulling.

She and Sarah walked through the humid, dimming streets, particles of powder and shimmer loosening, clinging to fine facial hairs, and then, with the air-rush of a passing lorry, let loose into the miasma of brick dust and carbon monoxide. Slowly the night dissolved her. In slow motion she would have looked like a runner, stripes of coloured air streaming behind her. But then in slow motion anyone has the potential for speed.

As they walked down the street to the tube they saw Londoners making their way, couples meeting, friends gathering, groups making and breaking in search of entertainment. In all of them she recognised the longing to be transported by drink or drugs or flirtation or drama. They were seeking eye contact with an actor, an upturn in fortune with a new underwired bra, inspirational uplift from the Philharmonic, communion in dance music or communal spirit from a musical. On the platform flocks of people were congregating, mocking, posturing, even vomiting already. The excitement in the air was palpable as the train drew closer to possible venues, the tube a bubble of multiple possibilities. And then Sarah and Beth arrived at Angel and the spark was temporarily lost in the darkness of the street.

A few hours later, long after Sarah and Beth had arrived at the sweaty Essex Road pub, Dan and Steve walked in. They stopped at the entrance, Steve searching for the mouthy blonde Sarah, Dan spotting Beth instantly, near the bar. This is what they call intervention, not coincidence he thought, and he noticed his heart skip fast to double its beat. And when Beth saw him watching her by the door she felt as if her responsibility for decisions had been lifted clear from her shoulders. She had a feeling of suspension. A willingness, once again, to be led. Deaf to the loud music, insensible to the shove of the bar queue, she remembered the transportation he offered with an almost physical relief. She opened her mouth and her lips moved slightly as if she were suddenly going to blow bubbles. He smiled and half-shrugged. Helpless too in the city's chaos of possible meetings. There was no point in either of them saying anything; they were too far apart to have heard each other over the music.

Dan held out his hand and Beth put down her drink. Steve had just spotted Sarah, who he had chatted up in the bar the week before, and, knowing nothing of what he had accidentally managed to set up, did a double-take. Sarah gave a bark of laughter, thinking her friend to have been swiftly seduced.

Dan held her properly, an arm around her back, hand gripping hers, bodies close, and he began to dance with her. She stumbled and held her knees rigid at first but then, consciously, submitted. Let him do the work for her. He led her legs, rotated her belly and pelvis, arched her spine with the pressure of his hand. They slowed imperceptibly and looked at each other and this time she kissed him. No reason, really, just a knowledge of the pleasure it would bring – and the aphrodisiac of being wanted.

He held her shoulders. He had a plan, you could see it in his stance. He said, close into her ear, 'What's your address?'

Beth told him, thinking he might write her a letter, which appealed. She had a whole box of letters from his father.

He nodded, committing the details to memory. 'I didn't know you'd be here. Honestly. I'm going to go because we didn't choose this place and it's grim and we can't talk, but I'm going to pick you up tomorrow and we're going to go for lunch. I want to see you in daylight.'

She nodded. Why not? She'd tried.

He looked at her shadowed face, a piece of hair that had slipped down to lie along her cheek, down in front of her neck, like a punctuation mark.

'You have no idea, do you?'

'What?' she said.

'No idea.' And then he left.

Beth's mother woke with a start the next morning. It was one of those very alert awakenings when she felt as if she'd been switched on. Unlike other days when she felt as if she were wading through waves of sleep. She heard a wood pigeon, a whimsically rural sound, and watched Roger's shoulders rise and fall. The rise and fall of Roger Standing. Not fair, she thought, the rise and rise of Roger Standing. Or maybe fall and rise. He was such an uncomplaining, brave man. Right now, unfairly, she was more worried about her falls than his. She felt overheated and sweaty. Panicked.

She remembered Beth was coming that afternoon. They'd not spoken since the morning after Jacob's party. Not an unusual length of time, but it had been a peculiar morning, a near argument, too close to the bone. They'd have no choice but to talk this evening. She hoped Beth would let her close. She let the worries out of the bag. They rolled like marbles around her head, swirling, malevolent glass eyes. The flutters started, leathery wings beating in her chest cavity, and what with the whizzing worries in her head and the bat-like palpitations in her heart she felt sure she would wake up Roger.

She got out of bed, folding back the Lenor-fragranced sheets and blankets into a careful wing. She noiselessly opened the door and walked down the landing to the bathroom. Her long pink cotton nightgown, peculiarly much wider at the hips than at the base, allowing a middle-aged woman room to grow but not to move, was damp with sweat. She began to run a bath. It was quite a big bathroom for a little house, which was good because Lizzie had never been entirely sure of the hygiene of having a toilet in the same room as a bath. It was all a bit close together.

She opened the medicine cabinet above the basin and took out the dental floss. She saw the bottle of Bach flower remedy she used occasionally. She'd stopped ever taking the valium ten years ago, when she'd read awful stories of zombie mothers in *Woman's Own*. But she figured that a day like today deserved a little flowery brandy at the very least, and she put three cold little drops on the back of her tongue.

'Eddie, no, I mean it. I shan't. If you think I'm goin' up there cap in hand, begging for forgiveness, you've got another think coming.'

Beth had at first suffered *The Archers* for Sarah's sake when they shared a flat together in their second and third years of university. And had then kept it close in the same way one continues to feed a hateful pet. It was daft and unrealistic, which in a roundabout way was the whole point. It was even more comforting than tea. Sarah's sexual epiphany had come when she'd seduced an actor one Saturday night, a passing member of *The Archers*' cast – a roguish wine salesman – and had fucked him again on the Sunday morning, reaching a thunderous climax in time for the theme tune.

Something was happening today but Beth couldn't seem to get beyond the whine of *The Archers* to remember what. She was happy like this, not awake enough to realise she was hot from the egg-yolk sun breaking over London. She played with sensations in her head, a remnant of a dream about Mike, the

198

sound of her own breathing through her nose, the feel of her duvet against her cheek. Her feet moved down and found a stretch of smooth, cool sheet, a good surprise like an unexpected patch of sun-warmed sea.

Slowly, she surfaced. Dan. That was what was happening. Dan, this morning. Alert now, but pleased. Give in to it, something urged. It was unavoidable now. And then . . . what came later, at home, would be later. No point in worrying now. Dan first, the rest later. Ignore the gnomic hammer of anxiety, it's just yesterday's wine draining through your system. Just let it happen, she thought, and dug deeper into her bed, seeking the sleep-sheen again.

He arrived at one on the dot. She was sitting waiting, ostensibly reading the paper, feeding words in, shoving more out.

He stood at her door in jeans, bearing a box of Neapolitan chocolates. They'd been their favourites as children and she seized them greedily as if they were a chance of skipping over the last twenty years back to innocence.

'Perfect,' she said with a big smile, 'we'll take them with us,' and without asking him in she stepped out into the dusty street, slamming the door behind her. 'I think we should take the first bus and see where we end up,' she said to Dan, who had booked a table at a smart Italian in Primrose Hill for one-thirty.

'Perfect,' he said back.

'Large, with bizarre, fluffy legs.'

'Fluffy?'

'Yeah, you know, feathery, like he's wearing trousers. Jester trousers not combat trousers.'

She giggled. They were talking about a breed of dog Dan coveted. Sometimes, on a slow day, he'd get out the *Hamlyn Book of Dog Breeds of the World* that he'd been given for his tenth birthday. That was his idea of fun. Row upon row of tan-coloured dogs, complete with neat histories and distinguishing marks. The two of them walked through a busy Hyde Park, not touching, like a couple in the early days of courtship. They navigated ducks, roller-bladers and children, everything in gaggles. A small boy threw a frisbee badly so that it travelled behind him instead of ahead and Dan bent to pick it up. Beth watched him, reaching in his grey T-shirt; handing it over with an equal smile, turning to look at her looking at him. He'd always had nice skin, even and slightly brown. Why did women like arms so much? she wondered. She'd never heard a man comment on a woman's arms. Only in old books, in praise of alabaster skin and sloping shoulders, back when they were, she supposed, the only bits you usually got to see.

'You always wore grey T-shirts,' she said, to no particular end.

'You wore a lot of frocks, and skirts with T-shirts tucked in,' he replied.

'Frock,' she said. 'An old-fashioned word.'

'We were quite old-fashioned. We were the very last of the non-computerised children. We're ancient,' he said, turning and walking backwards to her forwards. He grinned broadly and looked ridiculously young.

'Except this doesn't feel very long ago,' she said, 'you and me walking in a park, talking about dogs.'

'Should we talk about something grown-up?' he said. 'Should we go to the Serpentine and make intelligent noises and wander round planks of wood saying, "Hummm, but is it art?" Like they should have decided that *before* they put it in. Or perhaps we should talk about past lovers, or foreign policy? Or past policies and foreign lovers?'

'I think I'd rather go to the Serpentine.'

'Really?' He looked disappointed.

'You're the artist.' Beth was beginning to wonder if he wasn't

200

going to turn out to be rather a bad artist. But, as he'd just said, maybe the uncertainty was part of the process.

'Exactly.'

'Don't you like other people's work?'

'No . . .' he said, trying to be breezy. 'I just never saw the point of busman's holidays. Come on, I'm hungry; we're going to the Taj Mahal.'

He was delighted because she said she loved curries and they found a table with pink napkins and a pile of poppadoms. Inside there were a few tourists and local families but the majority of tables were taken up by purposeful men eating alone, face down to their dansaks. Beth and Dan ordered themselves great circles of naan bread, small silver bowls of red meat, trays of rice and beer with a cartoon name, and then talked about the past. As her chicken tikka separated into layers of oil and colour, Beth noted how little she'd chosen to remember. More specifically, how little she'd chosen to remember that had any joy in the retelling. And there were, she had to admit, even in her current state of ferment over Lizzie, some gently funny stories, as well as personalities, in Dan's reminiscence of her parents that she could hardly recognise. She would be back at home with them in four hours' time but she was as unable to describe her parents clearly as those Japanese tourists at the next table to pronounce the items on the menu. Yet they were people, people who might be met afresh, even welcomingly by other ordinary people. Sad that they were still as fragmented, as illogical as the constellations her father used to try and draw out of the sky for her.

Sarah and Steve were still in bed. They'd got up to answer the door to the take-away pizza man (American hot, meat feast, onion rings, coleslaw and beer) and had eaten the food in bed,

Steve licking the red grease drips off Sarah's chest. The curtains were half-drawn, the windows open as far as they would go, which was only an inch or so. It smelled like a school changing room in there, of bodies and sweat, but they didn't care. They played 'Ten things to do with an onion ring when you're in bed with a beautiful girl on a sunny afternoon' and at 2.35 p.m. Sarah said, 'Stop, stop, no, come back up here. Listen. You need to know this.'

'Oh, Sweet Jesus, what?' said Steve, expecting a declaration of love or a history of depression.

'I,' she said, her blonde hair floating with static, her lips swollen and stretched into the sweetest and broadest of smiles, 'am having *so much fun*,' and with a whoop she slid back under the bed covers.

Beth gave Dan an awkward kiss goodbye, on the cheek, at the bus stop. He touched her face lightly with tenderness and, she thought, a little longing. There seemed to be an unspoken agreement to go gently with each other. They agreed to speak again soon. She had decided in the lavatory earlier that if she did nothing more than kiss him goodbye on the cheek then she was allowed to see him again. She climbed to the top of a Routemaster, heading for Oxford Circus tube station. There were only two other people on the bus. A woman and a small boy in shorts who had a new toy in a plastic bag. She watched him rustle in the front seat, childishness suppressed by transport. She wondered why she found it so hard to take this as it was. Why it was so hard, these days, to experience each moment in isolation; why every passing landmark seemed to be a memory in the making. It was disconcerting, like the quotidian distortion of an insomniac. If things could just stop for a moment she might catch up, take a look around and get a clean footing. The bus trundled on, someone else climbed the stairs. The child walked down the aisle, the plastic bag banging at his bare legs, and Beth wondered if being old was like this, if it meant being unable to take a bus ride simply, slipping instead into a different era with each corner.

15. Show and Tell

Brighton, 1990

'I had very scabby knees. And a nasty trick, a way of getting what I wanted which involved breaking other boys' fingers. I was the kind of boy that serious little girls like you ran away from.'

'You're *sure* you weren't really just a mummy's boy?'

'Oh yes. That too. But it took me many years and some fiercely intelligent women before I was forced into admitting that. I loved my mum.'

'You look sad.'

'I am sad, sweetheart. I am sad about many things. I'm a sad, sad old man. So sad and so old that I often don't know what you want with me.'

'Don't be sad. Please. I love you.'

'I can't help it. I'm a man. You'll work that out as *you* grow older and fiercer; we have such high hopes when we are little that we can't be anything but.' Jacob reached across the bed, where they were lying listening to the sounds of Brighton's cars and waves, to stroke her face.

'I won't grow fierce,' she said and he looked at her, then rolled on to his back to face the ceiling.

'I worry that I'll be the one to make you lose your sweetness and your trusting. I worry that I'll end up hurting you.'

'Ssshusssh. I love you. It's enough.'

204

'Is it? Am I?' and then, suddenly, 'Eugggghhh, no more. We're on holiday. A two-day holiday to last a lifetime.' He rolled back towards her. 'Do you know how lovely you are, how beautiful and sweet and wise? And serious and sexy?'

'No. You haven't told me for at least half an hour.' They kissed and she whispered in his ear, 'Tell me a story.'

'What kind of story?'

'Something about you when you were a little boy. With scabby knees and bright eyes. And grey shorts?'

'Yes, grey shorts. And Aertex shirts. We didn't do casual back then . . .' He drifted a little mid-sentence. 'You had your school clothes and then your posh clothes and nothing in between.' He paused in thought: 'Have I told you about Art?'

'No.'

'So, Art was the dealer at the end of the road, scrap dealer not drugs. We didn't do them in the forties or fifties either. He had a collie dog and a horse called Agatha. And this dirty, old-fashioned yard. You don't really see places like that any more. There were bikes and bits of lorries and baths all piled up and toppling all over the place. It was magical. He gave me this bowling ball and it was pure Americana; it represented every-thing that London suburbs weren't at that time. You can imagine. Art had been in the RAF and was a bit silent. That's another thing you won't ever know, I hope. How quiet men who have come back from war are. How not present they are. How life is unbearably insignificant compared to what they have sacrificed for it.

'Anyway, Art had his ways of coping. Including women. Now, obviously, I didn't know this at first. Not until I went on a day trip with him to the south coast. Just outside Brighton, towards Worthing, to pick up a piano. I was playing hookey. Loving every minute of it up there in the lorry cabin, feeling like some miniature bloke, feet on the dashboard, watching the women on the way to the shops, being able to see over hedges.

'God, it was wonderful . . . I wonder if we could find it tomorrow. The house, I mean, the house we went to. It was a huge white 1930s house. By quite a famous architect; I can't remember who. It had curves and glass staircases and parquet floors and lawns in levels down the cliff. And incredible views of the sea. Like the set of a thirties Californian thriller.

'Anyway, we arrived and I left Art and the woman of the house to it and went for a wander. I thought they'd be fiddling over the piano we were picking up, talking about how to transport it. I presumed that Art would shout for help when he needed it. But he didn't shout and I got very, very hungry and rather cross at having been forgotten. I wanted a sandwich, you know. I was a growing boy and all that. So I went round the house looking for them. And it was all empty and there was piano music playing. I could hear the sea in the distance and I got this funny feeling about the place, like the furniture and all the expensive ornaments were moving around the floor when I wasn't looking, when my back was turned. It was eerie. I followed the music, thinking that perhaps it was her on the piano. And I climbed the stairs very, very slowly. A bit scared. I mean, I was a scruffy kid and this was an extremely grand house. And they had a sweeping staircase with a white carpet.

'I got to the top, looked both ways down the corridor, saw a door open and followed the music, some piano concerto. I'll recognise it when I hear it. And when I pushed open the door a little to see if they were in the room I saw them both on the bed.'

'No . . .'

He nodded. 'And they had no clothes on,' he said, as if he were telling a story of huffing and puffing and blowing houses down. 'No clothes on at all. I could see her back, undulating under her dark hair. And his leg was between hers, very white and hairy.' Jacob paused. 'They were holding each other mid-coitus, like a strange, painfully locked embrace, and then they rolled back and on her face was such intensity and such longing. I had never witnessed abandonment before, you see.'

'Then what happened?'

'I went back down the stairs and out the front door and went and sat in the van all alone and forlorn. I found a Thermos flask of tea and a greaseproof paper package with six sandwiches inside . . .'

'What kind?'

'Ohhh. Cheese, I suspect, and pickle.'

'Not ham?'

'No, not ham.'

'Too bad.'

'Very bad. I didn't like pickle and I opened each of the six sandwiches and took out the chunks of pickle and threw them under the seat where I thought they might go mouldy and smell and serve Art right.'

'How long did you have to wait?'

'Probably only twenty minutes, but I was a boy, a young boy. They're like dogs; each minute of waiting feels like seven.'

'Waiting for something to happen . . .'

'Waiting for something to happen to them.'

'And did you tell Art what you'd seen?'

'Of course I didn't. I knew which side my bread was buttered. That was the most exciting Tuesday I'd ever had.'

'And do you still like to think of it?'

'What?'

'The memory. Her face. The sound of the sea. Rooms made of glass. The idea of watching.'

'What do you think?'

'Right now, given the physical evidence, I'd have to say yes.'

There was a smiling pause in their hotel room. When you know what will happen there is no need to rush.

'Show me,' Beth said to Jacob, placing her full, loose weight on his soft body, the ripple of her flesh, slow-told memories, like pebbles dropped in pools of cream.

16. Faith

Beth sat on the tube, an unopened Sunday paper in her lap, heavy as an old cat. She felt tired with lunchtime beer, but also tense. It felt as though something were about to happen. She was terrified of change, yet she would scream if she had to live out the same strained evening she'd been doing for twenty years. She didn't know what she was more scared of – alteration or stagnation. She was scared of both, she thought, because she had nothing to fall back on, nothing to fuel her. She felt as if she were in limbo. And the only good thing was that Dan seemed happy to be there with her. A nun sat opposite her, eating a packet of cheese and onion crisps with quiet care. Beth watched her pull each crisp out slowly, look at it, then place it in her mouth. She was dressed in a casual habit and when she reached the end of the packet – at about Clapham Common – she folded it neatly into a small square and placed it inside her string bag. A very small pleasure, cleanly disposed of.

Next to a thin woman sat two men in black suits, the fabric shiny and thin like pages of a magazine. Beth tried to work out where they'd been. One carried a black case, a flute perhaps, but with his yellowing moustache, fat fingers and red face he didn't look like a flautist.

'I thought it was terrific, really terrific, your speech,' she heard him shout over the sound of the train.

The smaller, younger man, without a case, blushed and smiled slightly. He had the blow-dried hair of a game show host.

'You're enjoying it then . . . glad you're there?' asked the older.

'Ohh, yes,' the younger replied with feeling. Where? thought Beth. She stared unashamedly. The nun licked her lips.

'So,' said the elder, nudging the younger, 'you got someone for Ladies' night?'

'I hope so.' He looked concerned. 'She's funny about it though, she wasn't all for it. People don't really understand it, do they? And you can't explain it, can you? It's not really got a purpose . . . it's the ceremony that makes it, isn't it?'

'Ohh yes. Dead right,' said the elder, answering just the one question.

'But if I say I'm off to the Lodge she doesn't take an interest.'

'Get her along to the Ladies' night. It's the only way. She'll meet some smashing girls. We have a fabulous time, just fabulous.'

Of course thought Beth. Masons. Masons and Nuns. All that was needed now was the regular Northern Line evangelist, walking back and forth from Edgware to Morden, fuelled by conviction. Beth felt distant, as if she might be invisible among this collection of people in suits and wimples. She doubted she had it in her to belong to anything or anyone, to wear it or carry it in public. People are strange she thought. What bravery.

Beth'd not really thought about religion much. The closest she ever got to church was the National Gallery. She had a postcard up in her kitchen, a sixteenth-century version of a familiar theme. The three kings bringing their gifts to the Christ child, fulfilling roles as familiar as the seven dwarfs, robed in lavish gold and green and suede slippers. They trailed their wealth and soft feet over grubby broken tiles, fabrics brushing against the skinny whippets that lurked, shivering, in their corner, resisting the downward slide of perspective with knobbled paws and over-grown claws. The bovine Virgin's dress flowed over the furniture in a static spill, then rucked and spread over the ground. Beyond the clustering family, bound by a birth, the world could be sighted. But only in blue-mist miniature through a series of precisely designed arches.

Beth, in her kitchen, often peered through the arches at the far worlds. Turrets climbed above the back of a goat, echoing the plant which spiralled insolently out of the earth in the fore-ground. It was the painstaking placing that fascinated Beth. The ordering of faith. The structure of formal love. The mystery was what happened when you weren't looking – her own absence was hard to comprehend. What happened when someone broke the pose? When the goat moved and a burning building could be seen in the far, far city? How would they all behave if the scenery were to change? It was clear to Beth, what with their ornately protective clothes and heavy seating, they did not expect to have to make radical or sudden changes in the hierarchy.

Beth, slip-sliding home, travelled the escalator with heavy slowness. Stepped into the warm, windy evening where the day dimmed its way down to meet the small neon shop signs. The evening air was lighter outside than in, where TVs fluttered in darkened sitting rooms while the birds still sang clear in the dusk, the day's dying murmurs loud in the lowering light. She walked up the length of Delia Street, past a house which had once had a vicious terrier, another which had had a fire. Sidestepping bin-bags, observing home improvements, cal-culating the number of times she might have walked this street – when there, in front of his very own house, taking a bag out of a car, was Jacob. He bent over, his head lost in the boot, and her heart quickened with her soft plastic tread. He withdrew and straightened and turned and saw her, as easy-limbed and long-haired as ever. Something about a woman in the wind. She slowed down and for a moment she thought this could be a scene from a love story.

What was she to say when she'd shared his past and future? When she'd had every place but the present. This time, unlike at his party, there was just the two of them, which instantly jerked her back into memories of other stand-offs in other streets. He smiled and inclined his head slightly. If they had been old friends it would have been the preface to an embrace, but having done so much more to each other's bodies in the past there was no chance of that now.

'Beth,' he mouthed and she walked towards him. Once they had kissed like people coming home. They had slid so easily into each other, with the fluid collision of reaching and retreating waves.

'How are you?' they both said, then stopped again.

It really was so long ago, she thought. And yet years pass and fall. They don't necessarily take you further. There was something about the way he squinted and stared, a very concentrated gaze, that made her think she could probably be susceptible again. The thought gave her a warm flicker of pleasure. Faster than she could acknowledge, in the space between two sentences, she thought that maybe she had been right all along. Maybe he had always been the answer – maybe it was only ever him who could bring her to life. Bring life to her.

'I've just had lunch with Dan,' she said. It slipped out like a confession. But she just wanted a way in.

'Have you?' he said, puzzled.

'Yes,' she said, when a bubbling, painful cough distracted Jacob and he turned his head to wave at Mr Garland crossing the street in his wheelchair. There was a low electronic hum. 'I should go,' said Beth, standing still. Inviting him to talk to her.

He could see it in her face, in the way she was standing still, just looking. And he knew how it felt. He remembered feeling alone, feeling lost, and he felt sorry for her suddenly. Not for having left her, Christ no; that had been one of those things and he had been right to leave her alone to get on with her life. No, he felt sorry for her because she was still looking at him in a loaded way. He who had behaved like a bad sit-com adulterer, a middle-aged man with a belly, sagging breasts and a dissatisfaction that he tried to expel by having sex with younger women.

He felt sorry for her because even though she looked so young she wasn't really young at all. She must be thirty, almost the same age as Dan, in fact. The two of them living out their unhealthily extended youths, all neuroses and search. Casting shadows back on their parents rather than accepting their youth and getting on with it. Of course they had no children to make them just get on with it. He felt sorry for them because they hadn't yet been through and come out the other end. They hadn't even started, and no one could say he'd been scared of starting. Over and over again.

'Have you? So you're friends again now, after all this time? Have you been talking about me?' It comes out meanly but he's irritated by the idea of the two of them together. Was that fear of old secrets coming out or just anger at the way one's children never let things drop?

She could think of nothing to say in reply, the final end to a floating fantasy. Was that really all he'd been left with – a ten-year-old fear of discovery? Could he not bring himself to talk to her with recognition of what they had once been? This was no miraculous coincidence, this was a middle-aged man taking out the Tesco shopping in front of his own tatty terraced house. And she felt humiliated that for ten seconds, in her imagination, she had been his for the taking all over again.

She turned and walked away, and as she stood at her parents' door she was aware of Jacob still standing in the street, rubbing his hands over his eyes, stuck between two banks of brick houses. She plunged into the brightly lit hallway with relief. Funny, or not funny, how you end up running from the confrontations you've dreamed of.

It was five o'clock and the three of them were sat at the kitchen table. In the end it was Lizzie who told Beth that her father had had some bad news. Roger had said he wanted to tell her how the minor prostate problem had turned out to be an incurably serious one. But when it came down to it he couldn't. So Lizzie stepped into his ditching sentence. She watched Beth's face and reached for her, but Beth was faster and put her hands over her eyes. After a moment she looked up at Roger and said, 'Oh, Dad.'

Since Lizzie had accompanied Roger to each of his blood tests and appointments there had never been a moment when the truth of his illness had surprised her. The truth had crept up on them quickly, certainly. But the fact that people got ill, that they might die, was not quite such a surprise to her as it was to Beth. And Lizzie had had an added responsibility; she and Roger had had to get home, eat supper, keep on going, get through each night. The momentous, she knew, was always preceded, interrupted, followed by the superficial. But she was discovering that the minutiae were sometimes a useful vehicle. It was only late at night and early in the morning that Lizzie allowed herself to consider what was coming, and feel both rage and pity on behalf of them all.

'It's my decision,' Roger said quietly.

'Mum?' Beth looked at her.

'It is up to your father in the end.' Lizzie didn't mean to present a united front by that sentence but wanted to suggest that she too had tried to persuade him to follow treatment. But

Beth wasn't seeing things clearly and presumed only coldness. She became agitated.

'Have you seen another doctor? Maybe they're wrong . . .'

Her father shook his head and said with a tight smile, 'I don't think there's much doubt about it, Beth. They know their stuff. These specialists.'

'Oh, Dad,' she said again and just looked at him. His long thin face was still. His skin had slid over the years, perched on his cheekbones and eyebrows but losing its grip, sagging into pouches below the eyes, rippling down the planes of his cheek. He wasn't a man who'd ever laughed or joked much but his movements were always tender, considered. He had the down-ward gaze of a tall man and it was he she'd always wept to as a child. He didn't believe in over-reaction and would shush and pat her back to moderation. Get her to tell him the whole story when she was calm.

'How long have you known?' she asked.

'I guessed. But the results came back on Friday.' She got up and walked around the table and bent to put her arms around him. She was breathing too fast. He rubbed her back as she rested her face on his wiry wool jumper.

When she pulled away her eyes were brimming and her voice stretched with the effort of keeping control. 'I don't understand. Why won't you let them do anything? What about me?' Then she added quickly, 'What about Mum?'

'I do not want it.' He spoke each word with equal emphasis, with kindness rather than anger.

'What if I do?'

'Then you'll just have to respect my decision,' and suddenly, clearly, the scene was too much for him and he pushed his chair back and left the room.

There was a moment's silence. 'Mum,' said Beth accusingly, 'you can't let him do this. You can't.'

215

Lizzie turned around from the sink, where she had been washing up plates, and gripped stainless steel with one hand, saying with forced lightness, 'What do you expect me to do?' There was silence. 'We can't force him. He says he doesn't want to be in hospital for months. The doctors say the hormone therapy has only a five per cent success rate in cases like . . . like his. And that,' she paused to make the next phrase less harsh, 'it would only slow things down. Maybe for some years but not more than that.'

'Have you talked to him though? You haven't really talked about it, have you? You never do, Mum. You're always so sodding humble. And sodding stubborn.' Beth wanted to kick something and grabbed instead a dishcloth from the side and began to scrub viciously at the table.

'You don't like the way I do things,' Lizzie said quietly. 'You never have, I know. But this isn't your decision. This is about Roger.'

'He's my father,' said Beth, squaring up to her small mother in her apron.

'And he,' said Lizzie, with a sudden ferocity that silenced Beth, 'is my husband. How do you think I feel?'

Beth could not even begin to know how her mother felt; she'd never been able to guess and had given up trying long ago.

'I don't know. I don't know how you feel. I never do.'

'I know.' She started the washing up again. 'There's no reason why you should. I'm sorry.'

'What for?'

Lizzie didn't reply but waited for a moment and then turned around from the soapy remains of one meal and said brightly, 'So, will you stay and have your tea with us?'

Beth didn't know what to do. Either in general or in particular. She didn't know what to do in the house on a Sunday afternoon

216

when her father had announced that he was dying and tea was in order and no one was crying and everyone seemed to have assimilated the news before she'd got there. She moved out of the kitchen and into the sitting room where Roger was watching the television in his usual corner of the sofa. She sat down, closer than she needed, and he put his arm around his thirty-year-old daughter. Beth rested her head on his shoulder again, burrowing into the crook of his arm a little. But the angle just reminded her that her stomach felt strange and her head tense so she wriggled herself straight again.

Her eyes trawled the sitting room. It was only small; they'd never knocked through, bypassing the urge for spacious living like so much else. The mantelpiece was cluttered with photographs, proof of past living; so many of her and Roger, very few of Lizzie and then those small boys who had captured her curiosity. She had more important things to confront her mother with now.

It was all in here. The air was loaded with hundreds of different conversations and arguments. She remembered how as a child she had fantasised about funerals and high drama. A morbid girl, maybe. She'd always believed that with tragedy would come status, emotion and urgency. Like the misplaced child who believes they are adopted, she had been raised in such solemnity that she always felt a death was due.

And here it was now. A drama in the front room. And all she could do was watch the snooker with him. They watched in silence for one frame.

'My father took his time over dying,' he said quietly, emphasising the 'my'. 'Too much time. God, yes. He hated it – the drugs, the hospitals – and he was left with only bitterness at the world.' Roger's tone was moderated. 'If I could have found a doctor who would have finished it for him I would have. In the end he hated being alive. The whole thing was enormously

217

upsetting. Frankly, I'd rather not go through that myself. I don't believe in pointless fights. I'd rather you and your mother didn't have to go through it either.'

'What was actually wrong with him? What did he die of?' asked Beth.

'D'you know, I can't even remember.' He turned to look at her, almost amused by his admission. 'It was probably water somewhere, water on the something, pneumonia . . . that kind of thing. He'd had typhoid in the war. He'd always had a weak constitution and a bad temper. When I was about ten . . .' Beth knew this story. At eight one thing happens, at ten another. Talisman anecdotes, the stories selecting themselves, compiled into a personal canon. But she didn't want him to stop talking to her so she said 'Yes' eagerly.

'My mother and father gave me a train. I'd wanted a train set but a whole one, straight off, would have been very pricey so they thought they'd give me it bit by bit. They gave me the train to start off with. No track. And I was sulking, being an ungrateful child, and he stamped on it.' He still sounded shocked. Beth had never liked that story. Or the fact that Roger told it, like an old man admitting that the doll's house he'd spent years building in a shed had been rejected.

There was a pause and then he turned back to the TV. 'It's not going to stop, Beth. Not until I do.'

She realised she hadn't thought to ask something. 'Does it hurt? Are you in pain?'

'Only a little, sometimes,' he said.

'Surely they've given you something for that?' For the first time Beth felt an unexamined, unstoppable wave of panic. The sudden raw thought of her father's body stretched and raddled with pain made her want to be sick. She'd never felt this kind of fear before. She moved quickly to get the remote control, switched the TV off and rounded on him.

218

'People are cured, even very late on. Isn't it worth trying? Aren't we worth it?' She perched on the edge of the sofa, her face furrowed, too close for those kinds of questions and Roger got up to draw the curtains. He pulled one to and then stood there holding it lightly in his bony fingers.

'Sometimes you just have to let things be. It isn't always about you, you know.' He said this softly, not unkindly, but she'd have liked a little more to fight for and fewer lessons in life.

His words struck her, even in this crisis, as vastly unfair. She'd never thought it was all about her, or at least she'd never thought they lived for her alone. Her mother certainly never seemed to find much happiness in her. But her dad? Her dad did, in his own measured way. He was not a man who ever adopted a funny walk just to entertain a child. She didn't think he'd ever learned to skip, he never told her she was a princess but he never, ever forgot to tell her how proud he was of his only daughter. Oh shit, she thought to herself with absolute clarity, this is going to be awful.

Her dad was dying and she suddenly felt ashamed. She looked at him standing at the end of the room, a man who had once been a child, not just her father. A middle-aged person who was falling ill. She could see now, of course, that his hair was white-grey, no longer iron-grey, that he had red-rimmed eyes and a waxy pallor.

But standing up propelled the scene further away. Maybe they needed another cup of tea. Probably. She omitted to reply to her father and left for the kitchen.

Lizzie was putting a yellow quiche in the oven. Trying to keep things in motion.

'Lorraine,' she said brightly without turning around, 'you do like them, don't you?'

Good God Almighty, thought Beth.

PART THREE

17. Late

'I went for a drink with Steve last night,' said Dan.

'Where?' said Beth.

'What was that?'

'Me . . . moving the chair.'

'Oh. Pub round the back of Camden. Why are you moving the chair?'

'So I can put my feet on the table. They're weary, it *is* midnight. Not all of us are bar-flies like you,' she said.

He smiled. 'He got on my nerves.'

'Really?'

'Yes. He's funny about you. And I think he and Sarah are an odd couple too.'

'Can we not talk about them?' she asked.

'Why not?'

'It's incestuous. Boring.'

There was a pause.

'It's raining again,' said Dan. Funny how the banal shared with the chosen becomes enchanting.

'I can hear foxes,' she responded.

'In Camberwell?'

'Yes, in Camberwell. They sound like children crying. I dreamed about finding this boy crying in the street last night. I think it was because of the foxes.'

'Why was he crying?'

'Don't know. He just was, like you do in dreams. Like trains just drive through gardens and people arrive from nowhere.'

'What did you do with him?'

'Oh, I don't know, other people's dreams are very dull. They're always weird. Where's the interest?'

'Freud didn't think so.'

Beth laughed. 'What do you know about Freud?'

'Not much.'

'Didn't think so.'

He was laughing too. 'You needn't make it sound like a failing. Like not having read *War and Peace*.'

'I can't imagine you sitting still long enough to read Tolstoy,' she said sharply. He made an 'Ooh, get you' noise down the phone.

'I haven't read it either,' she said. 'Tell me what you are reading then. Tell me a good book.'

He didn't answer. Truth was, he wasn't reading anything. He very frequently wasn't. He liked detective thrillers, Chandler best of all. He didn't want to read about people like him, living like him, in an adolescent era of gender fascination.

'I'm reading sleeve notes voraciously,' he said and she laughed again. 'For your tape.'

'This tape has been a long time in development.'

'That's because it's going to be excellent.'

'Aren't you tired?'

'Aren't you?'

'I've told you. I can't sleep much at the moment.'

'Except to dream of little boys. I'm keeping you company. I like it. You know that.'

'I do know. I suppose I should say thank you. You've been very . . . very supportive. I've been a bit of a nightmare to everyone else. I don't want to talk to anyone properly.'

'I'm not—' Careful he thought. 'I'm happy talking to you.

224

I'm just sorry about Roger. Did you visit your dad today?'

'No, I went yesterday, and, oh, I don't know, you can't talk about it for ever. It's very bizarre – the more weeks he has the less of a tragedy it is supposed to be.' She paused. 'He's pottering around but he's bored and I think he finds it ridiculous to be visited daily by his thirty-year-old daughter. He keeps asking, "Haven't you got other things that need doing?" He told me he wasn't a child yesterday. I think he was cross.'

'I shouldn't think he was cross with you.'

'No, he was, he was angry. He was irritated by me and Mum. He heard us arguing and told me off as if I were a child. He told me to leave her alone.'

'Why were you arguing?'

'Oh,' it was a disgusted sound, 'because that's what we do. That's what we've always done. You'd have thought we might have stopped. We were arguing because I think they're not giving him enough painkillers. Because even if he takes nothing else, they don't know how long . . . how long it will take and so I think he should be allowed as much pain relief as he wants. And they've limited it and I wanted Mum to talk to them before he goes back in.'

'Does he want more?'

'He says he's all right. Again and again. "I'm all right, for God's sake."'

'But does he say he's in pain?'

'That's what I'm saying.' She'd raised her voice. 'He doesn't say anything. But sometimes he just closes his eyes suddenly. And that's the pain.'

Dan said nothing.

'He sits in the garden or listens to the cricket or Classic FM but obviously he can't do anything more. He's not strong enough to walk or talk for very long. Anyway . . . talk to me about something else. Tell me something new.'

It was quiet on their line.

'Are we still going to see each other? At the screening? Am I still invited?' he asked.

'If we're ready. We haven't finished the final edit yet.' She paused, then said, 'There was this woman in the episode we were finishing today and Mike kept saying we couldn't use her and I was disagreeing. And it was weird because, you know, she reminded me of my mother. She kept shutting down, which kind of made her not very good on camera, but she'd never before talked about how her daughter had died and she kept tuning out. She'd stop talking and just go into herself. And my mum always did that. She still does that.'

'But she is facing losing someone though . . . like you.'

'She doesn't seem to want to fight it. She saves her fights for me.'

'Mothers are meant to fight.'

'For you, not with you.'

'Maybe it's the same thing.'

'You're not helping, you know. You'll only end up pissing me off,' she said, but she didn't sound very angry.

'So we'll see each other on Monday,' he said, 'at the screening.'

'Couldn't we just talk to each other on the phone for ever?'

'No.'

She was silent, distracted. 'On top of everything else, Dad told me I have a lot to learn.'

'He did?'

'I was criticising Mum. I told you.' There was a pause. 'It would be expecting too much to ask you to call me every night and talk me to sleep for ever, wouldn't it?'

'It would be expensive, Beth. And you know my wallet isn't my strong point.'

'I haven't asked you much about your day.'

'What do you want to know? I'll tell you anything.'

'Anything?'

'Almost anything.'

'Not good enough.'

'The girl expects too much. If I were to *see* you I might know that I could tell you everything. I could confess anything and not shock you.'

'What could you possibly have to confess?'

'Just as much as you. We could match one for the other.'

'I think I'll stick with the phone calls.'

'Just so long as you know,' he said.

'I should go,' she said.

'Tomorrow, then.'

'You do know I know this is odd?'

'We'll get there,' he said with certainty. When he actually talked to Beth everything became less complicated in his head. Almost pure. But all she did was say goodnight and put the phone down.

It was past midnight one weekday in August, nearly five weeks since Beth had been told about Roger's illness. She sat in a chair, looking at her feet in their socks. She realised her shoulders were raised like hung puppets and she straightened herself and felt the stiffness groan. She might just stay up, it wasn't such an odd thing to do. There was no reason why she need feel madder and more alone at two in the morning than two in the afternoon. It was just that the unseen company was so poor. Mothers and foxes, rapists and policemen. And the unhappy – awaiting the light, anticipating the exhaustion.

When Beth was little and hadn't been able to sleep she'd played walking on the ceiling. She'd crossed the flat of the walls and right-angled up on to the foamy tiles above her head. They would give a little under her bare feet as if she were walking on paved clouds. The lightbulb and its shade with scalloped petals would rise taut on a white flexi-stem. She would have to bend to open the door to the landing and then she would step down into the gentle hum of the sleeping and cleaning thoroughfare (first floors are all about bodies). Each footfall would raise a small cloud of dust, the ashes of domesticity. It would be like walking on another planet. Curious, but nowhere to go. Step out the window and you would fall for ever, further and further from the irradiated London night into a bluer blackness than we know. A freefall equivalent to that elusive sleep.

She wouldn't talk about the fact that her father was dying. She was a modern enough girl to know that communication was meant to be a conduit to calm. But it took courage or a lack of inhibition to discuss sadness. Instead she set her face hard to the world for not knowing, not divining.

Meanwhile, something very odd was going on around her. People were pushing and retreating all over the place. She had never felt so alert, or so uncertain. So aware of life or so impotent. She could see every flicker in the eyes of the ones she loved as close up as if she were invisible. She wanted her dad. And watching his body fail was more shocking than anything she'd ever seen on the telly. Its progress was almost disgustingly intimate. She'd seen her father's yellowing toenails for the first time in fifteen years, a stretch of aged, white thigh as they all waited in a tiny consultant's office, a white baby's blanket on his knees. And the distant, latinate medical language they used of him reduced him to the status of yet another ageing man. And to each doctor she wanted to say, 'Yes, yes – he is my *father*, you see. This one is more important than the last.' Beth was forced to see her father as fallible. As an individual constructed of the same material as her. Although intellectually she'd never claimed he was invulnerable, she'd never imagined she'd have to watch the truth of it. It seemed so entirely the wrong way around. He hated being the invalid, being coddled and crowded. He sat listening to brass bands, thinking his way through the day.

His life and his story seemed painfully precious to Beth, as poignant as rain. If she couldn't keep him alive with will, could she keep all of him inside her? But she was only a part of him, something that cropped up over halfway through, and he was everything and always to her. The overlap was never balanced. If she had children of her own they might be everything to her but they'd come late and have to be left behind. How could it ever be anything but a process of passings?

Which was why, she supposed, she wanted someone of her own to learn the past and live the most part. And every passing day, about midnight, he phoned and said, 'So how was today then?' And the need to be reached out to overwhelmed her.

But obviously she was coping. There was so much worse that could be happening to them, so many worse stories she'd heard in waiting rooms. No one said it was meant to be easy, her mother had stated yesterday with that sudden glinting flash of anger masquerading as a truism. Beth wasn't sure whether Lizzie had meant living or dying.

18. Secret Garden

Early afternoons were the best. Even though Roger's days were no longer divided into awake and asleep, he and Lizzie would still pretend, go through the rigmarole of nightclothes and toothbrushes. He wondered sometimes what the point was of cleaning his teeth. To save them from a decay that was slower than the rest of his body's? So as not to have bad breath he supposed. He still shared a bed with his wife, they still embraced and touched – so that was the point. But in the mornings, after the sleeplessness and the getting up to visit the bathroom and the trying not to keep Lizzie awake, it was hard not to feel hollow and sick. However, by lunchtime he usually felt well enough to walk the few steps to the park, then return to sit in the garden with the radio on.

If the weather was warm and the music nice he would drift, dissolving into landscapes where past and present were confused, just a few elements vividly coloured, bright and flickering in his head like old home movies; Lizzie in a plum jumper, the day he first met her.

This afternoon someone was cutting the grass and, in the way that a taste of milk or the smell of wood can, it moved him with an inexplicable nostalgia for an unidentified era. Maybe it wasn't one period, maybe it was associations gathered like a cloud of balloons held in one hand. Or maybe it was nostalgia anticipated. This moment was as precious as any other, the brown

230

heads of his wife and daughter visible through the kitchen window.

They weren't looking at him, they were making tea. He could have been invisible. It was almost like watching them when he'd gone. It was hard to accept that people could do without you. They did though, they carried on all right; they might even be heard to laugh on the day you die.

What would he have done if it had been Lizzie who was ill? He thought about that a lot. Because, you see, in a selfish way he was glad it wasn't him being left behind. What would life be like without her? She would still be there every moment of every day. She would still surround him. But she would be so silent that it would be very sad.

Beth brought him a cup of tea in a bright, thick mug. She smiled broadly at him, matronly in her anxiety.

'You okay, Dad?'

'I'm all right. Just fine.' He knew she didn't believe him of course, but didn't know what to do about it. In a way this *was* all right he thought, numb with painkillers. It was life. You know. It's the way it goes.

Beth dragged a chair from the patio out on to the grass and Lizzie came out with a plate of small white sandwiches with no crusts. Beth told her mum to sit down and there was a little dance while she insisted and then it was Lizzie and Roger watching Beth retreat.

'She all right?' he asked Lizzie.

'Not really,' she said. Somehow she'd got blunter with age. With events. 'Girls and their fathers – it's not easy for her.'

'Are *you* all right?' Strange this, encouraging people through your own illness. The physical pain couldn't be shared and thus lessened so it had to be concealed, and the people you loved had to be protected from their beseeching futility. The disease spread but almost worst of all it isolated.

231

'No. Not really,' she said very slowly. Lizzie might not have been beyond believing in the importance of sandwiches, but she was beyond pretence. 'I'm very, very scared of reaching a point where I can't be of any help to you. You've always been there to help me. And I'm also scared of life without you.'

They held hands. Side plates in their laps. There was a silence and then she turned to him briskly as if she'd just met him in the street.

'And you, you all right?' And they had to laugh, because obviously he wasn't.

They chortled, a little shocked at themselves, and sighed and then let go of each other to eat their sandwiches. Roger said, 'Is she helping you, Beth? Is she, you know . . .'

'She and I are going to have to find a way. Aren't we? Left in a family of two. Not a grandparent or sibling between us. She's very mistrustful of me; I think she thinks I was a bad mother, or at least cold.' She smothered Roger's protest. 'But she's got a lot of learning to do. I worry about her. She has no idea how – well, how ruthless life is.'

'I think she's getting the idea,' said Roger, indignant on his daughter's behalf. 'Are you still going to tell her? About the boys? Like we discussed . . .' He nodded hopefully.

Lizzie didn't answer but looked blankly at the fuchsia bush.

'Roger, sometimes I think that not telling her was the one good thing I did do for her as a mother. It's hard to give that up. She did quite a lot for me, just by being there. But sometimes I look at her and think . . . well, you know what I mean. How much of it did she soak up? When she was a little girl. If I tell her then it's all been a bloody great waste, hasn't it?

'But then I also know that some people find telling everyone everything a great help. And even if I don't, I don't really see how she and I are ever going to have a proper conversation unless she knows the truth about me. And my nasty temper.' She flashed Roger a wicked smile.

And somehow Roger, not without sadness, realised she was going to be fine, in the end, without him.

19. Man-made

Dan had almost finished the third painting in his series. Each wonder was taking a long time – over a month. In fact, every one was taking weeks longer than the last. 'Happiness' had come out of somewhere. It had been the first ordering step. He had assumed that once it was finished everything else would follow easily. Paintings completed with the tumbling flourish of an acrobat. Unknown layers beneath their smooth surfaces.

But at this rate, thought Dan, it would be like a mathematical equation, each one taking twice as long as the last. He'd be on his deathbed before all seven were done. Before he'd worked it all out. Someone had once told him that you only have to fold a piece of paper in half 256 times before it reaches the moon. But then hadn't someone else once told him that you couldn't fold any sheet of paper, however big, more than seven times?

So far, there was a theme in the shaping of the pictures, in the acrylic smoothness that looked as if it were stuck in a Hockney era from a distance, then surprised the close inspector with its ragged reality. An idea placed and magnified, the image and the thought given wide but always contained attention. No one, though, had ever said they were beautiful.

Having left 'Happiness' facing the wall, he'd moved on to 'Innocence' and 'Man-made'. Next would come 'Landscape', 'Ignorance', 'Experience' and 'Love'. He liked the portentous words; loaded, poetic states which he could illuminate with a single image. He was well aware that illustrating the entire human condition within seven frames was an elaborately ambitious exercise. Almost bound to fail. But the complication of it, the scale of it still excited him. Right now, intoxicated by Beth, a little high as if she were a too sharp white wine, Dan felt he could take on the world.

The most recent was 'Man-made'. (What did he think the rest were? Angelic?) He'd had an idea of domesticity as mankind's most elaborate construction. The canvas edges framed an aluminium window set in red brick. It looked into a brightly lit room with a table. The shapes of sitting people were bent over it. They were blurred with movement, but also a whitish miasma of cloud, of steam from the potatoes, of dust, of ghosts. Someone was sitting, as they should do, at the head of the table, but it could have been anyone, a friend, father, stepmother, lodger, gas man or Jehovah's Witness.

Dan himself loved the contained, shadowy insight of Vermeer, the lacquered revelation of de la Tour's paintings, but he couldn't control himself so. There was so much space and movement at the corner of his eyes that he felt he must catch a view and then explode it huge.

He loved Stanley Spencer's paintings more than anything. He wanted to bring complications into coherence, humanity created from a hundred flaws. Beauty erupting from old things, scenes suffused with longing, a whole scape of possibilities within an inauspicious view. When Dan left the house he saw shrubs as hiding things, roads jammed with cars as necklaces of encased faces. It was a treasure trove out there.

He had hoped these paintings would calm him, detangle his head. Everything had always struck him as so precarious; he'd just thought it would be nice to know what he thought – have it there on a wall. Then he could stop having to worry about people he saw on the street, the way he loved and hated his father, feared and adored his mother. The way he loved to pursue a woman but refused to ever go to a supermarket with a girl-friend for fear he might catch resignation off the shoppers like a chill in the frozen food section. The way he would walk around London for a day just to observe people and then cry on the bus at the sight of a hopeless man. The way, whether he was in a city or the countryside, his eyes would flit from house to tree looking for signs that he could read.

But the paintings were complicated by the intent. The only emotion with any simplicity was the one he felt towards Beth. Which surprised him – he would never have described his intentions as pure.

He'd had to borrow money off his father to carry on these paint-ings since his wages from the bar didn't cover rent, drink, food, massive sheaves of canvas and pot after pot of paint. His father was due round the next morning with a cheque. Dan didn't like doing this but it wasn't as if he could get another job, or a whole new career. Someone had to step in. And the bank wouldn't give him anything more.

Not that he hadn't tried. He'd waited on the grey chair inside Lloyds Bankside, feeling singularly out of place among people whose affairs, probably even the illicit ones, were all in order. Outgoings carefully tailored to incomings. Saturdays saved for spending. Dan felt jealous of their existences for a moment, for the money they were being paid to work relatively hard and then stop at a set hour. But he didn't dwell on it; he'd never felt as if his choices were anything but his own fault. His father had enough money to help and unlike the bank manager had offered a sum without conditions. A bit of Dan felt that it was good for his father to continue to make amends.

That evening he was going to watch the first cut of Beth's documentary. They had seen each other once in the last month, for a cup of coffee, but they had continued to speak almost every day. In a way, with time, she had become more ordinary – in that she was more accessible. And yet more extraordinary because she spoke and thought and moved like no one else. Which was a discovery all of Dan's own and it gave him a possessive, painful joy. His phone calls were hopeful, careful – like gifts – but he felt anything but generous when alone. He was beginning to wonder if this was what real love was like. If he hadn't actually gone and fallen in love on the way.

Beth sat waiting for Dan in the cinema lobby, ready to watch the screening that she didn't want to see. She knew it inside out; she knew what had been left out and how each talking head had been edited to say what fitted the director's point best. And besides, she'd pointed out, a film about bereavement was a bit close to the bone. Worst of all she was beginning to realise how much more time and dignity each voice had deserved. They had packaged the raw into something palatable. They had left out the woman who'd found survival so consuming she could hardly talk because it didn't make for good viewing. Since when was grief supposed to make good telly? she asked. It wasn't that this kind of television warped reality. More dangerously, it pre-empted it – it had made her, and would make others, think they understood the extremities of other people's experiences. That she would recognise tragedy if it came to her, like a fairytale bogeyman knock-knocking at the door in the dark and the rain. Now she knew that she knew nothing and she was filled with a rare sense of awe.

Somehow, this last month, Beth had been aware of the fading relevance of Jacob. Memories that had seemed powerful in their distance now seemed simply distant. The past, she thought, may be as easily misinterpreted as the clairvoyant's future. The heavy golden weight she'd placed on moments she'd spent with Jacob had been her decision. Not necessarily divine. She remembered going to Devon with Jacob for a weekend in the winter. They were driving fast, rushing on the A303 to the gin and tonics, double beds and freedom that they had promised themselves. The sun was setting and he was driving faster and faster on the straight road to the south west – through the eerie, high flatness of Salisbury Plain. 'First one to see it,' he'd said and then, when he was looking down to change a tape, she'd seen it first – Stonehenge, small in the yellow-red striated sky. She'd said, 'There, there,' and claimed her reward in a lay-by outside Dorchester.

And recently she'd begun to wonder whether it wasn't too much to demand of him, and even of Stonehenge, to expect that kind of memory to sustain her as long as ten years.

Dan was the person in her life right now; him, her father and, obviously, her mother. And, strangely, surrounded by three people who ought to be, would soon be or had always been distant, she felt more included and essential than ever before.

Dan sat, excited, on the tube. There was an advert opposite for athlete's foot cream, saying that if women were made from sugar and spice and all things nice then why did their feet smell so nasty in tights? He wondered if Beth was made from sugar. He thought not – soapstone, more like; cream-coloured, smooth and sculptable. Steve was made from mozzarella – white and a little squidgy. The French girl sitting opposite him was made of conkers and Beth's friend Sarah from corn. Greg, with his strange blond curls, was made from wood shavings, while his mother had something of a thin, straight tree about her. His father was a brown powder; a spice, maybe – cinnamon, perhaps. He was rather enjoying himself when he realised he was at Tottenham Court Road and just managed to slip out between the closing doors.

He ran down Wardour Street, jay-walking past the pub parties, and was only two minutes late when he arrived. He grasped Beth with one arm where she stood talking to Mike at the door. She was wearing flip-flops and a green dress, emerald green with a deep V at the front and sleeves that only reached her elbows. She smiled sideways at Dan. Mike watched them and thought that they looked like brother and sister; tousled children with dark hair and bright eyes. They made him feel just a little bit grubby, as if his clothes smelled of fried food. He stood well back as he opened the door for the two of them to go in.

An hour and a half later they sat in the pub drinking fast pints, talking about one of the female, spot-lit representatives of grief. One of the ones whose sadness had been accessible enough and dramatic enough to make the cut.

'I wasn't sure about the Led Zeppelin background music,' said Dan.

'It was that woman's hair,' said Mike, both hands round his pint glass. 'It haunted me, I haven't quite got over it. They wanted to drop that bit and I said to Jim, "No, really, her hair is important" – I'm sure it means something.'

Beth hit Mike on the arm. 'Don't. Stop it.'

'No, but you know, I worked it out. She hadn't changed her hairstyle since her husband had died, which was, well, you know, she said, ten years ago. She was stuck with the perm thing. No one to say, "For God's sake, change it".'

'That's sad,' said Dan.

'It's awful,' agreed Beth. 'They open up and we end up laughing at them. It was such a lazy programme. Lazy. Aren't you ashamed? I am.'

'I'm not laughing,' said Mike indignantly. 'Can you see me laughing? I'm closer to crying.'

'Where do they find the people, the interviewees from?' asked Dan.

'They put adverts in newspapers, leaflets in hospitals, community centres. It's the same as everything on telly. Researchers are desperately in need of real people,' said Mike.

'We had plenty of real people. And then we manufactured them, made them fake things, repeat things, stage things. And then some of the real people we rejected for being just a little too consumed.'

Mike shrugged and got up to go to the loo.

Beth turned to Dan. 'Get me out of here? Please? Now?'

Down in Colliers Wood, Lizzie was busy. She'd come home from the hospital without Roger, and as well as fetching things for him – a washbag, his walkman, some of that nice freshening cologne she'd found on offer at the chemist's – she needed to get to grips with a small pile of letters and bills which he'd been going to answer and pay tomorrow. It wasn't a good sign, him having to stay in. But she didn't have time today to settle on it and worry herself to shreds.

He'd said to her, in between pauses, his voice poor and cracked, 'Bring them in. We'll do it together.' But, Lizzie had decided on the bus on the way home, over her dead body would she force Roger to write out cheques in hospital. She had never, ever paid one single bloody bill or done one single piece of sorting out like that since she'd been married to Roger. And it was about time she started. She'd have to let Beth know her dad was back in, and she was due to go into town tomorrow to start selecting fabric for her classes which would begin in little over a month. But that too would have to wait now. And, truth be told, she was glad to be pushed, glad to be stretched. She couldn't do that desperate, stuck kind of mourning ever again. She didn't have it in her to go to the very bottom all over again. And as she'd climbed carefully down the steps on to the pavement, thanking the bus driver, she'd thought of Rose, Gavin's mother, with sympathy – a round bustling woman who'd met her son's death with a fine tea for the funeral.

Her own mother had had to do all the bill-paying when Lizzie was a child. Moira had remained a widow for the rest of her life. There weren't that many men to go round she would say bitterly later on. But she'd struggled with a job and a daughter by herself, and Lizzie hadn't really ever experienced that. There'd always been plenty for the basics and a holiday. In that way, at least, she was a lucky woman.

She found the bills in the drawer Roger had said and, looking for a pen, went into the drawer below. There, on top of a serpentine tangle of elastic bands, ribbons and string, was a letter addressed to Beth. Lizzie took it out and placed it on the kitchen surface and stood looking at it with her hands on her hips.

Ever since she'd come back from the adult education centre in such a wicked rage and Roger had forced her to unravel what was going on, they had been talking about telling Beth about Martin and Paul. It had become a bit of a theme with Roger, only intensified by his illness. And as she'd told him the other day, while she saw the sense in being able to speak to her daughter with a clarity of heart, she was still scared by the idea. Of what might be left behind once everything was stripped back to the truth. And yet here he was writing her letters. Which just made her feel all the more left out between the two of them. She'd always known that Beth preferred him, respected him, went to him. She took the white envelope out. She wouldn't read it but she would ask him what he was playing at. But then, dear God, he was an ill man. He was allowed a sentimentality or two.

'D'you not think you should eat a bit more?'

Who the bugger was she? thought Roger.

'Just the mashed potato maybe? Hummm?'

If he'd had the strength he would have taken the plate and smashed it in her face.

Nice, sentimental Roger's day was being soiled by fetid air and bad food. And pain. He'd been brought in to see the consultant that morning and he hadn't been allowed to go home afterwards. On account of not being able to stand up. I, he thought in language he would never have uttered out loud, have bloody well had enough. The hospital nurses who had struck him as gentle and professional before were now patronising and thick-waisted.

The combination of pain, for which he refused to request enough medication, and humiliation gave him a strength of feeling that he'd thought was beyond him. In a way it was like being properly alive. Not in between. He was reluctant to relinquish it. So he was almost sad to see his wife return with his bits and pieces, wearing a light summer blouse and a purposeful look.

She kissed him lightly on his dry and cracking forehead. Good of her he thought. He'd seen himself in the toilet mirror yesterday.

'All right?' she said brightly.

'Super,' he said and he raised his eyebrows so that she couldn't help but laugh, even though he looked awful.

'Is your tea that bad?' she said glibly, gesturing towards the untouched tray.

'No,' he said, his head on the pillows, eyes to the ceiling, 'it's the service I object to.'

He knew this was mean on Lizzie but he thought she'd probably cope. It was more interesting than remaining neutrally brave. Up until now he'd been inhibited by all the attention.

'Probably better than my cooking,' said Lizzie, peering under one of the battered tin-plate covers.

He turned his head sharply, as if the television at the end of the ward had exploded.

242

'Don't say that, don't you bloody dare. I love your cooking.' His eyes filled with tears, which surprised both of them. 'I love your food.'

She took his hand and stroked his bony knuckles with her thumb. 'I know,' she said, 'I know,' thinking, I'm sorry, I'm sorry, my sweet.

'I need to go home,' he said and his tears leaked down to the pillows.

20. Sticky City

They headed for the underground, holding hands as they wove through gaggles of tourists and gangs of boys and girls out on the lash. They crossed over Shaftesbury Avenue, cars bumper to bumper, a double-decker rumbling in the jam. The claggy West End summer air absorbed the brightness from the car lights and neon signs and carried blackness to the redbrick theatres and restaurants so that there was no clarity to the city and as far as they could see, left and right, there was just an orange fug. The faces in the street blurred with the ducking speed of their walk, the women's make-up smudged and their eyes sleepy. They moved so fast through the sticky kitchen of Chinatown that they reached the escalator breathless. Dan stood on the step below her and facing Beth said, 'You look absolutely beautiful.' Raw in the electric lighting he could see her pores, the slip of mascara under her eyes, the red ruck of her lips, and he kissed her slowly, their mouths a bridge between their bodies, riding downwards in parallel. The architecture of desire.

They stood on the tube opposite the opening and shutting doors, wedged into a corner, so close they could feel each other's breath. He enclosed her from the rest of the home-goers while her flesh pressed against the smeared glass divide. 'I sat in the dark,' he said, 'and all I could think about was how close I was to you. I paid no attention to the film – d'you mind? I just

followed your breathing, the way your stomach rose and fell,'
and he put his hand to her and her fast breathtakes. They kissed,
their spit spreading, their damp, malleable, chewable faces
pressed to each other. Her textures – soft skin, hard teeth,
seaweed strands of hair – and his – skin scratch, bone edge and
wet, loose mouth.

They got off at London Bridge and weaved through traffic,
never letting go, into the small quiet streets she remembered
from before, where cobbled roads empty of cars made sharp
echoing sounds and lights winked in high converted warehouse
windows. They wound round dark corners until they were at
his doorway and they could stop and think – now we can begin.
And getting ahead of themselves her dress slid down over her
right shoulder and his hand slid to feel and press her breasts.
She pulled him into her so she could feel what it would be like
and undid his flies so that both of them stood grappling through
holes in their clothing. It suddenly struck them that if they just
opened the door and went upstairs they could undress each
other, not very slowly, and see how her breast joined to her
shoulder and her bum slid curving into the flesh of her thigh.
See how her neck became her breast plate, her ribs, her belly,
travelling to a mat of dark hair. And inside she could see, when
she'd unbuttoned his shirt, that his bones were close to his skin
and that his arms were tightly wrapped and that he had freckles
that gathered on his neck and then spread down to his back and
his stomach. And that his hands were rough and had the same
reptile scale as his elbows, his knees, and that the insides of
his thighs were unaccountably soft and unprotected by hair or
freckles.

They stood in the half-light of his bedroom, laying their hands,
following silhouettes. An image of Roger, prone on his bed, her
mother at his side, engaged in his disintegration, came into Beth's
head and she thought, perhaps for the first time, that her parents

245

too had once touched and tugged at each other with lust and intensity. 'I love this curve the best,' Dan said, bringing her back, following her waist, and she said, 'I love this line,' using one finger to travel from above his hip down to his groin. 'I'd like to be buried there,' she said and knelt down to press her face to the warmth and smell of him. She moved lower and he could see her from above, her dark head in his crotch, her viola back, her arse pointing to the window. She drew her head back and placed her lips around him. He was shocked at the heat of her mouth and at this view of she whom he'd spent so long not seeing, at her sudden freedom, at the insistent pull of her mouth. Above her he thought, this could end all too soon and so he took hold of her head, not entirely gently, pulled her back, took her by the arm and pushed her face down on to the bed. He brushed her hair off her back. There was so much of it – everywhere he went it invaded, trailing over her when all he wanted was to hold her moonshaped face below his and watch the edge of desire, impatience and fear in her eyes. He began to kiss each square inch of her. From the wing-like blades of her shoulders, round the forgotten sides of her – where her body was bound, usually hidden by her arms, soft like flesh beneath a shell – down the hair-trail dividing her buttocks. And when he was there, wanting to keep this as slow as he could, not wanting to ever be satiated by her, he raised her up with his left arm and with his right hand he felt for her.

He loved the fact that she was sliding wet by the time he got there, that he could feel her throb, feel her feet wriggle, watch her head bend inwards to catch a gasp. And for a while this pleasure of hers gave him a base joy, but then suddenly it wasn't nearly enough and he rolled her over so that he could see her face contort, her jaw jut forwards as he pushed into her, so hard that she thought she could quite possibly split beneath him and then he and she would have what they wanted, what everything had led them to believe they could have, mesh becoming merge.

Afterwards they lay on their backs, each with a hand collapsed on the other, on a chest, on a leg. His head turned towards her, mouth open, breathing, watching her watch the ceiling. He saw her blink, slow and languorous, cast in the moon's tomb light. If moments were ever longer, if they ever hung reluctant to leave, here was one. She was again her, linked to him only by an upturned hand. He had no idea if or what she thought. Come, come down and then please come back. Still, they were two within one bed, one room. Now they had something to share. From here on they could be anywhere and look at each other and, even involuntarily, feel the insistence of each other's body.

She suddenly breathed in sharply and turned her head to look at him. One might have thought they'd been paralysed. She had a strange, uncertain smile on her lips.

'Hello,' she said.

'Hello you,' he said.

There was a pause, 'Well, that's done it,' she said.

He raised himself out of effigy mode on to one elbow and kissed her again to silence her.

They slept on their sides facing each other, faces a millimetre apart, tired enough, serious enough not to find the body patterns of one another a problem – the flinches and farts and feet twitches.

Beth slipped into this sleep as if pressing pause, as if giving herself a present, as if there was no further point in being awake. As if it were too late now. Too late to go anywhere or track anything. Too late even for the nocturnal hunt of thought-beasts. Dan woke briefly at six, remembered the person pressed against him and thought that Beth in his bed was probably the strangest wonder of all.

At nine, after three hours of incoherent, greyhound dreams, he got up to make tea. When he came back to bed he found her lying on her front, arm hanging down the side of the bed, her back bare, the sheet twisted and tangled between her legs. Her arm hung perpendicular, heavy, hand trailing on the floor, the lines of her breaking clear from sleep's upholstery. 'I tried to get up,' she said into the pillow, half asleep, and he sat on the floor with his mugs of tea and took her hand and put his lips to the puffy creases of her cupped palm. She said it was like being woken by a dog, snout wet into your hand, and he said thanks very much *and* I made you tea, so she said thank you politely and they drank it propped up against his wall like a cartoon couple.

Beth was extraordinarily relaxed, still in a stupor of sex and sleep. She could feasibly spend all day in this light-filled room, eating, making love, looking at his paintings. She felt as if she'd been rewarded for resisting Dan so long, for being alone for so long. She felt an interesting combination of good and, still nakedly entwined with the sheet, smutty. It was a novel feeling and not without potential.

Dan squeezed her shoulder, a lazy gesture. He had her just where he had wanted her but now he recognised the familiar, inevitable tension in his gut. He wanted to spend the rest of the day with her; in fact, if put on the spot he might have declared that he wanted to spend the rest of his life with her. It was just that right now he'd rather be in bed alone. He didn't mind the to-ing and fro-ing, the negotiations − it was the potential for happiness that scared him. He had a pins-and-needles tension as if the building was being surrounded while he lay a-bed.

And there was something else − his father was due at 9.30 and it was imperative that she wasn't there to watch him lumber into the room, throw down his old satchel and get out a cheque book. If he'd had a separate bedroom he could have hidden her − but he didn't.

248

'Beth.'

'Ummm.' She smiled at him with anticipation.

'I expect you've got to get up now.'

She turned sharply to look at him. He didn't sound reluctant; it was a suggestion not a question. She felt a sharp plummet of disappointment. Fool she thought. Stupid of me she thought, livid and stony-faced as she clambered off the bed, stepping, sturdy-legged, giant-like, over Dan whose face was registering an ouch. She'd either trodden in his crotch or he'd remembered his manners. I must stop expecting things she thought. Things like love out of intimacy or honesty in bed. Stupid of me to think this was already something rather than part of the same hiding and seeking process it always was.

'Beth,' he said, stumbling, hopping into a pair of pants. 'I don't mean this minute, I just mean . . .'

'What?' she said wearily and then quickly, like asking for more was a mistake, 'Oh whatever, I have to get going anyway.'

'I just need to go to work.'

She stopped and looked at him. 'You work in a fucking bar. It's 9 a.m.'

'Deliveries,' he said, irritated by the assumption that he was lying, which he was.

She was collecting her clothes, putting herself back into them.

'What are you doing tonight?'

'I don't know.' She did up her bra. The reclothing so sadly functional. Dan picked the green dress from the floor and handed it to her but then didn't let go. 'I don't mean to throw you out.'

'Worse,' she said, removing his hand from the dress. 'You're making it worse.'

She turned away from him, groping for the zip at the back. He didn't remember it having a zip and he stepped in and did it up for her and then kissed the back of her cross neck. 'I'll call later,' he said and she simply stood still. She'd seen the large picture on the left wall facing the windows. Turning her head away from his kiss she'd caught sight of a face, a brown eye, a mouth. She walked slowly across the room, bare feet giving a soft flat slap.

Innocence was a painting of her as a child in a striped T-shirt. Done from memories of their holiday in Swanage. There was a huge expanse of grey mulching sea, rolls of grey waves like seal fat, and a girl, her, facing the horizon, just her head turned to the left to watch her chronicler. The wary surprise of youth was in her eyes, the unpredictability of a child's reaction, the moment's edge at the end of the land.

From afar she looked cartoonish and smooth, complete and alluringly caught in the surprise of her name called and the gaze behind her. As if the watcher had got a lucky break, a moment of attention before she turned back to the distance. She was much much larger than life and up close she became almost scary, a face with all its pores.

Beth positioned herself far back against the window and saw herself surprised, almost laughing, young enough to try and see the future at the end of the sea, young enough to flick-flack across a beach from one moment to another. I had it all along she thought. The freedom. All that following and searching, looking for sensation, for vividness, and she had it right there in her. Look at me. At that live strip of a creature. I had it all along.

'That's me. Years ago. I recognise the T-shirt,' she told him.

'Yes,' he said. 'D'you mind?'

'Not exactly. It's surprising.' She didn't look at him. 'It's like being out of your own body.' She looked at her eyes. 'Some cultures think it's stealing your soul.' If she hadn't felt so old she would have felt like Alice in Wonderland, strange truths and shapes lurking round corners. 'You're very . . .' She was going to say exhausting but she didn't mean that; it sounded as though she were bored by him. 'Demanding,' she said instead.

250

'I wanted a bit for myself, yes.' He was interested by her frozen reaction. This was an anti-portrait, taking a person without their permission in a moment they had left behind. It was both more and less real. He had made her, manhandled her, to suit his purposes. Love was not a gentle thing. He had become confrontational rather than canny.

Yet he watched Beth looking at herself as a child and thought that she looked less knowing now with her shadowed eyes and thin wrists than as a little girl, and suddenly wondered why he'd ever thought he'd portrayed innocence. It was a moment in a child's life. Surely that was description enough.

Right then he had no idea what she was thinking – he had led her to his present – would leave her to think – the fact that it was there and that she was looking at a relationship in itself – a bridge, like a gift or some carefully chosen words.

Beth felt suddenly spaced; picked up and displaced from all of it. She was very small in front of herself and she felt chafed and exposed by the frictions and caresses of last night. She felt as though her skin might be thinner, as if she had given away, even helped him shed, layers of her. And the reclothing had never come. How many layers were there to give away?

There on a chair was her bag, a collection of her things, little totems of identity – keys to her own door and the perfume she had decided she liked. She picked it up and left the room, saying that she, too, had to go to work.

On her journey to the tube station Beth saw a pigeon beaking through a patch of vomit. She stopped at the flower stall by the tube station and, blown by the stale air of the churning underground, bought a bunch of white camellias.

She sat holding them on the tube like an inappropriate bridesmaid. They had struck her as the most beautiful as she'd stood in front of the static kaleidoscope of the flower stall. So she'd bought them and for a few days the beauty would belong to her. People watched her on the tube; a woman looking for revelation in flowers. Somewhere in their neat technology, colour-drip shapes and tidy organs lay a lesson she thought. Something not man-made, something given.

Jacob rounded the corner into Dan's street and hoisted his leather bag from one shoulder to the other. He was on his way to a meeting with his accountant but first he was going to give his son some money. It was the first time he'd ever helped Dan financially and he didn't mind the feeling. He hadn't even begun to wonder whether his son did. With Laura had come structure and propriety and he felt a new potential for patriarchy. Next week he and Laura were going on holiday to the north-west coast of the States. They were going to start in Seattle and drive up into Canada. He wasn't expecting much from Canada except perhaps bears and motels. But it would be fun; Laura was good company in a car. She knew when to play a game and when to shut up.

Jacob knew he would never be unfaithful again. He wasn't different or wiser, he just knew himself and the repercussions better. And these days he got more of a kick from self-content than anything a one-night stand could offer. Also the opportunities were fewer, which did make him ache slightly – like a mild groin strain.

So as he climbed Dan's steps he felt pretty chipper, prepared to be sensitively generous, but Dan greeted him at the door without enthusiasm. Jacob suddenly wondered if he should have put the cheque in the post. He hadn't considered that. It was something he'd wanted to do in front of himself. Dan went into the kitchen and put the kettle on, and poured two steaming cups of tea down the sink. Jacob noticed how recently his son had had company and got his chequebook out. 'Right then,' he said and wrote his surname twice on the same slither of promised cash.

'Are the public going to get to see these ones then?' Jacob asked, suddenly avuncular, putting the lid back on his fountain pen. 'Can I have a preview?'

Fuck him thought Dan. He can't even do this without making a song and dance of it. He'd told his father he could put the cheque in the post last week. Equally Dan could have put him off last night before going to meet Beth. But, Dan had figured at the time, some things were unavoidable. Certain truths will always out.

With that in mind he pointed his father towards the two new paintings, hanging at right angles to each other on the left and far wall. Jacob walked into the main room towards 'Man-made' and saw people-type shapes through a window. He said nothing, best not to when his son was in this kind of mood. He could have looked for much longer, would have been happy to do so, but, wary of what he would be expected to discover, he turned to the second painting. The sea and then a girl, young probably but rid of purity by the art needed to create her, by the millions of brushmarks required to make her. A girl with brown eyes and dark hair standing looking at the sea, suddenly turning round to look at her portraitist. He would have liked to get a handle on it, been able to stand right back, one hundred feet away not fifty. It was kind of scary, looming. She was wearing a striped top and looked raw, unadorned, windswept. Something about a girl in the wind . . . It was Beth.

'It's Beth.' He looked at his son.

'Yes,' said Dan.

'Now?'

'No, much younger.' Jacob swallowed and nodded. He wasn't quite sure what was going on here. He knew they'd seen each other because Beth had said so. Why was he painting pictures of her?

'Are you . . . seeing much of each other?' There was a strange silence, and Dan's voice, when it came, was quiet.

'She just left.'

'She just left? What, now?'

'Yes,' said Dan, still and slow as if restraining himself from laughing at a stupid pupil.

Jacob said nothing. He just looked ahead into the mussed grey and the child's white face. His son said nothing. There was something happening here. Jacob was aware he was being challenged. But why would Dan be challenging him with her? Unless his son knew about Beth.

'Dan.' He turned to face him. 'I never told you this. I don't know how much you—'

'I know,' said Dan, interrupting. 'I've always known.'

And on his face Jacob thought he saw the end, or the beginning, of a slight smile.

21. Window-Cinema

December, 1991

Beth was in her third year at university when Jacob left her for his third wife. It was meant to have been the other way around. It made no sense within her landscape. The world became as surreal as one of those naff Dali posters that her male friends had on their college bedroom walls. Something must have happened, she reasoned, something had changed; she must have done something wrong, been too much or not enough. He had left her and clearly she was the root of the problem.

But if she was to have perched on a stranger's windowsill and watched the residents' stories unfold, with all the colourful silence of a Brueghel painting, she would have had no more control over those characters than the ones in her own life. A man in a red hat can carry multiple intentions.

Certain artists paint to discover the secrets of their own pictures. You'd have thought they'd have known in advance the machinations of their own created world but it's hard to divine true motives when we so rarely admit our own. More than anything adults want to trace some fairytale trail of crumbs to the source of their own hurts. And it takes effort to get off our own path on to another's. That's why creation, like kindness, is so hard.

Ages and ages of reason and we still think we're going to be enlightened by truth. But the physical truth of A's involvement with B gives no answer to 'Why?' One thing's for sure, you're not going to find the answer in letters of the alphabet. If they won't even reveal their identities how are they going to teach you anything?

It didn't occur to Beth that she had hardly even featured in Jacob's decision to leave her. That he now saw her as a symptom of his chaotic life, not the purpose. How could it? All she'd ever known was the anticipated hours, the bubble nights; the absolute inhabitation of being in love with someone who wasn't there. How could it possibly have occurred to her that while he had taken over her mind – so that nothing entered her head without being refracted through his existence – she had become just another duty to him.

Jacob hadn't had an aim in mind when he'd taken Beth in the Palace Hotel more than two years earlier. She'd caught his dissatisfaction and desire and like a silent marathon partner had quickly matched his longing with her own. What kind of love affair would it have been if they couldn't have sustained each other over those long distances? To make it work they'd needed to be full to the brim with infatuation, slopping longingly into each other so that they never fell below the watermark. Beth had watched out for their love as if she would have no other life but this one, no other future but a balding, tricky one. Any mud belch of boredom or deflation and she would panic and reclaim him with a heart-rending kiss when all he'd wanted was a cup of tea. She'd worked hard to turn it into the perfectly painful love affair. After all, why have an imperfect hurt?

It was her twenty-second Christmas. She was lying on her side on the floor of her parents' lounge, between the gas fire and the Christmas tree. A fallen fairy. Her black jeans and purple top shattered and reflected in a hundred little silver baubles. She was crying in a snotty, exhausted way. Jacob had left her. He

256

had found her heart, crystallised it and then broken it and she could think of nothing to do or say or be that would ever make it any better. And the simple thought of feeling like this for all unending time was a curse in itself. Stuck in the pit where the unhappy all go but taking no solace, only competitive displeasure at the company. Nevertheless, Beth still found a second to wonder why on earth her mother insisted on buying those vulgar tins of Quality Street when no one ate them any more. Bugger it she thought and, beyond caring but clearly not beyond salvage, she sat up, wiped her nose on her sleeve and began to eat her way through the tin.

Jacob drove away fast after dropping Beth off in Colliers Wood. The streets were empty apart from roving maroon mini-cabs. Everyone was at home defrosting turkeys. A faint mizzle fell on the windscreen, not enough to occupy the windscreen wipers, not dry or cold enough to feel like Christmas. He'd never liked Christmas, not since he was a child and his self-made world had been forced to close down for the holiday season when it was him and his mum left alone in the small house, making the best of an unsatisfactory situation. A post-war Christmas dinner for two was pretty meagre. He looked back at his childhood, every man's mythic period, through his own mizzle; sweet, grainy nostalgia for the streets, his innocence, his bravado and the ferocity of his mother's love. Yet even he couldn't keep away the blues that encroached as the nights ate into the day and December grew older. He'd always liked feeling different but that didn't mean he liked feeling alone. Depleted. Christmas made him feel depleted.

There had been a period, when the boys were young and his last infidelity had been far enough away to feel like the past, when he and Rachel would have sex in the fuzzy morning, then go down and find their children scavenging at the base of their

257

fir tree. And he had been able to still feel his wife's body on his, had been able to look at her in her new jumper and recall the curve of her thigh. He had stood in the doorway looking at the sweet creatures he had created from selfish lust. His and Rachel's intimacy now concentrated by the fact that they had easily woken children. (Jacob remembered from his own childhood that sex sounded disturbing, more like a boxing match than love.) Anyway, those mornings when he'd come down from the bed to happy children – that was a time when he'd felt replete.

Right now, he was supposed to be going straight to Jane's sister's house in Surrey for Christmas. She was waiting for him. They were waiting for him. He had presents in the back of the car. A juicer for Jane. Brandy for his brother-in-law, assorted crap for their kids. He'd had Beth's present in the back when he'd set off from their house in Ealing that afternoon. He'd used the same paper for everyone. The same for his girlfriend as his wife, which had seemed a bit obscene. It was quite nice paper – he'd chosen it with care. But he'd forgotten to buy more than three rolls in the same pattern. Beth's present was just another on the (mental) list.

What had happened? He'd dropped her back home, weeping, silent, and he'd looked at her and for the first time thought you are so young. So, so young. Younger than one of my sons. How could I have done this? How could I have let it come to this? All she'd ever done was follow his lead and love him.

Instead of turning left for the A3 and Surrey he turned right, northwards. From West to South to North, Jane to Beth to Rachel, all in one day. Leaving a quietly destructive wake behind him, like a slug's silvery trail. He need not be alone on a motorway on Christmas Eve, it was just something he was doing. It came naturally. Everything was so fucked by this stage, he thought, that another odd turning could be no worse than the last.

The shops he passed were the same shape as those of his childhood, but they were full of different things, new things, toys he would never have dreamed of as a child. They all paid homage to the season nonetheless, ruffles and fake snow and papier-mâché Father Christmases. In two days, when no one was looking, they would all be out of date.

What's happened? she'd kept asking. Why? Why? He didn't know, or at least he knew how he knew but he couldn't tell her that. Which was another symptom – she to whom he had once confessed everything now needed to be hidden from.

He knew he'd given up on her as the answer because he'd slept with someone else.

He'd a wife, a girlfriend and a one-night stand. And he wanted to do it again. Except Laura wouldn't because she was sensible, because she thought he was too much. Because she didn't like him for having all that, doing all three of them in the space of a week. And who could blame her? He couldn't.

Jesus Christ he thought, driving fast through London, what had happened? I have to sort this out. I have to start again.

He stopped at a service station on the M1. Turned the engine off and put his head in his hands. He'd driven so many miles in this car, always on his way to someone or something. Who had driven that many miles for him? Who had pounded tarmac in pursuit of him? He'd never sat still long enough to see. He wasn't about to now. What if no one came, if no one had noticed? Suddenly the fact that no one in the world knew where he was made him feel very scared. And it had always made him feel so liberated. He reached in his pocket for money for the pay phone.

Beth sat below the tree, her legs burning from the heat of the gas fire, and wondered what on earth she was supposed to do now. She would never see him again; he had said it would be better, that she was better off without him, that she had her whole

259

life ahead of her, that she deserved someone who could be with her all the time. Why can you not be with me? she'd said. Don't you love me enough? And he'd left it too long before saying it wasn't that simple. So she couldn't begin to believe in the complexities more than the straight fact that he couldn't have loved her enough. And Beth, surrounded by sweet wrappers, thought with considerable prescience that there was no way of getting over this one except time. She began to cry again with the failure of herself, that she could have been so not enough. And once not enough, how ever more?

Upstairs Lizzie could hear a small splutter and thought at first that it was the central heating. But as it continued she listened harder and could tell it was a human sound. Her daughter, weeping with quiet sobs like small upward steps. Lizzie never went to sleep before Beth got back. She never let Beth know she was lying awake – it was just her being a worry-bag. She wondered whether she should get up but the problem was she had a suspicion Beth was lying to her. She'd been out with Julie that night apparently. But there was no earthly reason for Beth to sit in Julie's father's car, or a mini-cab, talking for fifteen minutes. She would have thought it was one of her friends, some of whom had cars, except that this was far too grown-up a car for any of them. Of course, there was no reason at twenty-one why Beth should have to tell them what she was up to. She was in another city most of the year. At her age Lizzie had been married with a child. And lies, as Lizzie well knew, were usually about love. Beth would surely rather talk to anyone than her mother about that.

Jacob drove deeper and deeper into the countryside. It was thick black here at night. He thought he might be scared living here and wondered whether Rachel had ever been frightened. Surely she must have wondered what she'd done, coming mid-way through life to a strange village in a strange place? She'd trundled off into the wilds for herself and no one else. How extraordinary, he thought, and for the first time was impressed by the braveness of it. She'd had so little money, just the five hundred pounds a month he paid her. He'd been paying her the same for ten years and had seen it as a generous standing gift rather than an ongoing discussion, because she was the one who had left. He hadn't left. But then he hadn't been there much either. Ten years ago she'd left. Ten whole bloody years and look how far he hadn't come. God, he felt sorry for himself. He couldn't even bear to try and think how Beth felt. There was only one thought that he could bear and it was true, it really was; she was better off without him. He didn't even remember to think how Jane might feel. He was so used to the sense of being a disappointment to her. By now he simply presumed that knowledge of his behaviour would reach her through the ether.

Rachel, Dan and Greg were sitting drinking wine and beer in the kitchen when Jacob arrived unannounced. Greg was telling his mother and brother about the year he stole all his Christmas presents and Rachel was laughing loudly and freely because they were old enough now for it not to matter. Dan had come back from art college in Nottingham for the week but Dave was travelling through some hot, spicy and dope-laden city right now. She couldn't quite remember whether it was Jakarta or Yogyakarta this week. He had remembered to phone last night so for a few days she would be pleased to know he was still alive. Although, she reasoned, he could quite possibly have been murdered two seconds after he put down the phone. Still, she had two of them here. Large, mannish boys, giggling about the time Greg had given stolen breath freshener to his mother.

It was one o'clock in the morning and it was raining heavily outside. Rachel had just put more logs into the small fireplace and reached for one of the Christmas bottles that she had received from her chiropody patients. She'd qualified a year ago and treated her patients with unembarrassed, gentle humour. She'd been given a bottle of Baileys in return for bunion ease. Greg wrinkled his nose when she said this; he wasn't wild about the smooth phlegm texture of Baileys, particularly not when it was mixed with the image of a bunion in his head. He had just put his glass down when there was a knock on the door and they all stopped mid-clamour and looked at each other, a parody of Christmas Eve surprise.

Rachel rose and, mother to her overgrown children still, went to wrestle with the damp wooden door to see what had landed on her doorstep on this miserable night. She wrenched it open and could see nothing at first, just darkness and the glint of the falling rain lit by the lamp in the porch. Then something moved beyond, in the mud, and stepped into the light. Jacob. Jacket undone, hair flat wet to his head, not huddling from the rain but just taking the soaking as his due. He looked hopeless.

'Hello,' she said, thinking, of course, it would be him. 'You'd better come in.'

Dan saw who it was and like some corny flashback remembered years of Jacob's returns, late at night, a key in the door, always a surprise.

'Dad,' he said, 'you're soaking. I'll get you a towel.'

Greg said, 'Bloody hell, what are you doing here?'

Jacob saw them sitting around the table in a gentle light, faces relaxed with recent laughter, happy to be in one place, not waiting, not leaving, just sitting still in a place in which they belonged, and thought maybe, for once, he'd done the right thing.

Jacob took the rough towel and rubbed his head slowly as if he'd just swum the channel. What with the dog-droplets falling on the stone floor, no one realised his eyes were wet with tears.

'I thought I'd come and see you,' he said, and sat down and took a hefty gulp from Greg's abandoned glass.

In the end some old sense of routine had kicked in and Dan and Greg had trundled up the stairs to bed, aged eighteen and twenty-one, looking forward to a lie-in more than a Christmas stocking. They left their divorced parents sitting opposite each other at the kitchen table.

'Weird,' Greg said to Dan by way of a goodnight at the top of the stairs, and then, lightly, 'I haven't even got him a present yet.'

'He might not be here in the morning,' said Dan, shutting the bathroom door in his brother's face.

They looked at each other across the table, Jacob holding her gaze until he couldn't any longer. His eyes flickered down to the ridges between the wood, to the brown gunk of a million hot dinners that now held the table together.

'Why aren't you with Jane?' asked Rachel.

'Aren't you bored by me?' he asked. 'D'you really want to know? I don't. I'm bored by me. Dreariest man in the world.' He gave a tight, bitter smile.

'You can't just turn up in the early hours of Christmas Day and not expect me to ask what's wrong.'

'No, I suppose not,' he said glumly. 'Could we just not, though? Just go to sleep and wake up and pretend this is all very average. That there's nothing to discuss. I'm a bit tired, Rachel.'

'Oh good God, Jacob . . . why must you always mope around as if you're a victim?'

He was quiet for a minute and then, eyes down to the table, shoulders hunched, he said, 'You think I'm ridiculous, don't you? You always did.'

'No. I think there's something wilful about your unhappiness. Which is different.'

He shrugged. He always did this thought Rachel; invite care and love, make you chew over him and his personality, then turn on you for having an opinion. She knew what was going on though. She could recognise his mood.

'Are you seeing someone else?' She was harsher now.

He nodded. And Rachel shook her head angrily.

'Jacob, you *can't* carry on doing this. Look how much damage you'll do. If Jane and you break up that's another thing you take away from the boys.'

'I'm not sure they ever liked her that much.'

'That's not the point.'

'I don't know, I don't know anything . . . I'm sorry, I didn't come here to make you sort me out.'

'No?'

'I was so in love with her, Rachel, and I've hurt her so much. And I can't bear it. It's a mess. It's all a fucking awful mess and then I . . .' There was silence. 'And then I come back here. I can't even leave the past alone.'

'As long as the boys are here you're welcome. You know that.'

'And then?'

'I can't solve you, Jacob. You didn't want me. It was ten years ago.'

'I think I made the most awful mistake though.'

He looked at her again. Her hair was still long and dark. Her face had settled in on itself a little, creased into itself in places, lost flesh. They were the same beautiful bones beneath.

'You know what I miss? I miss making love to you and then being with our children. I miss that . . . the sweet carnality of us, us being a secret unit inside a family.'

Rachel got up and began clearing glasses. 'Don't.' She moved quietly around, putting things in the sink. 'You can sleep in Dave's room.' Jacob put his head in his hands.

'I'm sorry. I didn't want to barge in on your Christmas.' Rachel looked at him sitting there, small and damp, and felt frustration and the same old desire to bring him back to life. He was always putting himself beyond peace so that whoever he had charmed had to save him.

'You did want to barge in on our Christmas. Because we were the only ones not waiting for you. You thought you might find comfort but I know you – you didn't like the thought of us not wanting you. It's all right, Jacob, it's natural but, and I know it's dull, I think you have to start thinking of what you're doing to people.'

Dan, at the top of the stairs, caught the last sentence and, giving in to the distasteful appeal of adult truths, sat down and listened. The stairs were narrow and uncomfortable. He was probably too old to be doing this, eavesdropping through the banisters. He reckoned his mother would have probably said exactly the same to Jacob if he'd been in the room but Dan, while wanting to know all that happened, didn't actually want to witness it. Didn't want people to know he knew everything. His ontology was listen and learn and keep it to that.

Jacob listened to familiar words with an unfamiliar submission. He thought of Beth who had told him softly that he'd ruined it for her. What? he'd asked. Life, she'd said. Oh Beth, he'd said, glad to be able to retreat to patronage, you're so young, you have no idea. And she'd said no, not that, you've spoiled the rest because this was so lovely. How can I ever come back from that? And he hadn't known what to say. He who had always had so many words to plunder. She had been generous with love even in abandonment.

Rachel saw Jacob was making no movement other than playing with the same clump of hair, head low, elbow on the table. So she sat down again wearily. She fought internally between handling this well, helping the man, solving his problems, neatly reasserting her uniqueness in his life, and finally telling him that he was a reckless child of a man, not a bad man but one who might as well be. Actually, no; between telling him to learn to love himself and telling him he was a cunt. Because he was and somehow he'd managed to avoid hearing it.

'Was it serious, the affair?' she hedged.

'Over two years.'

'That doesn't quite answer the question.'

'Yes,' he said suddenly, unreasonably irritated. 'It was serious. But she was only eighteen when we met so there were always certain . . . certain inevitables.'

'Eighteen,' she hissed. 'Eighteen.' Again. 'Jesus, Jacob, that's younger than one of your own children.'

He looked at her hard and simply said, 'I know.'

There was a long silence. Dan, upstairs, thought that even he found eighteen-year-old girls a bit young. He was glad he didn't have a sister; it would have led to all sorts of strange analogies. A little bit of him was not unimpressed. The rest of him was disgusted, although he didn't really factor Jane into his thinking. Neither he nor his brothers ever did – as soon as it had become clear that she wasn't going to excel in the stepmother role instantly Jane had kept a very low, unengaged profile, away or busy over their weekend visits, never again at his side on the drive to Oswestry.

'Twenty-four months less and you could have been arrested.' She'd been doing the maths.

'I always wondered what it would take to shock you.'

'Oh, so *that's* a good aim in life.' She was almost enjoying this – years of calm, honest introspection had prepared her well. There was no doubt about it, she had the upper hand. The atmosphere was energised from a dull counselling session to something much more dangerous.

'Where did you meet her?'

Jacob felt cornered, defensiveness and pride boxing him in.

'You know her,' he said shortly. 'Beth, Beth Standing. They lived opposite us in Delia Street.'

'Ja*cob*,' said Rachel. She almost laughed. But then she remembered Beth as a little girl with Wellingtons and a sweet, solemn face.

At the top of the stairs Dan's eyes widened. Beth was his. His companion in his flashbacks to a London childhood.

In the kitchen Rachel decided for the second time in her life that she didn't want to spend her time feeding her ex-husband and got up from the table saying, 'I'm glad you came. I think you should sleep and then maybe do some thinking tomorrow.' She went to the slightly open door at the bottom of the stairs and added, 'Has it occurred to you that maybe you should just be by yourself for a while?'

Jacob reached for some extra smooth cream liqueur and pretended he could hear his family breathing.

22. Threes

It was quiet in the ward and Lizzie sat very still. She'd gone to a service in the chapel that morning, looking for some comfort somewhere, and a hymn was now running loud through her head. Louder and louder. 'LORD of all hopefulness, LORD of all joy, Whose TRUST, ever child-like . . .' Roger looked so ill it was extraordinary that he was alive. His skin was blotched and mottled from blue-white to purple. Gummy eyes and lips with a tide-line of scum. All his elements were out of kilter. There were drugs and drips and tubes, coming in, going out. It made her regard her own quietly functioning body with awe, seeing his so pushed to the limits.

He looked awful. It was a relief to admit it to herself. After six weeks of coping, of little sleep, of trying to relieve estimated discomforts, Lizzie felt as light-headed and exhausted as a new mother. But he was still her husband. And in his dilapidated state she felt so fiercely protective of him that it hurt not to be able to keep his appearance up, at least make him look fresh. But every time she left him the disintegration resurfaced.

She blew her nose with a clean white handkerchief, aware that she was a picture of tragedy – a weeping woman by a dying man's bed. But that wasn't really the point, was it, she thought, blowing her nose again angrily. This was Roger, her Roger. Her gentle husband.

She had been trying to explain it when she'd talked to the nurse last night. Sister George had said that he had a lovely face. She'd said that she expected Roger loved her very much. I bet you say that to all the near-widows Lizzie had said with a flash of nasty humour, and Sister George had raised her eyebrows. But no, Lizzie had continued, sitting down rather hard as she noticed a new drip being inserted, he *is* a lovely man. He's a quiet man who brings a bit of . . . And she'd not known how to say it to a professional woman like this sister . . . he brings a bit of magic. And he was good to me, she'd added.

Still holding the handkerchief to her nostrils, Lizzie leaned forward and said in a muffled way, 'You're my Roger and you are a good, good man.' Then she thought bugger it, and took away the handkerchief and said loud and clear to her drugged husband, 'You're a good, good man.' And she patted his hand, the one without the drips, and felt very slightly better. As if something was salvageable. As if the terrible sadness of his body was a temporary thing.

Because, although it was hard to feel positive about your husband dying, sometimes, after a cup of tea and a sugar boost from a packet of three bourbons, you could give it a go. If you kept away from the trigger points. The bad moments – his silent longing for another child; the hurt in his eyes when she screamed rough words at him; his embarrassed distaste for retirement. And then of course the good moments – his pleasure in Beth as a baby, the way he'd sat in the corner of the sofa with Beth resting from his hand to his elbow; his pure love of her, Lizzie's, own slight body; his pleasure in a good piece of music and his habit of conducting badly; his tendency to rush the crossword and his surprise at getting it wrong daily . . . If you avoided both the good and bad it was possible to think that he'd had a good life, that he wasn't in any pain, that this was better than spending five years dying, that . . .

The problem with death, thought Lizzie, was that there just weren't the words for it.

Beth had been coming twice a day for the five days Roger'd been in hospital. Sometimes she cried and sometimes she didn't. Lizzie had noticed the way she rocked herself slightly from side to side and she'd heard her say, 'You're my dad, my dad,' claiming him in the same way Lizzie did when Beth wasn't there. Which was fine, thought Lizzie, which was just as it should be. Beth had put on weight while managing to look more drawn each day. Actually, thought Lizzie, she simply looked unwell. But it wasn't surprising, this was her father. It was Beth's first loss and Lizzie hoped it was her hardest. She felt desperately for her daughter but it was like watching a tree from far away; you could see the tremors but you couldn't touch them.

Except that she couldn't rely on Roger to bridge that gap any more. It was harder even than that. Roger, Lizzie knew, was relying on her to bridge it before he died. So that he could at least think of them supporting each other when he'd gone. And Lizzie would have been lying if she'd denied that she didn't find his a rather simplistic, male approach towards people and personalities. But she also recognised that she and Beth needed to try and get along and that she, as the mother, should make the first step. Lizzie knew that the letter sat in the string drawer at home, like some clue in a treasure hunt, was for her in case she was unable to do it without him.

23. The Kiss

'Raymond Chandler said it. "Don't get complicated, because when you get complicated you get sad, and when you get sad your luck goes,"' quoted Martha Frock. She was a gallery owner and dealer and she had called Dan and asked to come round and view his work, having seen one of his paintings in an office. It was an unlikely stroke of luck since over the last few years Dan had averaged just one sale a year to Working Art, a company that bought paintings and sculptures and even installations for appearance-conscious offices.

Dan had explained to the small woman, who seemed to be wearing a grey tent, that there were only a few in the new series.

'How many?' she'd asked.

'Three,' he'd said. 'There will be seven.'

'You're sure about that?' she'd asked, laughing. 'Not six or eight?'

'No, there are seven wonders – so seven paintings.'

'Honey,' she'd said, even though she wasn't remotely American, 'I think the idea is that these days you can have as many wonders as you like.' There was silence while she watched Beth watching her.

'Then, of course, there's seven sins too,' she'd continued, 'and the significant seven of Judaism.'

'I prefer the wonders,' he'd said. 'It's an inventory; 'Sun', 'Sea' and 'Street' so far. I had thought they might be something else, more thematic than that. But then each picture turned out to be rather more independent than I'd planned.' And he'd laughed, his voice high in the air. He hadn't talked to anyone for a while. Not since his father two days ago. And he hadn't slept either. He was capable of getting very carried away and so he'd shut up suddenly – unusually – and then she'd said that thing about Raymond Chandler.

She'd asked him how he ate and, momentarily confused, he'd said well, standing up, usually. Then he'd understood and explained about the bar.

'Are you happy with this set up or would you rather not?'

'Of course I'd rather not,' he'd said.

'Well,' she'd said, reaching into her bag for her card. 'I like those two,' and she'd pointed at the two most recent. 'Kind of cartoonish and grotesque, but kind of beautiful. Incidental moments exploded. Personally I'd rather see the seven sins but that's me,' she'd added, smiling with half her mouth. She found him attractive. Like an experienced child.

'I'm not sure I've tried all seven,' he'd said, flirtatiously self-deprecating.

'They're too straight to be very fashionable, you know. Not sure everyone will like the naivety.'

'And there was me thinking I was very sophisticated. Never mind. I don't really care any more,' he'd said, scratching.

And she'd left saying remember Raymond Chandler and that she'd be in touch later in the week. He'd shut the door and thought, Thank fuck for that. I'm going to have to start putting out gifts for the just-in-the-nick-of-time God.

It wasn't funny being almost thirty with no tangible achievements. Bar job, ownership of a toaster and some paint brushes, and no girlfriend, car or home. It was probably even less funny being forty with none of the above, he'd thought warningly, but by then it was almost an achievement in itself.

272

* * *

'Really just a toaster?' Beth said when he was explaining this
to her on an escalator inside the Tate Modern Gallery. 'Kettle?'

'Steve's.'

'Ahh. Why do we have to start here? Why can't we start on
the floor below?'

'Because I want you to see something. It's very important,'
he said and took her hand and held it.

He had rung her straight after Martha Frock had left his flat.
He too had rung in the nick of time, which does of course spread
over a certain number of days, time being as subjective as any
emotion. That first night after she'd been with him she'd taken
her father the camellias in hospital. Then she'd gone home and
cried herself to sleep and woken up at four in the morning.
Losing Dan, or rather the future in him, felt predictable. It should
have been that she had no space to care about Dan because her
father was dying. Instead it all felt linked in its unravelling. She
just wanted to feel safe for one minute and she'd caught herself
about to clutch her mother goodbye – and had restrained herself
to their usual single kiss.

So when Dan *did* ring the last thing she was going to do was
sulk. His suggestion of a walk felt like an offer of hope. She
was due back in the hospital in the afternoon but it gave her
five hours with him. She changed into brighter clothes and at
least felt alive once again.

'If you ever have a show,' she said to him, 'I'll be in it. A whole
wall to myself.'

He grinned at her. She looked tired, pale, but she had hugged
him hard on arrival. He was suddenly flush with conviction that
maybe this was all going to be all right, that maybe he'd been
right in a roundabout sort of way when he'd seen a strange
woman in half a dress and thought I could fall in love with a

273

woman who stands like that. Maybe he'd needed to be driven by something, even if it wasn't the most honourable of explorations, to take that step off the precipice. He would explain to her that he'd overtaken himself, surprised himself, reached a place without knowing it. After all, her motives must have been mixed too.

They climbed to the top of the escalator on the second floor and he said, 'Close your eyes, I've got your hand.' She did, wondering whether they might possibly ever reach a stage where each meeting wasn't a process of revelations and surprises. Wondering why she always gave herself so happily to be led into the rust-orange distance of her eyelids. He held both her hands and led her ten steps in a direction that seemed left.

'There,' he said and in front of them was a large marble sculpture, grubby-white in the corner of the hall. For a moment she couldn't make out what this sculpture was over and above any other, and then she realised that this was their embracing couple, Rodin's 'The Kiss'.

'There you go,' he said, as pleased with himself as if he'd hewn the stone and lugged it to this corner himself. 'We've made a pilgrimage,' referring back to the newspaper piece he had given her that first night. She smiled, flushed with his planning, tip-toeing around her next words. She said nothing instead but walked slowly around the sculpture. Through the glass walls on to the main atrium Dan could see sunlight flooding into the high hall. A slipway of light, rising like steam.

She was pleased by the mysterious simplicity of the sculpture and set off in a slow circle, intrigued by the multitude of perspectives. It was novel, being able to change your mind with their attitude halfway round. 'Their history depends on where you stand,' Dan said when they met. 'From here he looks omnipotent. But from the back her determination is stronger than his. It looks as if she's jumped him.' They stood side by side, watching the way the outsized man's taut limbs held the woman carefully, the way hers wrapped and clasped, less powerful but more demanding than the man's. Waiting for the turn of the moment when she will either choose to push him down, or allow herself to be rolled back, an inverted arch over the uncomfortable plinth. Rodin's people; always club-footed, resting on rough-hewn end-stops, pedestals, strange super-humans somewhere in between earth and purgatorial heaven.

'He has the most extraordinary arms,' Beth said to a woman she thought was Dan. But he'd wandered away again, anti-clockwise. The woman looked at her and smiled but didn't say anything, then peered at the woman's buttocks and tentatively, checking round for uniforms, reached out and touched the skin at the base of the woman's spine.

'You think it's going to be soft,' she said to Beth and then walked off into the flat ladder of the Tate's rooms as if she'd been let down. It's not natural though, Beth thought, this completeness. She wanted to tell the woman – it's not the stone that makes it unreal, it's the stillness, the time you get to work it out. It's movement that reveals true potential. Concentrate on reality, she told herself; the corner of Dan's elbow, his haunch, five feet away. Slightly obscured but waiting for her. No one else. For once Beth didn't want to lose herself in the exhibits; there was more life inside her and beside her than anything she saw in front of her.

Just when Beth was thinking that maybe they need never discuss Dan's father, Dan was thinking that if they didn't talk about it now they never would. Right now he was lying to everyone. And he just wanted to hold her in the clear air of honesty.

'Beth,' he said first. 'We should try . . .' and he was fifteen again and it was his last chance all over again and he was bored of adult machinations and the clever ebbing and flowing of his behaviour. 'We haven't told each other everything. I haven't and you haven't either.'

She looked at him blankly and suddenly on display, on her plinth. She blanked out. Visibly. 'I don't know what you mean.'

People walked around them on their way to the next room. Some taking them in, some turning to look back, knowing a scene when they saw one.

'Yes, you do. I know about you and Dad. I've always known. I've known for years.'

Beth felt something crushing inside her and, as slow as escape in a nightmare, every moment with Dan was reworked. When he'd looked for her in Soho, followed her through the streets, made love to her as if he'd found an answer. It wasn't her story any more, it was his. She looked at him standing earnest in front of her. His posture pleading. Frowning in search of what . . . forgiveness?

'This is sick,' she said, cold and calm. 'What were you doing with me. Playing? Taking revenge? Proving you could?'

'No, no, I wasn't. I always wanted you but you stopped being just a challenge and became important. I began to care.' She registered his past tense. 'I don't think either of us knew what we were up to. What were *you* doing, Beth? When were you going to tell me?' She could understand he had a point but this was his responsibility. All she'd ever done was try to trust in the movement.

She turned and walked to the escalator, saying she had to get out of here, and she walked down it fast as if the gallery were about actual transport.

He followed her down one, then the other, out of the glass enclosure, not up the shining river of sunshine but through the ground floor exit where collegiate lawns bounced ice cream

276

cones and Coke cans. She didn't wait for him to join her so he had to run alongside the river to catch her up. There were still too many people. Tourists getting in the way, somehow managing to walk on the wrong side of the pavement as well.

Just past The Globe Dan stopped and grabbed her arm and said, 'Stop, for Christ's sake, will you? Will you just stop fucking walking?' At long last he actually sounded angry. Beth was surprised and blinked in silence. 'Where are you going?' he asked.

'Don't know,' she said. 'No, I do, I have to go and see Dad.'

'How long did you think we could keep doing this?'

She swallowed and with a clamped jaw like her mother's in her wilder moments just stared back at him.

'Did you have any intention of telling me?'

'I clearly didn't need to, did I?'

'Beth, I'm trying to make this work. I want us to make this work but we have to talk about this.'

Beth's feelings stopped and about-turned a little again. Marshalling themselves, everything a little out of step, behind the beat. He seemed to think this an issue, not an end, and she suddenly felt very, very angry. In that case, why had he played with her for so long? Why hadn't he discussed this before, if he hadn't just wanted to get a kick out of her, a fuck out of her, if he hadn't actually wanted to store up affection to effectively humiliate her?

'Don't you dare get moral with me.' She jabbed a finger in his face. 'I fell for you, I trusted you, with my dad and everything and you just watched and waited and sat on and held back like some . . .' Her syntax was slipping. 'Some con-man.'

He was stony livid now. He stared at her hard, his arms straight by his side, and said, very slowly, 'When were you going to tell me? I wanted you to tell me. I waited.'

She looked at him and on this erratically sunny day, despite all the lyricism she'd been credited with, the no small matter of the poetry of her soul, all she could think of to say was, 'You cunt.' And momentarily feeling she had restored the balance of power, she walked away from him.

This time he didn't follow. He had run out of things to say. He stood, a small sludge-coloured fixed point in the ebb of the street. Families, like water, divided around him. After a few minutes he walked to the railings and leaned on them, watching the weak lap of the brown waves. It wasn't so much that he had done anything worse than her, just that he had behaved more inexplicably than her. She had arrived and punctuated his life with the crash of a falling plane. He had taken the complexities as a starting point and then as a good omen. And he had tried to ignore the fact that, as well as lust and curiosity, what had driven him at the start was the chance of discovering, measuring, bettering Jacob.

And what had been going through her head? For the very first time he wondered if two weren't capable of playing his game. How much was he a route to Jacob also?

He didn't know. He felt like he didn't know anything so he went home to paint. Easier there in his quiet, familiar light.

24. Coming Home

Lizzie felt tense. There was a twisting clump in her gut, like a fur ball. She'd had three cups of coffee so far this morning and Roger had only said one word. ('Yes.') He slept most of the time now. Only it wasn't really sleep. It was more like stretches of time in which he practised dying. It didn't seem likely that he'd come home. They said it would be a lot of work for her. They weren't sure it was a good thing. She wondered how letting someone die could be regarded as harder work than giving birth. She had, after all, drawing herself up at the oncoming steps of the doctor, seen rather a lot of both in her time.

Yesterday they had started talking in periods of time. Weeks or days they'd said. She could have told them that. Every day he spoke less and looked worse. Starving thin, with little hair left, waxy yellow overall, purple in places – not human colours, rotten colours.

'Good morning, Mrs Standing.' She smiled at the group.

The consultant and his disciples talked low to each other. Then one of the junior doctors stepped forward, clasped his hands together and dropped his head. For one moment Lizzie thought he was going to say a prayer. She could have done with it.

'Mrs Standing,' he paused to smile, 'as I'm sure you know now, your husband's vital signs are failing. His heart will give out in the end. Possibly he will develop pneumonia. But either way we don't think he has more than a few days left. We understand you would rather he spent those at home?'

Lizzie suddenly didn't feel so sarcastic. Her eyes began to water. She nodded. 'It won't be easy. In fact –' he stumbled slightly on the words – 'in fact it may be extremely distressing on top of everything else. This is more than just palliative care, the last hours can be a struggle. It's not always peaceful – by any stretch. We will be able to arrange a nurse to visit, but do *you* have help?' he asked. 'Family?'

Lizzie nodded. 'A daughter.' She needed to appear strong. 'I . . . We would very much like him at home.'

He looked at her, at the consultant who shrugged and nodded, and said, 'Okay. I'll ask Sister Shone to talk to you about the practicalities. She'll fill you in on the liaison officers and counsellors – for afterwards.' The consultant had already begun to move off to the next bed. Lizzie wanted Beth there.

Beth arrived shortly after, trailing her bag and a grey cloud of misery behind her. Lizzie greeted her with a slight cry of pleasure, and, beyond thinking about it, rose quickly to meet her halfway down the ward, holding out her arms to embrace her. Beth's face began to crumple and she stepped into the circle of her mother's arms and laid her cheek on her shoulder and cried.

'Did they tell you?' said Lizzie, stroking her hair – she had someone to hold on to at last.

'What?' said Beth sharply, raising her head, panicked that her father might have died while she pissed around in an art gallery.

'That we're taking him home.'

'Oh God; right, no. Jesus.' And she moved away from Lizzie, thinking to pull herself together. 'Are you sure that's a good idea?' Beth was suddenly scared by the physicality of what lay ahead. It seemed unbelievable that they were meant to deal with this. That no one just stepped in and relieved one of the business of dying. There was surely always someone to take over –

wasn't there another authority, along the lines of doctors, policemen and lawyers?

'I want him at home with us,' said Lizzie and she looked crushed at having to explain.

After Sister Shone had detailed the sorry convoy of medical supplies that would arrive with Roger and the nurses who would visit over the next few days, she sent them to eat a meal in the canteen. 'You need a break,' she said. Beth felt sick at what they were undertaking and guilty at her fear of her father's body. They chose plates of macaroni cheese, a yellow-white glutinous mess that slipped and flopped from the fork to the mouth. Lizzie didn't even start the meal, she just sat still and small with her handbag in her lap, her hair flat and curling against her forehead in the unhealthy warmth of the hospital.

'Beth.'

'Yes,' said Beth. She wished she smoked. She was sure a brief escape, seven moments of smoky, illicit pleasure, would help. Add some poetry to the flat drama of hospitals. Except for the fact that the banished smokers outside the entrances looked so furtive.

'I'm sorry to do this now. It's a bit of a day, I know. I expect you'll think we should have done this before.'

'What? Take Dad home?'

'No, no, I've got something to tell you.'

Beth had had more than enough truth-telling for one day. She sat back in the canteen chair and folded her arms, weary as much as anxious. This would almost certainly be some minor complication of her mother's creation.

A hospital worker stacked plates in the background, scraping the throw-out into the bins, blunt knives dragged on cheap ceramic.

'Before you were born, I had two sons who died.'

281

A trolley rolled out from the kitchens. Beth looked nonplussed, almost unshocked. As if she had been told the milk had run out. Then she sat forward and said, frowning, 'What?'

'Before you were born, in the sixties. They died the year before you were born. In an accident. They were little, very little. Only seven and five. They . . .'

Beth waved her hand dismissively, to stop the flow. Lizzie had been about to tell her their names. Beth was flushed.

'You never said anything. Dad never said anything. Why didn't anyone say something? I don't understand.'

'Because I didn't want to tell you.' Lizzie looked down. 'It was before you were born, I didn't want you upset.'

Beth snorted with laughter. That was almost funny. Suddenly she felt sick and cold and . . . what? Undermined. Small. Stupid.

'How did they die?' she asked quietly.

'In a fire.'

Their eyes locked for a second.

'No wonder I never felt quite enough,' said Beth quietly. With more wonder than self-pity.

'They were your half-brothers . . .' Lizzie began but Beth was speaking low and fast, puzzled.

'You always do this. Hold things back and leave me out. You never ever tried to talk to me.'

'They were your half-brothers.'

'Half-brothers?' Now Beth looked shocked.

'I was married before. To a man called Gavin. They were his children.'

And it all began to make sense, settling into place as if it could never have been anything but. So why was she the last to know? She was humiliated to learn that what she suspected was true, that she was a poor substitute of a child. But none of this was her fault. All she ever used to do was try. Was she now meant to feel bad that she'd given up?

282

'You know what?' Beth stood up. 'I can't deal with this.' She sounded almost apologetic. 'All of a sudden you want to be open. I don't think I want to know. I don't think I can handle it now. I'm going back to Dad.' Beth began to walk away, then stopped and turned around and came back to add one more thing. She felt a flailing need to apportion blame. 'D'you know how angry you always were, how lonely I was, how much I wanted you to even just *like* me?' And then she stopped, suddenly ashamed to be a grown woman saying these things.

Lizzie reached for her handbag and took out Roger's letter. 'I know you weren't always happy. But I thought it was better not to tell you. I didn't want you to know what I'd lost, what you'd missed out on.' She held out Roger's letter. 'Will you take this and read it? It's from your dad.' Beth took it and turned away as Lizzie quietly said, 'I'm sorry.' Her daughter walked swiftly out of the canteen, leaving her alone with two full plates of macaroni cheese. Lizzie put her head in her hands. She felt old and tired. As if she'd had one too many such scenes in her life.

She knew Beth would be there though, would stick with them through the next days. For her father if no one else. And she was grateful for that. More grateful than she'd possibly ever managed to express. She just hoped Roger would be able to explain it better.

25.

30 August, 2000

My dear Beth

I don't know whether it's the drugs or the disintegration but these days, when I make my wobbling way down the street, I can see ghosts. I'm sure it is the drugs since I have never been a visionary man. The drugs are combined with a bludgeoned but very forceful sense of life, so that my slow saunters round the park feel like walking through dreams. All these people that I thought I had forgotten, and some I knew I hadn't, slip before me and behind me. I have begun to wonder if they weren't always here, that if I had only paid attention every time I had stepped on to the pavement I would have felt the company of the past. It is a strange feeling, a lifetime distilled into an afternoon. I can hear my mother in the air. She had a raw voice, or perhaps it was always the wind that carried her voice that was raw. There is no reason, I suppose, that droplets of her voice may not exist somehow still in the air. And in that way I can convince myself that the rushing of air I feel around my legs may be some leftover eddy of your childhood. You had a toy milk cart that you liked to pedal back and forth across my path. As if you wanted to prove that you were there. As if I could have ever doubted it.

When I met your mother I ran an old people's home in Harrogate. It was a funny old job. But I was an accountant who didn't like offices or figures very much. Some of the women in the home were sad and some were somewhere else. I was never quite sure where. I think now though that they were here, a place where the air is infused with millions of moments and voices and meetings. I met your mother in the home. We have never told you much of our past. I cannot remember why now. I think we thought it was to protect you. I think it was really to protect us. We thought that if we told you about your brothers who died it would contaminate your happiness. I think we thought it had to stop somewhere with someone. Though of course it didn't and hasn't and even now on these foolish walks of mine I imagine I can hear your brothers calling your mother.

There were two of them and they were your mother's first children. She was married to another man and she and I met and we fell in love. I have no doubt that this sounds trite, far too faded and aged to be shocking, but still, it's probably disturbing for you to think of us as people of impulses. But we did. We fell in love. She was the first person to have looked at me, in my strange job and unfashionable suit, as someone with a future. Thus far I had largely managed to side-step the embarrassment and confrontation of life, which meant missing out on much of the to-ing and fro-ing of relationships. I think perhaps I was old-fashioned. Anyway, your mother, who was, by the way, the prettiest woman I'd ever come across, and the kindest too, seemed to find me interesting. And suddenly, as if I'd actually all along been saving up my bravery for something, I seized on it and on her. I knew about her husband and her sons and of course I felt guilty. But just because you feel guilty doesn't mean something is necessarily wrong. And I thought that this had to be right. One day Lizzie came to visit her mother, and me too, I think, and that was the day your brothers, your half-brothers, and her first husband, Gavin, were killed in an accident. They tried to find your mother that night. But they couldn't find her because she was with me in my room where no one thought to look.

(I don't know how to tell this other than with facts.)

They died and your mother was pregnant with you. I went to find her in Leicester. She hadn't called me for weeks, just written to me telling me they had died. I rang her house one time and someone picked up the phone and started to say hello and then stopped. So I left Harrogate that day. I had to drive very slowly down to Leicester because I had such a rotten old car.

I am telling you this because I want you to know your mother. I want you to know that she has done the very utmost someone can, which is never move from loving you or never evade her first duty which was always to you.

I distrust death-bed wisdom but I am adamant that as you get older you pick up something worth knowing along the way. I have watched you and your mother and want to tell you this because I think I'm right in saying you don't understand each other as you ought. And as and when I die there is no point in waiting until you are older and ill to know that you had it all along, that you had her complete concentration, every ounce of her love as a mother all along. You should know it while you can appreciate it and grow to give back what you can.

I think you found us odd and undoubtedly dull. Which is every child's right. I seem to remember finding mine infuriating. My father had a habit of humming while he ate, my mother of eating her soup loudly and I was most unsympathetic at their ease with each other's noises. But I also think you found something distracted in us. I have a feeling you never quite forgave your mother for being a woman who was very private with her love, who had perhaps lost some of the courage to show it as you would have liked. I don't know. Who knows?

Sometimes I find it helpful to not look too closely into my head. I may be old-fashioned in that way but there are certain truths, Beth, which are unpalatable and irreconcilable with the way we've come to live our lives and expect our happiness, and your brothers' deaths was one. I think maybe we should have told you and then your life would have, perversely, been nearer a whole, but at the beginning we didn't because we didn't want you to feel the loss. I think families should talk, try and bridge the gaps. And parents aren't necessarily distant, they're just people who had a child, who gave him or her shape, but can't give them everything in the end. Blame is not a constructive thing.

Perhaps it would have helped us back then to recognise that the people suffering were us. Not the boys or their father. Perhaps it would have helped your mother to know that more than thirty years later they live on in her head, in the air around us, and in your imagination even though you never knew you knew it.

It's hard to separate grief at our own pain from grief at a future the dead don't know they're missing. Remember that when you're reading this. I will exist in you and your mother now.

I am worried about you. I want you and Lizzie to take care of each other. I know you will but by writing it I feel I have at least tried to do something. (Typical. I am pre-empting my absence already!)

A different woman might have found me pedestrian but

your mother and I worked out our happiness in the end. I wonder whether she ever managed not to blame herself for the accident. They did blame someone at the inquest – an individual in a brown suit – which seemed so incredible that Lizzie found it easier to blame herself. I am not sure she had the energy to direct her anger elsewhere. I think we needed each other, have always needed each other. Even before we met. And then after the accident especially – how could she or I look anyone other than each other in the eyes? I am so used to looking into her eyes, in understanding the good and bad and the generosity and selfish desire and the love and sorrow that is held in among the two of us, that I am afraid I have abandoned any hope of an afterlife. My sense of God has always been such a fuzzy thing, as nebulous as outer space, that it seems unrealistic to expect Him to provide me with real eyes to look into. Like asking a ghost to build a home out of heavy bricks. Being able to look into Lizzie's eyes and see all those things has meant living a full life to me. Anything that comes after will be as faint as a watermark. But then I suppose you never know what's in store. That's the magic. I could never have imagined I'd be blessed with your mother and you. I love your mother with a quiet ferocity and I have no doubt, have never allowed any doubt, that she feels that way about me.

I have no idea what comes after this. I think it might be like walking into that strange darkness we all hold beneath our eyelids. But what do I know? I don't feel especially resolved. Or especially calm. Things sometimes feel very slow and very clear and at others an almost nightmarish, and undeniably painful, blur.

I have not grown brave. I am not glad to leave you behind. But I am so, so glad to have something to leave behind. What a sorry end to evaporate entirely. I am a selfish, old-fashioned man and I like to think of my genes travelling through to newer, smaller people.

I like to think of you as a resilient and amused mother having a picnic in Colliers Park with Lizzie and your own children, who in my eye are brown like hazelnuts. I do not like the thought of my absence. But the thought of this picnic happening makes me very happy. Perhaps by imagining it in advance I am staking my place on the grass. Perhaps I am already there, waiting. And while waiting I will think of you with your heels dug into the snow on a winter's day in the garden, a sturdy little girl examining a sweet you've suddenly been given. You've always been a surprise to me. I was always amazed that I could actually do something so intrinsic, so important as become a father. Always surprised at your existence. But here I am scribbling and you're due here any minute so we must have got it at least a little bit right.

Sometimes I've watched you when you didn't know (we did watch, you know, much more than I think you think) and I've seen your face flicker and then fade, as if you were always reminding yourself that it could all be a big disappointment. Don't ever forget that cynicism is a cowardly thing and that happiness is yours to build. I want to see you fall in love, you see.

Forgive the sentimentality; I have never indulged in it much but I've discovered that there is one thing in death's favour. For once I can be sure of the last word.

Remember this – our love will pave your way.

Your Dad

Roger
x

26. Following

It is an early morning in September and the running stitch of trees along Delia Street shiver in the flood of daylight. Inside the houses heavy bodies stumble slowly out of dark rooms, splashing water and baptising themselves into the light. Somewhere beneath the stained pavements, telephone and TV cables piped subterranean rivers glug like a stomach.

Lizzie stands in the shower, welcoming the element with an open, amphibian mouth. She slops her feet round so that the hot waterfall drives into her back. She faces the wall in her little upright cell. She knows these tiles intimately. The grouting greying with her through the years.

She isn't alone in the house so she wraps a towel round her before unlocking the bathroom door and stepping on to the carpeted landing. She is aware of the soft synthetic knots beneath her feet and scrunches her toes back and forth as she sits down on the edge of her bed. She combs her shoulder-length hair that is brittle with years of brunette home dyes. She thinks maybe she will stop that now. The hair dyeing. Now that she is alone again.

She feels extraordinarily clear-headed and open to the day. She is aware of the wind sliding under the slightly open window, trickling on to her bare shoulders. She pulls them back, squares up to the future, stretching the skin between her breasts that has been folded by the tight wrap of the towel. There is a late butterfly lingering on the frame, slowly opening and closing its wings, a sly blinking at the sun.

Seven days before, Roger woke to find his wife sitting beside the bed in a chair. His hold on consciousness was ragged, inter-mittent. He sensed her presence and felt that she must have always been there, would remain there. Which made him think of something tall and green. He lay under a pale memory, a flickering scene of a house and a child, and felt a dry pressure on his hand. He blinked slowly, each one a careful gesture with the weight of a decade.

Lizzie watched him, knowing that at some point she would see the last flicker of his papery eyelids. He was so thin now. These last two days all they could do was administer painkillers when he seemed restless or seemed to be reaching for the switch himself. She and Beth used sponges to try to get some water past his lips. She wondered what strange dreams the drugs gave him – she hoped they were good ones. It would be so unfair to live calm and loved and then die under a nightmare. That was what had happened to her Martin and Paul and she didn't wish to imagine it again. He seemed calm. He seemed peaceful. Occasionally he would open his eyes and see Lizzie or Beth or both of them and smile.

So this is what it's like thought Lizzie. And if he were to have died suddenly she wouldn't have learned that death is neither here nor there. That the dying begins with life; that he will no more be gone than herself in another year, at a previous place. No more lost than her years as a child, than her life as a mother of her two boys. All of it, she felt, rested within her. Such life within one frame. She was silently amazed to have been at the beginning and end of so much. For a quiet woman, she thought, there is a great deal of history inside of me.

Beth was in the street having a conversation. The front door was open. How could someone be dying with the front door open, swinging slightly in the wind? It seemed extraordinary. Lizzie sat and watched her husband's thin, flaking face move slower and slower towards stillness. She had washed and changed his body the night before with such gentle tenderness, his bones so long and light and peculiarly mottled, that he had seemed infinitely more fragile than some fat baby. She had changed his pyjamas, with Beth's help, to a navy blue pair that swamped him in their respectability.

Beth was extricating herself from a conversation with Mrs Garland. Her father lay dying upstairs. Lizzie sat still on his bed, one hand on his. One hand slowly rubbing up and down her thigh. Something he would have done if he could. Lizzie could hear Beth's murmurings downstairs, she heard a car drive past and a groan in the house's heating innards. She could see a small fleck of tissue paper beneath Roger's nose move slightly, back and forth. Back and forth like a little puffball of dust, dodging the breeze. Back and forth, a millimetre up and down the deep pitted ridge between mouth and nose. She watched, mesmerised; this, the last sign of Roger's breathing. The body's fight was done. This was the only difference between life and death, the slight roll of a fragment of paper. And it struck her that when it stopped moving it would make no difference. That she would still feel his fingers between hers, his hand on her hip, the steady brown look of his eyes, the restraint and love of his arms. It struck her that she held him stronger and more vital inside, that he lived better in the air in the street, in the conversations below, in Beth's deep eyes, dark hair and familiar movements, in the vitality of the life that he gave her, in the routines of their marriage, in the photos and home-made shelves, than he did in this shamefully wasted body. Straight-backed and steady he had claimed her, named their future, and now all she would need to do was look around her. And then she would feel the rush of him within her.

292

'Beth,' she said, loud and urgent. He would stop very soon. Outside the wind picked up, and with the sound of the sea travelling the street Beth rushed up the stairs.

Lizzie was still wrapped in the white towel, laying out her brown, rather than black, outfit for the funeral later that day, when Beth knocked on the door offering a cup of tea.

'Did you sleep?' asked Lizzie, taking the tea.

'Yes. Straight out and heavy. Are you going to wear the hat this afternoon?'

'Yes. I quite like hats. Perhaps you could get married one day and then I could actually wear one for a nice occasion.' Lizzie turned her worn-out but just teasing face to her daughter.

Beth rolled her eyes and walked out with Lizzie's hairbrush in her hand.

They hadn't spoken about their conversation in the canteen for twelve hours after they'd got Roger home. They'd taken it in turns to sleep that first night, Beth from eleven until four, Lizzie from four until nine. There had seemed to be an unspoken agreement that they only had enough energy to concentrate on Roger.

The next morning had brought no revolution, or expressed resolution. Lizzie could only presume Beth had read the letter by now. There had been only this; Lizzie had felt Beth's attention. She had caught Beth watching her whisper into Roger's ear and kiss his forehead. Beth had watched intently the hardly touching lightness with which Lizzie wiped his face.

And then lunchtime came and Beth had gone to make them a cup of coffee. She'd returned instead with the single photo of Martin and Paul in her hand.

'This is them?' she'd said to Lizzie.

And Lizzie had nodded, wincing a little in anticipation. Beth had looked at the black and white picture closely, properly, for the first time. Two small boys in white jumpers and little nylon dungarees.

'They're very sweet,' Beth had said looking at her mum, her eyes glistening. It had been almost more than Beth could bear. One of them had an unruly tuft of hair, the other, smaller one was rounder and had a broad smile and big eyes. They would be large, strapping men with heavy shoes and belted trousers and their own kids by now. Beth had carefully propped the picture up on the mantelpiece, against a china figurine. Then she had moved to the side of the bed and picked up Roger's hand, kissed it and said, 'Look, I brought them up to see you,' and begun to cry.

Over the road, Mr and Mrs Garland were slowly beginning the day of Roger's funeral. Mr Garland was sitting, silent and grumpy, in the bath, letting the water drain out before shouting for his wife to come and help him out. Mr Standing's death had made him cry, and he sat crying even now, tears splashing on to his withered white legs. Death coming to call, slowly down the street. He was a good man, Mr Standing; not especially forthcoming, bit stuffy, bit of an accountant, Ted supposed. Another tear fell unwanted from his eye. Christ, he was getting sentimental. He would fill the bath back up again if he weren't careful, so he grasped the handles tightly, summoning reserves of determination, and called his wife's name.

There was a strong smell in Jacob's front garden. Browning tongues of buddleia brushed the shoulder of his suit as he left the house but it was the scent of the late summer roses that permeated. Deep pink with golden orange edges, they were voluptuous yet pubescent, breaking from bud to blossom. Jacob picked one gingerly and went back upstairs and placed it on the bare sheet by his sleeping wife. She would find it later when she rolled over and felt a small prick in her back.

After a meeting in W10 Jacob was going to pick up Dan and get some lunch. They had decided to go to the funeral together. It seemed at least truthful to turn up side by side. There wasn't much going on in the street as he shut the front door but it wasn't deserted. It was a Wednesday morning and the street now belonged to those without regular job hours. There were more and more of them, Jacob had noticed. The streets were being reclaimed, freelancers and homeless men wandering up and down their suburban lengths, no longer purely the province of schoolchildren, housewives or the elderly.

Jacob got into the car and drove off. After the service he would see the Garlands as still as stone in his rear-view mirror, waiting in vain in the church car park for the mini-cab they had carefully booked three days in advance. And he would say to them, opening his passenger door for Mrs Garland with a flourish, helping to fold Mr Garland's wheelchair, 'I can't believe it, you should have asked me for a lift. Or I should have thought to offer. I'm so sorry. Any time you need me, I'm at your service from here on in.'

The cars arrived at three o'clock. Long, black and gothic, they sat outside the diminished house. Lizzie popped to the loo. Beth waited at the bottom of the stairs for her mother. It was just the two of them, no one else left to emerge, straighten a tie, rattle the keys, start up the car. Just the two of them.

She had a hole in her stomach where her father used to be. Odd that he lived in her stomach, she thought. She wasn't sure how she felt beyond that. Unreal, as if she were breathing a thin, heady air. Unable to understand, in a very, very pure, childish way, how her father could be there and then suddenly not.

The last two days of his life had numbed her to most of her own. She had watched her mother nurse her father with an all-consuming tenderness and thought how extraordinary their silence, their self-sufficiency was, how she might never see the like again, how she would have to hold the sight of her father's still-warm hand in her mother's tight. He'd been conscious enough the day before to nod in recognition and return when she'd told him she loved him. Which had seemed almost a paltry, obvious thing to say until she thought about it, lying in her old bed, and couldn't remember having said it before.

Now that they had calmly chosen a coffin and hymns, she remembered with disgust how she had wished for some tragic drama as a child to lend her value and romance. But in retrospect it was obvious that something terribly damaging had happened in her mother's past. That something had happened to her father to limit the largesse of emotion that he just occasionally displayed. How could she have known? She couldn't. But, she thought with a new acuteness, it was typical that she hadn't thought to probe. She had a sneaking sensation of having used up a lot of people's energies in the past, had a memory of solipsism like a spiral, a situation with a limited scope pursued through tightening circles. Now that she really had something to mind about there wasn't much anyone could do. She knew that too. The days and months ahead took the shape of a bleak journey. He was still with her, of course, but it was his quietness she minded.

Once upon a time she thought she'd seen it all. Now she was shocked at how much she'd forgotten, let alone never witnessed. Six nights before, the day they'd taken his body away, Lizzie and she had had three glasses of sherry. And they'd almost got drunk, what with the high altitude of absence and the continued disinterest in Beth's sandwiches. She'd put too much mayonnaise and roughly chopped tomatoes in the ham sandwiches and they'd seemed too fleshy, too substantial to eat in this house. Hunger was the least of their problems.

They'd talked for hours. For the first time ever, Beth thought.

Lizzie had asked Beth whether she remembered something, an afternoon on holiday in Swanage when she and Dan had gone missing and Roger had quietly panicked and gone to find them on the pier before leading them back to the home-patch of mashed sand and wind-flipped towels. Beth had remembered and then seen other things as at the end of a kaleidoscope. Other days blending and separating with bright colours and cut-out shapes. Ducks that ate her mother's toes in Windermere. The pony that kicked her father on Dartmoor, leaving a horseshoe-shaped bruise which wasn't really funny, except, of course, that it was when he was all tall and thin, wearing his tight, striped swimming trunks with a drawstring at the top.

'You should have told me,' Beth had suddenly said of her half-brothers, with an exquisite embarrassment at talking this way with her mother.

'Don't you understand why at all?' Lizzie had asked.

'But it dominated anyway. Because of you, being so . . .' She had deliberately chosen what she thought was a kind word. 'Sad. You and I can, you know, talk and spend more time together, I suppose. But it means that I never knew about dad properly. And now he's gone. And that's not fair. It's just not fair.'

Lizzie hadn't said life's not fair, or even a variation on it. She'd chosen instead to say, 'Your father loved you so absolutely that whatever either of you said, he could never have loved you any more.'

'No, but he must have thought me so blind . . . and selfish. I just wish I'd been more . . .'

Lizzie had smiled at her pleading daughter and said, 'No one ever behaves selflessly to their parents throughout their entire life. It'd be worrying if they did. It's part of the process. Your dad didn't. Believe me. And you were here all the time for him in the last few months. He could have had no doubt of your love, or patience, or generosity.'

297

Beth had stared at her mother. No one had ever called her patient or generous before.

Lizzie came back down the stairs and as they reached the hearse she turned and smiled and gave her black-gloved hand to Beth.

The traffic moved slowly along the A3, wedged between schools, houses, homes, hospitals and playing fields, the pedestrians picking up speed as the traffic loosened. They drove straight into the sunlight, beneath trees dipped in gold. People and gardens and now a tunnel flickered past. They hadn't spoken and Beth felt a familiar tug of annoyance at her mother's silence. Unless she should have spoken first. So she said, 'Mum?' in an uncertain way. And her mother turned and looked surprised, not at the words but at the tone of voice. Lizzie had forgotten that someone could be so tentative about what was inside her head. So uncertain of her emotion. Beth never normally said Mum with a question in its inflection; she'd always said 'Mu-um' like a downward step. Funny.

'Are you okay?' said Beth.

Dan and his father gave each other a hug. Dan had the stagnant breath of someone who lived alone and hadn't spoken since drinking their morning coffee. Their embrace was important. The last time they'd met they'd argued and parted as if they'd both won, and the other was too sodding stubborn to realise it. It was over a month ago now, the day that Jacob had brought round the cheque and discovered that the girl who was obsessing his son was Beth.

Jacob had been shocked, and a little revolted. It had taken him some time and a lot of Laura to try and untangle the guilt from the distaste. To share a woman with your father seemed unnatural. The only woman whose insides had held both Dan and him was Rachel. Which, when it occurred to him, didn't help matters any further.

This collision, this collusion of child-adults, was like being discovered when he'd thought there was no longer a worry in it. In Dan's flat that morning he'd spluttered and invoked God and decency to an extent that Dan had had to laugh. Laugh and laugh in his father's face in a way that had shamed Jacob into livid, thin-lipped silence. What do you do when your son reveals a contempt that you'd never suspected? He'd never been faced with it since he had been a part-time father of teenagers, and never expressed it since his own father had never been there to provoke it. He'd always thought his continued existence in their lives was enough. He'd thought Beth was a mistake; he'd never thought that not talking about her was a mistake. Why would his sons want to know that side of him?

That day Dan had laughed at his father and dished out a few home truths. (They came as a shock to both of them.) All three of the boys knew why Rachel had left, knew it was his infidelities that had resulted in them leaving London. Dan had hated the fact that Jacob had assumed they would be all right about the women that followed after; actually, no, he'd hated the fact that Jacob had assumed they'd be all right in general, hadn't bothered to ask them anything ever. Or felt the need to explain himself to them ever. And the fact that he'd slept with Dan's friend Beth.

It had taken two goes for Jacob to apologise – he hadn't known which bit for exactly, he'd just felt the need to hear himself say 'Sorry'. The first time he'd rung they'd managed to make things worse. Picking up where they had left off, slamming the phone down. So Jacob rang again and forestalled his son by saying, 'Wait, wait, wait, let me just say this. I'm sorry for flying off the handle. It's up to you who you see. I suppose it's good that we argued and said what we said . . . and you know I do hope . . . I do want . . . well, I would like to see you in love with someone so—'

'Forget it, it's fine, it's not going to be Beth,' Dan had said quickly.

'Why?' Jacob had said, interrupted and confused.

'Why do you think?' Dan had replied. 'Because of you.'

Which had kind of left them back at square one.

Roger had asked to be buried. He didn't like the idea of burning, of spitting fat in the flames like bacon. He wasn't a Viking or a witch, he said, so he'd feel much more at home with a slow disintegration. The funeral was to be held in a church near Kingston, the local church for Wandle Comprehensive where he had worked for the last ten years. Just Beth and her mother were to watch the coffin being lowered. In the car Beth was trying not to think about his body, neatly suited and trimmed, in the wooden box. Such a familiar body now still and stiff and cold. She felt a sudden panic at the macabreness of all this.

However, when they walked slowly behind the coffin into the church, Beth forgot about the oddness of her father in a box, supported on strangers' shoulders, because as they stepped through the portico they saw not whitewashed walls and pews and carefully sewn kneelers but great numbers of people. Row after row of backs in browns and blues and greys, the odd solemn face turned round, bowed heads, shuffling shoulders. For one split-second Beth thought they might have the wrong funeral and turned, panicking, to look at Lizzie. But Lizzie simply said, 'Goodness,' and smiled and threaded her arm through her daughter's and took a step further on the path between the two blocks of bodies.

They sat, and as the vicar began Lizzie wondered whether it was wrong to know she'd survive, not to be sobbing at her husband's funeral. She knew it would flood out later, often at small stories of other people (lost tickets and homes, small crying boys and old men at windows), investing them with all that she missed. But right then she was sitting and feeling an annoying

300

ache in her back, the discomfort of the wooden pew, studying the embroidered scene of a maypole, children on the grass, a church spire in the background. Is this awful? she thought. Is it bad that I know I can live? Angry and aching, but alive. Is it bad to be more focused on providing a decent tea than on my misery? Does nothing scare me any more? What about the one thing left; what about Beth? And she turned to look at her daughter and thought, No, not even that any more.

Dan and his father sat next to each other seven pews back. For just a few seconds both of them watched Beth's head, their view-points converging on the spot of white window glare on the straight fall of her dark hair. Their four eyes fell on her and her head took the blessing unknowingly. She gazed clear-eyed on the flowers ahead. She couldn't cry yet, today seemed too shocking to be sad.

Jacob remembered the hair – the feel of it, the straight weight of it. But it wasn't important to him any more and he looked down again at his hands round the hymn book in his lap. Dan, though, was absorbed by being in the same building as her, by the desire to place his hand on her hair, to absorb the white light, to feel the heat of her scalp and the rise and fall of her breath. It was still there.

A colleague stood to speak of Roger and recreate him in everyone's eyes. Kind, tall, upstanding, literally, in a staff room, shop or garden. People shifted and coughed and thought of Roger and, intermittently, of their dinner, their bills and then their own fathers. And then they thought what a lot of people there were in this small church and wondered who they all were, what Roger was to them (more or less, or something else entirely?). And they wondered about their own funeral and what might be sung and who might come to shift and cough in their decent shoes for them. They thought about other funerals of the last few years, especially when they began to sing 'All Things Bright and Beautiful', which they'd heard too often because everyone thought it a cheerful sort of choice. Some took out a handkerchief or a tissue and used its corners to absorb tears that gathered like condensation in the rivulets between their nose and soft cheeks.

Trying to say the right thing at the end was difficult. People, as they kissed Lizzie, wanted to show her that they did care and they did feel. It was hard, the words were almost worn thin from use. But they knew, many from personal experience, that the appearance and the code was what counted. If we exist purely in each other's knowledge of us then the funeral is an arbitrary place to end. Yet the ceremony mattered to Lizzie because she wanted the summation of how he had grown and worked and loved.

Outside the church there was a busy clarity to the day. A whisking breeze and clear sky brought every movement into focus. The last sycamore pods spiralled panicky through the air and the branches of the large oak tree in the graveyard seemed to judder rather than sway. Dan too felt edgy and poked at the ground with his feet as he lingered with his father on the edge of the fractured gathering. Dan was telling his Dad that the paintings were going slowly, that in fact they had changed a bit. That they were more of an inventory, less of a personal top ten. One of them would appear alone in Frock's gallery and he said that he'd been a bit uncertain about that, about an individual appearing out of context without his explanation, as it were. But he'd begun to let go, he reckoned, begun to think there might be something interesting about a work in progress after all.

Beth saw the two of them, middle-sized men, standing near the chestnut tree and walked over to them. She tripped slightly on the edge of a stone grave surround and ended up in front of them with a smile that turned down at the edges and revealed more than she would have done before.

'Oops,' she said, embarrassed. Neither of them knew what to say so remembering her manners she said, 'Thank you for coming.'

She had a red nose and slight smudges of make-up under her eyes, and her eyes glittered slightly.

'I'm really sorry, Beth,' said Jacob. 'It's horrid, he was . . . he was a lovely man.'

Her face began to break up and she laughed through a down-turned mouth and watering eyes. 'Please don't be nice, I'll just start again. I was doing all right and then I started talking to someone he worked with, whom I'd never met, and he told me such lovely things that I didn't know about that it just seemed so sad that we were all here for him, and he would have enjoyed it, like a kind of party . . .' Then she was crying properly. Standing weeping in front of the two of them, aware of them but for once just not caring.

She looked so young and messy and raw, her shoulders shaking, fumbling with a fragment of a tissue, that it seemed inhuman not to just hug her, to attempt to absorb a little of the bone shake and sob. So Jacob did. He hugged her very tight and patted her on the back rhythmically as if she were just a child. Dan stood still, looking at the ground.

After a minute she quietened a little and pulled away. 'Sorry,' she said and made a face. 'I think I've got snot on your shoulder.' She swallowed and turned to look at Dan and said, 'Thank you for coming,' again.

He looked at her grimly. He didn't know how to put it into words, how to explain that losing her for those few weeks had seemed like the biggest, laziest mistake he'd ever made. 'Of course I've come,' he said blankly.

They looked at each other for a few seconds, her exhausted

and him scared. To Beth it was like looking at a refuge you can't have. She smiled and shrugged slightly and turned and walked away, avoiding the stone surround.

By the time Dan looked around, his father had begun to walk to the car. He caught him up in the car park and stood by the door to get in, but his father was looking at him.

'What?' Dan said defensively as if his father was the last thing he needed right now.

'You're done?' said Jacob.

Dan said nothing.

'I'm just surprised. I thought you said you were crazy about her.'

'It's a funeral, for Christ's sake; what am I supposed to do?'

Jacob's fist hit the top of the car with exasperation. 'You're meant to forget about yourself. Can you not do it for one single bloody moment?' he asked explosively and got into the car and locked the passenger door before his son could get in.

The two women stood by the graveside. Green baize (surely not the same as covers a snooker table) was spread over and then draped down into the hole. Politeness, Lizzie supposed, like a welcome mat. It wasn't a smooth process; the coffin jerked and wobbled down to the earth. Beside her Beth's shoulders drooped and she began to shrink, and Lizzie quickly put her arm around her waist very tight and very hard, which propelled the air out of her and then in again and then out again. She could hear some kind of harsh rook or crow as they emptied a fist of earth each on to the coffin. It fell and spread, small stones rolling outwards in dry ripples.

The sound of far traffic and trees ran through the graveyard, flowing over the still heads. Lizzie had a sensation of weightlessness, of cold, sharp air flowing into her. Everyone had been here, or would be, she thought. And yet each time it felt like such an unexpected journey. But then, Lizzie knew, you couldn't live in permanent anticipation of loss.

When it was over Lizzie and Beth slowly began to walk through the churchyard, two grown women side by side with the same brown eyes. Beth, with relief rather than anything excitable, noticed Dan waiting by the gate to the car park and pointed him out to her mother. Lizzie smiled and told her to go and talk to him, then continued on the path. Beth watched her walk away and at that moment Lizzie struck her daughter as a graceful figure – in her black coat and red glass brooch.

Theirs was the last service of the day and as Lizzie rounded the side of the church into the low stream of sun two women were shaking out a white altar sheet. It billowed in the late air and the sunlight on the fabric looked like water, patches of sea shifting. New water rising, overrunning and flowing past. There was no water, of course; it was only light, like liquid, fabric reflecting change. But the progress was there, in what we had seen, in how we were before and in how we stand after; the pleasure in the kinetic beauty of the moment. But the gift was the movement, on and on.

Lizzie walked slowly, swallowed by the sunlight, thinking of all that was to come.